Graveyard Clay

Graveyard Clay
Cré na Cille

A Narrative in Ten Interludes

MÁIRTÍN Ó CADHAIN

TRANSLATED BY LIAM MAC CON IOMAIRE

AND TIM ROBINSON

YALE UNIVERSITY PRESS ■ NEW HAVEN & LONDON

A MARGELLOS
WORLD REPUBLIC OF LETTERS BOOK

The Margellos World Republic of Letters is dedicated to making literary works from around the globe available in English through translation. It brings to the English-speaking world the work of leading poets, novelists, essayists, philosophers, and playwrights from Europe, Latin America, Africa, Asia, and the Middle East to stimulate international discourse and creative exchange.

Yale University Press books may be purchased in quantity for educational, business, or promotional use. For information, please e-mail sales.press@yale.edu (U.S. office) or sales@yaleup.co.uk (U.K. office).

Set in Electra and Nobel types by Tseng Information Systems.
Printed in the United States of America.

Library of Congress Control Number: 2015951050
ISBN 978-0-300- 20376-9 (cloth : alk. paper)

A catalogue record for this book is available from the British Library.
This paper meets the requirements of ANSI/NISO Z39.48-1992 (Permanence of Paper).

10 9 8 7 6 5 4 3 2 1

CONTENTS

An Introductory Note   Liam Mac Con Iomaire   vii

On Translating *Cré na Cille*   Tim Robinson   xxxv

List of Characters and Dialogue Conventions   xxxix

Graveyard Clay   1

Bibliography   317

A Biography of Máirtín Ó Cadhain (1906–1970)

Cré na Cille (*Graveyard Clay*) is the most acclaimed work by Máirtín Ó Cadhain, writer, teacher, academic, and language activist, who was born in the townland of Cnocán Glas (green hillock) near An Spidéal (Spiddal), in the coastal region known as Cois Fharraige (by the sea), in the south Conamara Gaeltacht (Irish-speaking region). In spite of its proximity to Galway city, about twelve miles away, Cnocán Glas was wholly Irish-speaking. Because the formative years of his life were spent in this community, Ó Cadhain escaped the influence of a secondary boarding school in an English-speaking area, to which most Irish speakers were of necessity subjected at an early age, if they were to get any post-primary education. That accounts, in part, for the depth of his knowledge of the spoken language, but his parents, of course, were a major influence. Both his mother, Bríd Óg Nic Conaola, and his father, Seán Ó Cadhain, were traditional storytellers, as were his grandfather and his uncle and other relations; and his brother Seosamh, who assisted in the editing of the *English-Irish Dictionary* (Dublin, 1959), had a remarkable knowledge of the vocabulary and idiom of Conamara Irish.

Ó Cadhain himself declared in *Páipéir Bhána agus Páipéir Bhreaca* (Blank Papers and Speckled Papers), a public lecture he delivered to Cumann Merriman, the Irish cultural organisation, in 1969, at which time he had come to be considered by many as the foremost modern Irish writer, in Irish or English: "The most valuable literary instrument I got from my people was the spoken language, the natural earthy pungent speech, which sometimes starts dancing and sometimes weeping, in spite of me" (translated from the Irish).[1] In later life he acquired many other languages, including English, Scottish Gaelic, Welsh, Breton, Russian, Spanish, German, French, and Italian.

At the age of eighteen he won a scholarship to St. Patrick's College in Dublin, the largest primary teacher training college in Ireland, where he spent the years 1924–1926, after which he returned to the Galway Gaeltacht and taught in various schools there until 1936. A copy of the magazine *Honesty*, which he had read while at the training college, had aroused his interest in republicanism.

His earliest contribution to scholarship was a collection of folktales he made for the Irish Folklore Commission, recorded mainly from his parents. Some of these folktales were published in *Béaloideas: The Journal of the Folklore Society of Ireland* in December 1933, December 1935, and June 1936. Ó Cadhain was a lifelong collector of old songs in Irish. A rich collection of traditional Conamara songs he had made while principal at Camas National School in the late 1920s, edited by Ríonach uí Ógáin, was published by Iontaobhas Uí Chadhain (the Ó Cadhain Trust) and Coiscéim in 1999, entitled *Faoi Rothaí na Gréine* (Under the Wheels of the Sun).

He never relaxed in his efforts in the defence of the Gaeltacht (Irish-speaking) communities against the ever-increasing pressures from outside. In the early 1930s he was pivotal in persuading the Irish government to acquire better holdings in County Meath for Irish-speaking families from his native Conamara, thereby forming the nucleus of what was to become, in his own lifetime, the vibrant Ráth Chairn Gaeltacht. In later life in Dublin in 1966 he led Misneach (Courage), a small group of likeminded young people, in protests against the government's neglect of the Irish language, and shortly

---

1. Ó Cadhain 1969, 15. The full titles of works cited in the footnotes may be found in our bibliography at the end of the book, which lists texts written by Ó Cadhain, editions of *Cré na Cille*, translations, secondary literature, and selected audio-visual materials.

before he died he travelled all over the Conamara Gaeltacht, canvassing support for the newly formed Gaeltacht Civil Rights movement and its candidate for the Galway West constituency in the 1969 general election.

In 1936 his membership of the proscribed Irish Republican Army led to his dismissal from Carnmore National School in East Galway by his clerical manager, Canon Patrick J. Moran, and the then bishop of Galway and Kilmacduagh, Dr. Thomas O'Doherty. Blacklisted as a national teacher, Ó Cadhain found employment in the Fáinne Office in Dublin, where a ring-shaped badge, or "fáinne," could be purchased, to be worn on the collar of one's coat or jacket as a sign of one's ability and willingness to speak Irish to other Irish speakers. He also worked as a labourer on a building site in Dublin and on a government employment scheme, stacking and distributing turf (peat) in Phoenix Park during the Second World War.

In 1937 his special knowledge of the Irish language was recognised by the Department of Education when he was invited to contribute to a projected Irish dictionary. His collections of words and phrases from the living speech of Conamara were used extensively in the preparation of the department's *English-Irish Dictionary* (1959) and again in its *Irish-English Dictionary* (1977).

In 1939 his first book, *Idir Shúgradh agus Dáiríre* (Between Jest and Earnest), a collection of short stories, was published by An Gúm (Government Publications). In it his own people in Conamara are portrayed with insight and sympathy, and with an honesty that makes no attempt to conceal the harsh realities of life in a depressed rural community. Although the book was favourably received, Ó Cadhain himself knew he hadn't yet found the style or form of writing that suited him. Nevertheless, in these early stories he begins to explore narrative forms of various lengths, while experimenting with established literary conventions. Around this time, in the latter half of 1939, he had a momentous experience that steeled his resolve to be a writer:

One day I found an old copy of a French magazine, for a penny I think, in a bookshop in Aungier Street in Dublin, something that was as much of an eye-opener to me as what happened to Saint Paul on the road to Damascus! In it I came across a French translation of a story by Maxim Gorky, *Harvest Day among the Cossacks of the Don.* I jumped up off the bed where I was lying down reading it. I hadn't read the like of it before. Why didn't anybody tell me there were such stories? "I would be able to write that," I said to myself. "That's work my people do, except that they have different names." A sort of hunger came over me, a hunger that was much more unbearable than the sort that was in my stomach at times. Cois Fharraige, with its stony ground, its bare rocks, its inlets, streams, pools, lakes, mountains, with the faces of man, woman and child, began creating itself behind my closed eyelids. That magazine was in my pocket, and very little else, the day I was arrested.[2]

Ó Cadhain was arrested in September 1939 under the Offences against the State Act and spent nearly five years between three or four prisons; most of that time was spent in the internment camp on the Curragh of Kildare. While in captivity he read widely in many languages and taught himself the sort of dialogue he was to use afterwards in his two novels. Influenced by Gorky and others, he set about developing his own particular kind of short story, and he wrote *An Bóthar go dtí an Ghealchathair* (The Road to Brightcity) and *An Taoille Tuile* (Floodtide) in the Curragh Camp; they would not appear in print until much later. "Those were really the days," he said, "I started writing in earnest."[3] He edited the internees' (news)paper *Barbed Wire* in the camp for a period and wrote for it in Irish and English. He translated many songs into Irish, including the "Red Flag" and the "Internationale" and other songs that were popular with the internees, such as "The Shawl of Galway Grey," "Moonlight in Mayo," and "The Boys of Kilmichael."

During his internment he had been very successful in teaching

---

2. Ó Cadhain 1969, 26.

3. Ó Cadhain 1969, 27.

spoken Irish to adults of very varied educational backgrounds. In the first of many letters Ó Cadhain wrote to his fellow Irish-language writer Tomás Bairéad in Dublin, he states (translated from the Irish): "There wasn't a language spoken in Babel that isn't being taught by us here: Irish, French, Spanish, German, Latin, Welsh, Breton. . . . There's a fair amount of Irish speakers here, and every trade and faculty, except barbers!"[4] A collection of those letters in Irish, twenty-three in all, was published by Sáirséal agus Dill, a small, bespoke publishing house in Dublin, entitled *As an nGéibheann* (Out of Captivity, 1973), leaving us a rich personal account of his years behind barbed wire. More personal references to his years in the Curragh Camp are available in *TONE — Inné agus Inniu* (TONE — Yesterday and Today), based on a lecture Ó Cadhain gave to the Wolfe Tone Association in the Mansion House, Dublin, in 1963, edited by Bernadette Ní Rodaigh and Eibhlín Ní Allúráin, published by Iontaobhas Uí Chadhain (the Ó Cadhain Trust) and Coiscéim in 1999. Both his father and his mother died during his years in captivity.

On his release in July 1944, Ó Cadhain was asked by the then Taoiseach (head of government), Éamon de Valera, to continue with his work on the *English-Irish Dictionary*. In 1945 he married Máirín Ní Rodaigh, a national teacher and fluent Irish speaker from Cavan, and a gifted teacher of Irish to the infant classes in Scoil Lorcáin in Monkstown in south Dublin for many years. They settled permanently in Dublin and had no children of their own.

In March 1947 Ó Cadhain was appointed to Rannóg an Aistriúcháin (the Parliamentary Translation Staff) in Dublin, which at the time had been given the task of forming a standardized spelling and morphology of Irish, based on the spoken dialects as well as on the written language. He made no small contribution to this difficult task, although, of course, his suggestions were not always adopted (as is evident in his article "Forbairt na Gaeilge" published in the monthly magazine *Feasta* in December 1951). His period with the Parliamentary Translation Staff provided him with valuable experi-

---

4. Ó Cadhain 1973, 46.

ence of the problems involved in the adaptation of a spoken rural language (with three major dialects) to the requirements of modern urban society.

His second collection of short stories, *An Braon Broghach* (The Cloudy Drop) was published in 1948, meriting the following praise from the writer and poet Eoghan Ó Tuairisc, who would later translate a selection of these stories into English: "One feels a certain exultation of spirit in his 1948 collection of stories: the born teacher discovering himself as the born writer."[5]

Cré na Cille (*Graveyard Clay*), Ó Cadhain's third book and first novel, was published by Sáirséal agus Dill in 1950 to critical acclaim, and was serialised over a seven-month period in the national daily broadsheet newspaper the *Irish Press*. In the public lecture delivered to Cumann Merriman, Ó Cadhain said (translated from the Irish): "A few years after being set free I wrote *Cré na Cille* and another novel *Athnuachan*, which won the Club Leabhar Prize (1951). When I began writing *Cré na Cille* I felt confident that I could write a better novel than had previously been written in Irish."[6] *Cré na Cille* was chosen by UNESCO as an outstanding work, with a recommendation that it be translated into other European languages, and Ó Cadhain was elected a member of the Royal Irish Academy, the first Irish-language writer to receive the honour.

Athnuachan (Renewal) remained unpublished, at the author's own behest, until after his death. The writer and critic Tomás Ó Floinn, on behalf of a panel of judges appointed by An Club Leabhar (the Book Club), noted (translated from the Irish): "Nothing has been written in Irish to date that is as powerful, as moving, as certain chapters in this book . . . only a real artist could handle this subject as it has been handled here."[7] And when the book was eventually published by Iontaobhas Uí Chadhain (Coiscéim, 1995), the writer and critic Breandán Ó Doibhlin wrote in the preface (trans-

---

5. Ó Tuairisc 1981, 8.

6. Ó Cadhain 1969, 28.

7. In Ó Cadhain 1995, xv and back cover.

lated from the Irish): "I think it is no exaggeration to say that *Ath-nuachan* is on a par with *Cré na Cille* as far as its energy and force of dialogue is concerned, in its comic depiction of the utter absurdity of the human race."[8]

Ó Cadhain's third volume of short stories, *Cois Caoláire* (By the Firth—that is, by Galway Bay), published by Sáirséal agus Dill in 1953, added further to his reputation and marked a new departure in his writing. The volume contained some earlier material that An Gúm had deemed unsuitable to include in *An Braon Broghach*, a decision that sufficiently rankled with Ó Cadhain for him to remark on Raidió Éireann several years later (on 11 May 1952) that his readers would be the ultimate arbiters on the isssue. The collection contained several searing studies set in Conamara, but it also marked a change in emphasis from the rural towards the urban and the suburban, which opened up a new canvas on which Ó Cadhain could examine the individual on the margins.

From 1953 to 1956, he contributed a weekly column to the *Irish Times*, and a collection of those articles entitled *Caiscín* (Brown Bread), edited by Aindrias Ó Cathasaigh, was published by Iontaobhas Uí Chadhain (Coiscéim, 1998). A collection of his writings in the monthly magazine *Feasta* entitled *Ó Cadhain i bhFeasta*, edited by Seán Ó Laighin, was published by Clódhanna Teo. in 1990, and a collection of his writings in the monthly magazine *Comhar* entitled *Caithfear Éisteacht!* (It Must Be Heard!), edited by Liam Prút, was published by *Comhar* in 1999.

In 1956 Ó Cadhain was appointed lecturer in Irish at Trinity College Dublin, where he inspired his students with such dedication and enthusiasm for the Irish language that they responded with an esteem and affection that was as remarkable as it was unusual at the time. His long-playing record *The Consonants of Irish* (*Ceirníní na Gaeltacht*, published by SPÓL in 1961) marked a departure from traditional teaching and was accompanied by a text for learners that bore characteristics typical of Ó Cadhain's creative work—humour,

---

8. In Ó Cadhain 1995, x.

satire, and a sense of the ridiculous. Reading the text aloud sounds not so much like an educational tool as like a hilarious surrealist fantasy rooted in the life-world of *Cré na Cille*.

Ó Cadhain's wife, Máirín Ní Rodaigh, died in October 1965. In 1967, following a public competition, Ó Cadhain was appointed associate professor of Irish at Trinity College Dublin, and in 1969 he proceeded to the chair of Irish as Established Professor. The publication of *An tSraith ar Lár* (The Fallen Swathe) that same year won for him the valuable Butler Award of the Irish-American Cultural Institute. He was to receive the distinction Fellow of Trinity College Dublin in 1970, the year he died. The other two collections of short stories in the *Sraith* (Swathe) series were to follow: *An tSraith dhá Tógáil* (The Swathe Being Raised), published in 1970, and *An tSraith Tógtha* (The Raised Swathe), the very last book he wrote, published posthumously in 1977. All three are different, both in style and in content, to his first two collections, with the emphasis shifting to stories based on material from the Bible and to a more existential examination of the individual. All three *Sraith* collections were published by Sáirséal agus Dill.

Ó Cadhain was a formidable controversialist and satirist, and perhaps some of his best writing is to be found in articles such as "Do na Fíréin" (For the Faithful, in *Comhar*, March 1962) and "Béaloideas" (Folklore, in *Feasta*, March 1950), in which he ridicules a folklorist who feeds off the people of the Gaeltacht while hoping for their speedy extinction in order to enhance the value of his own collections. His published lectures, articles, and pamphlets on literary, language, and political problems are essential reading for anyone who would understand fully the contemporary Irish scene. A collection of satirical essays, *Barbed Wire*, which Ó Cadhain considered "the best bit of writing I ever did,"[9] was published posthumously by Iontaobhas Uí Chadhain, edited by Cathal Ó Háinle (Coiscéim, 2002). *Barbed Wire* was the eventual product of Ó Cadhain's increasingly bitter polemic in the early 1960s, and it presents an unsympathetic portrait of Ire-

---

9. Ó Cadhain 1969, 29.

land in the Séan Lemass era. The commentary on the contemporary Irish-language movement is scathing, and the virtuosity of the prose is exceeded only by its vitriol. *An Ghaeilge Bheo, Destined to Pass* is a bilingual, personal, and passionate account he wrote in 1963 of the decline of the Irish language from the Flight of the Earls in 1607 to the early 1960s. Edited by Seán Ó Laighin after Ó Cadhain's death, it was published by Iontaobhas Uí Chadhain (Coiscéim, 2002). (Following the defeat of the Irish chieftains and their Catholic allies at the Battle of Kinsale in 1601, and the ensuing planting of their lands by the victorious English, the Earls of Tyrconnell and Tyrone, O'Donnell, and O'Neill, together with their families and followers, were forced to leave Ireland in 1607 and seek refuge on the Continent.)

Ó Cadhain had parted company with An Gúm since it had refused to publish some of his best writing, including *Cré na Cille*. Luckily for him and his readers, Seán Ó hÉigeartaigh, together with his wife, Bríghid Ní Mhaoileoin, had founded Sáirséal agus Dill in 1947 to cater for a new generation of Irish-language writers whose work An Gúm refused to publish. Ó Cadhain said in *Páipéir Bhána agus Páipéir Bhreaca* (translated from the Irish): "Around the time I was writing *Cré na Cille* I got to know Seán Sáirséal Ó hÉigeartaigh. . . . I am certain that I would have stopped writing altogether, or at least stopped writing in Irish, were it not for Seán Ó hÉigeartaigh. Were it not for him I would not have been entered for Duais an Bhuitléaraigh [the Butler Award].[10] It was he who brought news of the Award to me in the Mater [Hospital] in Dublin. He used to come in to me for a while every evening, correcting proofs of a script of mine on modern Irish literature and proofs of *An tSraith ar Lár*. . . . He came in the day he died."[11]

When Seán Ó hÉigeartaigh died suddenly in the Sáirséal agus Dill office on 14 June 1967, Ó Cadhain rose from his hospital bed to deliver a moving graveside oration in Templeogue cemetery in Dub-

---

10. The Butler Literary Awards are given by the Irish American Cultural Institute in support of works in the Irish language.

11. Ó Cadhain 1969, 29.

lin, where he told the mourners (translated from the Irish): "If there is an Irish language literature since 1940 it is because Seán Ó hÉigeartaigh saw to it that it would be so."[12]

Three years later, Máirtín Ó Cadhain died in the Mater Hospital in Dublin, on 18 October 1970. Seán Ó hÉigeartaigh's son, Cian Sáirséal Ó hÉigeartaigh, in his graveside oration in Mount Jerome cemetery in Dublin, spoke for many when he said (translated from the Irish): "He [Máirtín Ó Cadhain] was the greatest man to emerge from the Gaeltacht since the whole of Ireland was a Gaeltacht."[13]

Tomás de Bhaldraithe, professor of Irish at University College Dublin and editor of the 1959 *English-Irish Dictionary,* wrote in an obituary after the death of Ó Cadhain: "When many a learned academic will be forgotten, Máirtín Ó Cadhain will be remembered for his contribution to Irish life in general, and in particular for his efforts, both literary and political, which put new heart into the young people of Conamara, and for his creative writing which has given such pleasure and encouragement to readers of Irish."

The Publication History of *Cré na Cille*

The history of the text is intricate and unusually so for a work of the modern period. *Cré na Cille* was written during the period 1945–1947 and then submitted to the annual Oireachtas literary competition in 1947. This entailed the production of multiple copies by hand.[14] The novel was then serialised between February and September 1949 in the *Irish Press* (*Scéala Éireann,* in Irish), which enjoyed a wide urban and rural circulation. The newspaper had close associations with Éamon de Valera and the Fianna Fáil party and was also a literary platform of some significance in the postwar period.

Following serialised publication to considerable acclaim, the manuscript was submitted to the state publications agency, An Gúm.

---

12. I heard Ó Cadhain speak these words at the graveside.
13. I heard Cian Ó hÉigeartaigh speak these words at the graveside.
14. Costigan and Ó Curraoin 1987, 73.

Faced with such a radical departure from established literary convention as having corpses squabbling in their graves, An Gúm gave it a lukewarm reception. The text, and author, ultimately found a champion in Sáirséal agus Dill, the small publishing house in Dublin owned and managed by Seán Sáirséal Ó hÉigeartaigh (1917–1967) and his wife, Bríghid (1920–2006). Established in 1947, Sáirséal agus Dill had already gained a reputation for publishing quality contemporary fiction of literary merit. For a fledgling enterprise, its standards of design and production were also of the highest calibre.

The publication of *Cré na Cille* in book format was flagged by Comhdháil Náisiúnta na Gaeilge as early as March 1948 in a publicity blurb about Máirtín Ó Cadhain in the literary journal *Comhar*. Despite a printed publication date of 1949 in the first edition, the book did not actually appear until 10 March 1950.[15] It must be said that this has not been generally taken into account in the assessment of the earliest published reviews. The first edition was published in hardback, with black publisher's cloth boards, in octavo format, with a grey dust jacket carrying a depiction of a graveyard by Charles Lamb, an associate of the Royal Hibernian Academy. The text runs to 364 pages. Lamb also provided uncluttered, nuanced portraits of the text's primary characters: Caitríona Pháidín, Tomás Inside, the Big Master, the priest's sister, Big Brian, and Nell Pháidín. The biographical notes in Irish, unmistakably written by the author himself, are noteworthy for both their brevity and their content, especially from a writer who has been criticised for being excessive with words:

Máirtín Ó Cadhain
Gaillimheach a bhfuil an saol feicthe aige. Seal ina mhúinteoir, seal ina thimire teangan agus muirthéachta, seal ag cruachadh móna i bPáirc an Fhionnuisce agus seal ag tógáil tithe. Chúig bhliana ina ghéibheannach ar an gCurrach.

(A Galwayman who has seen the world. Spent a while as a teacher, a while as an organiser of language and of revolution,

---

15. Ó Cathasaigh 2002, 118; Ó Háinle 2006, 22; Cló Iar-Chonnacht 2009, 11.

a while stacking turf in the Phoenix Park, and a while building houses. Five years in captivity in the Curragh.)

Charles Lamb
Ultach a tháinig go Baile Átha Cliath agus a lonnaigh i gConamara. Ag léiriú saol an Iarthair ó shoin, agus clú fhada leitheadach air dá bharr.

(An Ulsterman who came to Dublin and settled in Conamara. Depicting life in the West since, and is famous for it far and wide.)

The book was reprinted with no apparent textual changes in 1965. The original dust jacket designed by Lamb was now featured on a grey publisher's cloth hardback. The publisher had also provided copious extracts from a selection of the reviews of the work in minuscule font on the inside front and back covers. As was common practice with many Sáirséal agus Dill publications, the hardback was sold in a clear, transparent plastic dust cover. Reprints were also issued in 1970 and 1979. The reprints of 1965 and 1970 were slightly reduced compared to the first edition, but the 1979 reprint reprised the size of the original publication and also carried an international standard book number (ISBN 0 901374 01 6).

The publisher Caoimhín Ó Marcaigh (1933–2014) acquired Sáirséal agus Dill in 1981. *Cré na Cille* remained out of print for a considerable period, and controversially so. A second edition in hard and soft covers was published in 1996, the text running to 321 pages. The text of this edition was the subject of considerable comment and criticism on publication. It appeared that a deliberate policy of normalisation had been attempted, of both orthography and accidence, but the sheer scale of typographical errors in the edition rendered the text unreliable. The publication is thought to be the last book designed by Liam Miller (1924–1996) and retains all of the original drawings by Charles Lamb, though the frontispiece portrait of Tomás Inside (Tomás Taobh Istigh) surveying the graveyard has been transposed to the book's interior.

The third edition of *Cré na Cille* was prepared by Professor Cathal Ó Háinle and published by Sáirséal Ó Marcaigh in 2007 in hard and soft covers. This text, running to 347 pages, was substantially revised and heavily amended. The editorial principles by which these revisions were implemented are enumerated in a brief paragraph on the dust jacket. We are told that the original manuscript is no longer available but that a copy of the first edition, amended by the author's own hand in 1950, appears to have formed the basis for many changes to the second edition's punctuation and orthography. Reference is also made to syntactical and word changes, and the basis for normalisation implemented in the second edition appears to have been adopted as well. It is understood that the rationale for such departures from the text as originally published relates to accessibility, ease of reference, and the desire to facilitate a new generation of readers whose capacity to read non-standardised Irish may be diminished. The dust jacket and soft cover carry a line drawing of Máirtín Ó Cadhain, by Caoimhín Ó Marcaigh.

In 2009, following the acquisition of Sáirséal Ó Marcaigh by Cló Iar-Chonnacht, the 1965 reprint was used as the basis for a softcover print run. The first edition contains a colophon in Irish on the end page:

> Arna chur i gcló do Sháirséal agus Dill Teo. ag Foilseacháin Náisiúnta Teo., Cathair na Mart, idir Lá Fhéile Muire sa bhFómhar agus Lá Nollag, 1949.

> (Printed for Sáirséal agus Dill Teo. by Foilseacháin Náisiúnta Teo., Westport, between 15th August and 25th December 1949.)

This text also appears in the second, third, and fourth reprints, with the additional information that the book was being printed by Dill agus Sáirséal Teoranta in Dublin, with a minor amendment to the wording of the formula in the third and fourth reprints. In a nod to publishing history, the 2009 reprint, under the imprint of Cló Iar-Chonnachta (*sic*) and designated generically as *An Cló Seo* (This Print), contains a colophon on the end page, which replicates the formula:

Arna chur i gcló do Chló Iar-Chonnachta Teo., ag Clódóirí Lurgan, Indreabhán, idir Lá Fhéile Muire sa bhFómhar agus Lá Nollag, 2009.

(Printed for Cló Iar-Chonnachta Teo. by Clódóirí Lurgan, Indreabhán, between 15th August and 25th December 2009.)

Translations of *Cré na Cille*

Cré na Cille was translated in full by Joan Trodden Keefe (1931–2013), and the translation formed the basis for a doctoral degree granted by the University of California, Berkeley, in 1984. As part of the dissertation, Trodden Keefe provided an introduction and notes to the translation. The graduate research was supervised by Professor Daniel Melia, and the dissertation was examined by Brendan P. O Hehir and Robert Tracey. This translation has been available for consultation in university libraries on microfiche but has not been in general circulation. Trodden Keefe proceeded to publish an extended literary analysis of *Cré na Cille* in the journal *World Literature Today* in 1985.[16]

Another translation of the text was undertaken by Eibhlín Ní Allúráin (1922–2010) and Maitiú Ó Néill (1921–1992),[17] who were closely associated with Máirtín Ó Cadhain. The translation was substantially completed but has not been published. An extract of this translation was published in the literary journal *Krino* 11,[18] and also appeared in the *Field Day Anthology of Irish Writing*.[19] Sections of the text have been translated by literary scholars for the purposes of explication or pedagogy, as in the case of Alfred Bammesberger, who included extracts from twentieth-century writers, including an extract from *Cré na Cille*, in a language teaching manual published

---

16. Trodden Keefe 1985.
17. Ó hÉigeartaigh and Nic Gearailt 2014, 186.
18. Mac Póilín (ed.) 1991.
19. Deane (ed.) 1991.

in Heidelberg, Germany, in 1984.[20] Philip O'Leary, Robert Welch, Declan Kiberd, and Brian Ó Broin have all provided their own versions of extracts in the course of scholarly commentary in English on aspects of the narrative.[21] By their very nature, these extracts are relatively brief and serve primarily to cater for a non-Irish-speaking readership.

The Dirty Dust is Alan Titley's version of *Cré na Cille*, published by Yale University Press in 2015 in the Margellos World Republic of Letters series, which treats especially of previously overlooked works of cultural and artistic significance. Initial enthusiasm regarding access to the narrative may ultimately be tempered by a more guarded analysis of the translation's "free-wheeling" nature in general and a markedly creative interpretation of the text's "rich and savage demotic base" in particular.[22]

Translation of Ó Cadhain's other works has been sporadic, but versions of *Cré na Cille* have been made available in Norwegian[23] and Danish,[24] offering interesting challenges for the translators in choosing suitably responsive target registers for their readership. A relatively limited number of Ó Cadhain's short stories have been translated. Eoghan Ó Tuairisc (1919–1982) made a study of stories from the earlier corpus, the collection *An Braon Broghach* in particular.[25] Some twenty-five years later, in 2006, a further two stories were translated by Louis de Paor, Mike McCormack, and Lochlainn Ó Tuairisg and published by the Cúirt International Festival of Literature.[26] Ó Cadhain's novella *An Eochair*, a study of a minor civil servant and his literal and metaphoric entrapment, from the narra-

20. Bammesberger 1984.
21. O'Leary 2010; Welch 1993; Kiberd 2000 and 2005; Ó Broin 2006 and 2008.
22. See Alan Titley in the *Irish Times*, 30 March 2015.
23. Rekdal (trans.) 1995.
24. Munch-Pedersen (trans.) 2000.
25. Ó Tuairisc 1981.
26. de Paor, McCormack, and Ó Tuairisg 2006.

tive collection *An tSraith ar Lár,* was translated by Louis de Paor and Lochlainn Ó Tuairisg and published by Dalkey Archive Press in 2015.[27]

Michael Cronin made an impassioned plea for "*Cré na Cille* in English" in the *Irish Times* in 2001: "Translation excites desire, it does not cancel it. The better the translation, the more compelling the case for going to the original."[28] The relative paucity of translations can be ascribed to a reluctance to embroil oneself in copyright difficulties, and to the notion held by many critics that Ó Cadhain's Irish and use of language is "difficult." There is also a sense of linguistic piety or cultural decorum that has served to warn off potential translators. A translator may very well take the view that one tampers with canonical texts at one's peril; however, Tim and I took Michael Cronin's plea to heart and committed ourselves to producing this English-language translation of *Cré na Cille.*

The Language

When it was established that folk or popular idiom, "caint na ndaoine," would be the medium of modern literary Irish, emerging authors and critics became keenly aware of the importance of mastery of the registers of Irish as spoken in the Gaeltacht, the regions where primarily Irish is used. The extent of dialectal variation in Irish, the slow development of Irish language literacy in post-independent Ireland, the absence of a standardised orthography, and the inadequacy of available dictionaries meant that for many readers texts from authors such as Máirtín Ó Cadhain and Séamas Ó Grianna were cherished as lexical treasure troves, to be revered as regionalised glossaries as much as literary masterpieces. The *Irish-English Dictionary* of the Reverend Patrick S. Dinneen (1927) was regarded as a superb work of scholarship, and, while it is probably more representative of

---

27. Máirtín Ó Cadhain, *The Key/An Eochair,* Dual Language Edition, translated by Louis de Paor and Lochlainn Ó Tuairisg. Dublin: Dalkey Archive Press.

28. Cronin 2001, B13.

Munster Irish than other dialects, Ó Cadhain praised it profusely, advising all writers of Irish that there is no better bedfellow than Dinneen's dictionary.[29]

The appearance of *Cré na Cille*, whose narrative consists entirely of dialogue, was bound to present challenges for ordinary readers and literary critics with only a scant familiarity with Connacht, much less Conamara, Irish. It is also worth noting that the seminal monograph series on Irish phonetics and accidence published by the Dublin Institute of Advanced Studies began appearing during the 1940s. All these factors served to emphasise a lexical, as opposed to a literary, analysis of the text in the first instance.

Reception and Interpretation

In the early reviews by Tomás Ó Floinn, Daniel Corkery, and David Greene in 1950 we are told that the author has excelled in the crafting of his medium, that this medium is heavily indebted to the speech of his native Conamara Gaeltacht, and that, while this is a criterion of excellence in itself, the text is difficult.[30] This has been challenged by Róisín Ní Ghairbhí, who states that syntactical structures are relatively straightforward, and while individual words or phrases may be rare or unusual, their significance and meaning are not beyond the resources of a reasonably alert reader.[31] Other critics have pointed out that *Cré na Cille* "is not simply a *tour de force* of conversational Irish,"[32] and that "Ó Cadhain has been criticised unjustly by critics who didn't understand what he was saying."[33] An Aran Islander and native Irish speaker himself, Breandán Ó hEithir went on to say: "*Cré na Cille* is a great comic work and by far and away the funniest in modern Irish, as Ciarán Ó Nualláin [brother of Myles na gCopa-

---

29. Ó Cadhain 1969, 17.
30. Ó Floinn 1950, also in Prút (ed.) 1997; Ó Corcora 1950; Greene 1950.
31. Ní Ghairbhí 2008, 49.
32. Ó Corráin 1988, 143.
33. Ó hEithir 1977, 74.

leen] pointed out when it was published. Apart from Evelyn Waugh and Jaroslav Hašek no author makes me laugh as heartily and as regularly as Máirtín Ó Cadhain in *Cré na Cille*."[34]

The initial reaction to *Cré na Cille* must be measured carefully, however, against the constraints of literary and periodical journalism of the day. Several analyses exist, in English and in Irish, of critical responses to the publication in book format of the text.[35] As the publication was only made generally available in March 1950, the considered reviews of critics such as Tomás Ó Floinn (April 1950), Daniel Corkery (May 1950), and David Greene (May 1950) must be regarded as relatively rapid responses to editorial demands. In that light, the quality of insight demonstrated by all three of these critics stands the test of time, by and large, although it is fair to say that all three reviews tell us as much about the critical culture of the time as they do about the actual text. Gearóid Denvir, of a younger generation of critics, suggests that the text is "an acerbic, satiric and darkly comic depiction of some of the rather less pleasant side of human nature, told with earthy, Rabelaisian humour."[36]

The temptation to read *Cré na Cille* as a faithful record and authentic representation of contemporary Gaeltacht life still features in criticism now, as it did then. Breandán Ó Doibhlin, however, in his reappraisal of the novel in 1974, makes a particular study of the comedic aspects of the text. He downplays the role of satire and any sense that the purpose of the novel is a realistic depiction of Gaeltacht communities, and sees *Cré na Cille* as a general statement about the human condition, enabled by laughter and filtered through humour (translated from the Irish): "To tell the truth, this novel is a prime example of the comedic *genre*. Máirtín Ó Cadhain chose his subject so meticulously that he has been accused of sordidness (suarachas); his characters can only talk about parish gossip, futile disputes about the GAA [Gaelic Athletic Association] and the Treaty, backbiting

---

34. Ó hEithir 1977, 75.
35. O'Leary 2010; Welch 1993; Kiberd 2000; Titley 1991; Denvir 2007.
36. Denvir 2007, 222.

and petty jealousy of the meanest kind. . . . The author avoids any kind of subject—pity, affection, idealism—that would interfere with laughter, because the reader must not have any empathy with the character."[37]

The Graveyard

The geographic location of *Cré na Cille* is fixed very much in the author's own Cois Fharraige in south Conamara during the Second World War, a generation after partition and independence, during the Emergency, as World War II was called in Ireland. The characters are a motley collection of locals, including some who were in real life killed by a German mine that drifted ashore in Cois Fharraige in June 1917, and some victims of a typhus epidemic in the Spiddal area in the winter of 1942. There are also a couple of stray corpses like Dotie, the woman from East Galway who moans longingly for the lush green plains where she wished to be buried, and the French pilot whose plane came down in Galway Bay and who is now learning Irish from the local corpses.

The French airman may be regarded as a rather exotic species in the graveyard, but it has been argued that he "is a reminder that Ireland has made itself marginal to the fight against continental European fascism."[38] An attempt has also been made to identify a real-life source for the character: Pilot Officer Maurice Motte alias Remy of the Free French forces, who was interned in the Allied Officers' section of the Curragh Military Camp, having landed in County Waterford in June 1941 after running low on fuel.[39] Whether the character had a basis in reality is an interesting question in itself, but he is a representative of an external dimension and wider world beyond the graveyard, Conamara, and Ireland itself.

The graveyard is divided into three sections—Áit an Phuint (the

---

37. Ó Doibhlin 1974, 48.

38. Kilfeather 2006, 93.

39. Ó Briain 2013, 281.

Pound Place), Áit na Cúig Déag (the Fifteen-Shilling Place), and Áit na Leathghine (the Half-Guinea Place), and commentary on the social status of each section is supplied on the hustings before the graveyard election. Locating the graveyard in that context offers multiple possibilities for informed historical, political, and sociocultural criticism. The discourse in general reflects the passions, anxieties, and preoccupations of an intimate rural community, warts and all. Land, social status, love, lust, greed, and visceral hatred all feature strongly in the exchanges, extending the significance of the text beyond temporal and regional contexts.

The Story

The action, which is nearly all verbal, is helped along by the regular arrival of fresh corpses, bringing fresh news from the world above. Many of the characters can be identified only by their recurring peculiarities of speech, thus focusing attention on the characters themselves. In a lecture Ó Cadhain delivered to Cumann Merriman the year before he died, he said (in translation): "The most important thing now in literature is to reveal the mind, that part of a person on which the camera cannot be directed. Speech is much more capable of this than observations about his clothes, his complexion. . . . It is not what covers a person's skin that is important, or even the skin, but that which he is walking about with inside his head. We know more about the stars in the firmament than about what's going on under that small skull beside you."[40]

As to where the idea for Cré na Cille came from, Ó Cadhain went on to say:

> When I was released from the prison camp I was at home that winter. A neighbouring woman died during the short dark days around Christmas. There was a deluge of rain and sleet so that the grave couldn't be dug until the day she was being buried.

---

40. Ó Cadhain 1969, 30–31.

Five or six of us went to dig it, so as to hurry the job. We dug up two graves but didn't find the right coffins. The map of the graves was sent for but it was like a child doing sums in the ashes on the hearth. It was late in the day and the funeral would soon be upon us. We said we'd dig one more grave and that would be it. On our way home one of my neighbours said: "Do you know where we sneaked her in eventually," he said, "down of top of a person whom I will call Micil Rua." "Oho!" said another, "there will be some *grammar* there alright!"[41]

The story (or stories) is in ten parts described as interludes (*eadar-lúidí*). The dialogue is augmented by snippets of verse, occasional parodies, and the distinctive passages uttered by *Stoc na Cille*, the Trump (Trumpet) of the Graveyard, at the beginning of interludes 3 to 8, which then peter out into textual insignificance.

Critical opinion on these distinctive passages varies from complete dismissal to wondrous admiration, but there is general agreement that the prose is markedly denser and intentionally metaphoric, and appears to have no discernible impact on the graveyard inhabitants.

Daniel Corkery criticised these passages as an extraneous romantic affectation, an attempt by Ó Cadhain to add depth to the narrative.[42] "Rather purple punctuation marks" is how Breandán Ó hEithir chooses to describe the Trump's exclamatory pronouncements,[43] and a combination of "Father Time" and the Fates is another surmise.[44] Concepts of playfulness,[45] mockery,[46] and practical jokes[47] are also alluded to. But more serious intent is posited by scholars who note the

---

41. Ó Cadhain 1969, 33.

42. Ó Corcora 1950, 14.

43. Ó hEithir 1977, 83.

44. Ó Dochartaigh 1975, 14.

45. Ó Murchú 1982, 19.

46. Nic Pháidín 1978, 22.

47. Denvir 2007, 50.

development of death as a primary motif in the passages: "dreochan atá i saol na mbeo"[48] (living is but decaying), and "dreo an fhómhair agus reo an gheimhridh"[49] (decay of autumn and freeze of winter). "The Trumpeter adds a further dimension to the work," says Ailbhe Ó Corráin. "His is the only contemplative voice. It is he who introduces the central themes of regeneration and decay and gives the work much of its suggestive power. You might say that he brings a little gravity to the grave."[50] Róisín Ní Ghairbhí also argues that *Stoc na Cille* provides a marked contrast to the dialectal exchanges of the graveyard and seeks to offer an alternative model of authority, parallel to the graveyard chatter.[51] Declan Kiberd has described *Stoc na Cille* as "an entirely playful, ironical invention" that functions as "a debunking of the cult of the author."[52] Joan Trodden Keefe argues for the validity of several purposes for these passages, which are "clearly satiric" in her view and could possibly be based on "a parody of the 'Bugle' and 'Loudspeaker' announcements of the Curragh, where the voice of authority is ever-present but ultimately ignored by the camp inhabitants, and so also in the graveyard."[53] The present translation of these high-flown passages reflects our conviction that, as invocations of the great cycles of life and death, they are to be read with extreme seriousness.

Various narrative strands in the novel involve three sisters: Caitríona Pháidín, the chief protagonist, a seventy-one-year-old widow with a married son called Pádraig Chaitríona; Nell Pháidín, Caitríona's younger sister, who married the young man Caitríona was in love with; and Baba Pháidín, their eldest sister, who has been left a legacy in Boston, whose death is imminently expected, and whose last will and testament is the subject of constant transatlantic corre-

---

48. Nic Eoin 1981, 49.
49. Ó Doibhlin 1974, 47.
50. Ó Corráin 1988, 144–45.
51. Ní Ghairbhí 2008, 50.
52. Kiberd 2000, 583, 584.
53. Trodden Keefe 1985, 371.

spondence—the Big Master (An Máistir Mór) writing for Caitríona, and the priest (An Sagart) writing for Nell. A relation of these sisters, Tomás Inside, is an easy-going bachelor who avoids any form of labour while drawing a weekly pension, and is playing both sisters against each other, with their eye on his patch of land.

Caitríona was in love with Jack the Scológ, who could enchant the young women of the village with his repertoire of songs and traditional (Sean-Nós, or Old Style) singing. But Nell stole him away from them all, married him in triumph, and has kept Jack and his songs to herself ever since. Caitríona has carried her hatred and envy of Nell into the grave with her, along with her love and longing for Jack the Scológ. Jack and Nell are still above ground.

When reacquainted with Muraed Phroinsiais in the graveyard, Caitríona makes a seemingly innocent statement of intent: "Anything concerning me personally, anything I saw or heard, I brought it to the grave with me, but there's no harm in talking about it now, as we are on the way of truth." (Being "on the way of truth," *ar shlí na fírinne* in Irish, is a common expression for being dead.)

Muraed functions as a safe foil, allowing Caitríona to engage in full, frank, and extensive disclosure about her relatives and in-laws, safe in the knowledge (for most of the time) that Muraed was a good friend and neighbour above ground. Hardly anybody else escapes the lash of Caitríona's tongue, but her son Pádraig's mother-in-law, Nóra Sheáinín, with her aspiring notions of culture and grandeur, is a constant target of Caitriona's, especially when Nóra boasts of having an *affaire de coeur* with the Big Master, and puts her name forward as a candidate in the graveyard election.

The Big Master dominates large parts of the book. He marries his assistant but soon after falls ill and dies. Shortly after his burial a new arrival tells him that his widow is being consoled by Billyboy the Post (Bileachaí an Phosta), then he hears that they have married, and after that again that Billyboy is at death's door, all of which inspires the Big Master to scale new peaks of invective and vituperation, culminating in what is probably the longest litany of curses ever uttered in a graveyard.

Adaptations of *Cré na Cille*

Cré na Cille has had a life beyond the confines of its covers and has been the subject of several dramatic, stage, and film adaptations in addition to substantial critical documentary features on television and radio. Shortly after the establishment of Raidió na Gaeltachta in 1972 *Cré na Cille* was adapted as a serialized drama for radio by the poet and writer Johnny Chóil Mhaidhc Ó Coisdealbha (1929–2006). This was an ambitious project for the fledgling Gaeltacht radio service and involved the production of twenty-five separate thirty-minute instalments that were broadcast between 6 February 1973 and 24 July 1973. Recorded by Tadhg Ó Béarra (†1990) and produced by Maidhc P. Ó Conaola, the series required the services of an extended cast, designated as Aisteoirí Chonamara, some of whom were located in Dublin and travelled weekly to the headquarters of Raidió na Gaeltachta in Casla in Conamara for the recording sessions. The part of Caitríona Pháidín was played by Winnie Mhaitiais Uí Dhuilearga (†1982) from Béal an Átha, Mine, Indreabhán, with eloquence and élan. This dramatic version was remastered by Máirtín Jaimsie Ó Flaithbheartaigh and rebroadcast on a weekly basis between January and June 2006 as part of the commemoration of Ó Cadhain's birth by RTÉ, Ireland's national television and radio broadcaster. The series was then issued as a publication by Cló Iar-Chonnacht and RTÉ in 2006 and is contained in a set of eight CDs with production notes and short biographies of the cast. Charles Lamb's portrayal of the graveyard is reworked and reinterpreted by Pádraig Reaney's artwork on the CD publication.

Cré na Cille has been the subject of a number of successful adaptations as a stage drama, primarily thanks to the intelligent and sensitive reworking of the novel by the actor and writer Macdara Ó Fátharta. The Abbey Theatre premiered an adaptation of Ó Fátharta's in Coláiste Chonnacht, Spiddal, County Galway, on 29 February 1996. Directed by Bríd Ó Gallchóir, it was apparently the first production of Ireland's National Theatre to open outside Dublin. Bríd Ní Neachtain (Caitríona Pháidín), Máire Ní Ghráinne (Nóra

Sheáinín), Peadar Lamb (Tomás Taobh Istigh) and Breandán Ó Dúill (1935–2006) (An Máistir Mór) formed the mainstay of the cast and the well-received production toured various venues throughout the Gaeltacht in addition to Derry and Belfast.[54] A further production by the Irish-language theatre company An Taibhdhearc in March and April 2002 was again based on a script by Macdara Ó Fátharta. The play was directed by Darach Mac Con Iomaire, and the set was designed by Dara McGee. Caitríona Pháidín was played by Bríd Ní Neachtain, and the cast included Joe Steve Ó Neachtain, Diarmuid Mac an Adhastair (1944–2015), and Macdara Ó Fátharta himself— all of whom would go on to feature in the film adaptation in 2006.

Cré na Cille went on to be produced as a full-length feature film by Ciarán Ó Cofaigh of ROSG productions, directed by Robert Quinn. It was first shown in Galway in December 2006 prior to its broadcast by the Irish-language public service television station, TG4, in 2007. Nominated for four Irish Film and Television Awards (IFTAs), the film was based on a script by Macdara Ó Fátharta, with photography by Tim Fleming, production design by Dara McGee, and editing by Conall de Cléir. The role of Caitríona Pháidín was played forcefully and effectively by Bríd Ní Neachtain, who has also played this role in adaptations for the stage. Gearóid Denvir, in a glowing critique of the adaptation, notes the introduction of scenes from life above ground and the absence of *Stoc na Cille*, and re- marks that "the film remains true in the main to the original storyline and overall message of the novel, while at the same time successfully making the *genre* leap from page to screen to produce what is un- doubtedly one of the best—perhaps even the best—film ever made in the Irish language."[55]

A literary portrait of Ó Cadhain with special emphasis on *Cré na Cille* was the subject of a detailed and nuanced television documen- tary broadcast on RTÉ in October 1980 to mark the tenth anniversary of his death. *There Goes Cré na Cille!* was directed by filmmaker Seán

---

54. *Irish Times*, 24 February 1996 and 1 March 1996.
55. Denvir 2008, 222.

Ó Mórdha and scripted by Breandán Ó hEithir (1930–1990). In the absence of a full-scale monograph on Ó Cadhain's work at the time this film successfully interrogated many of the critical myths associated with *Cré na Cille* and introduced the novel to a mass audience that was primarily English-speaking. The measured assessment of the film's contributors combined with the critical insights of both scriptwriter and director did much to introduce Ó Cadhain to mainstream Irish critical and academic culture. Ó Cadhain's life and achievements were revisited in 2006 in Macdara Ó Curraidhín's extended television treatment *Is mise Stoc na Cille*, produced by ROSG and broadcast by TG4, and in 2007 in *Rí an Fhocail*, an RTÉ commission that was scripted by Alan Titley and directed by Seán Ó Cualáin and Macdara O Curraidhín.

RTÉ Raidió na Gaeltachta marked the sixtieth anniversary of *Cré na Cille*'s appearance in print on 10 March 2010 with a sixty-minute radio documentary, *Cré na Cille: Seasca Bliain os cionn Talún* (sixty years above ground). This documentary, produced by Dónall Ó Braonáin, contains a useful synopsis of critical thinking on Ó Cadhain's masterpiece and features contributions from Éamon Ó Ciosáin, Lochlainn Ó Tuairisg, Róisín Ní Ghairbhí, Louis de Paor, Gearóid Denvir, Alan Titley, Máire Ní Annracháin, and Cathal Ó Háinle. Another television film is worthy of particular note: *Ó Cadhain ar an gCnocán Glas*, which was produced and directed by Aindreas Ó Gallchóir (1929–2011) for RTÉ and broadcast on 13 February 1967. The then single-channel national television service was a relatively recent arrival (1962) to the Irish media scene, but many interesting literary documentary features were produced in the initial years of RTÉ television. *Ó Cadhain ar an gCnocán Glas* is a short but arresting autobiographical portrait and features a visit by Máirtín Ó Cadhain to his native village and ancestral home approximately one mile west of Spiddal. Through a series of direct confessional pieces to the camera, short reflective voice-overs and unscripted, informal conversations with his neighbours, Ó Cadhain's playful and humorous personality reveals itself in the course of twenty-four minutes. The film was shot in black and white by Will Warham, edited by Merritt Butler, remastered and rereleased by RTÉ Archives, and published in a DVD set with *Rí an Fhocail* by Cló Iar-Chonnacht in 2007.

Focal Scoir/Final Word

The last word is best left to Máirtín Ó Cadhain himself. In a contribution to a symposium entitled "Literature in the Celtic Countries" in Cardiff in 1969, he told of coming into the Hogan Stand in Croke Park on All Ireland Day as the teams waited for the parade:

> In passing, a man whom I did not know, said in the Queen's English and pointing his finger at me, "There goes *Cré na Cille*." In pre-television days few writers of English, if any, would have been so recognised. The man said it as if he had a claim on me, as if he felt I was one of his own, one he could kick around, as the burly Kerry full-back was kicking the football about at the same moment. And of course I was. Whether he spoke Irish or not, he felt I belonged to him in a special way, one who was beyond yea or nay his own. This is worth more than all the money and all the sales in the world. It is recognition . . .[56]

Liam Mac Con Iomaire

---

56. In Caerwyn Williams, JEC (ed.), *Literature in Celtic Countries* (Cardiff: University of Wales Press, 1971), 151.

ON TRANSLATING *CRÉ NA CILLE*

More talked about than read, for over threescore years *Cré na Cille* has been the buried treasure of modern Irish-language literature. Our aim in this translation is modest: to give the Anglophone reader the most accurate answer we can provide to the question, What is in this book? There is ample space in the shadow of Ó Cadhain for "versions," subjective interpretations, radical transpositions into other settings and periods, even parodies; these things will follow. But, be faithful to Ó Cadhain has been our first commandment. This of course involves much more than word-for-word equivalence. In English the words are often lacking, Ó Cadhain being a word addict with access to a world that feasted upon its verbal riches, having little else. So it has often been necessary to jump out of the footsteps of the Irish text, run round it, and fall in with it again at the next corner.

A word on our working method. My Irish was picked up in Aran and south Conamara in the middle of a busy life, when I was exploring and mapping those intricate landscapes; it was serviceable enough then for discussing states of the tide, the gossip of the townlands, and the promise of the potato crop, but nowadays it is hardly fit for public use. Hence the basis of our translation was produced by Liam, and then the two of us worked through it repeatedly, almost phrase by phrase. In searching for the English words that would most clearly convey Ó Cadhain's meaning, we have tried to avoid flattening out his extravagances, his anarchic wit, his otherness, his sheer strangeness. At an early stage parts of our text were circulated among anonymous readers by the publisher, eliciting a wide range of comments and suggestions, for all of which we are grateful, and some of which we have adopted, while feeling that their mutual contradictoriness left us free to follow our own lights, which implies that the shortcomings of the present version are entirely our own. Nevertheless we gratefully acknowledge the guidance of Éamon Ó Ciosáin and Gearóid Ó Crualaoich in negotiating some particularly tangled corners of Ó Cadhain's thorny masterpiece, and of Pádraig Ó Snodaigh, who read through and helpfully commented on our translation.

One of the most frequent and urgent recommendations made to us concerned what is almost an established practice with weighty precedents, of leaving personal names and placenames untranslated, in order to root the text in its original setting in time and space. There is point to this; one doesn't want to be pretending that Caitríona and her neighbours are buried in some present-day English graveyard. But there are other ways of preserving a whiff of the book's setting, its irreducible foreignness, across the linguistic gulf. The countless mentions in *Cré na Cille* of little stony fields, seaweed harvesting, holy wells, and so on, and the occasional references to a motor car, a movie, a woman in trousers, sufficiently locate it in a rural seaside community at a period when its folk ways are being invaded by modernity. (Also, if precedent is to be given weight in this debate, there is on the side of translation the splendid example of Brightcity, Eoghan Ó Tuairisc's version of Ó Cadhain's name for the city of Galway, in "An Bóthar go dtí an Ghealchathair.") The point is this. Placenames are semantically two-pronged. The placename on the one hand denotes a location, and on the other bears a load of connotations with it, including the associations that make a place, an element of a life-world, out of the bare location. But the places mentioned in *Cré na Cille* are fictional, which complicates the relationship between denotation and connotation; the only existence of these places is in the text, and all we know of them is what the text tells us, which it does partly through the placename itself. What is denoted is constituted by the connotations. Of Lake Wood, all we know is that there is or was a lake and a wood; but given the general setting we can imagine the place. Pasture Glen, the Common Field, Mangy Field,

Flagstone Height, Donagh's Village, West Headland, Colm's Cove, Woody Hillside, the Deep Hollow, Roadside Field, the Hill Field, and so on, and so on—cumulatively these names paint a picture of a small-scale, well-worked countryside intimately known to its inhabitants. To replace them all with strings of letters the non-Irish-speaking reader will not even be able to pronounce would entail a tremendous loss of texture, of precious discriminations, of meaning. Of course there are difficult choices to be made in translating some of them. To avoid a touch of the English suburban estate we have rendered Lake Wood as Wood of the Lake, and Pasture Glen as Glen of the Pasture, for instance. Also, it's not possible to give the full sense of *tamhnach* in one or two English words—but such obstacles are just the usual ones that make translation a joy frustrated.

A similar argument applies to personal names, but in the present text it is not so pressing, since the English or anglicised equivalents of most of them—Cáit, Bríd, and the like—are obvious anyway. A few that are just English names spelled in the Irish phonetic system, such as Jeaic, we have let revert to their English forms. However, we found it necessary to translate nicknames, as they are indicative of status, appearance, ancestry, or the community's attitude towards the person named. So we have "Siúán the Shop" and "Máirtín Pockface," for example. As with placename elements there are some puzzles, of course: what exactly is implied by the nickname of Tomás Taobh Istigh we think we know, but the ambiguity of Jeaic na Scolóige's name is not just in our minds but commented on (unrevealingly) by other characters in the book.

Translation theorists speak of the "target language." I don't like the aggressive term; I'd rather think of a "host language" and what variety of it might most generously welcome this demanding but rewarding text. The formal principle—a bold invention—of Ó Cadhain's novel is that it is entirely composed of direct speech, with no explicit indication of who is speaking. So, for the reader to be able to ascribe each speech to the right speaker by its tone and vocabulary as well as its content, a dialect of English with a notable range of expressive means is called for, and of course in Ó Cadhain's own territory a Hiberno-English that has for centuries been living next door to and borrowing household items from the Irish language offers itself. The English of the Conamara Gaeltacht can range from bardic frenzy to cocksure modernism; but it is a potent brew, to be used with discretion; it is no use translating Irish into an English that itself calls for translation or has been debased by Paddywhackery.

Finally, and despite our sense of the enormity of what we have undertaken in opening to non-Irish readers' eyes a book so long aureoled in distant respect, I must say what a pleasure the task has been. I hope too that our partners Bairbre and M have found that their considerable contributions have been repaid in the wild humours of Ó Cadhain's *Graveyard Clay*.

Tim Robinson

CHARACTERS AND DIALOGUE CONVENTIONS

CAITRÍONA PHÁIDÍN Caitríona (daughter of) Páidín. Newly buried

PÁDRAIG CHAITRÍONA Pádraig (son of) Caitríona. Her only son

NÓRA SHEÁINÍN'S DAUGHTER Pádraig Chaitríona's wife. Living in same house as Caitríona

MÁIRÍN Girl-child of Pádraig Chaitríona and Nóra Sheáinín's daughter

NÓRA SHEÁINÍN Nóra (daughter of) Seáinín. Mother of Pádraig Chaitríona's wife

BABA PHÁIDÍN Baba (daughter of) Páidín. Sister of Caitríona and Nell. Living in America. A legacy from her expected

NELL PHÁIDÍN Sister of Caitríona and Baba

JACK THE SCOLÓG Jack (son of) Scológ. Nell's husband

PEADAR NELL Peadar (son of) Nell and Jack

BIG BRIAN'S MAG Daughter of Big Brian. Wife of Peadar Nell

BRIAN ÓG Young Brian. Son of Peadar Nell and Big Brian's Mag

BIG BRIAN Father of Mag

TOMÁS INSIDE Relative of Caitríona and Nell. The two of them contending for his land

MURAED PHROINSIAIS Muraed (daughter of) Proinsias. Next-door neighbour and life-long bosom friend to Caitríona

Other Neighbours and Acquaintances

Guide to Dialogue Conventions

— Speech beginning

—... Speech in progress

... Speech omitted

GRAVEYARD CLAY

Time

Eternity

Place

The Graveyard

Regimen

Interlude 1: The Black Clay
Interlude 2: The Spreading of the Clay
Interlude 3: The Teasing of the Clay
Interlude 4: The Crushing of the Clay
Interlude 5: The Bone-Fertilising of the Clay
Interlude 6: The Kneading of the Clay
Interlude 7: The Moulding of the Clay
Interlude 8: The Firing of the Clay
Interlude 9: The Smoothing of the Clay
Interlude 10: The White Clay

CAITRÍONA PHÁIDÍN

Interlude One

THE BLACK CLAY

1

I wonder am I buried in the Pound Plot or the Fifteen-Shilling Plot? Or did the devil possess them to dump me in the Half-Guinea Plot, after all my warnings? The morning of the day I died I called Pádraig up from the kitchen: "I beseech you, Pádraig, my child," I said. "Bury me in the Pound Plot. In the Pound Plot. Some of us are buried in the Half-Guinea Plot, but even so . . ."

I told them to get the best coffin in Tadhg's. It's a good oak coffin anyway . . . I have the scapular[1] mantle[2] on. And the winding-sheet. I had them left ready myself . . . There's a spot on this sheet. It's like a daub of soot. No it's not. A fingermark! My son's wife for certain. It's like her sloppiness. If Nell saw it! I suppose she was there. She wouldn't have been, by God, if I could have helped it . . .

Little Cáit made a botch of cutting out the shroud. I've always said not to give a drop of drink to herself or Bid Shorcha till the corpse was well away from the house. I warned Pádraig not to let them cut out the shroud if they had drink taken. But Little Cáit can't be kept away from corpses. Her greatest delight every day of her life was to have a corpse anywhere in the two townlands. The crops could rot on the ridge once she got the whiff of a corpse . . .

---

1. Two small squares of cloth attached by two strings and worn over the shoulders around the neck as a pious practice.

2. A long strip of cloth with an opening for the head, worn hanging before and behind over the habit on a corpse.

The crucifix is on my breast, the one I bought at the mission . . . But where's the black crucifix Tomáisín's wife got blessed for me at Knock Shrine[3] the last time Tomáisín had to be tied? I told them to put that one on me too. It's much better looking than this one. The Saviour on this one is crooked since Pádraig's children dropped it. The Saviour on the black one is gorgeous. But what's the matter with me? I'm as forgetful as ever! There it is under my head. It's a pity they didn't put that one on my breast . . .

They should have knotted the rosary beads round my fingers better. Nell herself did that, for sure. She'd have been delighted if they'd fallen on the floor when they were putting me in the coffin. Oh Lord God, that one would keep well clear of me . . .

I hope they lit the eight candles over my coffin in the chapel. I had them left ready for them, in the corner of the chest under the rent papers. That's something no corpse in that chapel ever had: eight candles. Curraoin only had four. Liam Thomáis the Tailor had six, but he has a daughter a nun in America.

Three half-barrels of porter I told them to get for my wake, and Éamonn of the Hill Field promised me personally that if there was any drop of the hard stuff[4] to be had on the Mountain[5] he'd bring it himself without waiting to be asked. It would all be needed, with so much altar-money.[6] Fourteen or fifteen pounds at the very least. I sent someone, or a shilling, to many places I didn't owe a funeral visit at all in the five or six years since I felt myself failing. I suppose all the Mountain crowd came. It would be a poor show if they didn't.

---

3. Knock is a village in Co. Mayo where the Virgin Mary and other sacred personages are said to have appeared in 1879. It has long been an important Catholic place of pilgrimage.

4. *Poitín*, illicitly brewed barley spirits.

5. In Conamara "mountain" (sliabh) means rough uncultivated land, not necessarily elevated. *Poitín* was and is secretly made in such areas.

6. A church collection for the priest after a funeral Mass. A shilling coin was the most common contribution among the poor. The custom has been largely abandoned.

We went to theirs. That's the best part of a pound for a start. And the Wood of the Lake crowd would follow the in-laws. That's the best part of another pound. And the whole of Glen of the Pasture owed me a funeral . . . It wouldn't surprise me if Sweet-talking Stiofán didn't come. We were at every single funeral of his. But he'd say he didn't hear about it till I was buried. And the song and dance he'd make of it then! "I assure you, Pádraig Ó Loideáin, if it cost me my life's blood I'd have been at the funeral. I owed it to Caitríona Pháidín to come to her funeral even if it was on my two knees. But devil a word I heard about it till the night she was buried. A young lad . . ." A right blatherer, the same Sweet-talking Stiofán! . . .

I wonder was I keened[7] well. No word of a lie but Bid Shorcha has a fine tearful wail, if she wasn't too drunk. I'm sure Nell was sponging around there too. Nell crying and not a tear on her cheek, the puss-face! That one wouldn't dare come near the house while I was alive . . .

She's happy now. I thought I'd live another few years and bury the bitch. She failed a lot since her son was injured. Even before that, she was going to the doctor fairly often. There's very little wrong with her. Rheumatism. That won't kill her for a long time. She takes good care of herself. Which I didn't do, and it's now I know it. I killed myself toiling and moiling . . . If only I'd seen to that pain before it became chronic. But once it hits you in the kidneys your goose is cooked.

I was two years older than Nell, anyway . . . Baba, then me, then Nell. A year last Michaelmas I got the pension. But I got it before my time. Baba is bordering on seventy-three. She's close to death now, for all her efforts. Our people weren't long-lived. When she gets word of my death she'll know she hasn't long left herself, and she'll make her will for certain . . . She'll leave every single penny she has to Nell. The pussface got the better of me after all. She has milked Baba well. But if I'd lived till Baba had made her will I'd say she'd have given me

---

7. Anglicisation of *caoineadh*, to lament aloud over a corpse. Certain women were highly regarded for their abilities in this ancient and now extinct Gaelic form of mournful chant.

half the money in spite of Nell. Baba is fickle-minded. I was the one she wrote to most, these last three years since she moved out from Big Brian's people in Norwood and went to Boston. It's a great relief that she parted company with that nest of vipers at any rate . . .

But she never forgave Pádraig for marrying that scold from Mangy Field and turning his back on Big Brian's daughter Mag. She wouldn't have gone next or near Nell's house, that time she was home from America, if Nell's son hadn't married Big Brian's Mag. Why would she! . . . A little hovel of a house. And a filthy little hovel at that. Not a house fit for a Yank at any rate. I don't know how she put up with it at all, after our house and those grand American houses. But she didn't stay there long before taking off over again . . .

She won't come to Ireland again in her lifetime. She's done with that now. But who knows, she might get itchy feet again when this war is over, if she's still among the living. As for Nell, she'd charm the honey from a hive, she's so sly and cunning. Blast Baba for an old hag! Even though she parted from Big Brian's family in Norwood, she still has a great regard for his daughter Mag . . . Wasn't my Pádraig the silly little fool not to take her advice and marry the ugly wretch's daughter. "It's no use going on at me," said the little fool. "I wouldn't marry Big Brian's Mag if she was the last woman in Ireland." Baba went off up to Nell's as if she'd got a slap in the face, and she never came near our house again, except to step in for a moment the day she was going back to America.

—. . . Hitler is my darling. He's the man for them . . .

—If England is beaten this country will be in bad shape. We've already lost the market . . .

—. . . You Breed of the One-Eared Tailor, it's you who left me here fifty years before my time. The One-Ear Breed were always ready with the foul blow. Knives, stones, bottles. You wouldn't fight like a man, instead of stabbing me . . .

—. . . Permission to speak! Permission to speak . . .

—Jesus, Mary and Joseph!—Am I alive or am I dead? Are these here alive or dead? They're all giving out as much as they did above ground! I thought that once I was laid in the grave, free from chores and household cares and fear of wind or weather, there'd be some peace in store for me . . . but why all this squabbling in the graveyard clay? . . .

2

—. . . Who are you? Are you long here? Do you hear me? Don't be shy. Feel as free here as you would at home. I'm Muraed Phroinsiais.

—For God's sake! Muraed Phroinsiais who lived next door to me all my life. I'm Caitríona. Caitríona Pháidín. Do you remember me, Muraed, or do you lose all memory of life here? I haven't lost mine yet at any rate . . .

—And you won't. Life's the same here, Caitríona, as it was in the "ould country," except that all we see is the grave we're in and we can't leave the coffin. You won't hear the living either, or know what's happening to them, apart from what the newly buried dead will tell you. But we're neighbours once again, Caitríona. Are you long here? I didn't hear you coming.

—I don't know if it was on St. Patrick's Day I died or the day after, Muraed. I was too worn out. And I don't know how long I'm here either. Not very long anyway . . . You're a good while buried yourself, Muraed . . . You're right. Four years come Easter. Spreading a bit of manure for Pádraig in the Hollow Field I was, when a young girl of Tomáisín's came down for me. "Muraed Phroinsiais is in the throes of death," she says. And then, believe it or not, wasn't Little Cáit already going in the door of the house by the time I got to the top of the haggard![8] You had just expired. It was I closed your eyelids with my own two thumbs. Myself and Little Cáit laid you out. And indeed, everyone said you looked lovely. No one had call to grumble. Everyone who saw you said you made a beautiful corpse. There wasn't so much as a hair out of place on you. You were laid out as smoothly as if you'd been ironed onto the board . . .

---

8. A walled enclosure beside a farmhouse, where the hay and corn were stacked for winter fodder for the animals.

. . . I didn't linger long, Muraed. My kidneys had been failing for a long time. A blockage. I got a terrible pain there five or six weeks ago, and I caught a cold on top of that. The pain went into my belly and from there up into my chest. I only lasted about a week . . . I wasn't that old at all, Muraed. I was only seventy-one. But my life was nothing but hardship. It was, God knows, and the signs are on me. When it hit me it hit me hard. There was no fight left in me . . .

You can say that indeed, Muraed. That hussy from Mangy Field didn't help matters at all. What possessed my Pádraig to marry her in the first place? . . . God bless your innocence, Muraed dear, you don't know the half of it, for not a word of it ever passed my lips. It's three long months now since she as much as lifted a finger . . . Another child. She only just pulled through. She'll never survive the next one, I'd say . . . There was a clutch of children, and not an ounce of sense between them, apart from Máirín, the eldest girl, and she was at school every day. I used to potter around as best I could myself, washing them and keeping them away from the fire and giving them a bite to eat . . . You're right, Muraed. Pádraig will have no house left, now that I'm gone. Certainly that hussy isn't fit to keep a house, a woman who spends every second day in bed . . . Now you've said it, my friend! Pádraig and the children are to be pitied . . .

I had indeed. I had everything left ready, Muraed, shroud, scapular mantle and all . . . Honestly, Muraed, there were eight candles over me in the chapel, and that's the truth . . . I went into the best coffin in Tadhg's. I'd say it cost every penny of fifteen pounds . . . But there are three plaques on this one, Muraed, not just two . . . And you'd think each one of them was the big mirror in the priest's parlour . . .

Pádraig told me he'll put a cross of Island limestone[9] over me like the one over Peadar the Pub, and an inscription in Irish: "Caitríona Bean Sheáin Uí Loideáin . . ." Pádraig himself said that straight out, Muraed . . . I wouldn't have dreamed of asking him, Muraed . . . And

---

9. The limestone of the Aran Islands, some ten miles off the south Conamara coast, was highly prized for tombstones in south Conamara, which is largely underlain by rocks harder to carve, such as granite.

he said he'd put a railing round the grave like the one round Siúán the Shop, and that he'd plant flowers over me—damned if I can remember what they're called—the sort the Schoolmistress had on her black outfit after the Big Master died. "It's the least we could do for you," said Pádraig, "after all the hardship you endured for us . . ."

But tell me this, Muraed, what part of the graveyard is this? . . . Upon my soul you're right, it's the Fifteen-Shilling Plot . . . Now, Muraed, you know in your heart I wouldn't expect to be buried in the Pound Plot. If they did bury me there I could do nothing about it, but as for asking them to . . .

Nell, is it? . . . By Dad, I nearly buried her before me. If only I'd lived just a little longer I'd have done it . . . Her son Peadar's accident set her back a lot . . . A lorry knocked him down, back at the Strand, a year or a year and a half ago, and made pulp of his hip. They didn't know for a week in the hospital whether he was coming or going . . .

Oh! You've heard about that already, Muraed . . . Faith then, he spent six months on the flat of his back . . . The devil a tap of work he did since he came home, just going about on two crutches. Everybody thought it was all up with him . . .

The children are no help to him, Muraed, apart from the eldest scamp, who's a blackguard . . . Why wouldn't he be! Taking after his grandfather, his namesake Big Brian, the ugly streak of misery. Not to mention his little granny Nell. Nell's people haven't made a spring sowing worth mentioning for the past two years . . . The injury is a hard blow for Big Brian's Mag and for Nell. Serves the pussface right! We had three times the potato crop she had this year.

Oh! God bless your innocence, Muraed, wasn't the road as long and as wide for him as it was for everyone else, to keep out of the lorry's way . . . Nell's son lost the case, Muraed. "I won't give you a red cent" said the Justice . . . He took the lorry driver to the Sessions since, but the judge wouldn't let Nell's son as much as open his mouth. He's to take the lorry driver to a High Court in Dublin soon, for all the good that will do him. Mannion the Counsellor told me personally that Nell's people wouldn't get a brass farthing. "For what?" says he. "On the wrong side of the road!" . . . It's true for you, Muraed. The law will take the last penny off Nell. Serves her right! She won't be going past our house so often from now on singing "Eleanor of the Secrets"[10] . . .

Poor Jack isn't keeping at all well, Muraed. Of course, the devil a bit of caring Nell ever gave him, or Big Brian's daughter either, since she moved in there . . . Isn't Nell my very own sister, Muraed, and why wouldn't I know? She never took the slightest bit of care of poor Jack. She was all for herself. She cared for nobody else in the whole wide world . . . I'm telling you, Muraed, and I'm telling you the truth, Jack had a hard life at the hands of that little bitch . . . Tomás Inside, Muraed? The same as ever you saw him . . . He's still in his little hovel. But it will fall in on top of him any day now . . . Well, indeed, didn't my Pádraig offer to go up and put a layer of thatch on it for him. "Now, Pádraig," says I, "don't demean yourself by going thatching for Tomás Inside. Let Nell thatch his house for him if she wants to. If she goes thatching for him, then so will we . . ."

"But Nell doesn't have a soul to help her since Peadar injured his leg," says Pádraig.

"Everyone has enough to do to keep his own house thatched," says I, "never mind that useless old Tomás Inside's little hovel."

"But the house will fall in on him," says he.

"Then let it fall," says I. "Nell has enough to do now without stuffing Tomás Inside's big gob. Hold on now, Pádraig, my fine man!" says I. "Tomás Inside is like a rat in a sinking ship. It's to our house he'll have to run from his leaking roof . . ."

Nóra Sheáinín, did you say? That I would be pleased to get acquainted with her again here! Too well acquainted I am with that one, and with every one of her breed . . . She's listening to the schoolmaster every day? To the Big Master, the poor man . . . The Big Master reading to Nóra Sheáinín! . . . To Nóra Sheáinín . . . Ababúna![11] . . . Isn't it little respect he has for himself as a schoolmaster, reading to Nóra Sheáinín . . . Of course, there isn't a word of learning in that

---

10. "Eleanor of the Secrets," a well-known Irish love song.

11. Caitríona's personal expression of surprise or consternation.

one's head. Where would she get it? A woman who never set foot in a schoolhouse unless she went there on polling day . . . Upon my soul it's a strange world if a schoolmaster is having conversations with Nóra Sheáinín. What did you say, Muraed? . . . That he's very fond of her, even? He doesn't know what sort she is, Muraed . . . If he had her daughter in the same house with him for sixteen years as I had, then he'd know the sort she is. But I'll tell him . . . about the sailor and everything . . .

—. . . "Mártan Sheáin Mhóir[12] had a daughter
        And she was as broad as any man."

—. . . Five times eight is forty; five times nine is forty-five; five times ten . . . I can't remember, Master . . .

—. . . "He went ranting after women
        And he headed for the fair."

—. . . I was twenty, and I led with the Ace of Hearts. I took the King off your partner. Murchaín hit me with the Knave. But I had the Nine, and my partner had the fall of the play . . .

—I had the Queen and a saver.

—Murchaín was about to lead with the Five of Trumps and he would have swept your Nine. Wouldn't you, Murchaín?

—But then the *mine*[13] blew the house up . . .

—But the game would have been ours all the same . . .

—Don't be so sure of that! Were it not for the *mine* . . .

—. . . God help us, now and forever . . .

—. . . A bald-faced mare.[14] She was the best . . .

—Muraed, you can't hear a finger in your ear in this place. Oh!

---

12. Mártan (son of) Big Seán. The opening line of a bawdy rhyme.

13. The explosion of a German mine that drifted ashore in June 1917, killing nine local men, is still remembered in Cois Fharraige in Conamara. *Mine* appeared in English in the original Irish text. We use italic for all words that were not in Irish in the original text.

14. Mare with a white front to the head.

Blessed Son of God tonight . . . "A bald-faced mare." May yourself and herself go bald if you don't stop talking about her . . .

—I was fighting for the Irish Republic . . .

—Nobody asked you to . . .

—. . . He stabbed me . . .

—If he did, it wasn't in the tongue. A plague of baldness on the pair of you! . . . You have me demented since I came into the graveyard. Oh, Muraed, if only we could find a quiet nook to ourselves! Above ground, if you didn't like your company you could leave them and go elsewhere. But alas and alack, the dead will never leave their place in the graveyard clay . . .

3

. . . And I was buried in the Fifteen-Shilling Plot after all! In spite of my warnings . . . Nell must have been grinning all over her face! She'll go into the Pound Plot herself for sure now. I wouldn't be a bit surprised if it was Nell got Pádraig to bury me in the Fifteen-Shilling Plot instead of the Pound Plot. She wouldn't have had the cheek to come next or near the house until she knew I was dead. She never set foot inside my door since the day I got married . . . unless she sneaked in unknown to me when I was in the throes of death . . .

But Pádraig is a bit simple. He'd give in to her sweet talk. And Pádraig's wife would go along with her. "Indeed now, you're perfectly right, Nell dear. The Fifteen-Shilling Plot is good enough for anybody. We're not landed gentry . . ."

The Fifteen-Shilling Plot is good enough for anybody. She would say that. What else would she say? Nóra Sheáinín's daughter. I'll take it out on her yet. She'll be here on her next childbirth for certain. I'll take it out on her, by God. But in the meantime I'll take it out on her mother—I'll take it out on Nóra Sheáinín herself.

Nóra Sheáinín. From over there in Mangy Field! Mangy Field of the puddles. We always heard they milk the ducks there. The upstart! Learning from the Master now! Faith then, it was time for her to start, so it was. A schoolmaster wouldn't speak to her anywhere else in the world but in the graveyard, and he wouldn't speak to her even there if he knew who she was . . .

It's her daughter has left me here twenty years before my time. I'm worn and wasted for the last six months minding her plague of children. She's sick when she's having a child and she's sick when she's not. The next one will carry her off for certain . . . Poor Pádraig would be better off rid of her, whatever way he'd manage without her. Pádraig himself was the unbiddable son. "I'll never have anyone else, mother," says he. "I'll go off to America and let the place go to wrack and ruin, since you've no liking for her . . ."

That was when Baba was home from America. She begged and implored him to marry Big Brian's Mag. Very concerned indeed she was, for that matter, about the ugly little skin-and-bones. "She took good care of me in America," says she, "when I was very sick and far away from all my own people. Big Brian's Mag is a good resourceful young woman, and she has a well-lined purse of her own apart from what I'll be giving her. I was fonder of you, Caitríona," she says to me, "than of any of my other sisters. I'd rather see my money in your house than with anyone else belonging to me. I'd like to see your son Pádraig bettering himself. The choice is in your hands now, Pádraig," says she. "I'm in a hurry back to America, but I won't go till I see Big Brian's Mag settled here, since she wasn't getting her health over there. Marry her, Pádraig. Marry Big Brian's Mag, and I'll not leave you in want. I have more than I'll ever see spent. She's already asked for by Nell's son. Nell herself was talking to me about it the other day. She'll marry Nell's son if you don't marry her, Pádraig. Either that or go and marry whoever you want, but if you do . . ."

"I'd sooner go begging for my keep," says Pádraig. "I won't marry any woman on the face of the earth but Nóra Sheáinín's daughter from Mangy Field . . ."

And he married her.

I myself had to put a shirt on her back. She didn't even have the marriage fee, not to mention a dowry. A dowry from the Filthy-Feet Breed! A dowry in Mangy Field of the puddles, where they milk the ducks . . . He married her, and she's there with him ever since like the shadow of death. She's not able to raise a pig or a calf, a hen or a goose, not even the ducks she'd have been used to in Mangy Field. Her house is dirty. Her children are dirty. She can't work the land or the strand[15] . . .

There was full and plenty in that house until she came into it. I kept it scrubbed clean. There wasn't a Saturday night in the year I didn't have every stool and chair and table out by the stream to wash. I spun and I carded. I had yarn and I had sackcloth. I raised pigs and calves and fowl . . . for as long as I had the energy to do it. And when I hadn't, I shamed Nóra Sheáinín's daughter into not letting everything go by the board completely . . .

But how will the house be now without me? . . . The bold Nell will be satisfied at any rate . . . So well she may. She has a good woman in her house for baking and spinning: Big Brian's Mag. It's easy for her to laugh at that little fool of a son of mine who has nobody but that untidy slut. When Nell's going up by our house now, won't she often be saying: "Indeed we got thirty pounds for the pigs . . . It was a good fair if you had cattle raised for it. We got sixteen pounds for the two calves . . . Even though it's not the laying season our Mag still manages to collect eggs. She had four score eggs in Brightcity[16] on Saturday . . . Four broods of chicks hatched for us this year. All the hens are laying a second time. I set another clutch yesterday. 'The little clutch of the ripening oats,' Jack called it when he saw me putting them under the hen . . ." She'll have a right swagger in her bottom now, going by our house. She'll know I'm gone. Nell! The pussface! She is my sister. But may no corpse come into the graveyard ahead of her! . . .

---

15. Such tasks as collecting seaweed as manure for the fields, and collecting limpets, cockles, mussels, and periwinkles for food.

16. The translation of *Gealchathair*, Ó Cadhain's name for Galway, introduced by Eoghan Ó Tuairisc in *The Road to Brightcity* (1981), in his English version of selected short stories from Ó Cadhain's earliest collections.

4

—. . . I was fighting for the Irish Republic, and you killed me, you traitor. Fighting for England you were, the time you fought for the Free State . . . An English gun in your hand, English money in your pocket, and an English spirit in your heart. You sold your soul and the heritage of your ancestors for the sake of a "bargain," for the sake of a job . . .

—That's a lie! A criminal you were, rising up against a legitimate government . . .

—. . . By the oak of this coffin, Muraed, I gave Caitríona the pound . . .

—. . . I drank two score pints and two . . .

—I remember it well, Glutton. I twisted my ankle that day . . .

—. . . You stuck the knife into me between the lower and upper ribs. Through the edge of my liver it went. Then you gave it a twist. The foul blow was always the mark of the One-Ear Breed . . .

—. . . Permission to speak! Let me speak . . .

—Are you ready for the hour's reading now, Nóra Sheáinín? We'll make a start on a new novelette today. We finished *Two Men and a Powder-puff* the other day, did we not? The title of this one is *The Red-Hot Kiss*. Listen now, Nóra Sheáinín: "Nuala was an innocent girl until she met Charlie Price in the nightclub . . ." I know. There's no peace or seclusion or opportunity for culture here . . . and as you say, Nóra, paltry trivialities is all they ever talk about . . . cards, horses, drink, violence . . . he has us demented with his little mare, day in day out . . . You are perfectly right, Nóra dear . . . There's no opportunity here for one who wants to cultivate the intellect. That is the absolute truth, Nóra. This place is as bad-mannered, as dull-witted, as barbarous as the Wastelands of the Half-Guinea Plot down there. We're truly in the Dark Ages since the *sansculottes* who accumulated piles of money "on the dole" began to be buried in the Fifteen-Shilling Plot . . . This is how I would divide up this graveyard now, Nóra, if I had my own way: university people in the Pound Plot, and then . . . Isn't that so, Nóra? It's a crying shame indeed that some of my own pupils are lying up here beside me . . . It depresses me how ill-informed they are, when I think of the diligence I wasted on them . . . And they can be quite disrespectful at times . . . I don't know what's coming over the young generation at all . . . You're right, Nóra . . . Lack of cultural opportunities, I suppose . . .

"Nuala was an innocent girl until she met Charlie Price in the nightclub." A nightclub, Nóra? . . . You were never in a nightclub? Well, a nightclub is not unlike this place . . . Ah no, Nóra. The places frequented by the sea-going fraternity are not the same as nightclubs. "Dives" is what those places are, Nóra, but cultivated people go to nightclubs . . . You would like to pay a visit to one of them, Nóra? . . . It would be no bad thing, to give your education the final touch, a bit of polish, a *cachet* . . . I was in a nightclub in London myself that time the teachers got a pay rise, before the two cuts. I saw an African prince there. He was as black as a berry, and drinking champagne . . . You'd love to go to a nightclub, Nóra? Aren't you the shameless one . . . Naughty girl, Nóra . . . Naughty . . .

—You brazen hussy! Seáinín Robin's daughter from Mangy Field! What was that place she said she wanted to visit, Master? . . . May she not live to enjoy it! Take care that you pay no heed to her, Master dear. If you knew her as well as I do you'd sing dumb to her. I've spent the last sixteen years bickering with her daughter and herself. You're poorly employed, Master, squandering your time on Nóirín Filthy-Feet. She never had a single day's schooling, Master, and she'd be more familiar with the track of a flea than her ABC . . .

—Who is this? Who are you . . . ? Caitríona Pháidín! Is it possible you're here, Caitríona! . . . Well, no matter how long it takes, this is the last shelter for all of us in the end . . . You are welcome, Caitríona, you are welcome . . . I'm afraid, Caitríona, you are . . . what shall I say . . . a little too hard on Nóra Filthy . . . on Nóra Sheáinín. Her mind has much improved since the time you used to be . . . what was the expression you used, Caitríona? . . . Yes . . . bickering with her . . . It is difficult for us here to keep track of time, but if I understand you rightly, she has been here for three years now, under the beneficial influence of culture . . . But tell me this, Caitríona . . . Do you remember the letter I wrote for you to your sister Baba in America? . . . That was the last letter I ever wrote . . . I was struck down by my fatal illness the following day . . . Is that will under discussion still?

—It's many a letter came from Baba since you were writing for me, Master. But she never confirmed or denied anything about the money. We got her reply to that letter you spoke of, Master. That was the last time she mentioned a will: "I did not make my will yet," she said. "I hope I will not suffer a sudden or accidental death as you were imagining in your letter. Do not worry. I will make my will in due course, when I consider it necessary." When that letter came I said to myself, "It must have been a schoolmaster wrote that for her. Our people never had that sort of talk."

It's the Small Master—your own successor—who writes for us now, Master, but I'm afraid the priest writes for Nell. That hag can get round him with her chickens and her knitted stockings and her backhanders . . . She's the one who's good at that, Master. I thought I'd last another few years and bury the bitch before me! . . .

Anyway, you did your best for me about the will, Master. You had a hand for the pen, Master. I often saw you writing a letter, and I used to think that your pen was able to blacken paper with words as fast as I could put stitches on a stocking . . . "May the Lord have mercy on the poor Big Master," I used to say. "He was so obliging. If God had granted him more time he would have got the money for me . . ."

I think the Schoolmistress—your wife I mean, Master—will soon be setting up house again. And why wouldn't she? A strong active young woman still, God bless her . . . I beg your pardon, Master! Don't heed anything I say. I'm always rattling on like that, but sure a person can't help that . . . Master dear, I shouldn't have told you at all. You'll be worrying about her. I thought it would warm the cockles of your heart to hear the Schoolmistress was getting married again . . .

Now Master, you'll have to forgive me . . . I'm not a gossip . . . Don't ask me to name the man, Master. Ah now, Master dear, don't ask me that! . . . If I'd known it would upset you so much I wouldn't have mentioned it at all . . .

So she swore and she promised that if you died she'd never marry another man! Ah! Master dear! . . . Did you never hear: after the vows the women are easiest . . . You weren't even cold, Master, when she had her eye cocked at another man. I think, between ourselves, she was always a bit flighty . . .

The Small Master? . . . Indeed it's not . . . The Wood of the Lake Master? . . . That's a decent man, Master. Never touches a drop. Himself and the Parish priest's sister are to be married soon—that dark miserable little slip who wears trousers. They say he'll get the new school then . . .

Indeed it's not the Red-haired Policeman either. They say he has a fine stump of a nurse on a string in Brightcity . . . it's not the seed potato man[17] either . . . Guess away now, Master. I'll tell you if you guess right . . . Padeen's gone to England, Master. The lorry was taken off him and sold. There wasn't a road he travelled buying turf that he didn't leave a string of debts after him. Guess again, Master . . . The very man himself, Master, Billyboy the Post! You did well to guess him. You have a great head on you, Master, whatever anybody says . . .

Look out for yourself with Nóra Sheáinín. I could tell you things, Master . . . Oh! Put that bit of news out of your mind, Master, and don't let it bother you in the least . . . I'm inclined to agree with you, Master. It was more than letters brought Billyboy round the house . . . Ah! Master, she was always a little bit flighty, your wife was . . .

5

—. . . They were sent over as plenipotentiaries to arrange a peace treaty between England and Ireland . . .

—I tell you that's a damned lie. They were only sent as delegates, and they exceeded their authority. They committed treachery and the country bears the marks of it . . .

---

17. The official who distributed seed potatoes supplied by the Department of Agriculture.

—. . . A bald-faced mare. She was the best. It was no bother to her to pull a ton and a half . . .

—. . . By the oak of this coffin, Nóra Sheáinín, I gave Caitríona the pound . . .

—. . . "Mártan Sheáin Mhóir had a daughter
And she was as broad as any man
She'd stand away up on a height . . ."

—. . . Oh! To hell with your England and her markets. Worried you are about the few pence you have in the bank. Hitler is my darling! . . .

—. . . Now Cóilí, I am a writer. I have read fifty books for every book you have read. I'll have the law on you, Cóilí, if you suggest that I'm not a writer. Did you read my last book, *The Jellyfish's Vision?* . . . You did not, Cóilí? . . . I beg your pardon, Cóilí. I'm very sorry. I had forgotten that you cannot read . . . It is a mighty powerful story, Cóilí . . . And I have three and a half novels, two and a half plays and nine and a half translations sent to An Gúm,[18] and another short story and a half, *The Setting Sun.* It is my greatest regret that *The Setting Sun* was not in print before I died . . .

If you intend to take up writing, Cóilí, remember that it is taboo for An Gúm to publish anything that a daughter would hide from her father . . . I beg your pardon, Cóilí. I am sorry. I thought you intended to write. But for fear you should ever experience that divine urge . . . There is not a single Irish speaker who does not feel it at some time of life . . . The elements on these western shores are to blame, they say . . . I'll give you a few bits of advice. Now, Cóilí, don't be unmannerly. It is a moral obligation on every Irish speaker to find out if he has the gift of writing, especially the gift of short-story writing, of drama and of poetry . . . These last two gifts are much commoner even than the gift

---

18. The Government (Irish Language) Publications Scheme. Many Irish-language writers including Ó Cadhain earned a pittance writing or translating works for An Gúm ("the Scheme").

of short-story writing, Cóilí. Poetry, for example. All you have to do is start writing from the bottom of the page up . . . or else start writing from right to left, but that is not nearly as poetic as the other way . . .

I beg your pardon, Cóilí. I am extremely sorry. I forgot that you cannot read or write . . . But the short story, Cóilí . . . I will explain it to you like this. You have drunk a pint of porter, have you not? . . . Indeed, I understand . . . You often drank a pint of porter . . . Never mind how many you drank, Cóilí . . .

—I drank two score pints and two, one after the other . . .

—I know that . . . Wait a minute now . . . Good man! Let me speak . . . Cóilí, have an ounce of sense and let me speak . . . You have seen the head on a pint of porter. Froth, is it not? Worthless dirty froth. And yet, the more of it there is the greedier people are for the pint. And when a person is gulping the pint he'll drink it dregs and all, insipid though it be. Do you see now, Cóilí, the beginning and middle and end of the short story? . . . Mind you don't forget, Cóilí, that the end must leave a bitter taste in your mouth, the taste of the divine hangover, the urge to steal fire from the gods, the longing for another bite at the forbidden fruit . . . Look at the way I would have ended *The Re-Setting Sun*, which I was working on when I dropped dead with a spasm of writer's cramp:

"After the girl had uttered that fateful word, he turned on his heel and went out of the stuffy room into the evening air. The western sky was darkened by thick clouds pressing in from the sea. And a little hang-dog sun was going to ground behind Old Village Hill . . ." That is the *tour de force*, Cóilí: "little hang-dog sun going to ground"; and I may as well remind you that after the last word the final line must be generously sprinkled with dots, writer's dots as I call them . . . But perhaps you would have the patience, Cóilí, to listen while I read you the whole work . . .

—Hold on now, my good man. I'll tell you a story: "Long long ago there were three men . . ."

—Cóilí! Cóilí! There's no artistry in that story: "Long long ago there were three men . . ." That's a hackneyed beginning . . . Now,

Cóilí, hold on a minute. Allow me to speak. I consider myself a writer . . .

—Shut your mouth, you windbag. Go ahead, Cóilí . . .

—"Long long ago, and a long time ago it was, there were three men. There were three men long ago . . ."

—Yes, Cóilí . . .

—"There were three men long ago . . . Indeed there were three men long ago. Apart from that, we don't know what became of them . . ."

—. . . "And by my book,[19] Jack the Scológ[20] . . ."

—. . . Five times eleven is fifty-five; five times thirteen . . . five times thirteen . . . we don't learn that one at all . . . Now then, Master, don't I remember them! . . . Five times seven, is that your question, Master? Five times seven is it? . . . five times seven . . . seven . . . hold on a tick now . . . five times one is five . . .

6

—. . . But I don't understand it, Muraed. *Honest Engine*,[21] I don't. She gave me a bad name with the Big Master, Caitríona Pháidín did. I wouldn't mind but I never did anything to deserve it. You well know, Muraed, I never interfere in anybody's business, being always busy with culture. And I have a fine flashy cross over me too. *Smashing*, as the Big Master says. To insult me, Muraed! . . .

—It's time you were well used to Caitríona's tongue, Nóra Sheáinín . . .

—But *honest*, Muraed . . .

---

19. A snippet of an impromptu satirical song of the kind still composed in Conamara. The book is the Bible.

20. The word can mean scholar, manservant, farmer, a yeoman; *scológ cheoil*, snatches of song. See the Introductory Note.

21. Thus in the original; a local mishearing of the American-English phrase "Honest Injun."

—... "Like an eel in a net Caitríona was set
    To grab by the hair Nóra Sheáinín."

—But she's forever getting at me, time after time. I don't understand it. *Honest* . . .

—... "Ere the morning grew old Nóra Sheáinín came over,
    Into Tríona she tore in the guise of a shark . . ."
    — "My fine gentle daughter, if she married your Pádraig,
    Her dowry put order and shape on your shack . . ."
    — "Caitríona, you're shameless, you're mean and
    outrageous,
    You tried to defame me and ruin my name . . ."

—... Her lies, Muraed! *Honest to God!* I wonder what she said to Dotie . . . Dotie! . . . Dotie! . . . What did Caitríona Pháidín say to you about me? . . .

—God bless us and save us forever and ever. I don't know who ye are at all. Isn't it a pity they didn't take my earthly remains back east of Brightcity and lay me down with my own people in Temple Brennan, on the fair plains of East Galway . . .

—Dotie! I told you before, that sort of talk is "sentimental drivel." What did Caitríona say? . . .

—She said the most vindictive thing I've ever heard, about her own sister Nell. "May no corpse come into the graveyard ahead of her!" she said. You wouldn't hear talk like that on the fair plains of East Galway . . .

—Dotie! But what did she say about me? . . .

—About your daughter . . .

—... "She had no bodice or a wedding garment
    But what I bought her from out my purse . . ."

—She said you were of the Filthy-Feet Breed and infested with fleas . . .

—Dotie! *De grâce* . . .

—That sailors used to be . . .

—Parlez-vous français, Madame, Mademoiselle . . .

—Au revoir! Au revoir! . . .

—Mais c'est splendide. Je ne savais pas qu'il y avait une . . .

—Au revoir. Honest, Muraed, if Dotie didn't know me she'd have believed those lies . . . Dotie! "Sentimentality" again. You are my fellow-navigator on the boundless sea of culture, Dotie. You should be able to filter every misjudgement and every prejudice out of your mind, as Clicks put it in *Two Men and a Powder-puff* . . .

—. . . It was the Poet composed it, I'd say . . .

—Oh, was it that cheeky brat? . . .

—Indeed then, it was not. He wouldn't be able to. It was Big Micil Ó Conaola composed it:

> "Nursing an old Yank there was Baba Pháidín
> And no finer damsel could be found in Maine . . ."

—Honest, Muraed, I have forgotten everything concerning Caitríona's affairs on the plain above us. Culture, Muraed. It elevates the mind to the lofty peaks and opens the fairy palaces in which is stored the protoplasm of colour and sound, as Nibs says in *Sunset Tresses*. One loses all interest in the paltry trivia of doleful life. A glorious disorder has filled my mind for some time now, brought on by an avalanche of culture . . .

—. . . "And no finer damsel could be found in Maine.
> She came home dressed in gaudy clothing
> For she coaxed the hoard from the grey-haired dame . . ."

—. . . Baba Pháidín never married, as she was looking after the old hag ever since she went to America. What do you think but didn't the old hag leave her all her money—or almost all—when she was dying . . . Baba Pháidín could fill every grave in this graveyard with golden guineas, Dotie, or that's the reputation she has . . .

—. . . Cóilí himself made up that rigmarole. Who else:

> "'Oh, Baba my dear,' said Caitríona's cat,
> 'Don't heed her my dear,' said the cat of Nell.

'If I got the gold,' said Caitríona's cat,
'It's mine now my dear,' said the cat of Nell."

—Caitríona would sooner do Nell out of Baba's will than get a thousand leases on her own life . . .

—. . . "'I've a lovely pocket,' said Caitríona's kitten,
'I've a lovely pocket,' said the kitten of Nell."
"'For an old hag's money,' said Caitríona's kitten,
'You've no promise from Baba,' said the kitten of Nell . . .'"

—She had all the schoolmasters for years back worn out with writing to America for her . . .

—And Mannion the Counsellor . . .

—The Big Master told me he wrote very cultural letters for her. He picked up a lot of Americanisms from the cinema . . .

—The time he used to bring the Schoolmistress into Brightcity in the motor car . . .

—What's galling Caitríona now is that she died before Nell. When I was alive I often heard her going along the boreen muttering to herself, "I'll bury Nell before me in the graveyard clay" . . .

—. . . Tell the truth, Cóilí. Was it yourself made up that rigmarole?

—It was Big Micil Ó Conaola composed it. It was he composed "The Song of Caitríona" and "The Song . . ."

—. . . But Nell is still alive. She'll get Baba's inheritance now. There's no other brother or sister but herself . . .

—Don't be so sure of that, Muraed. Baba was very fond of Caitríona.

—Do you know what my better half used to say about the Páidín clan: "Weathercocks," he'd say. "If one of them went to the fair to buy a cow he'd come home in half an hour with a donkey. And the first person to pass some remark about the donkey, he'd say to him: 'I wish I'd bought a cow instead of that old lazybones of a donkey! She'd be of more use . . .'"

—. . . "Would you yourself come home with me?
   There's room beneath my shawl;
   And by my book, Jack the Scológ,
   We'll have songs forevermore . . ."

—. . . Why would it be a peculiar nickname for a person, Dotie
. . . Yes. "Jack the Scológ." He's up there above the townland where
Caitríona and myself lived . . . I saw the Scológ himself, Jack's father
. . . The Scológ. He was one of the Ó Fíne clan by right . . . It's no
laughing matter, Dotie . . . Dotie! "Scológ" is as good as "Dotie"
any day of the year. Let me tell you that even if you are from the fair
plains of East Galway we weren't hatched out under a hen either . . .
   —*De grâce* Marguerita . . .

—. . . "'I'll marry Jack,' said Caitríona's dog,
   'I'll marry Jack,' said the dog of Nell . . ."

—Caitríona refused many a man. Big Brian was one of them. He
had a tract of land, and a wealth of stock on it. Her father asked her to
move in there, but she wouldn't have given the potato-water for him.
   —. . . Begin that song again and sing it properly . . .

— "Up got Son of Scológ . . ."

—. . . You wouldn't think God had put a soul into Jack the Scológ
until he began to sing. But if you heard his voice just once it'd haunt
you for the rest of your life. I don't know how to put it now . . .
   —A dream of music.
   —That's it, Nóra. Like a strange dream, exactly. You're in distress
on a clifftop. The abyss yawns beneath you. You're trembling with
fear . . . Then you hear Jack the Scológ's voice coming up to you out
of the depths. The singing overcomes your fear. You're letting yourself go . . . Feeling yourself sliding down . . . down . . . to draw closer
to that voice . . .
   —*Oh my,* Muraed! *How thrilling! Honest* . . .
   —I never saw anyone who could remember which song it was
she heard Jack the Scológ sing. We'd forget everything but the passion

he could put into his voice. There wasn't a young woman in the neighbouring townlands who wasn't wearing the rugged path smooth up to his house, tracing his footprints. I often saw young women above on the bogs, and as soon as they got a sight of Jack the Scológ on his own bog or working round the house, they'd be stealing away, crawling through mud-holes and marshes for love of hearing him singing to himself. I saw Caitríona Pháidín doing it. I saw her sister Nell doing it . . .

—*Smashing*, Muraed! The eternal triangle is the cultural name for that . . .

> —. . . "Up got Son of Scológ in the morning with the day,
> And flirting after women he headed for the fair . . ."

—. . . It was indeed on the Day of the Great Pig Fair that Nell Pháidín and Jack the Scológ eloped. Her people were raging, for all they could do about it. I don't know if you had that custom in East Galway, Dotie, that the eldest daughter must marry first . . .

> —. . . "She carried him through swamp-holes,
> Through marshes and through mud,
> And no one cared but curlews
> That were driven off their brood . . ."

—Up on the moor Jack lived, with nothing but wasteland and quagmires . . .

—Well, Muraed Phroinsiais, I never in all my life saw a path as rocky as the one up to the Scológ's house. Didn't I twist my ankle that night coming home from the wedding . . .

—. . . You did, because you made a glutton of yourself there, as you often did . . .

—. . . The night before the wedding in Páidín's, Caitríona was stuck in a corner of the back room, with a face on her as long as a shadow at midnight. There was a bunch of us there. Nell was there. She started a bit of fun with Caitríona: "Bedamn, Caitríona, but I think you should marry Big Brian," says she. Caitríona had refused him before that . . .

—I was there, Muraed. "I've got Jack," says Nell. "We'll leave Big Brian for you, Caitríona."

—Caitríona went crazy. She tore out, and she wouldn't go near the room again till morning. Nor would she go near the chapel next day . . .

—I was cutting a ropeful of heather that day, Muraed, and where did I see her but wandering about up in the marsh at Yellow Hillock, even though the wedding was going on in the Scológ's house . . .

—She didn't set foot across the threshold of Jack the Scológ's that day or any day since. You'd think Nell had the spotted plague the way Caitríona used to pass her by. She never forgave her about Jack . . .

—. . . "Briany is handsome, with land, stock and wealth,
    And outside of marriage he won't get his health . . ."

—. . . But in spite of all his wealth that same Big Brian was a complete failure at getting a wife. Devil a bone in his body but came asking Caitríona again . . .

—. . . "'By the devil,' says Tríona, 'Here's a fine pig for scalding,
    The kettle off the fire, to welcome the stalwart.'"

—The pot-hook is what they used in cases like that east of Brightcity. The time Peats Mac Craith came . . .

—That mode of refusal is found west of Brightcity too, Dotie. *Honest*. Myself, for example . . .

—Did you hear what the Tailor's sister did when some old loafer from Wood of the Lake came in asking her to marry him? She got a long knife out of the chest and began to sharpen it in the middle of the house. "Hold him down for me," she said . . .

—Oh, she would do that indeed. The One-Ear Breed . . .

—What do you think, after all that, but didn't Caitríona marry Seán Thomáis Uí Loideáin from our neighbourhood without a yea or a nay when he came to ask for her . . .

—By God, Muraed, Seán Thomáis was too good for her . . .

—He had a big holding of the best sandy land . . .

—And he was the man to work it too . . .

—He had a grand big house . . .

—It was the place she coveted, of course. To have more means and money than Nell. To be close enough for Nell to see, every day that dawned, that Caitríona had more means and money than she herself would ever have . . .

—. . . "'I've a fine big haggard,' says Caitríona's kitten,
'I have strippings[22] of cows, butter and fat . . .'"
— "'I'm gentle and useful, loving and decent,
Which cannot be said for Nell's little cat . . .'"

—To show Nell it wasn't Caitríona that drew the short straw, and that Nell was welcome to the leavings and the longings. From Caitríona's very own mouth I heard it. That was her revenge . . .

—*Oh my*, but that's an interesting story. I think I won't bother with the Big Master's reading session today . . . Hey, Master . . . We won't bother with the novelette today . . . I have other intellectual work on hand. *Au revoir* . . .

—Caitríona was hard-working and thrifty and clean in Seán Thomáis Uí Loideáin's house. I should know it, since I lived next door to her. The rising sun never caught her in bed, and her card[23] and her spinning-wheel often chattered into the night . . .

—Her house was the better for it, Muraed. She had wealth and means . . .

—. . . Dropping into Barry's the Bookmakers in Brightcity. My hand in my pocket as bold as if there was something in it. And me down to the one shilling. Making a great rattle throwing it down on the counter. "'Golden Apple,'" I said. "The three o'clock race. A hundred to one . . . It might win," says I, putting my hand in my pocket and turning it out . . .

---

22. The last few drops milked from a cow, considered to be the best for cream and butter.

23. An implement like a pad with bristles on one side, used in carding raw wool, i.e., aligning the fibres in preparation for spinning. Two cards are needed, pulling one against the other, with the wool in between.

—... A pity it wasn't me, Peadar the Pub, I wouldn't have let him away with it. It wasn't right of you to let any black heretic insult your religion like that, Peadar.

> "Faith of our fathers holy faith,
> We will be true to thee till death,
> We will be true to thee till death . . ."

You had no red blood in you, Peadar, to let him away with talk like that. If that had been me . . .

—To hell with yourselves and your religion. Neither of you has shut his mouth in the last five years but arguing about religion . . .

—... Indeed, Muraed, they say that after all Caitríona's bitching about Nell she was glad to have her, after her husband died. She was in a bad state at that time, for Pádraig was still fairly young . . .

—That I was glad to have Nell! That I was glad to have Nell! That I'd accept anything from Nell! Sweet Jesus tonight, that I'd accept anything from that pussface! I'll explode! I'll explode! . . .

7

—... The nettly groves of Donagh's Village, you said.

—Even nettles wouldn't grow on the hillocks of your village, there are so many fleas on them . . .

—... I fell off a stack of oats . . .

—Faith then, as you say, the Menlo man and myself used to write to each other . . .

—... "I wonder is this the War of the Two Foreigners?"[24] says I to Paitseach Sheáinín . . .

—Wake up, man! That war's over since 1918 . . .

—It was still going on when I was dying . . .

—Wake up, I tell you. Aren't you nearly thirty years dead? The second war is on now . . .

—I'm thirty-one years here. I can boast of something that none

---

24. The reference here is to World War I (1914–1918).

of you can boast of: I was the first corpse in this graveyard. Don't you think the oldest inhabitant of the graveyard should have something to say? Permission to speak. Permission to speak . . .

—. . . Indeed then, Caitríona had wealth and means, Muraed . . .

—She had. But though her place was much better than Nell's, Nell never left a tithe unpaid either . . .

—Oh, God bless your innocence, Muraed. The devil a tap of work herself or Jack ever did but looking into one another's eyes and singing songs, till their son Peadar was strong enough to cultivate some of the moor and the bog and clear those wild wastelands.

—Nell didn't have a brass farthing till Big Brian's Mag's dowry came into her house.

—For all your criticism of her place, what stood to her in the end was its nearness to the river and the lake and the grouse. There's no telling the amount of money fowlers and anglers from England left with that one. I saw the Earl myself pressing a pound note into her hand one day—a brand new pound note . . .

—. . . "Fens" is what you call marshes, on the fair plains of East Galway, Dotie. I also heard that your name for the cat is "rat-hunter," and "fireside son" for the tongs . . . Oh indeed then, Dotie, that's not the real Old Irish . . .

—God help us forever and ever . . .

—. . . "'We'll send pigs to the fair,' said Caitríona's cat,
      'It's the bullocks are dearest,' said the cat of Nell."

—. . . I'm not exaggerating when I say Caitríona used to put an extra aspiration into her prayers to bring want and waste down on Nell. She used to be delighted if a calf of hers died or her potatoes failed . . .

—I wouldn't tell a lie about anyone, Muraed. May God forbid that I should! But the time the lorry injured Peadar Nell's leg Caitríona said to my face, "Why didn't he stay clear of it? The road was long and wide enough for him. That's the stuff for her, the puss-face! . . ."

—"Nell has won that trick," she said, the day Seán Thomáis Uí Loideáin, her husband, was buried.

—'Twas in the east cemetery he was buried. I remember it well and I have good reason to. I twisted my ankle when I slipped on a flagstone . . .

—When you made a glutton of yourself, as you often did . . .

—. . . To have more potatoes than Nell; to have more pigs, hens, turf, hay; to have a cleaner, neater, house; to have better clothes on her children: It was part of her revenge. It was all revenge . . .

—. . . "She came ho-ome dressed in gaudy clo-oth-ing
For she coaxed the ho-ard from the grey-haired dame."

—Baba Pháidín got a bout of sickness in America that brought her to death's door. It was Big Brian's Mag who looked after her. She brought Mag home with her . . .

—. . . "'Twas in Caitríona's house that Baba took shelter . . ."

—She seldom went near Nell. She was too far up and the path was too rugged for her, after her illness. She felt more at home with Caitríona somehow . . .

—. . . "Nell's little house is an ugly hovel
And she has no conscience in whispering lies.
She had the fever there but won't admit it,
And if the plague will hit you it will end your life . . ."

—. . . There was only the one son, Pádraig, in Caitríona's house.

—Two daughters of hers died . . .

—Three of them died. There was another one in America: Cáit . . .

—It's well I remember her, Muraed. I twisted my ankle the day she left . . .

—Baba promised Pádraig Chaitríona that he wouldn't see a day's hardship for the rest of his life if he married Big Brian's Mag. Caitríona had an undying hatred of Big Brian, as she had of his dog and his daughter as well. But Mag was to get a big dowry, and Caitríona thought Baba would be more inclined to leave all her money in Caitríona's own house on account of Mag. To get the better of Nell . . .

—. . . "'Twas in Caitríona's house that Ba-a-ba took sh-e-elter
  Till Pádraig re-e-jected Big Brian's Mag.
  'Tis Nó-ra Sheáinín has the neat-handed daugh-ter,
  I lo-oved her always without go-old or land . . ."

—*High for* Mangy Field! . . .

—Nóra Sheáinín's daughter was a fine-looking woman, by God . . .

—. . . That's what turned Caitríona against your daughter from the beginning, Nóra Sheáinín. This talk about the dowry is only an excuse. Since the day your daughter stepped into her house married to her son, she went at her like a young dog with its paw on its food when another one challenges it. Didn't you often have to come over from Mangy Field, Nóra . . .

—. . . "Ere the morning grew o-old Nóra Sheáinín came
  o-over . . ."

—*Oh my!* We're getting to an exciting part of the story now, Muraed, aren't we! The hero is married to his sweetheart. But the other woman is still there in the background. She's defeated in battle now, but there are more upsets to come . . . anonymous letters, insinuations about the hero's affairs, murder maybe, divorce for certain . . . *Oh my!* . . .

—. . . "I wouldn't marry Big Brian," said Caitríona's kitten . . ."

Put in another line yourself now . . .

— "'To scald him you tried,' said the kitten of Nell . . .
— 'His daughter I'd marry,' said Caitríona's kitten . . .
— 'I won't give you the chance,' said the kitten of Nell."

—'Tis well I remember, Muraed, the day Peadar Nell married Big Brian's Mag. I twisted my ankle . . .

—... "'Twas in Caitríona's house that Ba-a-ba took she-e-elter
    Till Pádraig re-e-jected Big Brian's Mag ..."

—It hurt Caitríona even more that Baba moved up to Nell's
house than that Nell's son got the money and the dowry promised to
her own son Pádraig ...

—'Tis well I remember, Muraed, the day Baba Pháidín went
back to America. Cutting hay in the Red Meadow I was when I saw
them coming down towards me from Nell's house. I ran over to say
goodbye to her. I'll be damned but as I jumped a double ditch didn't
I twist ...

—Would you say, Muraed, it's twenty years since Baba Pháidín
went back to America? ...

—Sixteen years she's gone. But Caitríona never took her eye off
the will. That's what has kept her from being in her grave long ago.
The satisfaction she got from snarling at her son's wife gave her a new
lease of life ...

—Yes, Muraed, and her obsession with going to funerals.

—And Tomás Inside's land. ...

—... Listen now, Curraoin:

"Much altar-money was small consolation ..."

—Don't pay any heed to that brat, Curraoin. He's not able to
compose poetry ...

—The story is pretty flat now, Muraed. *Honest*. I thought there'd
be much more excitement ...

—... Listen, Curraoin. Listen to the second line:

"And a good pound grave, will's proud donation ..."

—... *Honest*, Muraed. I thought there'd be murder, and at least
one divorce. But Dotie can analyse all my misjudgements ...

—... I have it, by Heavens, Curraoin. Listen now:

"A cross on my grave will make Nell's poor heart pine,
And in graveyard's cold clay grief's triumph is mine ..."

8

Hello Muraed . . . Can you hear me, Muraed? . . . Hasn't Nóra Sheáinín a nerve, talking to a schoolmaster . . . But of course she is, Muraed. Everyone knows she's my in-law. I wouldn't mind but in a place like this where there's no privacy and nobody has any discretion. Good God above! A bitch! She's a bitch! She always was a bitch. When she was in service in Brightcity before she got married, they say—we renounce her!—that she was keeping company with a sailor . . .

Of course I did, Muraed . . . I told him. "Pádraig dear," says I, like this. "That one from Mangy Field you're so eager to marry, did you hear that her mother used to keep company with a sailor in Brightcity?"

"What harm?" says he.

"But Pádraig," says I, "Sailors . . ."

"Huh! Sailors," says he. "Can't a sailor be as decent as any man? I know who this girl's mother was going out with in Brightcity, but America's farther off and I don't know who Big Brian's Mag was going out with over there. A *black*, maybe . . ."

Of course, Muraed, the only reason I asked my son to bring a daughter of Big Brian's into my house was that I didn't want to give Nell the satisfaction of getting the money. By God, Muraed, I had good reason for not liking Big Brian's daughter. The night Nell got married, that's what the pussface threw in my face. "Since I have Jack," she says, the pussface, "we'll leave Big Brian for you, Caitríona."

Believe you me, Muraed, those few words hurt me more than all the other wrongs she did me put together. That remark was like a plague of weasels snarling back and forth through my mind and spitting venom. I didn't get it out of my head till the day I died. I didn't, Muraed. Every time I'd see Big Brian I'd think of that night, of the room at home, of that mocking grin on Nell's face in the arms of Jack the Scológ. Every time I'd see a son or daughter of Big Brian's I'd think of that night. Every time anyone mentioned Big Brian I'd think of it

. . . the room . . . the grin . . . Nell in the arms of Jack the Scológ! . . . in the arms of Jack the Scológ . . .

Big Brian asked me twice, Muraed. I never told you that . . . What's this you said Nóra Sheáinín calls it? The eternal triangle . . . the eternal triangle . . . That's like her stupid grin all right . . . But, Muraed, I didn't tell you . . . You're mistaken. I'm not that sort of person, Muraed. I'm no gossip. One thing about me, anything I saw or heard, I carried it into the graveyard clay with me. But it's no harm to talk about it now that we're on the way of eternal truth[25] . . . He asked me twice, indeed. The first time he came I was no more than twenty. My father wanted me to move in there. "Big Brian is a good hard-working man with a warm house and a fat purse," he says.

"I wouldn't marry him," says I, "if I had to get the loan of the shawl from Nell and stand in the middle of the fair."

"Why not?" says my father.

"The ugly streak of misery," says I. "Look at the goaty beard on him. Look at the buckteeth. Look at the stopped-up nose. Look at the club-foot. Look at his dirty little hovel of a house. Look at the layers of filth on him. He's three times my age. He could be my grandfather."

It was true for me. He was nearing fifty then. He's nearing the hundred now, and still above ground, without a day's illness, apart from the odd twinge of rheumatism. He was going for the pension every Friday when I was still above ground. The ugly streak of misery! . . .

"The wilful child will follow his own counsel!" says my father, and he said no more about it.

It wasn't long after Nell got married when he came in again. I was just going to make a drop of tea before nightfall. I remember it well. I had set the teapot down on the hearth while I was raking out a bed of embers to put under it. This man comes barging in on top of me before I had a chance to see who it was. "Will you marry me, Caitríona?" he says, not beating about the bush. "I've earned you well,

---

25. *Slí na Fírinne*, the way of truth, is a common phrase for the afterlife.

having to come twice. But since I'm not getting my health for want of a strong lump of a woman . . ."

Upon my soul, that's exactly what he said.

"I wouldn't marry you, you ugly streak of misery, if I was covered in green scum for the want of a man," says I . . .

I'd laid down the tongs and I had the kettle of boiling water in my hand. Without a moment's wavering, Muraed, I ran at him in the middle of the floor. But he had made it out the door.

I'd have you know, Muraed, I was hard to please when it came to men. I was good-looking and I had a good dowry . . . To marry Big Brian, Muraed, after what Nell had said . . .

—. . . "It could win," says I, putting my hand in my pocket and turning it out. "It's all or nothing now!" says I, collecting the ticket from the girl. She smiled at me: an innocent smile from a young heart without guile. "If 'Golden Apple' wins," says I, "I'll buy you sweets and I'll take you to the cinema . . . or would you prefer a caper of a dance . . . or a couple of drinks in the privacy of the lounge bar in the Western Hotel? . . ."

—. . . *Qu'est-ce que vous dites? Quelle drôle de langue! N'y a-t-il pas là quelque professeur ou étudiant qui parle français?*

—*Au revoir. Au revoir.*

—*Pardon! Pardon!*

—Shut your mouth, sourpuss!

—If I could get over as far as that drake I'd shut him up! Either that or make him talk like a Christian. Every time Hitler is mentioned he starts spluttering, with a torrent of talk coming out of him. If one could understand him, I think he's not at all grateful to Hitler.

—Don't you hear, every time Hitler's name comes up he says "meirdreach"[26] on the spot. He's picked up that much Irish anyway . . .

—Oh, if I could only reach as far as him! *High for* Hitler! *High for* Hitler! *High for* Hitler! *High for* Hitler! . . .

—*Je ne vous comprends pas, monsieur* . . .

---

26. Presumably the Frenchman says "merde," meaning "crap," which is misheard as *meirdreach*, prostitute.

—Who is that, Muraed?

—That's your man who was killed out of the aeroplane, don't you remember? Your man who fell into the Middle Harbour. You were alive at the time.

—Oh, didn't I see him laid out, Muraed... He had a fine funeral. They say he was some sort of a hero...

—He keeps on babbling like that. The Master says he's a Frenchman and that he could understand him if only his tongue weren't sluggish from being so long in the salt water...

—So the Master doesn't understand him, Muraed?

—The devil a bit of him then, Caitríona.

—I always knew, Muraed, that the Big Master had no learning. Don't heed him if he doesn't understand a Frenchman! I should have known that a long time ago...

—Nóra Sheáinín understands him better than anyone else in the graveyard. Did you hear her answering him a while ago...

—Oh, have a bit of sense, Muraed Phroinsiais. You mean Nóirín Filthy-Feet?...

—*Ils m'ennuient. On espère toujours trouver la paix dans la mort, mais la tombe ne semble pas encore être la mort. On ne trouve ici en tout cas, que de l'ennui...*

—*Au revoir. Au revoir. De grâce. De grâce.*

—... Six times six, forty-six; six times seven, fifty-two; six times eight, fifty-eight... Now amn't I good, Master! I know my tables as far as six. If I'd gone to school as a child there'd be no stopping me. I'll say the tables for you from the beginning now, Master. Two times one... Why don't you want to hear them, Master? You've been neglecting me this last while, since Caitríona Pháidín told you about your wife...

—... By the oak of this coffin, Curraoin, I gave Caitríona Pháidín the pound and I haven't seen sight of it since...

—Ababúna! That's a lie, you old hag...

—... *Honest,* Dotie. You wouldn't understand: a stranger from the plains of East Galway. This is the truth, the honest truth, Dotie. I was going to say "By the blessed little finger," but that's tramps' talk.

I'll say "Cross my heart" instead, Dotie. Muraed told you about herself and Nell, but she didn't tell you what dowry I gave my daughter when she married into Caitríona's house. You should know that now, Dotie. The rest of them here already know it. One hundred and twenty pounds, Dotie. *Honest!* One hundred and twenty pounds, in golden guineas . . .

— Ababúna! Muraed! Muraed! Do you hear? I'll explode! I'll explode, Muraed! I'll explode, Muraed! Nóra Sheáinín's daughter . . . one hundred and twenty . . . dowry . . . into my house . . . I'll explode! I'll explode! Oh, I'll explode! I'll expl. I'll exp. I'll ex . . .

Interlude Two

THE SPREADING OF THE CLAY

1

You were asking for it. If I hadn't stabbed you someone else would have, and isn't the fool as good as his servant? If you were to be stabbed, it was better for a neighbour to do it than a stranger. The stranger would be buried far away from you, on the fair plains of East Galway maybe, or up in Dublin, or even the North. What would you do then? Look at the satisfaction you get scolding me here. And if it was a stranger buried beside you, you'd be in a bad way not knowing what to throw in his face, since you wouldn't know his people for seven generations back. Have sense my good man! I wouldn't mind, but I stabbed you cleanly . . .

—The One-Ear Breed were known for stabbing people cleanly! . . .

—. . . A white-faced mare . . . She was the best . . .

—. . . By the oak of this coffin, Siúán the Shop, I gave Caitríona Pháidín the pound . . .

—. . . I left it at that. Went up to the bookie's around three o'clock. "'Golden Apple,'" I said. "It could win," putting my hand in my pocket and turning it out. Not a farthing in it . . .

The clock struck three. The race was run. "Golden Apple" won: a hundred to one. Drew my five pounds. The young girl gave me that smile again: a bright smile from a young heart without guile. That meant more to me than the five pounds. "I'll buy you sweets, or I'll take you to the pictures or a dance . . . or would you prefer . . ." I felt embarrassed and didn't finish the sentence. "I'll meet you outside the Plaza at a quarter past seven," said I.

Went home. Shaved, cleaned, washed, preened myself. Didn't even have a celebratory drop. I had too much respect for that sweet smile from a young heart without guile . . .

Went to the Plaza at seven. Broke my five pounds buying her a box of chocolates. The chocolates would bring more joy to that young heart without guile, and her smile would be like a rose in the first virginal sunrays of morning. What a shame I'm such a tough myself! . . .

— Hold on now till I read you the Declaration issued by Éamon de Valera to the people of Ireland: "People of Ireland . . ."

— Hold on yourself till I read you the Declaration issued by Arthur Griffith to the people of Ireland: "People of Ireland . . ."

— . . . I drank two score pints and two that night, one after the other. And I walked home afterwards as straight as a Spanish reed . . . as straight as a Spanish reed, I tell you. I pulled a calf out of the speckled cow, that had been stuck between its bones for a couple of hours. I drove the old donkey out of Curraoin's oats . . . and it was me who tied Tomáisín. I had taken off my boots on the hearth and I was just going on my knees to say a smattering of prayers, when in comes the little girl. There wasn't a puff of breath in her. "My Mammy says you're to come over straight away," she says, "the madness has struck Daddy again."

"The devil take his madness, doesn't he pick the right time for it," says I, "and me just about to say my prayers. What the hell is wrong with him this time?"

"Poteen whiskey," says she.

I went over. He was stark raving, and the whole lot of them not able to tie him. A spineless lot, it has to be said.

"Come on!" says I. "Get me the rope quickly before he grabs the hatchet. Can't you see he's got his eye on it . . ."

— I remember it well. I twisted my ankle . . .

— The game was ours.

— It mightn't have been. Only for the *mine* flattened the house . . .

— . . . "I washed my face with the dew,
And the comb I had was the wind . . ."

It's still not right, Curraoin. There's a limp in that line. Hold on now:

> "I washed my face with the dew . . ."

That much is beautiful, Curraoin. I used it before in *The Golden Stars*. Hold on now . . . Listen now, Curraoin:

> "I washed my face with the dew,
> And I combed my hair with the wind . . ."

That's perfect. I knew I'd get it right in the end, Curraoin . . . Are you listening now?

> "I washed my face with the dew,
> And I combed my hair with the wind . . .
> The rainbow was a lace in my shoe . . ."

Hold on, Curraoin . . . hold on . . . Eureka! . . .

> "And the Pleiads held up my trews . . ."

I knew I'd get it, Curraoin. Listen to the whole verse now . . .

—May the devil pierce you and don't be annoying the people! You have me demented with your trivial verses for the past two years. I have other things on my mind, though if it's God's will I shouldn't complain: my eldest son is keeping company with Road-End's daughter, and that wife of mine at home could be on the point of handing over the big holding to him. And, for all I know, Glutton's donkey or Road-End's cattle could be in my oats at this very moment.

—'Tis true for you, Curraoin. Why in the name of God didn't they bury the dirty scoundrel in the east cemetery. That's where Maidhc Ó Dónaill is buried, the man who made "The Song of the Turnip" and "The Chicken's Contention with the Grain of Oats" . . .

—And Big Micil Ó Conaola, who made "The Song of Caitríona" and "The Song of Tomás Inside" . . .

—And "The Lay of the Cats." "The Lay of the Cats" is a fine piece of work. You wouldn't be capable of composing it, you impudent brat . . .

—. . . Eight times six, forty-eight; eight times seven, fifty-four . . . You're not listening at all, Master. Your mind is wandering these days . . . I'm making no progress! . . . Is that what you said, Master? It's no wonder, Master, and the way you're neglecting me . . . Tell me this . . . How many tables are there, Master? . . . Is that all? Oh, if that's all, then! Arrah, I thought they went up to a hundred . . . to a thousand . . . to a million . . . to a quadrillion . . . We have plenty of time to learn them in any case, Master. I've always heard it said that we owe the clay many a day. He who made Time made plenty of it . . .

—. . . God help us! A pity they didn't take my earthly remains east of Brightcity and lay me down with my own people in Temple Brennan on the fair plains of East Galway! The clay is gentle[1] and welcoming there; the clay is crumbly and smooth there; the clay is friendly and tender there; the clay is protective and cosy there. The decay of the grave would not be decay there; corruption of the flesh would not be corruption there. But clay would receive clay; clay would kiss and caress clay; clay would coalesce with clay . . .

—She's having another attack of "sentimentality" . . .

—You never saw anyone so full of life till this foolishness comes over her . . .

—Her nature, God help us! Caitríona is much worse, once she starts talking about Nell and Nóra Sheáinín . . .

—Arrah, Caitríona is completely out of order. Big Brian was right when he called her a *jennet*[2] . . .

—Big Brian was not right. *Honest*, indeed he was not . . .

—What's this? Have you turned against the streak of misery too, Nóra? . . .

—*Honest*, he was not right. The *jennet* is a very cultured animal. *Honest*, it is. The Redheads in Donagh's Village had a *jennet* when I was going to school long ago, and he used to eat raisin bread out of the palm of my hand . . .

---

1. East of Galway the underlying limestone gives rise to fertile and hospitable plains, unlike the harsh Conamara terrain of granite and metamorphic rocks.

2. The offspring of a female donkey and a horse.

—Going to school long ago! Nóra Filthy-Feet going to school! Raisin bread in Mangy Field! O woe, woe forever! Muraed, did you hear what Nóra Filthy-Feet, daughter of Seáinín Robin, said? Oh, I'll explode . . .

2

. . . Hey! Nóra Sheáinín! . . . Nóra Sheáinín! . . . Nóra Filthy-Feet! . . . You weren't content to leave the nasty habit of telling lies above ground but you brought it underground with you too. Indeed, the whole graveyard knows that the devil himself—we renounce him!— gave you the loan of his tongue when you were on your mother's breast and you've used it so well ever since that he never asked for it back . . .

As for giving a hundred and twenty pounds of dowry to that little scold of a daughter of yours . . . Well! Well! . . . A woman who didn't have a stitch of clothes to cover herself with on her wedding day, until I bought an outfit for her . . . A hundred and twenty pounds from Nóra Filthy-Feet . . . There wasn't ever a hundred and twenty pounds in the whole of Mangy Field. Mangy Field of the Puddles. I suppose you're too posh now to milk the ducks . . . A hundred and twenty pounds . . . A hundred and twenty fleas! No, more likely a hundred thousand fleas. That was the most plentiful livestock the Filthy-Feet Breed ever had. Indeed then, Nóirín, if fleas were dowry that stupid little fool who married your daughter would have so many lambs he would have been knighted nine times over. She brought a good flock of them into my house with her . . .

It was a day of woe for me, Nóirín, the first day I ever saw yourself or your daughter under the roof of my house . . . The scrawny little thing, and that's exactly what she is. Indeed, Nóra, she's no credit to you: a woman who's not able to put a wrap around her child or make her husband's bed, or clean out the week's dead ashes or comb her matted head . . . It was she who put me in the clay two score years before my time. She'll put my son there too before long, if she doesn't come here herself on her next childbirth to gossip and keep you company.

Arrah! Haven't you the mocking gob today, Nóirín . . . "We'll be . . ." How did you put it? . . . "We'll be O.K. then." . . . O.K.! That's like your cheeky rump alright, Nóirín . . . "We'll be O.K. then. You'll have your son and I'll have my daughter, and all of us will be together again below ground as we were above." . . . That devil's plaything in your gob is full of mockery today, Nóirín . . .

When you were in Brightcity . . . I'm a liar, you say? You're the one who told a damned lie, Nóirín Filthy-Feet . . .

—Stump!

—Bitch!

—Whore!

—Filthy-Feet Breed . . . Duck milkers . . .

—Do you remember the night Nell was sitting in Jack the Scológ's lap? "We'll leave Big Brian for you, Caitríona . . ."

—I never sat in a sailor's lap anyway, thanks be to God . . .

—You never got the chance, Caitríona . . . I'm not a bit afraid of you. Your villainy and lies won't burn a hole in my coat. I'm better known and respected in this graveyard than you are. I have a fine decent cross over me, which is more than you have, Caitríona. *Smashing! Honest!* . . .

—Oh indeed, if you have, it wasn't your money that paid for it. You can thank that fool of a brother of yours who put it up when he was home from America. It would take a long time to make up the price of a cross from Mangy Field's duck milk . . . What are you saying, Nóra? Out with it . . . You haven't the courage to say it to me . . . I have no culture? . . . I have no culture, Nóirín? . . . I have no culture, then! That's true for you, Nóirín. It's on the Filthy-Feet Breed I've always seen the culture of lice and nits . . .

What's that you say, Nóirín ? . . . You don't have time to swap insults with me . . . that you were wasting your time swapping insults with me. Ababúna! You have no time to be swapping insults with me, Nóirín . . . You have other things to do, then! Now, what do you know? You've got to listen to another piece of . . . what did she call it, Master . . . Master . . . He doesn't hear me. His head is in a whirl since he heard about his wife . . . yes, on my soul . . . *novelette* . . . this is the time the

Master reads a bit of the . . . *novelette* to you every day? If the Master heeded me . . . Oh, Mary Mother of God! . . . A *novelette* in Mangy Field . . . A *novelette* among the Filthy-Feet Breed . . . Muraed! Hey, Muraed! Do you hear? A *novelette* among the Filthy-Feet Breed . . . I'll explode! . . . I will! . . .

3

—. . . By the oak of this coffin, Glutton, I gave Caitríona Pháidín the pound . . .

—. . . God help us forever and ever! My death would not be death to me there: for it is the warm soft clay of the plain there; robust clay that can be gentle with the strength of its strength; proud clay that does not need to decompose, decay or dissolve the treasure of its womb to fertilise itself; rich clay that can afford to be generous with its takings; productive clay that can change and reshape all it eats and drinks without consuming, deforming and despoiling it . . . It would recognise its own . . .

The pleasant buttercup would grow on my grave there, the gracious hemlock, the conceited primrose and the tough bent-grass . . .

I'd have gentle birdsong above me instead of the cacophony of breakers, of waterfall or sedge, or of the cormorant glutting itself on a school of fry. Oh! Clay of the plain, oh! To be under your mantle . . .

—The "sentimentality" has come over her again . . .

—. . . Pearse[3] said, O'Donovan Rossa said, Wolfe Tone said it was Éamon de Valera was right . . .

—Terence McSwiney said, James Connolly said, John O'Leary said, John O'Mahony said, James Fintan Lalor said, Davis, Emmet, Lord Edward Fitzgerald and Sarsfield said it was Arthur Griffith was right . . .

—Owen Roe O'Neill said it was Éamon de Valera was right . . .

—Red Hugh O'Donnell said it was Arthur Griffith was right . . .

---

3. The listed political and historical figures are here all regarded as heroes of the age-long struggle for Irish independence.

—Art MacMurrough Kavanagh said it was Éamon de Valera was right . . .

—Brian Bórú, Malachy, Cormac MacArt, Niall of the Nine Hostages, the two Patricks, Brigid and Columkille and all the saints of Ireland, no matter where they are—on earth, at sea or in the sky—and all the martyrs of Erin from Dunkirk to Belgrade, and Finn McCool, Oisín, Conán, Caoilte, Deirdre, Gráinne, Ollav Fódla and Gael Glas said it was Arthur Griffith was right . . .

—You're a damned liar, they did not . . .

—I say you are the liar, and they did. The truth is bitter . . .

—You murdered me treacherously, and me fighting for the Republic . . .

—It served you right. Neither the Law of God nor that of the Church permits the attempted overthrow by force of a lawful government . . .

—I have nothing to do with politics myself, but I do have a fondness for the Old IRA[4] . . .

—You coward you, under the bed you were when Éamon de Valera was fighting for the Republic . . .

—You spineless thing, under the bed you were when Arthur Griffith was . . .

—. . . "And flirting after women he headed . . ."

—. . . Hold on now, my good man, till I finish my story:

"'. . . Send out to me John Jameson,[5]
    And now I am without that same son.'

"A fairy lover abducted John Jameson into the fairy fort, out of which there was no deliverance. At that very time the Emerald Isle of Ireland, its islands and territorial waters ran dry, all except two bottles of Portuguese sparkling water washed ashore on the Blasket

---

4. The Irish Republican Army of the War of Independence and the Civil War, as opposed to the IRA of more recent "Troubles."

5. A brand of Irish whiskey.

Island,[6] and a keg of Spanish holy water given off a trawler to a fisherman on Brannock Island[7] in exchange for half a hundredweight of potatoes . . .

"The fair maid of the brown tresses was in Dublin at that time . . ."

—The version I heard from the old folks in our own village, Cóilí, is that it was a nurse in Brightcity . . .

—A woman in a bookie's office is what I heard . . .

—Oh! How could that be? She was up in Dublin. Where else! "I have an arrow," she said, "that will release John Jameson if he promises to give me as dowry a hundred and one big barrels, a hundred and one puncheons, and a hundred and one hogsheads of the best poteen whiskey . . ."

—Now Glutton, where's your two score pints and two? . . .

—Cóilí, hold on a moment. This is how I would have finished that other story if I hadn't died . . .

—. . . When Hitler invades England he'll make them eat dead cats . . .

—Indeed, the world will be at its worst ever then. Not a cow nor a calf will be worth a penny. May God help the poor if the price of cattle falls any further. I have a bit of land at the top of the village and it'll never be beaten for fattening cattle. It'll go to waste, I'm afraid, if the price of stock slumps . . .

—"It'll never be beaten for fattening cattle!" If you let two rabbits loose on all the land in your village, and left it to themselves for five years, there'd still be only two rabbits, if even the two . . .

—You had no blood in you, Peadar. I wish it had been me. By the book, I'd have given him a good answer. If I had a pub, Peadar, and black heretics came in insulting the faith like that . . .

—. . . We—the Half-Guinea[8] Corpses—are putting forward a joint candidate in this election too. Like the other two groups—the Pound Corpses and the Fifteen-Shilling Corpses—we have nothing

---

6. Off the coast of Kerry.
7. At the western end of the Aran Islands.
8. A guinea was a coin worth one pound one shilling.

to offer our fellow corpses. But we are taking part in this Graveyard Election because we—the Half-Guinea Party—have a policy also. If an election is of benefit to the community above ground it should be of benefit to us here. Election is the essence of democracy. We here in the graveyard clay are the true democrats.

The Pound Corpses are the Party of the Gentry, the Party of Conservatism, the Party of Big Shots, the Party of Reactionaries, the Party of Restraint and Control. The Fifteen-Shilling Corpses are the Party of Commerce and Trading, of the Poets and Artists, of the *Bourgeoisie* and the Middle Classes, of Property and Wealth. But we, Fellow Corpses, are the Party of the Labouring Class, of the Proletariat, the Rural Rent-Payers, the Party of the Unfree and the Bond Tenants and the Old Thatched Cabin, the Party of the Great Dispossessed: "hewers of wood and drawers of water." It is our task to fight for our rights boldly and fearlessly as becomes ex-men (knocking of skulls in the Half-Guinea Plot) . . .

—. . . The joint candidate that we—the Fifteen-Shilling Party—put forward in this election is a woman. Don't let that frighten any of you, friends. Her husband was never a Member of the Irish Parliament. She is a woman who established herself in this cemetery by her own intellect and good sense. Three years ago when she came into the graveyard clay she was as ill-informed as any of those windbags spouting nonsense down there in the Half-Guinea Plot. But in spite of what the Half-Guinea Party says, everybody in this graveyard has equal rights and equal opportunity (knocking of skulls). Our joint candidate is proof of that. She has culture and learning now. My Corpses, I wish to introduce to you our joint candidate . . . Nóra Sheáinín (great knocking of skulls).

—Nóra Filthy-Feet! The bitch. Duck milkers . . . Hey, Muraed! . . . Hey, Muraed! . . . Nóra Sheáinín . . . I'll explode! . . . I'll explode! . . .

4

. . . Nóra Filthy-Feet standing for election! Good God above, they've lost all respect for themselves in this cemetery if the best they

can offer is Nóra of the Fleas from Mangy Field . . . She won't get in
. . . But then, who knows? Cite, Dotie and Muraed are always talking
to her, and Peadar the Pub, and even Siúán the Shop at times. As for
the Big Master, of course it's a public scandal the things he says to
her every day . . . He says they're in the book, but nobody would have
the indecency to put those things in a book:

> "Your flowing curly hair,[9]
> Your dewy bright eyes,
> Your delicate round white breast
> Attracting eye's desire."

. . . That's fine talk for a schoolmaster! The Schoolmistress and
Billyboy the Post are driving him mad. But he must have a screw
loose to be singing Nóra Sheáinín's praises: "Her mind has greatly
improved," he says, "she's cultured now . . ."

She wasn't long reminding me of the cross over her grave. "I have
a fine decent cross over me," says she, "which is more than you have,
Caitríona." Her grave would be a long time without a cross only for
that fool of a brother of hers paid for it, and I told her so. Down there
in the Half-Guinea Plot among the riff-raff of Sive's Rocks and Wood
of the Lake, without headstone or slab she'd be. And that's where she
should be if justice were done. She most certainly was never praised
till she died. When did anyone ever have a good word to say for any
of her breed? Never. Never in living memory. It didn't happen. Out
from under the dock leaves that lot crawled . . .

But a cross over your grave here is as good as having a big slated
house above ground, with a name over the door — Badger's Den View,
Paradise Refuge, Banshee Residence, Lovers' Way, Eye of the Sun,
Saints' Abode, Leprechaun Lawn — and a cement wall around it,
trees and blossoms up to the edge of the flower-bed, the little iron
gate with the archway of branches above it, success in life and money
in the bank . . . Railings around a grave are equal to the big walls

---

9. A phrase from a love song.

around the Earl's[10] house. Every time I looked in over the Earl's walls my heart would flutter. I always expected to see some wonderful sight: the Earl and his wife with their wings on, just landed back from dining in Heaven. Or St. Peter, and the Earl and his wife alongside him, escorting him to a table in the shade of the trees; a net in his hand after being fishing on the Earl's Lake; a golden salmon in the net; his big keys making a clatter; the Saint opening his book and consulting the Earl about which of his tenants should be allowed into Heaven. I thought then that to have a clean sheet in the Earl's books was to have a clean sheet in the books of Heaven . . .

Those people above ground are very simple-minded. "What good will it do the dead to put a cross over their grave?" they'll say. "Devil a bit! The same crosses are nothing but snobbery and vanity and a waste of money." If they only knew! But they don't understand till they're buried in the graveyard themselves, and then it's too late. If they understood above ground that a cross on your grave here makes even the Filthy-Feet Breed respectable, they wouldn't be so neglectful . . .

I wonder when will the cross be put over me? Surely Pádraig wouldn't let me down. He promised me faithfully:

"It will be up within a year, or even before that," says he. "It would be ungrateful of us not to do that much for you . . ."

A cross of Island limestone, with an inscription in Irish . . . The Irish language is more genteel for crosses nowadays . . . and nice flowers . . .

It's many a warning I gave Pádraig:

"I reared you tenderly, Pádraig," says I. "I always kept a good house for you. Our Lady knows it wasn't always easy. I never told you about all the hardship I endured after your father's death. I never demanded the least thing in return. I would often get the urge to buy a bit of bacon to boil with a head of cabbage; or a handful of raisins to

---

10. Lord Kilannin's big house and grounds in An Spidéal (Spiddal) were major features of the neighbourhood.

put in the bread; or to go into Peadar the Pub's when I felt my wind-pipe parched with dust from spring-cleaning, and order a half-glass from one of those golden bottles that smiled at me from the windows every time I passed . . .

But, Pádraig, my dear, I didn't. I put by every penny . . . I wouldn't like to give Nell or Big Brian's Mag the satisfaction that I wouldn't be buried properly. Get me a grave in the Pound Plot. Put a cross of Island limestone over me. Have it up within a year of my burial at the latest. I know all this will cost money, but God will reward you . . .

Don't heed your wife if she's grumbling about the expense. She is your wife, but I'm the one who brought you into the world, Pádraig. This is the only trouble I've ever caused you. Then you'll be finished with me. Make sure you don't give Nell the satisfaction . . ."

And after all that he didn't bury me in the Pound Plot. The wife . . . or the wife and that other little pussface, Nell. But Pádraig can be headstrong too, when he wants to. He promised me that cross . . .

I wonder what sort of funeral I had? I won't know till the next corpse I'm acquainted with arrives. It's high time now for someone to come. Bid Shorcha was ailing. But I'd say she's in no danger of death yet. There's also Máirtín Pockface, Beartla Blackleg and Bríd Terry, and of course the ugly streak of misery Big Brian, may God protect us from his heap of bones . . . Tomás Inside should have his death from the leaking roof any day now. His hovel should have fallen in on him by now, if Pádraig heeded my advice.

My son's wife will be here for certain on her next childbirth. Nell is very stricken since Peadar was injured, and the rheumatism is at her, the pussface. But even if it is, it won't kill her. According to herself she was often at death's door, but the seven plagues of Egypt wouldn't kill some people. May no corpse come into the graveyard ahead of her . . .

I don't know if there was any letter from America since. I'm afraid Nell will have an easy ride with Baba's will now. If only I'd lived another couple of years, even . . .

Baba was always fonder of me than of any of the rest of us. When we were little girls together long ago, herding the cows in the Little Field of Haws . . . It would never occur to her to put a cross over me, like Nóra Sheáinín's brother did for Nóra . . .

—. . . Do you think this is the "War of the Two Foreigners"? . . .

—These chatterboxes always get a fit of talking just when a person is longing for peace and quiet. What a load of rubbish they speak in the world above: "She's gone home now. She'll have peace and quiet from now on, and she can put all memory of the world out of her head in the graveyard clay." . . . Peace! Peace! Peace! . . .

—. . . If you elect me as a representative I promise you I'll do all a man can do—I mean all a woman can do—for the cause of culture and to cultivate an enlightened public opinion here . . .

—Muraed! Muraed! Hey, Muraed . . . Did you hear what Nóra Sheáinín said? . . . "If you elect me" . . . I'll explode! I'll explode! . . .

5

—. . . "Tomá-ás Inside was there with an urge to ma-arry
As often ha-a-ppens when he's ta-aken a drop . . ."

—. . . Isn't it funny, Dotie . . . Tomás Inside is a nickname everybody calls him . . . He lives on his own in a little cabin at the top of our village. He never married. He's an old man now. There's nobody related to him alive—in Ireland at any rate—except Caitríona and Nell Pháidín . . . Damned if I know, my dear, not to give you a short answer, what relation he is to Nell or to Caitríona, although I've heard it often enough . . .

—First cousins once removed, Muraed. Caitríona's father, little Páidín, and Tomás Inside were first cousins.

—. . . "I've a patch of la-and and a cot that's co-osy . . ."

—Tomás Inside's patch of land borders on Nell's, and it means more to her than to Caitríona. Caitríona's land is well away from it, and she already has a big holding anyhow . . .

—. . . "And two people I kno-ow who'll pay-ay my rent . . ."

—Caitríona was forever pestering Tomás Inside, trying to coax him down to her own house, not just because she coveted his land but to prevent Nell getting it . . .

—Oh, indeed Muraed, didn't I see how she had Pádraig driven crazy . . .

—Even if his own crops were rotting on the ridge she'd still be at him to go up and help Tomás Inside . . .

—Pádraig Chaitríona is a decent man . . .

—And the best of neighbours, to give him his due . . .

—He never had any designs on Tomás Inside's land . . .

—Sometimes he only went up there against his will, just for the sake of a quiet life . . .

—. . . "Nell's a great one for stone-wall bui-il-ding . . ."

—. . . I don't think I ever saw anything so funny in all my life . . .

—You never saw anything so funny, indeed . . .

—But you didn't see the half of it . . .

—I saw enough . . .

—If you'd lived in the same village with them . . .

—I was close enough to them. What I didn't see I heard about. Wasn't the whole country talking about them? . . .

—Devil a person in our two villages wasn't in stitches with them from morning till night. You wouldn't believe the half of it if I told you . . .

—I would indeed believe it. Nearly every Friday after collecting the pension didn't Tomás Inside and myself go into Peadar the Pub's for a few drinks and he'd tell me every single thing that had happened . . .

—Keep your voice down. You know that Caitríona was buried recently—in the Fifteen-Shilling Plot. She might hear you . . .

—Let her hear. Let all of them in the Fifteen-Shilling Plot hear me if they want to. What do I care about them! Themselves and their fine airs. You'd think we were filthy scum . . .

—All the same, I wouldn't want Caitríona to hear me. I lived in the same village as her all my life, and indeed she was a good neighbour, except that she was seething with hatred for her sister, Nell. It was Tomás Inside who reaped the benefit of their spite . . .

—Didn't he often tell me that, when we were having a drink . . .

—You'd see Caitríona setting out early in the morning to drive the cows to the top of the village. On her way back she'd take a roundabout route, just to pass Tomás Inside's cabin:

"How are you feeling today, Tomás? . . . I see your pair of turf-creels are in bad shape. Now that I think of it, we have a couple of creels we have no use for any more, somewhere around the house, as Pádraig was basket-making the other day and he made a new pair . . ."

So Tomás would get the creels.

Caitríona would hardly be down past Meadow Hill when down comes Nell:

"How are you feeling today, Tomás? . . . I see the trousers you're wearing are in poor shape. They badly need a few patches . . . But I don't know if they're not too far gone. They're quite frayed. Faith then, there's a pair of trousers up at the house that are as good as new from the little wearing they ever got. They were made for Jack, but the legs were too narrow and he never put them on again . . ."

So Tomás would get the trousers . . .

—Didn't he tell me that himself? . . .

—Another day Caitríona would go up again:

"How are you feeling today, Tomás? . . . I see the walls of your field back here have been knocked to the ground . . . The donkeys of this village are an awful nuisance. They are indeed, because they're not tied up in the barns where they should be. Glutton's old donkey and Road-End's lot are bad enough, but the worst of all are this one's donkeys"—meaning Nell—"and she lets them wander at will . . . A poor old man like you, Tomás, isn't able to go chasing after donkeys. Faith then, you have plenty of other cares from now on. I must tell Pádraig the walls are down . . ."

So the walls would be built up for Tomás Inside.

—Well indeed, didn't he tell me that . . .

—Nell would come down to him:

"How are you feeling today, Tomás? . . . You're not making much headway with this field, God bless you. Good God, you've only sown a corner of it. It will take you another two weeks to finish it. It's difficult, of course, to make any progress on your own. It's a bit late now for sowing potatoes. Isn't it nearly May Day already! . . . It's a wonder that crowd down there" — meaning Caitríona's crowd — "wouldn't do a day's work for you, since they've finished their own sowing for the past two weeks . . . I must tell Peadar to come over tomorrow. The ideal place for the two of us now Tomás, for the rest of our lives, is in the two chimney-corners by the fire . . ."

So the rest of the potato field would be sown for Tomás Inside . . .

—Do you think he didn't often tell me that? . . .

—All the same, nobody could really know it all but someone who was living in the same village with them . . . Caitríona was forever trying to get him to move into her own house, lock, stock and barrel. But not a hope of it! I'm telling you there were no flies on Tomás Inside, even if some people tried to make fun of him . . .

—Do you really think I don't know that? . . .

—No one who wasn't living in the same village with them could rightly know . . . Tomás was as attached to his little hovel of a house as a king to his throne. If he moved in with either of the sisters, the other would turn her back on him. And neither of them would have much time for him just as soon as he'd parted with his patch of land. So he didn't. A cunning old cadger, Tomás Inside . . .

—Do you think I don't know? . . .

—You do not indeed, nor does anyone else who didn't live in the same village with them. But it was when he had drink taken — on a fairday or a Friday, or any other day — that there'd be great fun. He'd take a notion to marry.

—The devil spare you, do you think I didn't often see him in Peadar the Pub's, and him half drunk? . . .

—I saw him there one day and, if I did, it was a comic sight. It's a little more than five years ago, the year before I died:

"I'll marry," says he. "I've a nice patch of land, a half-guinea a week pension, and I'm still in the full of my health. By the docks, I'll marry. I'll marry, I will indeed, my friend . . . Give me a bottle of whiskey there, Peadar," — Peadar the Pub was alive then — "the very best of whiskey, now. By the docks, I'll go looking for a wife."

— It's well I remember that same day. I twisted my ankle . . .

— In walks Caitríona and whispers in his ear:

"Come on home with me, Tomás, and our Pádraig will go and ask on your behalf, when the two of you have put your heads together . . ."

In walks Nell and whispers in his other ear:

"Come on home with me, Tomás dear. I've a bit of meat and a drop of whiskey. Our Peadar will go asking for a wife for you as soon as the two of you have a bite to eat . . ."

Tomás went roaring off over to Nóra Sheáinín's house in Mangy Field. "A widow she may be," says he to Nell and Caitríona, "but by the docks she'll do me fine. She's still a young woman. Her daughter that's married to your Pádraig, Caitríona, is not much more than thirty-two or three. By the docks, my dear, that workhorse of a mother of hers is young enough for me." That's what he said, faith. Did you know that? . . .

— Why the hell do you think I didn't know it? . . .

— Oh, how would you know it, and you not living in the same village with them . . . They were lucky Tomás had only a little cabin or they'd be robbed thatching it, because no other house under the sun was thatched as often. Pádraig Chaitríona did the north side from gable to gable one year. Pádraig is the best of thatchers. Sedge is what he put on it. And it wasn't the worst sedge either. That side wouldn't need another bit of thatch for fourteen or fifteen years. The next year Peadar Nell came with his ladder and mallet. Up with him on the north side. And do you know what he did with the thatch Pádraig had set the year before? Pulled it all out and threw it about on the ground. May I drop dead right here if I tell a word of a lie. There wasn't a pick of Pádraig's sedge between the two gables that he didn't drag off.

"You'd soon have the rain dripping down on you, Tomás," says he. I swear by the book I heard him say it! "Last year's thatch was no good," he said. "I'm surprised it kept out a drop at all. The half of it is only short heather. You can see it there for yourself. Devil a bit of trouble he gave himself cutting it either, staying on firm ground. If

TOMÁS TAOBH ISTIGH

you want good sedge you have to go into the deep hollows and get your feet wet. Have a look at the sedge I have there now; that came out of the middle of the Red Sedge Hollow . . ."

He thatched both sides of the house and, if he did, a slipshod job he made of it. The worst you ever saw. It didn't last three years even. It was a complete waste . . .

—Damn it, anyone listening to you would think I didn't know that . . .

—No one would know it, all the same, except one who was in the same village with them . . .

Another time I saw the two of them on the roof of the house: Pádraig Chaitríona and Peadar Nell. Pádraig was on the north side with his ladder and mallet and his heap of sedge. Peadar was on the south side with his own ladder and mallet and a heap of sedge. And you could call it work, the way those two were hard at it. Tomás Inside was perched on the big rock at the eastern gable, puffing his pipe to his heart's content and keeping up the chat with both of them at once. I came by, and sat myself down on the big rock beside Tomás. You wouldn't hear a finger in your ear with the noise of the two mallets.

"You'd think," says I, "one of you would stop thatching and go and pass the sedge up to the other, seeing that Tomás here is not assisting either of you; either that or take it in turns to thatch and to assist . . ."

"Hold your tongue," says Tomás. "By the docks, they're working neck and neck now, God save their health! They're great thatchers. I wouldn't say there's a nail or an inch between the two of them . . ."

—To listen to you, anyone would think I didn't know that . . .

—Well indeed, you don't know it, nor a bit of it . . .

—. . . "Nell's a great one for stone-wall building
        And Caty's an expert on roofs to mend . . ."
—. . . "Tomás Inside was laughing always
        At Caty Pháidín who had paid his rent . . ."

—He was not! He was not! He was not! Hey, Muraed! Muraed! I'll explode! I'll explode! . . .

6

—. . . The Gravekeeper! He's as big an imbecile as he ever was . . .

—It's a wonder, Caitríona, if he has a map, that he wouldn't know one grave from another . . .

—In the name of God, man, what map! That fellow's map is no better than the way the man from East-Side-of-the-Village divided the land with the tongs in the ashes, at the time of the "striping"[11] long ago . . .

—Faith then, Caitríona, I held on to my patch of land at the top of the village in spite of you all, when every mother's son of you wanted it for himself. There's no beating it for fattening cattle . . .

—Oh! Do you hear that gadfly at his blustering again? . . .

—It's a wonder, Caitríona, if corpses are being buried in the wrong graves, that someone wouldn't inquire into it: report it to the Government, or tell the priest or the Red-haired Policeman . . .

—Oh! God help your Government! That's the sort of Government we've had since Griffith's crowd were thrown out . . .

—You're a liar . . .

—And you're a damned liar . . .

—Didn't Big Brian say: "They're pitching them into any old hole in that graveyard back there, as if they were fish guts or periwinkle shells . . ."

—Oh, the ugly streak of misery . . .

—If you don't have a cross over you in this graveyard, so that your grave is well marked, not a day will go by without someone opening it . . .

—I'll have a cross over me soon. A cross of Island limestone, like there is over Peadar the Pub and Siúán . . .

—A cross of Island limestone, Caitríona . . .

---

11. Rationalisation of the tangled holdings of little fields characteristic of the ancient "rundale" system, so that each tenant had his or her holding in one piece, often in the form of a strip running inland from the shore to the beginning of bog or commonage land.

—They wouldn't let any wooden crosses be put up, would they, Caitríona?

—They'd be thrown out on the road the next day . . .

—Do you think it's the people who sell the other crosses are responsible for that? . . .

—Arrah! Who else? Everybody's drawing water to his own mill. If wooden or cement crosses were allowed there'd be no demand for their own crosses. Then everybody could make his own cross . . .

—I'd sooner have no cross at all than a wooden or cement one . . .

—You're right. I'd die of shame . . .

—This Government is the cause of all that. They get money in taxes on the other crosses . . .

—You're a liar! That game was going on before this Government . . .

—It's an awful thing to do, bundling your own kith and kin down into the ground beside a stranger . . .

—The bones want to be with their own, sure enough . . .

—That's the Government for you now . . .

—You're a liar . . .

—I heard they squeezed Tomás the Tailor's son down on top of Tiúnaí Mhicil Tiúnaí last year . . .

—Oh, didn't I kick the murderer off me! Another one of the treacherous One-Ear Breed who stabbed me . . .

—Last year I was at the funeral of Jude from our own village. She was laid down on top of little Dónall the Weaver from Sive's Rocks. They didn't know they were digging the wrong grave until they unearthed the coffin. I'm telling you the honest truth; I was there . . .

—You're right. Don't we know you're right. They dug up four graves for the Poet, and in the end they sneaked him in beside Curraoin . . .

—May the devil pierce him! He has me demented with his silly verses. May he roast in hell; couldn't he have stayed alive another while till I had a cross over me . . .

—Oho! The cheeky brat . . .

—I wouldn't mind but I was worried that my wife at home would have given my fine big holding to the eldest son . . .

—Did you hear about Micil Chite's wife from Donagh's Village, who was nearly buried on top of Siúán the Shop. There was no cross over Siúán at the time . . .

—Oh! Siúán, you poor thing . . .

—Poor Siúán, you must have been in torment . . .

—I shouted up at her, straight out, to get away from me into the Half-Guinea Plot or the Fifteen-Shilling Plot. The last thing I needed was that lazy lump laid on top of me. The smell of nettles off her would have killed me . . .

—Didn't they try to bury someone on top of you too, Cite? . . .

—Some insignificant little thing from Sive's Rocks whom I'd never known, nor her parents either. By the oak of this coffin, I made her take herself off in a hurry! "I was badly got if the beggars of Sive's Rocks are going to be my companions in the graveyard clay in the end," said I . . .

—*Honest.* They had my grave dug up too. Some woman from Hillside Wood. "Ugh!" I said, "to put that coarse-grained barbarian from Hillside Wood down alongside me! Now, if it was someone with a bit of culture! . . ."

—Oh! Do you hear the little bitch from Mangy Field of the Puddles belittling Hillside Wood? Oh, don't talk to me! I'll explode! . . .

7

—. . . I fell off a stack of oats . . .

—. . . God help us forever and ever! If only they'd taken my earthly remains back east of Brightcity . . . The setting sun there would not have to slink and slant in order to reach me. The rising sun would not appear like a poor woman of the roads on her first begging mission, ashamed to venture beyond the obscure tracks of hill and cliff. The moon would not have to watch its step on an impossible tangle of hill, hummock and harbour when she desired to come and kiss me. I would have the vast expanse of the plain spread out like a multi-coloured carpet before her. The rain would not come darting down like shots from a rambling ruffian blazing away on rough mountainy paths, but like the stately triumph of a queen whose presence among her people confirms the rule of law and prosperity . . .

—Dotie! "Sentimentality"!

—That foolishness again . . .

—. . . Look at me! The murderer gave me a bad bottle . . .

—. . . Went to the Plaza at seven . . . She came. That bright smile again. Accepted the chocolates. A flick . . . She'd already seen the flick at the Plaza—seen all the flicks in town. A stroll or a dance . . . She'd been on her feet in the Bookie's since morning . . . Tea . . . She'd just got up from her tea . . . The Western Hotel . . . Certainly, a short rest would do her good . . .

"Wine," says I to the waiter.

"Whiskey," says she.

"Two large whiskeys," says I . . .

"Two more large whiskeys," says I . . .

"I've no more whiskey," says the waiter. "Do you know how many whiskeys you've drunk since seven o'clock: twelve large ones each! Whiskey is scarce . . ."

"Stout," says I.

"Brandy," says she.

"Two large brandies," says I . . .

"Do you know," says the waiter, "that it's away past one o'clock, and even though you're in the Western Hotel we still have to keep an eye out. There might be a police raid . . ."

"I'll escort you home," says I, as the waiter closed the door of the Western Hotel behind us.

"Escort me home?" says she. "By the look of you it's me will have to escort you. Smarten yourself up there or you'll fall in through that window. You can't take it, is that how it is? Look how sober I am, and I had a large brandy more than you! You wouldn't think I had a drop taken, would you? . . . Mind you don't bump into that pole . . . Come on, walk. Let me take your arm and I'll escort you to your own door.

We might get a few more drinks in Simon O'Halloran's on the way up. It's pay-night and he won't close till morning . . ."

I managed to get a look at her in the half-light of the street. She had that bright smile on her face. But I was putting my hand into my pocket and turning it out. Down to the one shilling . . .

—You silly fool . . .

—. . . Faith then, as you say . . .

—. . . I'm telling you the truth, Peadar the Pub. Caitríona Pháidín came in to me. I remember it well. It was late in the year, in November. It was the year we put winter manure on the Rape Field. Micil was spreading seaweed the same day. I was expecting the youngsters home from school any minute, and I turned the batch of potatoes I had roasting in the ashes for them. Then I sat down in the chimney-corner turning the heel on a stocking.

"God bless all here," she says. "Well, the same to you," says I. "You're welcome, Caitríona. Sit down."

"I can't stay for a proper visit," says she. "I'm up to my eyes preparing for the priest. It's only nine or ten days now till he'll be in on top of me. I won't beat about the bush, Cite," says she. "You sold the pigs last fairday. Ours won't be ready for selling till the Feast of St. Brigid,[12] if the Lord spares them . . . It's a lot to ask for, Cite, but if you can spare it till St. Brigid's Fairday, you would do me a great favour if you could give me a pound of money. I'm getting the chimney fixed and I'm thinking of buying a *roundtable*[13] for the priest's[14] breakfast. I have two pounds of my own . . ."

"A *roundtable*, Caitríona?" says I. "Nobody around here has a *roundtable* for the priest, except the big shots of course. Wouldn't he eat just as well off an ordinary table, as we've always seen the priests do?"

"The last time he was in our Nell's," says she, "she had a silver

---

12. The 1st of February. Marks the beginning of spring.

13. Thus in the original, with some inconsistencies later on.

14. When Mass was celebrated in a private house the priest had to be entertained to breakfast afterwards.

teapot Big Brian's Mag brought home from America. I'll get the loan of Siúán the Shop's silver teapot, Cite, because I'd like to keep neck and neck with Nell and even a nose ahead of her. The brazen upstart!"

I gave her the pound. She bought the *roundtable*. Things were cheap at the time. She laid out the priest's breakfast on it, and she made his tea in Siúán the Shop's silver teapot.

By the oak of this coffin I gave her the pound, Peadar the Pub, and I never got another sight of it from that day to the day I died, whatever Siúán the Shop did about the teapot . . .

—You're a liar, you Hag of the Ash-Potatoes. Don't believe her, Peadar dear. I gave every single penny of it back to her, into the palm of her hand, when I sold the pigs the following Feast of St. Brigid . . . It's in your nature, of course! It wasn't often your own mother told the truth . . . I died as clean as crystal, thanks be to God . . . Nobody can ever say Caitríona Pháidín owed as much as a red farthing when she died, which is more than can be said about you, stingy Cite of the Ash-Potatoes . . . Yourself and your people before you always left a heap of debt behind you wherever you went. You have a nerve to talk! You killed your family and yourself with your ash-baked potatoes . . . Oh, don't believe her, Peadar . . . Don't believe her . . . I gave her every red penny of it into the palm of her hand . . .

I didn't, you old hag? . . . I didn't, you say?

Hey, Muraed! . . . Muraed! . . . Did you hear what Cite said? . . . I'll explode! I'll explode! . . .

Interlude Three

THE TEASING OF THE CLAY

1

I am the Trump[1] of the Graveyard. Let my voice be heard! It must be heard . . .

For I am every voice that was, that is and that will be. I was the first voice in the formlessness of the universe. I am the last voice that will be heard in the dust of Armageddon. I was the muffled voice of the first embryo in the first womb. When the golden harvest is stacked in the haggard, I am the voice that will summon home the last gleaner from the Grain-field of Time. For I am the first-born son of Time and Life, and steward of their household. I am reaper, stack-builder and thresher of Time. I am storeman, cellarer and turnkey of Life. Let my voice be heard! It must be heard . . .

There is neither time nor life in the Graveyard. There is neither brightness nor darkness. There is no sunset, springtide, changeability of wind or breaking of weather. Nor is there lengthening of the day, or manifestation of the Pleiads and the Plough; nor the growing creature attiring itself in the cloak of Joy and Festivity. The lively eyes of the child are not there. Nor the extravagant desire of the youth. Nor the rose-tinted cheeks of the maiden. Nor the gentle voice of the nurturing mother. Nor the serene smile of old age. Eyes, desire, cheek, voice and smile all dissolve into one amorphous sameness in the unsqueamish alembic of the earth. Complexion has no voice there, nor voice complexion, for the indifferent chemistry of the grave has

---

1. Poetic or archaic word for "trumpet," as in "last trump" or "trump of doom."

neither voice nor complexion. It has only bones crumbling, flesh decaying, and body parts once vital decomposing. It has only the wardrobe of clay where the discarded suit of life rots under the moth . . .

But above ground a heat haze hangs lightly on the air. The springtide is pulsing constantly in the channels of the shore. The meadow is as if a can of green milk had been spilt on its grass. Hawthorn, bush and boundary hedge array their formal gowns like ladies-in-waiting before entering the presence of the King. There is a soft lonely ring to the blackbird's song in the groves. The children's eyes widen as they handle the toys tumbling from the treasure-chest of the virgin year. The torch that rejuvenates all hope glows in the cheek of the pubescent youth. Foxgloves plucked from the meadows of eternity bloom in the modest cheeks of the maiden. Whitethorn blossom foams in the tender countenance of the mother. The children play hide-and-seek in the haggard, their laughter ringing like chimes of joy, the pitches of their voices rising and falling as if trying to draw Jacob's Ladder back down from Heaven. And the intimate whisper of courtship escapes from the seclusion of the boreen like a gentle breeze wafting over beds of cowslips in the land of youth . . .

But the old man's trembling is chronic now. The young man's bones are seizing up. The smear of grey washes over the gold in the woman's hair. Cataract, like snake slime, is quenching the child's eyesight. Gaiety and gambolling give way to grumbling and groaning. Weakness is driving out strength. Despair is overcoming love. The grave-cloth is being stitched to the cradle-cloth, and the grave to the cradle. Life is paying its dues to death . . .

I am the Trump of the Graveyard. Let my voice be heard! It must be heard! . . .

2

—. . . Hey! What's that? Who are you? Are you my son's wife? Wasn't I right when I said she'd be here on her next childbirth . . .

—Seáinín Liam is what they used to call me in the last place, indeed—unless I have to be christened again here. The heart . . .

—Seáinín Liam. Ababúna! They're burying you in the wrong grave, Seáinín. This is Caitríona Pháidín's grave . . .

—Arrah, isn't that always the way in this cemetery, Caitríona my dear? But I can't speak to a living soul. I have more to worry me. The heart . . .

—What sort of funeral did I have, Seáinín Liam?

—Funeral? The heart, Caitríona! The heart! I had just been to collect the pension. Devil a thing I felt. I drank a drop of tea. Down I went to the Common Field to fetch a creel of potatoes. When I was easing it off me inside the house, the strap handle slipped and the creel came down lopsided. I gave my side a little wrench. There wasn't a puff of breath left in me . . .

—What sort of funeral did I have, I'm asking you?

—The heart, God help us! The heart is a serious matter, Caitríona. A weak heart . . .

—To hell with your heart! You'll have to give up that nonsense here . . .

—Bedamn but the heart's a poor thing, Caitríona. We were building a new stable for the colt we bought after Christmas. We had it finished except for the roof. I wasn't able to give the young fellow much help, but little and all as it was he'll miss me. I wouldn't mind but the weather was great for a long time now . . .

—Weather! Time! Those are two things that won't worry you here, Seáinín. You were a dimwit all your life. Tell me this much! Why don't you pay attention to me? Did I have a big funeral?

—A fine big funeral!

—A big funeral, you say, Seáinín . . .

—A fine big funeral. The heart . . .

—May the devil and all his demons take that same heart of yours, if it's such a treasure! Do you hear me? You'll have to quit that blathering. They won't listen to that sort of talk here, I'm telling you. How much altar-money was collected at my funeral?

—A fine big funeral . . .

—I know, but how much altar-money? . . .

—A fine big collection . . .

—How much, I ask you? You always were a dimwit. How much altar-money?

—Peadar the Pub had a big collection, and so had Siúán the Shop and Muraed Phroinsiais and Cite . . .

—Don't I know that! But that's not what I'm asking you. Wasn't I above ground myself then? But how much was collected at my own funeral, Caitríona Pháidín's funeral. Altar-money. Seventeen pounds, sixteen pounds, fourteen pounds? . . .

—Ten pounds, twelve shillings.

—Ten pounds! Ten pounds! Now, Seáinín, are you sure it was ten pounds, not eleven pounds or twelve pounds, or . . .

—Ten pounds, Caitríona! Ten pounds! A fine big collection, indeed. No word of a lie to say it was a fine big collection. Everybody said so. I was talking to your sister Nell: "Caitríona had a fine big collection," she said. "I thought she wouldn't come within two or three pounds of it, or four indeed." The heart . . .

—Blast and damn your heart! Now Seáinín, stop that nonsense for God's sake! . . . The Mountain crowd weren't there?

—She said that, faith: "I thought she wouldn't come within two or three . . ."

—The Mountain crowd! They didn't hear about it. Pádraig was going to send them word: "Arrah," says Nell. "Why would you be dragging the creatures down, walking all that distance." That's what she said. The heart. A weak heart . . .

—I wish to God your heart was a lump of poison stuck in the pit of Nell's stomach! The Glen of the Pasture people weren't there? . . .

—Not a sight of them.

—The Wood of the Lake people?

—That cousin of Siúán the Shop in Wood of the Lake was being brought to the church the same day . . . I wouldn't mind but the weather was great for a long time now, while we were working on the stable . . .

—Sweet-talking Stiofán wasn't there, of course? . . .

—A colt we bought after Christmas . . .

—For the love of God, Seáinín, don't let the whole graveyard know you're so stupid! . . . Was Sweet-talking Stiofán there?

—Not a bit of him, but Pádraig told me he was talking to him last fairday and what he said was: "I assure you, Pádraig Ó Loideáin," says he, "If it cost me my life's blood I'd have been at the funeral. I owed it to Caitríona Pháidín . . ."

—"to come to her funeral even if it was on my two knees. But devil a word I heard about it till the evening she was buried. A youngster belonging to . . ." A right blatherer, that same Sweet-talking Stiofán! . . . What sort of coffin did they put me in?

—Ten pounds, Caitríona. A fine big collection.

—Are you talking about the coffin or the collection? Why don't you listen? . . . What sort of coffin did they put me in? Coffin . . .

—The best coffin in Tadhg's, three half-barrels of porter and a good dash of poteen. There was enough drink there for twice as many. Nell told him so, but nothing would do him but to get the three half-barrels. Indeed there was lashings of drink there. Even though I was an old man myself I drank twelve mugs that night, not to mention all I drank the day you were brought to the chapel, and the day of the funeral. To tell you the truth, Caitríona, for all the respect and affection I had for you, I wouldn't have risked drinking that much if I'd known the heart was weak . . .

—You didn't hear that Pádraig said anything about burying me somewhere else in the cemetery?

—I gave my side a little wrench and there wasn't a puff of breath left in me. The heart, God help us . . .

—Will you listen to what I'm saying, Seáinín. Listen to me. You didn't hear that Pádraig said anything about burying me . . .

—You wouldn't have been left unburied anyhow, Caitríona, no matter how much drink there was. Even myself who had a weak heart and all that . . .

—You're the biggest dimwit since Adam ate the apple. Did you hear that Pádraig said anything about burying me somewhere else in the cemetery?

—Pádraig was to bury you in the Pound Plot, but Nell said the

Fifteen-Shilling Plot was good enough for anyone, and that it was an awful thing to put a poor man to that expense.

—The bitch! She would say that! She was at the house so?

—A fine big colt we bought after Christmas. Ten pounds . . .

—Was it for the colt you paid the ten pounds? You told me before there was ten pounds of altar-money . . .

—There was ten pounds in your altar-money for certain, Caitríona. Ten pounds, twelve shillings. That was it exactly. Big Brian came along as the funeral was turning at the head of the boreen, and he was pressing a shilling on Pádraig but Pádraig wouldn't accept it. That would have been ten pounds, thirteen shillings if he had . . .

—Rammed down his throat it should be! Big Brian! If the ugly streak of misery was looking for a woman he wouldn't be late . . . But now, Seáinín Liam, listen to me . . . Good man! Was Nell at the house?

—She didn't leave it from the time you died till you were brought to the church. She was the one attending to the women inside the house the day of the funeral. I went back into the room myself to fill a few pipes[2] of tobacco for the Mangy Field crowd who were too shy to come in. Nell and myself began to talk:

"Caitríona is a fine corpse, may the Lord have mercy on her," says I. "And you laid her out beautifully . . ."

Nell drew me into a secluded corner: "I didn't like to say anything," says she. "She was my sister . . ." Faith then, that's what she said.

—But what did she say? Out with it . . .

—When I was easing it off myself inside the house I gave my side a little wrench. There wasn't a puff of breath left in me. Not a puff! The heart . . .

—Oh, the Lord bless us and save us! Yourself and Nell were in the corner of the room and she said: "I didn't want to say anything, Seáinín Liam. She was my sister . . ."

—Faith then, that's what she said. May I not leave this spot if

---

2. It used to be the custom to distribute clay pipes and tobacco to the mourners at a wake or a funeral.

she didn't: "Caitríona was a rough and ready worker," says she. "But she wasn't the cleanest, may the Lord have mercy on her. If she were, I assure you she would be laid out beautifully. Look at the dirt on that winding-sheet now, Seáinín. See the spots. Isn't that disgraceful! You'd think she could have washed her grave-clothes and laid them aside. If she'd been lingering for a long time I wouldn't mind. Everybody's noticing the spots on the winding-sheet. Cleanliness is a grand thing, Seáinín . . ."

—Ababúna! Holy Mother of God! I left them as clean as crystal in the corner of the chest. My son's wife or the children must have soiled them. Or else whoever laid me out. Who laid me out, Seáinín?

—Nóra Sheáinín's daughter and Nell. Little Cáit was sent for but she wouldn't come . . . The heart, God help us . . .

—What heart! Wasn't it her back she was complaining of? You think that because your own old heart was rotten everyone else's heart is rotten. Why wouldn't Little Cáit come ? . . .

—Pádraig sent his eldest girl to get her. I don't remember her name. I should remember it indeed. But I died too suddenly. The heart . . .

—Máirín is her name.

—That's right. Máirín. Máirín it is . . .

—Pádraig sent Máirín back to get Little Cáit, did he? And what did she say? . . .

—"I'll never go over to that village again," says she. "I'm finished with it. The way's too long for me now with the sort of heart I have . . ."

—It's not the heart but the back, I tell you. Who was it keened me?

—The stable was finished except for the roof. Little and all help as I was able to give the young fellow . . .

—You won't be giving him even that much any more . . . But listen now, Seáinín. Good man yourself! Who keened me? . . .

—Everybody said it was an awful pity Bid Shorcha didn't come, and when she'd have had her fill of porter . . .

—Ababúna! So Bid wasn't there to keen me?

—The heart.

—The heart! How could it be the heart! The kidneys were Bid Shorcha's complaint, the same as myself. Why didn't she come?

—When someone was sent for her, what she said was: "I wouldn't stir a foot for them. I cried my eyes out for them, and did I get any respect for it? No: 'Bid Shorcha's a sponger. Sponging for drink. I'll warrant you won't hear a wail out of her till she has drunk enough to put a billy-goat in kid. She'll keen woefully enough then alright.' Let them keen themselves now, if they want to. From now on I'm only going to keen certain people." That's what she said . . .

—A right bitch, that Bid Shorcha. But I'll let her have it when she comes here! . . . Was Nell whispering in the priest's ear at the funeral?

—The priest wasn't there at all. He went to Siúán the Shop's cousin's funeral, as she was fine and close to him. But he lit eight candles . . .

—That's something no corpse ever had before, Seáinín.

—Except that one of them went out, Caitríona. Snuffed . . .

—Snuff the lot of them!

—And he said the world of prayers, and he sprinkled the holy water five times on the coffin, a thing that was never seen before . . . Nell said he was blessing the two corpses at once, but I wouldn't say so myself . . .

—Arrah, Seáinín, why would he do that? May the Lord reward him. Even that much, it's great revenge on Nell. How is her son Peadar?

—Poorly enough. Poorly enough. The heart . . .

—Oh musha,[3] musha, musha! What's that nonsense about the heart! Wasn't it his hip was hurt. Or did it go to his heart since? That's better still . . .

—The hip, Caitríona. The hip. There's talk of the law case being heard in Dublin in the autumn. Everybody says he'll lose, and that he'll leave Nell and Big Brian's daughter without a brass farthing . . .

---

3. *Muise*, a common exclamation in Irish and in Hiberno-English: *Muise! Muise!* Well, well!

—May he do just that! May God grant it . . . What did you say about Tomás Inside?

—After I'd collected the pension I had a drop of tea and I went down to the Common Field . . .

—Don't worry! You'll never again set foot there . . . Listen. Listen, I say. Tomás Inside . . .

—Tomás Inside? Full of life. The cabin was about to fall in on him for want of a roof. Nell came to your Pádraig recently: "It's an awful shame for you to leave that poor old man with the rain down on top of him," she said. "Only for what happened to my Peadar . . ."

—And the little fool gave in to the bitch . . .

—He was busy, but he said he'd put a bit of straw here and a bit there on the worst leaks till he'd get a chance to give it a proper cover . . . The heart . . .

—'Tis true for you. The heart. Pádraig has a good heart. Too good . . . You didn't hear him say anything about putting a cross over me?

—A brand-new cross of Island limestone, Caitríona . . .

—Soon?

—Soon indeed . . .

—And my son's wife?

—My son's wife? . . . My son doesn't have a wife, Caitríona. I told him that when the new stable for the colt is finished a young fellow like himself could do worse than . . .

—To go to a doctor about his heart, Seáinín, for fear he had caught the disease from you. My son's wife. My son Pádraig. Nóra Sheáinín's daughter. Do you understand me now? . . .

—I do. Nóra Sheáinín's daughter. Sickly. The heart . . .

—That's a damned lie. It's not her heart; she was sick . . .

—Sickly, Caitríona . . .

—Thanks for the news! I knew that much myself. I thought she might be showing some signs of coming here. She'll be here on her next confinement for sure. Did you hear anything about Baba?

—Your Baba in America. She wrote to Pádraig sympathising about your death. She sent him five pounds. She didn't make any will yet. He told me that eldest girl of his — what's this her name is? I don't remember. I should remember, but I died too suddenly . . .

—Pádraig's eldest girl. Máirín . . .

—That's her, Máirín. The nuns somewhere down the country are taking her to make a schoolmistress out of her when she has enough learning . . .

—Máirín going to be a schoolmistress! May God save her. She was always very fond of the books. That's great revenge on Nell . . .

—. . . Our joint candidate in this Election . . .

—May the Cross of Christ protect us! Don't tell me there are elections here too, Caitríona. There was one above ground the other day.

—How did our people vote?

—I gave my side a little wrench. The heart . . .

—See how he wanders off again! Listen to me! How did our people vote?

—The old way. How else? Everybody in the village voted the old way except Nell's people. Everybody in her house changed over to this other crowd . . .

—May God send her no luck, the pussface. Of course she would turn her coat. She was always treacherous . . .

—They say this other crowd promised her a new road up to the house . . . But indeed there's not a bother on her yet. 'Tis younger she's getting. I never saw her look better than the day you were buried, Caitríona . . .

—Be off with you, you old sourpuss. None of your people ever had a good word to say, so they didn't . . . Be off with you. This isn't your grave at all . . . The cemetery must be upside-down entirely when the likes of you was going to be buried in the same grave as me. Be off with you down to the Half-Guinea Plot. That's where you belong. Look at all the altar-money there was at my funeral. Look at the respect the priest showed me. Your coffin didn't cost a penny over five pounds. Off with you. You and your old heart. The cheek of you! . . . Your people seldom brought good news. Clear off now! . . .

3

. . . And ten miserable pounds is all the altar-money there was, after all my efforts putting money on altars for every lazy good-for-nothing in the country. Nobody—living or dead—is worth doing a good turn for . . . And the Mountain crowd didn't come to my funeral . . . or the people of Glen of the Pasture or Wood of the Lake . . . And of course Sweet-talking Stiofán didn't come, the big-mouth. They'll answer for this some day. They'll be coming here . . .

What chance did anyone have of coming, with that pussface Nell building a nest in Pádraig's ear, advising him not to tell anyone about my death. And there she was laying me out and handing round drink at my funeral. She knew well I wasn't alive, so she did. The dead person can't do a thing about it . . .

I wouldn't mind but Little Cáit and Bid Shorcha didn't come. I'll let them have it hot and heavy for that. It wouldn't surprise me in the least if Nell had approached them beforehand and put them up to not coming to our house at all. She would do it, the pussface. Any woman who said I didn't have clean grave-clothes set aside to be laid out in . . . May no corpse come into the graveyard ahead of her! . . .

But Baba sent five pounds to Pádraig. Even that much is a great help to him. It will coax that hussy of a daughter of Nóra Sheáinín's, and now she won't be able to say she'll be the only one out of pocket with my cross. It's no bad sign either for Baba to be writing to us . . . If only I'd lived another few years to bury that bitch Nell before me . . .

It's great that Máirín is going to be a schoolmistress. That will madden Nell and Big Brian's Mag: for us to have a schoolmistress in the house and them not to have one. A schoolmistress earns great money, I believe. That's what I've always heard. I must ask the Big Master how much his wife was earning. Who knows but Máirín might be teaching in our own school, if the Big Master's wife left, or if anything should happen to her. That's when we'd have revenge on Nell. Máirín going up the church every Sunday morning with her hat, her pair of gloves, her parasol, a Prayer Book the size of a turf-creel under her arm, walking up to the gallery with the priest's sister, and playing the piano. Let Nell and Big Brian's Mag eat their heart out — if they're still alive. But they say it's up to the priest to appoint schoolmistresses. If that's so, I don't know what to say, as Nell is so friendly with him . . . But who knows. Maybe it won't be long till he leaves, or till he dies . . .

And that hussy of a wife of Pádraig's is still sickly . . . It's a great wonder she doesn't die. But she will, on her next childbirth for certain . . .

A pity I didn't ask Seáinín Liam about the turf and the sowing, and about the pigs and the calves, or how the fox is faring these times. I was all set to ask him, then . . . But what chance did a person have of asking him anything, with all his gibbering about his old heart? I can easily get a chance to speak to him from now on. He was sneaked in just near here . . .

—. . . Patience, Cóilí. Patience. Listen to me. I am a writer . . .

—Hold on, my good man, till I finish my story: "Oh, the blackguard," says Fionn.[4] "It wouldn't occur to him to leave Niamh of the Golden Tresses to his poor father whose nights are so lonely since Gráinne, that inconstant lump of a daughter of Cormac son of Conn, took off with Big Macán, son of the Black Warrior from Holly Wood of the Fianna . . ."

—. . . The most difficult man I ever dealt with in the line of insurance was the Big Master. There wasn't a trick in my book I didn't try. I came at him from the northwest and from the southeast. From sunlit seas and frozen mountains. Out of the eye of the wind and by tacking against it. As a pincers, as a ring, as a sledgehammer, as Cuchulainn's spear, as an atomic bomb. As a fawning pup and as a thief in the night. With a shipful of human kindness and with a bellyful of satirical reproach worthy of Bricriú.[5] I gave him unheeded invitations to the

---

4. Fionn, Fianna, Niamh, Gráinne: Fionn Mac Cumhaill (Finn Mac Cool) was the mythical leader of a band of warriors, the Fianna; Niamh and Gráinne figure in legends about the Fianna.

5. Mythical satiric poet in stories of the Ulster Cycle who caused dissension and strife among the warriors of Ulster at drinking feasts, one of which is known as the Feast of Bricriú.

snug in Peadar the Pub's. I gave him cigarettes for free and lifts in the car for free. I brought him exact reports of the prowling of inspectors and the latest gossip about the rumpus between the Schoolmaster and Schoolmistress of Grassy Upland. I told him mouth-watering stories about young women . . .

But it was no use. He was afraid that if he took out an insurance policy with me it would be his total ruination. Nobody could persuade him to part with a farthing . . .

—But I did . . .

—You did, and so did I. Hold on. He was the biggest miser who ever wore clothes. He was so shrewd he could herd mice at a crossroads, as they say. The only wild deed he ever did was that trip to London when the teachers got the rise . . .

—That was the time he was in the nightclub.

—It was. He spent the rest of his life telling me about it, and warning me to keep my mouth shut about it. "If the priest or the Schoolmistress heard about it!" he would say . . .

Then he married her: the Schoolmistress.

"Maybe," said I to myself, "I'll succeed in locating some generosity in him now. The Schoolmistress would be a great backing to me if I could only cajole her. And it is possible to cajole her." There isn't a woman born who hasn't that kernel of vanity, if one can only uncover it. I didn't spend time selling insurance without knowing that.

—I know it too. It's easier to sell to women than to men if you have your wits about you . . .

—I'd have to allow some time for the novelty of the marriage to wear off a little. But I couldn't leave it too long either, because he might not be so amenable to his wife's advice if he was beginning to lose interest in her charms. Insurance people know these things . . .

—And booksellers too . . .

—I gave him three weeks . . . It was on a Sunday. Himself and herself were sitting out in front of the house after their lunch. "Here I come, you rascal," says I . . . "By the bone marrow of my forebears I'll do business today! . . . You have the week's work schedule prepared by now, and the notes you're forever talking about. You're stuffed with

AN MÁISTIR MÓR

food, and if the wife is at all favourable it will be easier to play on you than another time . . ."

We had a bit of chat about the affairs of the Realm. I said I was in a hurry. "Sundays and Mondays are all the same to me," said I. "Always prowling, 'seeking whom I may devour.' Now that you're married, Master, the Mistress should make you take out a policy on your life. You're more valuable now than you were before. You have the responsibilities of a spouse . . . I'm of the opinion," says I to the wife, "that he doesn't love you at all, but you serve his purpose, and if you die he'll take another one."

The two of them laughed heartily. "And," said I, "as an insurance man I have to tell you that if he dies there is no provision made for you. If I had a 'gilt-edged security' like you . . ."

She turned a little sulky: "Yes," she said to the Master, half in jest and half in earnest, "if anything should happen to you, the Lord between us and all harm . . ."

"What could happen to me?" says he, in a disgruntled voice.

"Accidents are as common as air," says I, "it's the duty of the insurance man always to say that."

"Exactly," says she. "I hope nothing will happen. May God forbid! If anything did happen to you, I wouldn't survive without you. But, the Lord between us and all harm, if you should die and if I didn't die at the same time . . . what would become of me? It's your duty . . ."

And, believe it or not, didn't he take out a life insurance policy! One thousand five hundred pounds. He had only paid four or five instalments, I think—big instalments too. She made him take out another two hundred and fifty at the time of the last instalment. "He won't last long," says she with a smile, and she gave me a wink.

She was right. It wasn't long before he wasted away . . .

I'll tell you about another big *coup* I had. It wasn't half as good as the one with the Big Master . . .

—You got one over on the Big Master just as Nell Pháidín did on Caitríona about Jack the Scológ . . .

—Ababúna! I'll explode! I'll explode! I'll ex . . .

4

Hey, Muraed! Hey, Muraed! . . . Can you hear me? . . . They were burying Seáinín Liam on top of me. Indeed they were, Muraed . . . Oh, have a bit of sense, Muraed! Why would I allow him into the same grave as me? I never had to pick and sell periwinkles. Didn't he and his people live on periwinkles, and I'd remind him of that too. Even in the short time I spent talking to him he nearly drove me mad going on about his old heart . . . It's true for you, Muraed. If I had a cross on my grave it would be easily recognised. But I'll have a cross soon now, Muraed. Seáinín Liam told me. A cross of Island limestone like the one over Peadar the Pub . . . My son's wife, is it? Seáinín Liam said she'd be here on her next childbirth for certain . . .

Do you remember our Pádraig's eldest girl, Muraed? Yes. Máirín . . . That's right, Muraed. She'd be fourteen now . . . You're right. She was only a plump little thing when you died. She's in college now. Seáinín Liam told me . . . to become a schoolmistress! What else! You don't think she'd be sent to college to learn how to boil potatoes and mackerel now, or make beds or scrub the floor? That old scrubber of a mother of hers could do with that, if there was such a college . . .

Máirín was always fond of school. She has a great head on her for a child of her age. She was away ahead of the Schoolmistress—the Big Master's wife—before the Master died. There's nobody in the school who's any way near her, Seáinín Liam tells me.

"She's extremely advanced in learning," he says. "She'll be qualified a year before everybody else."

Upon my word, he did, Muraed . . . Now Muraed, there's no need for talk like that. It's not a wonder at all. Why do you say it's a wonder, Muraed? Our people had brains and intellect, even if I say so myself . . .

—. . . But that's not what I asked you, Seáinín.

—Ah, Master, the heart! The heart, God help us! I'd been for the pension. Devil a thing I felt . . . Now Master, don't be so irritable. I can't help it. I fetched a creel of potatoes. When I was easing it off me . . . But Master, I'm not saying a word but the truth. Of course I know damn all about it, Master, but what I heard people saying. I had more to worry about, unfortunately. The creel came down lopsided. I gave . . . What were the people saying, Master? Our people had no time for saying anything, Master, or listening to anything. We were building a new stable for the colt . . .

What were the people saying, Master? You know yourself, Master—a man like you with so much education, God bless you—that there are some people who can't live without gossiping. But a person who has a weak heart . . . Amn't I telling you what they're saying, Master, if only you'd have a bit of patience and not be so ratty with me. I wouldn't mind, but the weather was great for a long time while we were building the stable . . . The people, Master? They're saying more than their prayers, Master. But a person who has a weak heart, God help us . . .

The Schoolmistress, is it? I never saw her looking better, Master, God bless her! 'Tis younger she's getting, so it is. She must have a great heart . . . People used to be talking indeed, Master. There's no denying that. But faith, myself and the young fellow were busy with the stable . . . Don't be so ratty with me, Master dear. Of course, everybody in the country was saying Billyboy the Post was never out of your house.

It was a fine big colt, Master . . . What's the use of being so ratty with me, Master. There's damn all I can do about whatever happens to the whole lot of you. I had more to worry about, God help . . . He spends time in the house, is it? On my soul, he does indeed, Master. I wouldn't mind that, but in the school as well. He calls into the school every day and gives the letters to the children, and himself and the Schoolmistress go out into the hall for a chat. Arrah, God bless your innocence, Master. You don't know the half of it. But I had more to worry about. There wasn't a puff of breath left in my body. The heart . . .

—. . . But Cóilí, Cóilí . . .

—Let me finish my story, my good man:

"'There's nobody can inform me about this case now,' says Daniel O'Connell,[6] 'but one person—Biddy Early—and she's seven hundred miles from here, working charms for distillers whose poteen is being robbed of all its powers by the fairies, in a town they call Bones of the Horse[7] in the County of Galway back in Ireland. Saddle and bridle the best horse in my stable till I go and fetch her to London in England riding pillion behind me . . .'

"Off he went. 'Miss Debonaire,' says he to her . . . 'How dare any son of a hag take liberties with my name?' says she . . ."

—. . . Now then, Siúán the Shop! Looking for votes for Peadar the Pub! Why wouldn't you? Your son is married to his daughter above ground. And even if he weren't, yourself and Peadar would be as thick as any pair of thieves . . .

—This is the thanks I get now. You'd have died years before your time only for I gave you credit. Running into me begging each day: "For the honour of God and His Blessed Mother give me a grain of flour till I sell the pigs . . ."

—I paid dearly and direly for that same flour, my sharp little Siúán. All the people were saying: "Siúán the Shop is good and charitable. She gives credit." You did, Siúán, because you knew you'd get paid, and if the odd person wouldn't pay you, a hundred others would . . .

—The same basic principle applies in insurance . . .

—I'd get a bag of flour for a pound if I paid on the nail. If I waited till fairday or sold before the fair, it cost me one pound, three shillings. If I wasn't able to pay for six or nine months, it cost me one pound,

---

6. The Irish Catholic political leader Daniel O'Connell (1775–1847) is the subject of much folklore. Biddy Early (d. 1874, Co. Clare) was a widely known herbal healer reputed to be gifted with second sight.

7. Unidentified place.

seven shillings. You were smooth and sweet to the big shot. You were cruel and contemptuous to the person who didn't have his penny in the palm of his hand. Thanks be to God the day has come that we're not afraid to say it to your face . . .

—Arrah, Siúán, you little toady—toadying to the well-off—you little toady Siúán, it was you who killed me four score years before my time. For want of *fags*[8] . . . I saw you giving them to the sergeant, who didn't shop with you at all but in Brightcity. I saw you giving them to a lorry driver that nobody knew where the devil he came from, and that you never made a penny on. You kept them under the counter. "Just the one," says I. "I'll make do with that for now and maybe they'll be more plentiful from tomorrow, the beginning of the month . . ."

"Where would I get *fags?*" says you. "Don't you know I don't make them! . . ."

"If I could afford four or five shillings a box for them," says I . . . "Keep them!"

I went home.

"You should gather up that scattering of seaweed you left down there and spread it on the field over here," says my mother.

"Seaweed!" says I. "My seaweed spreading is over, mother."

I threw out a spit. It was as stiff as a male briar. May I not leave this spot if it wasn't. There was a kitten on the hearth. He began to lick at the spittle. He took a fit of coughing. May I not leave this spot if he didn't.

"This doesn't look good," says I. I took to my bed. I didn't get up any more. For the want of *fags*. My death is on your head, toady Siúán, toadying to the well-off . . .

—And so is my death! Your *clogs* were my killer, you cheating Siúán. I handed out my two pounds, five shillings into your hand. It was in the blackest depths of winter, and us building the road in Donagh's Village. Drawing stones[9] on a hand-barrow I was, in that wet

---

8. Cigarettes.

9. Two workmen carrying stones on a wooden hand-barrow, one in front and one behind.

hollow to the south. May the same hollow smother and drown forever and ever! It was there I was fated to die. I put on the *clogs*. Oh, the devil as much as one drop did they keep out after the second day . . .

I rested the barrow.

"What's wrong with you?" says my workmate.

"There's plenty wrong with me," says I. I sat down in the fork of the barrow and I pulled my drawers up above my ankle. The small of my foot was as blue as Glutton's nose. By Heavens, it was.

"What's wrong with you?" says the big boss when he came by.

"There's plenty wrong with me," says I.

"There's plenty wrong with you, I'm afraid," says he.

"Siúán the Shop's *clogs*," says I.

"May they smother and drown forever," says he. "If she lives much longer I won't have a road-worker left who isn't in the cemetery."

I went home. I lay down on the bed. The doctor was sent for that night.

"You're finished," he says. "The feet . . ."

"I'm finished indeed," says I. "The feet . . . *clogs* . . ."

"Siúán the Shop's *clogs* indeed," says he. "As long as she lives I won't be idle . . ."

The priest was sent for the following morning. "You're finished," he says. "The feet . . ."

"Finished indeed," says I. "The feet . . . *Clogs* . . ."

"Siúán the Shop's *clogs* indeed," says he. "As long as she lives I won't be idle. But you're finished anyhow . . ."

And of course I was. A week from that day I was laid out. Your *clogs*, you cheating Siúán. My death is on your head . . .

—My death is on your head, you ugly Siúán. Your coffee. Oh, your damned coffee! Your jam. Oh, your damned jam, you ugly Siúán. Your coffee instead of tea: your jam instead of butter.

It was the sorry day for me—if only I could have helped it—the day I left my coupons with you, you ugly Siúán:

"No tea came this week. I don't know what's wrong with them that they didn't send me any."

"No tea came, Siúán?"

"Devil a grain, then."

"And the people can't get any tea this week, Siúán?"

"They can't indeed. But you'll get two weeks' rations next week."

"But you said that often before, Siúán, and we were never compensated for the weeks it didn't come . . . For the honour of God and His Blessed Mother, a grain of tea, Siúán. A little grain. As much as would cover a fingernail, even . . . The coffee has me poisoned . . ."

"Don't you know it's not me that manufactures tea. If you're not satisfied you can take your coupons to . . ."

And you knew right well I couldn't, you ugly Siúán. Saving up the tea for those who could pay you three times the price for it: houses that kept Irish-language learners, tourists, big shots and so on. You gave it to the Priest's housekeeper in front of my two eyes, and you gave a quarter of a pound to the sergeant's wife. Trying to get the priest not to denounce your roguery from the altar; trying to get the sergeant not to denounce your roguery in court . . .

I brought the coffee home with me. The old woman put down a dash of it.

"I won't drink it," said I. "The blessings of God on you . . ."

"You'll have to take something soon," she says. "You haven't taken a thing since yesterday morning."

"Let it be," said I. I got up a lump of phlegm. It was like leather, begging the graveyard's pardon. The dog began sniffing around it. But not for long. He took off and wasn't seen again for two days.

"My stomach juices are not what they should be," I said. "I might as well die right now. I'll die if I drink that scour of a coffee, and I'll die if I don't . . ."

And I did die. I wouldn't have a word of speech now only for I sweated the stuff out of me while I was laid out . . . your coffee was the cause of my death, you ugly Siúán. My death is on your head.

—And my death!

—And my death!

—And my death!

—. . . I won't vote for you, Peadar. You let a black heretic insult the faith inside your public house. You had no blood in your veins. If it had been me . . .

—You were a crook, Peadar the Pub. You charged me four four-penny bits for a half-glass of whiskey and I was so green I didn't know what I should pay.

—Your wife would know. Many is the half-glass she drank in my pub. But that was another thing you didn't know till now, it seems . . .

—You were a crook, Peadar the Pub. You were watering the whiskey.

—I was not.

—I say you were. Tomás Inside and myself went in to you on a Friday after collecting the pension. This was before the war. The country was awash with whiskey. As soon as you saw Tomás was a bit merry you started talking about women to him. "It's a wonder you wouldn't marry, Tomás," you said. "A man who has a nice patch of land . . ."

"By the docks, but I have that, my friend," says Tomás. "You might as well give me the daughter."

"By God, there she is, and I'm not keeping her from you," you said . . . There was such a day, Peadar. Don't deny it . . .

Your daughter came into the pub at just the right moment. She took a crock of jam from the shelf. Do you think I don't remember? "That's her now," says you. "She can do whatever she likes . . ."

"Will you marry me?" says Tomás, moving in close to her.

"Why wouldn't I, Tomás?" says she. "You've a nice patch of land, and a half-guinea pension . . ."

We spent some time joking like that, but Tomás was half in earnest. Your daughter was wriggling about and fiddling with her neckscarf . . . There was such a day, Peadar the Pub. Don't deny it . . .

Your daughter went into the kitchen. In went Tomás after her, to light his pipe. She kept him in there. But soon she was back in the pub again getting another swig of whiskey for him. "That old eejit will soon be blind drunk, and he's ours till morning then," she says.

You took the glass she had in her hand. You put a good half of water into it from the jug. You filled it up with whiskey then . . . There was such a day, Peadar . . .

Do you think I didn't see you at it? I knew well what was going on between you and your daughter behind the counter. Do you think I didn't understand your whispering? Your daughter plied Tomás Inside with watered whiskey throughout the day. But he paid the price of whiskey for the water, and he was drunk in the evening all the same ... Your daughter spent the day coaxing him. He soon began to order glasses of whiskey for her, and she only filling them with water. A lorry driver would have run into him that evening only for Nell Pháidín, Jack the Scológ's wife, came in and brought him home with her ... There was such a day, Peadar. Don't deny it. You were a robber ...

—You robbed me too, Peadar the Pub. Your daughter gave me change out of a ten-shilling note instead of a pound, and then she was ramming it down my throat that ...

—You robbed me too, Peadar the Pub. Your daughter brought me into the parlour, letting on she was fond of me. She sat in my lap. A crowd of squireens[10] from Brightcity came in and they were sent into the parlour along with me, and this fool was buying them drinks all night. The next day she did the same thing. But there was no squireen from Brightcity around. Instead, she gave the nod to the scroungers off the corner to come in; they were brought into the parlour, and this stupid fool had to stand them drinks ...

—I remember it well. I twisted my ankle ...

—until I didn't have as much as a coin that would rattle on a flagstone. It was part of your roguery, Peadar the Pub: your daughter pretending to be fond of every knock-kneed fool who might have a couple of pounds, till they were spent ...

—You robbed me like everybody else, Peadar the Pub. I was home on leave from England. I had a hundred and twenty pounds of my earnings in my breast pocket. Your daughter brought me into the parlour. She sat in my lap. Some infernal stuff was put into my drink. When I awoke from my drunkenness all I had left in Christendom was a two-shilling piece and a heap of halfpennies ...

—You robbed me like the rest of them, Peadar the Pub. I had

---

10. *Boicíní*, rakish young men of money.

twenty-one pounds fifteen shillings I'd got for three lorryloads of turf that evening. We went in to you to seal the bargain with a drink. At half past ten or eleven o'clock I was on my own in the shop. What did you do but take yourself off. That was part of your cuteness: letting on you noticed nothing. I went into the parlour with your daughter. She sat in my lap. She put her arms around me under my oxters. Something that wasn't right was put in my drink. When I came to my senses all I had left was the change out of a pound I got earlier, that was in the pocket of my trousers . . .

—You robbed me too, Peadar the Pub. No wonder your daughter had a big dowry when she married Siúán the Shop's son. Straight out, Peadar, I wouldn't give you my vote . . .

—I had intended from the beginning to conduct this Election in a decent manner on behalf of the Pound Party. But since you, the Fifteen-Shilling crowd, have brought up unsavoury personal matters—things I thought I would only have to reproach the Half-Guinea Party for—I am going to divulge information that is not very complimentary to Nóra Sheáinín, your own joint candidate. Nóra Sheáinín was a friend of mine. Although I oppose her politically, that doesn't mean that I couldn't respect her and be on cordial terms with her. For that reason, I hate to talk about this matter. I find it painful. I find it repugnant. I find it distasteful. But it was yourselves, the Fifteen-Shilling crowd, who started this incivility. Don't be upset if I give you the stick you cut for yourselves. The bed you have made for yourselves, let you sleep in it now! I was a publican above ground. Nobody but a damned liar can say my pub was not a decent one. You are very proud of your joint candidate. She could hold her head up in any company for decency, honesty and virtue, if what you people are saying is true. But Nóra Sheáinín was a drunkard. Do you know that hardly a day went by without her coming in to me—especially on Fridays when Tomás Inside was in the pub—and drinking four or five pints of porter in the snug at the back of the shop.

—It's not true! It's not true!

—That's a damned lie! That's a damned lie, Peadar . . .

—You're spouting lies! It's not true! . . .

—It is true! Not only did she drink, she sponged for drink. I often gave her drink on credit. But it's not often she paid me for it . . .

—She never took a drop of drink . . .

—It's a damned lie . . .

—It's not true, Peadar the Pub . . .

—It is true, Fellow Corpses! Nóra Sheáinín was a secret drinker. Usually when she had no business in any other shop in the village, she would come over by the old boreen, down through the little wood and in the back entrance. And she used to come on Sundays as well as weekdays, after closing time at night and before opening time in the morning.

—It's not true! It's not true! It's not true!

—Hurrah for Nóra Sheáinín! . . .

—Hurrah for the Fifteen-Shilling Party! . . .

—Hurrah, hurrah, hurrah for Nóra Sheáinín! . . .

—May God save your health, Peadar the Pub! Let her have it where it hurts! Oh by God! And I never knew she was a secret drinker! What else would she be! Keeping company with sailors . . .

6

—. . . The heart! the heart, God help us . . .

—. . . God help us forever and ever . . . My friends and relations and my kith and kin would come and kneel at my grave. Kindred hearts would break into a blaze of prayer and sympathetic souls would compose an *Ave*.[11] Dead clay would answer living clay, the dead heart would warm to the love of the living heart and the dead voice would comprehend the bold utterances of the living . . .

Familiar hands would repair my grave, familiar hands would raise my memorial and familiar tongues would accord my funeral rites. The clay of my native Temple Brennan! Sacred clay of my Zion . . .

But there can't be a Kelly in Gallough, or a Mannion in Menlo,

---

11. "Ave Maria," Hail Mary, a prayer to the Virgin Mary.

or a Clan McGrath left on the Plain, for if there were my earthly remains would not be left to decompose in the rude clay of the granite, in the inhospitable clay of hills and harbours, in the barren clay of stones and cairns, in the sterile clay of bindweed and sandweed, in the lonely clay of my Babylon . . .

—She's very bad when the foolishness comes over her . . .

—. . . Hold on you, my good man, till I finish my story:

". . . The speckled chicken began clucking around the yard at the top of its voice: 'I laid an egg! I laid an egg! Red hot on the dung-heap. Red hot on the dung-heap. I laid an egg! . . .' 'Bad scran to your little egg, and don't deafen us with it,' says an old laying hen that was there. 'I've laid nine clutches, six second clutches, four broods, three score odd eggs and a hundred and one shell-less eggs since the first day I began to cluck on the dung-heap. I was felt for an egg five hundred and forty six times . . .'"

—I wish it had been me, Peadar. You shouldn't have allowed a black heretic to insult your faith . . .

—. . . I drank two score pints and two, one after the other. You know that, Peadar the Pub . . .

—. . . I'm telling you there were no flies on Tomás Inside . . .

—Do you think I don't know that . . .

—May the devil take your futile verses. And for all I know at this very moment the old woman at home could be handing over the big holding to our eldest son and Road-End's daughter . . .

—. . . "Mártan Sheáin Mhóir had a daughter . . ."

—. . . A bad bottle the murderer gave me . . .

—Faith then, as you say . . .

—The elder of the graveyard here. Permission to speak . . .

—*Qu'est-ce qu'il veut dire*: "Permission to speak"? . . .

—. . . But I was putting my hand in my pocket and turning it out . . .

—. . . Your *clogs*, you cheating Siúán . . .

—. . . Oh, Dotie dear, the Election has me exhausted. Always questioning and quibbling. Votes! Votes! Do you know, Dotie, an election isn't half as cultural as I expected? *Honest* it's not. The talk is barbarous and insulting. *Honest!* And all lies. *Honest!* Did you hear what Peadar the Pub said about me: that I used to drink four or five pints of porter every day above ground. *Honest!* Porter! If he'd said whiskey, even. But porter! The most uncultured drink of all. Ugh! . . . Of course you don't believe that I drank porter, Dotie! It's a lie! Filthy, black, uncultured porter. It's a lie, Dotie! What else. *Honest Engine* . . .

And that I got drink on credit . . . Scandal-mongering, Dotie. Scandal-mongering. And that I was sponging. Ugh! Lies and scandal, Dotie. Who would think it of Peadar the Pub? I was friendly with him, Dotie. He was a man who had cultured people coming in and out to him . . . Mud-slinging is what cultured people call it. As the Big Master says, that elemental beast fettered and repressed within us—the "old man" as Saint Paul called it—is let loose at election time . . . I feel my own culture diminished since I came into contact with the *demos*[12] . . .

Tomás Inside, Dotie? Peadar said that too. He said that I was never as keen to go in to him as when Tomás Inside was there. It's easily known what sort of reputation he was trying to give me . . . *Honest*, Dotie, I had no need to run after Tomás Inside. It was he who used to run after me. *Honest!* There are certain people who are destined for romance, Dotie. Did you hear how Kinks expressed it to Blixen in *The Red-Hot Kiss?* "It was Cupid created you out of his own rib, my tweetie-sweetie . . ."

There was never a time that there wasn't a plague of lovers haunting me. In my youth in Brightcity, as a widow in Mangy Field, and now here, I've an *affaire de coeur*, as he calls it himself, with the Big Master. But it's quite harmless: Platonic; cultural . . .

Dotie! Sentimentality! Never mind the fair Plains of East Galway. You must understand what I'm saying so that you can rid your mind of every misjudgement and prejudice. That is the first step in

---

12. Ancient Greek for the common people.

culture, Dotie . . . I was a young widow. I married young too. Romantic fate once more, Dotie. Tomás Inside lost every spark of sense over me when I was a widow:

"By the docks, but I have a cosy cabin," he would say. "I have indeed, dear, and a nice patch of land. Heads of cattle and sheep. I'm still a strong and supple man myself. But I find it difficult to attend to every call on me: cattle, sowing, thatching. The place is going to wrack and ruin for want of a good housewife . . . You're a widow, Nóra Sheáinín, with your son married in the house, and it's no benefit to you to be in Mangy Field any more. By the docks, marry me . . ."

"*De grâce*, Tomás Inside," I'd say. But it was no use saying "*De grâce*" to him, Dotie. He was at my heels everywhere. As Pips puts it in *The Red-Hot Kiss*: 'True love knows no obstacles.' He was always pressing me to come in for a drink every time we met in the village. *Honest!* "*De grâce*, Tomás," I used to say, "I never touched a drop . . ."

Honest I didn't, Dotie . . . But the things he used to say to me about love, Dotie:

I'll marry you, Nóra Sheáinín . . .

> "My star of light and my sun of harvest,
> My locks of amber and my earthly store . . ."

Honest he did, Dotie. But I knew it was only an Indian summer of romance for both of us, and I used to say:

"Little moon, little moon of Scotland, it's lonesome you'll be this night, tomorrow night, and long nights after, and you pacing the lonely sky beyond Glen Lee, looking for the trysting-place of Deirdre and Naoise,[13] the lovers . . ."

He came to Mangy Field to me a few weeks before I died and a bottle of whiskey with him. *Honest* he did. He was so hot for marriage he was to be pitied. I don't know that I wouldn't have encouraged him too, Dotie, but for the obstacles to true love. I told him so:

"The little moon of Scotland will never find our trysting-place,"

---

13. Ill-fated lovers in one of the best-known of Irish myths, Oidhe Chlainne Uisnigh (the Fate of the Sons of Uisneach).

I said. "Naoise and Deirdre are not fated ever to keep a tryst again, or to taste the harvest festival of their love under the pleasant rocks of Glen Lee of the lovers." "By the docks, why not?" said he. "The obstacles to true love," said I. "Others have something to gain by keeping me and my true love apart till death. The only trysting-place in store for us is that of the graveyard. But we'll spend the harvest festival of everlasting love there for all eternity . . ."

It broke my heart to tell him, Dotie. But it was true for me. *Honest*, it was. Caitríona Pháidín came between me and my true love. Petty worldly concerns. She didn't want to see any woman coming into Tomás Inside's house. She wanted his land for herself. There wasn't a thing under the sun she didn't steal from him. *Honest* . . .

—That's a damned lie, you bitch! I didn't rob and I didn't steal from Tomás Inside, or from anyone else. You bitch! You were a secret drinker in the snug in Peadar the Pub's . . . A secret drinker! . . . A secret drinker. Don't believe her, Dotie! Don't believe her! . . .

Hey, Muraed . . . Muraed . . . Hey, Muraed . . . Did you hear what that bitch Nóra Sheáinín said about me? . . . I'll explode! I'll explode! I'll explode! . . .

Interlude Four

THE CRUSHING OF THE CLAY

1

I am the Trump of the Graveyard. Let my voice be heard! It must be heard . . .

Here in the graveyard the spectre of Insensibility is violating coffins, grubbing up corpses and kneading the decayed flesh in his cold earth-oven. He cares nothing for cheek of sunlight, fairness of complexion or the pearly teeth that are the maiden's pride. Nor for the stout limb, the nimble foot or the sturdy chest that are the pride of the youth. Nor the tongue that beguiled the multitudes with enchanting words and sweet cadences. Nor the brow that bore the laurel wreath of triumph. Nor the brain that was once the guiding star for every seafarer "on the wide seas of high learning" . . . For these are tasty morsels in the wedding cake he is baking for his family and his assistants: the fly, the maggot and the worm . . .

Above ground the tufts of bog-cotton are on every hummock of the marsh. The meadowsweet is a divine pharmacist in every meadow. The fledgling seagulls are fluttering gently in the wrack of the shore. The playful voice of the child in a pen can be heard in the proud growth of the ivy on the house gable, in the boastful branching of the thorn-bushes in the hedgerow and in the protective roof of the trees in the grove. And the milking-woman's lively song at sunset from yonder seashore pasture is the cheerful music of rediscovered happiness in the Land of Gold . . .

But the foam-flakes on the brink of the gushing stream are being dragged into the river's channels and turned into mud. The pale chaff of mountain-grass on the windswept moor is being carried into the hidden gullies at the will of the wind. The humming of the bee on its journey to the hive from the empty honey-store of the foxglove is a grumble of hopelessness. The swallow is preening its feathers on the copestone of the barn, and its song echoes the loneliness of the wind that screams through desolate expanses of desert. The mountain ash is cowering before the withering wind . . .

The feet of the sprinter turn sluggish, the whistling of the cowherd sounds hoarse, and the reaper lays down his sickle in the swathe that is still uncut . . .

The graveyard must have its dues from the living . . .

I am the Trump of the Graveyard. Let my voice be heard! It must be heard . . .

2

—. . . What's this? Another corpse, I declare! My son's wife for sure! 'Twas easily known . . . It's a cheap coffin too. If you really are my son's wife . . .

Bríd Terry! I don't believe it. It's a long time ago you should have been here. You had tremors and phlegm and heart trouble for as long as I can remember . . . You fell into the fire? . . . and you didn't have the strength to get yourself out of it. You've had it bad enough, indeed . . .

Listen here to me! . . . You didn't come here for news, Bríd? Well now, what do you know! . . . Oh! Looking for peace, are you? That's what they all say when they arrive. You heard that the cross is to be put over me soon, Bríd? That it's ordered. But when? Two weeks? A month? . . . You don't know? To tell the truth, Bríd, you seldom knew much about anything . . .

I know. You already told me you fell into the fire . . . They didn't leave anyone at home to mind you? Musha now, they'd have better things to do! An old hag like you. There's no harm done, Bríd. You might as well have it over with . . . But you won't fall here! Or if you do, you won't have far to fall . . .

Listen here to me, Bríd . . . Now, Bríd, have a bit of decorum and don't be making a Seáinín Liam of yourself, who has the graveyard demented since he arrived, about his rotten old heart . . . My son's wife is sickly all the time, you say? . . . She had another little one! Is that true? . . . And it didn't kill her! It's a hell of a great wonder, then. But she'll never survive this pregnancy . . . I'll bet you anything you like, Bríd, she'll be here on her next confinement . . . A girl-child . . . Ababúna, Bríd! . . . They called her Nóra . . . Named her after Nóra Filthy-Feet! She knew well I wasn't alive! . . .

My son's wife and Little Cáit had a scolding match? . . . Pulling each other's hair out, you say! Had-dad,[1] indeed! That's it now, Bríd! Nobody would believe how that slut from Mangy Field treated me, since she was shoved into the house on top of me. The tea she used to give me! And the bedclothes, only for I used to wash them myself! She has to turn her snappishness on someone else, now that she doesn't have me, Bríd. Faith then, Little Cáit is no pushover, I'm telling you . . .

There'll be a court case, you say? Faith then, there'll be contention and conflict and costs over that . . . Little Cáit said that? That Máirín's college clothes were bought from Cheap Jack in Brightcity! My son's wife didn't give her half enough, so! How would Little Cáit know, only that her tongue was too long? And even if they were, what's that to her? Hasn't she little shame, to be passing remarks about the poor girl who's going to college? It would be a long time before anyone belonging to her could become a schoolmistress. The law will settle her, you just wait and see! I hope Pádraig will have the sense to hire Mannion the Counsellor against her. That's the fellow who'll wring the cider out of her . . .

Peace is what you want, you say. Isn't that what we all want? But you've come to the wrong place looking for peace, Bríd . . . That's all the potatoes my Pádraig has sown this year, the Root Field? Why, there aren't two decent patches of soil in the whole lot of it . . . Nell has the two Meadows under potatoes! . . . Well now, Bríd, those two

---

1. A common exclamation of delight in someone else's misfortune.

fields are pretty big, but they're a long way from the seven patches you say there are . . .

What's that last thing you said, Bríd? . . . Never mind your falling in the fire, just wake up and stop slurring your words . . . What are you saying about Nell's son? . . . Right as rain again! Ah! . . . Doing the odd job, is he? Ababúna! I thought, from what Seáinín Liam said, that he'd never do another day's work! . . .

He was cured at St. Ina's Well? Not likely! How well that pussface of a mother of his knew where to bring him for a cure. That pussface can see her own future! But indeed I wouldn't believe it was at St. Ina's Well he was cured. Nor would I believe there's any cure at all in St. Ina's Well. My son's wife wore out her kneecaps on pilgrimages there. Sure, there isn't a well from our own well at home to the Well at the End of the World[2] she didn't visit, for all she has to show for it. Always sickly. Her next child will give her enough to do, I'm telling you.

That's only a bit of Nell's trickery, bringing him to St. Ina's Well and then saying he was cured there. That pussface and the priest are thick as thieves! . . . Arrah, God bless yourself and your St. Ina's Well, Bríd! Not at all. It was your man, the priest. Who else? He gave her son the St. John's Gospel.[3] That's how he was cured, Bríd. How else! The priest. Someone else will have to die in his place now, on account

---

2. The Well at the End of the World is a medieval folktale motif, which suggested to William Morris his fantasy novel, *The Well at the World's End*.

3. *Leabhar Eoin* (John's book) in the original. The opening words of the poetic prologue to St. John's Gospel, written by a priest in Latin on a piece of paper, folded and wrapped in scapular form about the neck or concealed in clothing, came to be used in Christian devotion throughout the Middle Ages as a protective and healing charm. In later Irish tradition, a verse quatrain composed extempore on request by a priest could also function as such a charm text and was known as Leabhar Eoin (John's Book). The incorrect use of the Leabhar Eoin was regarded as involving possible misfortune to the priest who provided it and could even lead to "transferred" death in cases where it was used to save the life of an otherwise mortally stricken individual (as is the case in this text).

of him being cured by the St. John's Gospel. Death will have its due. We've always heard it said . . .

God bless your innocence, Bríd! As if Nell herself would be the one to go! It's no wonder you fell in the fire, Bríd, you're such a simpleton. Devil a bit of danger of Nell going . . . Or Big Brian's daughter either. Or any of her brood. Jack the Scológ is the one they'll shift. You may be sure it was Jack she told the priest to kill in return for curing her son. God help us! Poor Jack has had a hard life with that pussface. That one didn't give him the slightest bit of care. Mark my words, Bríd: the bad luck falls on Jack now, and you'll see him here before long. It doesn't bother Nell or Big Brian's daughter. Won't they get a heap of insurance money on him! . . .

Is that so? The law case is still going on, so . . . They'll be going to Dublin in the autumn? Faith then, going to Dublin is expensive business, Bríd . . . Oh, they say it will go to a retrial even then! It'll leave Nell stony broke in the end, and may it do so! But Bríd, if her son is cured he can't go looking for money . . . Oh, he only works on the sly, is that it? . . . He keeps the crutches by him wherever he's working! . . . He has doctors' certificates that his hip won't get better? He would! Not only that, he brings the crutches with him into the garden and out on the bog! More of Nell's trickery. She was always treacherous.

There's talk now of building a road in as far as her house? So the priest and the Earl will be able to get to it in a motor car. May she not live to enjoy her road, then! . . . Arrah, the devil a road or a bit of a road ever, Bríd! What could shift those big boulders?

You want peace and quiet again, do you! You'll be a laughing-stock here if you keep on talking like that . . . Bid Shorcha is badly crippled, you say? The kidneys still at her! Good enough for her! Apart from Nell and my son's wife, there are very few people I'd rather see coming here than her . . . And Little Cáit's back is bad again? May the devil take her! She's as bad as the rest of them . . . Big Brian is as frisky as a donkey in May, you say. Not wishing to demean him! . . . He's still able to go for the pension? Don't some people have all the luck! He's old enough to be my grandfather — may God forbid, the ugly streak of misery! . . .

Now Bríd, it's many a one as well as you fell into the fire. Your time was up. It's not too serious, seeing you didn't burn the house down as well . . . Two of Pádraig's calves died? . . . Of blackleg![4] Musha, God help us! Isn't it strange that they had to be Pádraig's calves! . . . Nell dosed hers in time. Some spirit is watching over that pussface. I wouldn't mind only that her land was always a nest for blackleg. It's the priest . . .

Pádraig cut hardly any turf this year, you say? How could he cut turf when he has to care for that hob-hatching wife of his? He should smother her under a pot like a cat, if she won't die of her own accord . . . Five of our hens gone in the one day! By Dad, that hurt! . . . And it didn't take as much as one hen from Nell? Weren't the rocky places around her up there always a breeding-ground for foxes! Of course she has Big Brian's daughter in her house, a woman who can keep hens, which is more than can be said for Nóra Sheáinín's daughter from Mangy Field. I believe that even the fox is afraid to touch Nell's hens. It's the priest . . .

Pádraig has no pigs now, is that so? Oh, the pigs went since I went, Bríd. I used to turn out two batches of pigs every year . . . Nell got thirty-five pounds for her own! Ababúna! . . . Yours were better than them, and you only got thirty-two pounds fifteen? Nell would get the highest penny, of course. The priest . . .

No word came from Baba in America recently, you think . . . Not that you've heard of? Big Brian says Nell will get all of Baba's money . . . Is that what he said, Bríd? "Who would Baba give her money to, but her only sister Nell? In any case she can hardly give it to a woman who's thrown into a hole in the ground" . . . Of course, what else would he say, and his own daughter married to Nell's son! . . .

You heard them saying that Tomás Inside is still mad to get married? The useless yoke! He'd be better employed preparing his soul for eternity . . . You think Pádraig doesn't visit him as often as he did when I was alive? I always had to keep on at him to do anything at all for Tomás. That's the sort Pádraig is. He won't keep house with me

---

4. A serious disease of cattle caused by a bacterium.

gone. Nell will play on him . . . You tell me Nell paid a man to cut Tomás Inside's turf for him this year? Ababúna! What's that you said, Bríd? Don't mumble like that, I tell you . . . Tomás Inside said that if he doesn't marry he'll leave his patch of land and the cabin to Nell! "Caitríona wasn't half as good-hearted as Nell," he says. "Faith, then, she wasn't. After my patch of land Caitríona was" . . . Well, the dirty, useless, rattle-brained packman, that same Tomás Inside! . . .

A fine story you have, Bríd Terry! Doesn't the whole of Ireland know that Nell's land lies alongside Tomás Inside's land? . . . The way you're talking, Bríd, you'd think Nell is more entitled to his land than my Pádraig . . . Don't I know as well as you do, Bríd, that Nell's land is all stones and boulders . . . By God, you have a nerve, Bríd, to say a thing like that up to my face. What is it to you who gets Tomás Inside's land? What have you got to lose? . . .

Peace and quiet again! You don't deserve it, you slut . . . What are you saying, Bríd? That I should squeeze down in the grave and make room for you? You'd think, listening to you, that the grave was your own. Do you know that I had my fifteen shillings paid for this grave a year before I died? Wouldn't I have a fine piece of goods stretched alongside me: a scorched woman! . . . What's the world coming to that yourself or any of your breed should be buried up here in the Fifteen-Shilling Plot! But it's easy for you now. There are five of you drawing the dole in your house . . .

You want me to leave you in peace! Have your peace, so! But you're not going to sneak yourself up against my thigh here. I had the best coffin in Tadhg's and three half-barrels of porter, and the priest shook the holy water . . .

Now, you slut, if you push me that far I'll tell you in front of everybody in the graveyard who you are . . . What are you saying? . . . "As rare as a cat with a straddle,[5] one of the Páidín clan buried in the Fifteen-Shilling Plot!" Well now, Bríd, look who's talking: one of the beggar-folk. Wasn't it I reared your father? Coming over to me night

---

5. A wooden saddle for a horse or donkey, from which turf-creels and so on could be suspended on either side.

and day sponging cups of tea, when there was nothing to be had at home but potatoes and salted water? And the stuck-up talk of you now! No doubt about it, the dunghills are coming up in the world these days . . . What's that, you slut? . . . There isn't a cross over me yet as fine as Nóra Sheáinín's? Be off with you, you slut . . .

3

. . . Bríd Terry, the Slut . . . Bid Shorcha, the Sponger . . . Cite of the Ash-Potatoes . . . Little Cáit, the Grinner . . . Tomás Inside, the Good-for-Nothing . . . Big Brian . . .

It's easy for the ugly streak of misery to be boasting, now that his daughter's husband is doing well again. Was that winkle-picker Seáinín Liam telling the truth when he said he'd never do another tap of work as long as he lives? Cured at St. Ina's Well! Cured indeed! Faith, then, if he was cured, it was that pussface of a mother of his got the St. John's Gospel from the priest for him. Poor Jack the Scológ is the one who'll pay the piper. His name will be in the raven's book now, on account of the St. John's Gospel. He'll be here soon. And I'm sure they didn't even warn him. Good Lord, have they no scruples at all?

The priest and Nell and Big Brian's daughter whispering in low voices:

"Faith, then, Father," Nell would say, "if anyone has to go it's old Jack should be sent on his way. He'll be off soon anyway. He's unwell for a long time. But let's not say a word about it. It would worry him. Nobody wants to part with life, God help us . . ."

That's what she'd say, the pussface . . . My son's wife had another baby. It's a wonder it didn't kill her. But that scullion is tough. Tough as the rocks of Mangy Field, that the roadwork bosses were always cursing because no explosive could break them . . . But she'll be here on her next childbirth. I'd bet anything on that . . .

And they called the infant Nóra! What a pity I wasn't there! My son's wife tried the same trick when Máirín was born. I had her in the baby-blanket ready to bring her to the font. Muraed Phroinsiais was there: "What will you call the little bundle, God bless her?" says she.

"Máire," says I. "What else? My mother's name."

"Her mother back there in the bed says to call her Nóra," said Pádraig.

"Nóra Filthy-Feet!" says I. "Naming her after her own mother. What else would she say? Why should we, Pádraig?"

"You have no shortage of names," says Muraed. "Caitríona or Nell or . . ."

"May the pussface smother and drown," says I. "I'd rather give her no name at all than call her Nell. There's no name more suitable for her, Pádraig," says I, "than her grandmother's name: Máire."

"Is the child mine or is it yours?" says Pádraig, flying into a rage. "Nóra is what she'll be called."

"But Pádraig, my dear," says I, "think of the child and the life ahead of her. Didn't you hear what I told you before? Sailors . . ."

"Shut your mouth, or may the devil take my soul . . ."

It was the first cross word I ever heard him say to me, I think. "If that's how it is," says I, "carry on. But it won't be me will bring her to the font. I have some respect for myself, thanks be to God. If you call her Nóra, go ahead. It's enough for me to have one Nóra calling to the house without having another there permanently. If that's the way it's to be, I'll not be staying. I'll take to the roads . . ."

I handed Muraed the infant and I grabbed my shawl off the back door. Pádraig went back into the room to Nóra Sheáinín's daughter. He was back out again in the flick of an eyelid. "Let you call her whatever name ye want to," he says. "Call her 'Hi Diddle Diddle[6] the Cat and the Fiddle' if you want to. But don't be making a show of me any more. The pair of you have me between hammer and anvil every day of my life . . ."

"'Twas your own fault, Pádraig," says I. "If you'd taken my advice and Baba's advice . . ."

He had stormed out of the house. From that day till the day the thumbs were placed on my eyelids there wasn't another word about

---

6. *Amhráinín síodraimín siosúram seó* in the original, a nonsense refrain from a children's song.

calling any of the infants Nóra. But that hussy of a wife of his knows that I'm gone now . . .

The cross is ordered anyhow. Pádraig is a good scout, though he's probably left penniless by that stiff-jointed wife of his who's not able to raise a calf or a pig or go out into a field or on a bog. I know in my heart it's hard for him to attend to everything. When Máirín is a schoolmistress she'll be able to help him out.

Wasn't Bríd Terry[7] ready with her tongue when she said, "There's no cross over you yet as fine as Nóra Sheáinín's." But there will be, you slut. A cross of Island limestone like the one over Peadar the Pub, and railings like Siúán the Shop's, and flowers, and an inscription in Irish . . .

Only for I don't like to, I'd tell Peadar the Pub about the cross. Amn't I more entitled to talk to him—seeing as I'm voting for him— than Muraed or Cite or Dotie. They're the ones with the crosses, of course. I wouldn't mind but for all the attention he paid to Nóra Filthy-Feet! But the porridge is spilt now. Good Lord, they gave each other a right scolding the other day. If Peadar the Pub had heeded me in time I'd tell him who Nóra Filthy-Feet is. But it's not easy to talk to that lot in the Pound Plot. They have far too high an opinion of themselves . . .

I'll leave Peadar the Pub alone for the moment. He's too busy with the Election anyhow. I'll tell Siúán the Shop, and she'll tell the Pound crowd. I'd better say that the cross will be put over me within . . .

—. . . He stabbed me through the edge of my liver. The One-Ear Breed were always a treacherous lot . . .

—. . . Wasn't it stupid of us to let go of the English market, Curraoin? . . .

—. . . "It's the War of the Two Foreigners, Paitseach," says I . . .

—. . . *Honest*, Dotie! Our people had great intellects. Myself, for example . . . My son, who's married at home in Mangy Field, has

---

7. *Bríd Thoirdhealbhaigh* in the original. The name Toirdhealbhach is customarily shortened to Terry in the Gaeltacht.

a young lad who was going to school to the Big Master, and he told me there was no surpassing him. Literature was his pet subject: "He had culture in his bones," he said. "I knew by looking at him." *Honest*, that's what he said, Dotie. You know that daughter of mine who's married to Caitríona Pháidín's son. A young girl of hers has just gone off to be a schoolmistress. 'Twas from my daughter she got the brains. It wasn't from the Loideáin or from the Páidín clan at any rate . . .

—That's a damned lie, you bitch! Drinking secretly in Peadar the Pub's snug! Drinking secretly! Sailors! Sailors! . . . Hey, Muraed! Hey, Muraed! . . . Do you hear that? . . . Do you hear what Nóra Filthy-Feet said! . . . I'll explode! I'll explode! . . .

4

—. . . Would you for the love and mercy of God, Nóra Sheáinín, leave me alone. It's a fine time you pick for novelettes! I must have a conversation with my old neighbour Bríd Terry. I didn't have a chance to talk to her since she came, what with yourself and your culture and your elections! . . .

Are you there, Bríd Terry? . . . Fell into the fire! That was always the first science lesson I taught in school, Bríd, how important it is to keep air away from a fire. Air is what nourishes a fire, Bríd. That should be widely understood . . . Oh, nobody was left at home who could have kept the air off you, Bríd? In a case like that the best thing to do would be . . . I'm afraid science would have no remedy for a case like that, Bríd . . . Oh, looking for peace, are you, Bríd? . . . I'm afraid science has no remedy for a case like that either . . . What's that, Bríd? . . . The whole country was at the wedding, Bríd! . . .

—That's the truth, Master. The whole country was at the wedding. You can be proud of your wife, Master. There was lashings of everything: bread, butter, tea, six kinds of meat, porter, whiskey, and Seán Payne,[8] Master. Seán Payne, Master. When our fellow—Séamas—got fed up drinking whiskey and porter, into the parlour he

---

8. *Seán Péin* in the original; a comic mishearing for champagne.

goes to drink the Seán Payne, Master. Every bit as good as Éamon of the Hill Field's poteen, he said.

Don't worry, Master, it was a lavish wedding—as lavish as if you'd been alive yourself. She's a generous woman, the Schoolmistress, Master. She came up to our place two nights beforehand to invite the whole household down to the wedding. Myself, I wasn't able to stir, Master. By the book, if I were, I'd have been there, not a word of a lie. "Maybe you could spare a can of fresh milk, Bríd," says she. "Indeed I could and two cans, Mistress," says I. "Even if it were much more than that, you'd be welcome to it, and so would your poor husband who's in the graveyard clay—the Big Master—the Lord have mercy on him!" says I.

"I mean to make it a good wedding, Bríd," says she. "Billyboy the Post and myself were talking about it," says she: "'A good wedding,' says Billyboy the Post," says she. "'That's the way he'd prefer it himself, the Lord have mercy on him!'"

"'I'm sure if the Big Master knew that I'm getting married again, Billyboy,' says I, Bríd," says she, "'that's what he'd tell me, to make it a good wedding. He wouldn't begrudge it to the neighbours. And of course he wouldn't begrudge it to myself.' And he wouldn't, either, Bríd . . ."

"Bedad then, Mistress," says I to her—I don't know if I should have said it at all, Master, only for my tongue being too loose—"Bedad then, Mistress," says I, "I thought you wouldn't marry again."

"Well indeed, Bríd my dear," says she, "I wouldn't either—no fear of me—only for what the Big Master said to me a few days before he died. I was sitting on the edge of his bed, Bríd. I took his hand. 'What will I do,' says I, 'if anything happens to you?' He burst out laughing, Bríd. 'What will you do?' says he. 'What would you do—a fine active young woman like you—but marry again?' I began to whimper, Bríd. 'You shouldn't say a thing like that,' says I to him. 'A thing like that?' says he, and he was deadly serious this time, Bríd. 'A thing like that!' says he. 'It's exactly the right thing. I won't rest easy in the graveyard clay,' says he, 'if you don't promise me that you'll marry again.' Faith then, that's what he said, Bríd," says she.

—The harlot! . . .

—May God forbid that I'd tell a lie about her, Master. That's what she said. "You're going to great expense, Mistress," says I. "You're in the way of money, and of course the postboy isn't badly paid, may God spare you both to earn it," says I, "but faith a wedding's an expensive undertaking nowadays, Mistress."

"Only for what he had put aside himself before he died, and the insurance I got on him, I wouldn't have a hope of doing it," says she. "The Big Master was a thrifty man, may God be good to him," says she. "He wasn't given to drink or debauchery. There was a pretty penny in his purse, Bríd . . ."

—The harlot! The harlot! She wouldn't spend half as much on putting a cross over me . . .

—Isn't that what I told her, Master: "But you shouldn't do anything till you've put a cross over the Big Master first."

"It's a better place the Big Master is in, the poor man," says she. "The Big Master is on the path of truth, and seeing that he is, it's not crosses he'll be worrying about. But I'm sure, Bríd, if he knew about myself and Billyboy the Post, who are still on the path of untruth, he'd tell us not to bother with a cross, but to give ourselves every comfort we can. It was no lie to call him the Big Master, Bríd," says she. "He was big in his heart and in everything." Upon my soul that's exactly what she had to say, Master . . .

—The harlot! The thieving harlot! . . .

—. . . I fell off a stack of oats . . .

—. . . The heart! The heart, God help us! . . .

—. . . I'm absolutely certain it was Galway won the All-Ireland football final . . .

—In 1941, is it? If you mean 1941, they didn't . . .

—In 1941 is what I'm saying. But they can thank Concannon. The devil his like of a footballer was ever seen. He smashed and he thrashed and he bashed and he gashed the Cavan players one after another. He was a powerful footballer and a stylish one! I was watching him that day in Croke Park in the semi-final . . .

—They won the semi-final against Cavan, but they didn't win the final . . .

—Oh indeed they did! Concannon won it on his own . . .

—Do you mean in 1941? Because if you do, Galway didn't win the All-Ireland final. They beat Cavan by eight points, but Kerry beat them by a goal and a point in the final.

—Oh, for the love of God, how could they? Wasn't I in Dublin watching the semi-final against Cavan! Three of us went up on the bicycles. I'm not telling you a word of a lie: on the bicycles every bit of the way. It was midnight when we got there. We slept in the open that night. We didn't even get a drink. You could have wrung the sweat out of our clothes. After the match we nipped in to the footballers. I shook hands with Concannon myself. "My life on you," says I. "You're the greatest footballer I've ever seen. Wait till the final a month from today. I'll be here again, with the help of God, watching you beat Kerry," . . . and of course they did . . .

—1941, is it? If it is, Galway didn't beat Kerry but Kerry beat Galway . . .

—For the love of God! Tell that to a supporter. "Kerry beat Galway." What sort of an eejit do you take me for? . . .

—In 1941, was it? Were you watching the final?

—I wasn't, so I wasn't. But I was watching the semi-final against Cavan, I tell you. What sort of an eejit are that you don't understand me? We came home again that Sunday evening on the bicycles. We were hungry and thirsty. There was never such hunger! Devil a town we passed through that we didn't shout "Up Galway!" It was broad daylight on Monday morning when we got home. I came down off the bike at the head of the boreen. "If it turns out," says I to the other two, "that we've recovered from our hunger and thirst in a month's time, by God we'll go up again. I'd love to be watching Concannon beat Kerry." And of course he did. It was no bother to him . . .

—1941, was it? I tell you Kerry won. Surely you were at the final? . . .

—I wasn't. I was not. How could I be? Don't you think I would if I could? What sort of an eejit are you? That day after coming home from the semi-final wasn't I taken ill! I got a cold from the sweat and sleeping in the open. It turned chronic straight away. Five days from that day I was here in the graveyard clay. How could I have been at the final? You're an awful eejit . . .

—And what are you blathering about so, that they beat Kerry?

—It was no bother to them, of course . . .

—1941, was it? Maybe you're thinking of some other year.

—1941. What else? They beat Kerry in the final . . .

—But I tell you they didn't. Kerry beat them by a goal and a point. A goal and eight points for Kerry and seven points for Galway. The referee was unfair to the Galway men. And if he was, it wasn't for the first time, either. But Kerry won the match . . .

—May God grant you an ounce of sense! How could Kerry win the match when Galway won it? . . .

—But you were dead. And I was watching the match. I lived for nine months after that. The match was no help at all to me. There wasn't a day from that day on that I wasn't ailing. Only for I was watching them getting beaten . . .

—For the love of God! You're the greatest eejit I ever saw! If you'd watched them a hundred times Kerry didn't beat Galway. Wasn't I at the semi-final in Croke Park! If you'd seen them that day beating Cavan! Concannon! Oh, he was a powerful footballer! The only lease of life I wanted was to watch him beating Kerry a month from that day . . . Beating them was no bother to him, of course . . .

—The 1941 final, is it?

—Yes. What else? What sort of an eejit are you?

—But they didn't beat them . . .

—They did so. They did so. Concannon would have beaten them on his own . . .

5

—. . . Hey, Muraed . . . Do you hear me? . . . Why aren't you talking? Or what has come over you all recently? There's not a squeak or a squawk out of any of you since the election. Bríd Terry will have peace now. May she not enjoy it, then! The little hag! Strife is better than solitude, after all . . .

Surely you're not disappointed that Nóra Filthy-Feet was defeated in the election, Muraed. It'll teach her not to be so full of herself in future. She'd lose the run of herself entirely if she'd got in . . .

I voted for Peadar the Pub, Muraed. Who else? Of course, you wouldn't expect me to vote for Nóirín of the Sailors, the secret drinker. I have more respect for myself than that, Muraed. To vote for a woman who used to drink in secret, is it?

And the Master is very prickly with her these days, Muraed. It's the devil of a job to keep him underground at all since Bríd Terry told him about his wife's marriage. Do you know, Muraed, what he said to Mangy Nóirín the other day when she was all grumpy because he wouldn't read a bit of a novelette to her? "Leave me alone, you bitch," says he. "Leave me alone! You're not fit company for man, beast or corpse . . ."

On my solemn oath he did, Muraed . . . What's the use in arguing, Muraed? Didn't I hear him?

But Muraed, you're all very gloomy in this part of the graveyard, and you're not talking like you used to be . . . Turning to clay, is it? . . . The writer's tongue is decaying, is it? Cóilí won't complain about that, I'd say. He had him demented . . . Oh, Cóilí himself is turning to clay, is he? Do you know what, Muraed, I'm sorry to hear it. That story he had about the hens was nice and homely. I used to make money on hens, not like the hussy I left behind me, my son's wife . . . 'Tis God's justice, Muraed, for him to have a worm in his throat, a man who drank two score and two pints . . .

Oh, so that fellow is totally decomposed, Muraed . . . The Half-Guinea crowd told you he was decomposed? I thought, Muraed, you didn't speak to the Half-Guinea crowd? Arrah, how else could he be but decomposed? A corpse couldn't be any other way down there: a Half-Guinea grave. Is it any wonder! It seems to me, Muraed, there's a peculiar smell coming up from the Half-Guinea Plot now and again. If I were you, Muraed, I'd leave them well alone . . .

What's that shouting, Muraed? . . . The Half-Guinea crowd . . . Celebrating the election of their candidate. They'll deafen the grave-yard. The beggars! Thieving ill-mannered rabble! Oh, do you hear the goings-on of them! God bless us and save us! It's a poor plight to be in the same cemetery with them at all. But, by God, I'm better pleased to see the Half-Guinea man elected than Nóra Filthy-Feet. If there was no alternative I'd have voted for him myself, to spite her . . .

—. . . There was such a day, Peadar the Pub. Don't deny it . . .

—. . . That awful murderer who gave me a bad bottle . . .

—. . . A white-faced mare. At the Fair of St. Bartholomew I bought her . . .

—I remember it well. I twisted my ankle . . .

—. . . Hitler! Hitler! Hitler! Hitler! Hitler! Hitler!

—. . . A pity they wouldn't bring my earthly remains . . .

—. . . It's true for you. She's the most cheerful woman in the graveyard till that silliness takes over . . .

—She had always intended to go back to the Plains of East Gal-way . . .

—She knew the cat-o'-nine-tails[9] was waiting for her. Having put a gash in a poor old man's head with the fire-crane . . .

—Maybe he deserved it. She says herself that he didn't give her a moment's peace since the day she married his son . . .

—. . . Permission to speak! . . .

—. . . But the funniest of all was to see them thatching the house for him.

—. . . That bright smile was on her face . . .

—May the devil pierce yourself and herself! On the devil's hoof-prints to hell with her! What use is her bright smile to me? You're every bit as boring as this cheeky poet here. Bright smile! Doesn't Road-End's daughter have the same bright smile? May the devil pierce her, hasn't she led my eldest son into temptation? She has his eyes bewildered or some damned thing. Totally bewildered! She's in

---

9. The rope whip with nine knotted lashes that would figuratively await her; i.e., she would be most unwelcome.

the Freemasons or some cursed thing. Trying to get a foot in on my big holding . . .

—. . . Wait till I tell you how I sold the Big Master the books . . . I went into Peadar the Pub's. The Big Master wasn't long in the place at the time. I made discreet inquiries about him. They weren't particularly fond of him in Peadar's. He only went in there once in a blue moon. He was a stingy fellow. But he was crazy about the Schoolmistress.

"I have it," said I, "I have the bait to hook you, my boyo."

"The World's Finest Love-Stories," says I to him. He went at them as greedily as a hungry suckler at the teat. "Five guineas for the set," says I. "They're very expensive," says he. "What do you mean, expensive?" says I. "A half-guinea on the nail, and instalments to suit yourself. It's a substantial set. You'll never be ashamed to have them in your personal bookcase. Look at the paper! And they're the top class of love-story. Have a look here at the contents: *Helen and the Trojan War; Tristan and Isolde; The Fate of the Sons of Uisneach; Dante and Beatrice* . . . You're not married? . . . You're not! . . . You've reached the age you are and never read these love-stories: about Helen, *'the face that launched a thousand ships and burnt the topless towers of Ilium,'* and *The Only Jealousy of Deirdre*:[10]

> 'As Scotland's nobles drank one day
> With the Sons of Uisneach in friendly bliss,
> From the daughter of Lord Bravesfort
> Naoise stole a secret kiss . . .'

"Picture yourself, man . . . Down there in a creek by Galway Bay, a golden beauty in your arms and you not able to tell her one of the world's finest love-stories . . ."

He began to waver. I tightened my grip. But the devil a bit of good that did. "They're too dear for the likes of me," says he. "Don't you have any second-hand books?"

"We are a reputable company," says I. "We wouldn't put the

---

10. Fictional woman of great beauty in one of the great Celtic romantic legends.

health of our travellers or our clients at risk. Who knows but they might infect yourself or your wife? . . . I see. You're not married. But you will be, please God, and that's when you'll realise what a set like this is worth. Sitting up late, the wind howling outside, yourself and the wife cosy by the fireside . . ."

Wasting my words I was . . .

I called in at the barracks. No one there but the Red-haired Police-man. "Books!" says he. "I've a roomful of them up there. I'll have to burn them soon if someone doesn't come looking for scrap paper."

"What sort are they?" says I.

"Novels," says he. "Rubbish . . . The dregs . . . But they kill the time for me all the same, in this flea-bitten place . . ."

We went upstairs. There was the world of books there. The dregs, as he said. The sort of trashy romances silly young girls devour. To tell the truth, most of them bore the name and surname of a nurse of my acquaintance in Brightcity. I took the best of them—the cleanest-looking ones—and I cut the front page out of each one of them. I did a tour of the other schools in the area and in a few days' time I came back to the Big Master. I was sorry by now that I'd been so disparaging about second-hand books.

"I'm travelling away back west today, Master," says I, "and I thought I might as well call on you again. I've a collection of roman-tic novels here. Second-hand. I bought them specially from a friend of mine in Brightcity who was selling his library, in the hope that they might suit you. They've been disinfected."

The gaudy covers appealed to him, and the romantic titles: *The Red-Hot Kiss, Two Men and a Powder-puff, Sunset Tresses* . . .

"Two pounds, ten shillings to you, Master," says I. "That's exactly what I paid for them myself. There's no profit for me in it, as they're not company books. If you turn them down I'll be out of pocket . . ."

The haggling began. He wanted to push me to the very limit. Eventually I told him to take it or leave it but that I wouldn't part with them for less than two pounds. I got that much out of him, if only just. Of course they weren't worth a damn . . .

—You knew the tricks of the trade, you boy you. But I knew them too. I never told you about this *coup:*

There were two sisters living near me. One of them was called Nell Pháidín. The other was called Caitríona. She's here now. The two of them hated each other . . . Oh, you heard the story before? The devil a bit of me but headed off up to Nell's one day. Her son's wife was there too. I lectured them on insurance for children: that they would get so much money when they'd be of such an age, and so on. You know the tricks. The two of them were very suspicious. I showed them forms some of the neighbours had filled in. It was no good. "There's no sharp practice in this," said I, "but there's a lot to be gained by it. Ask the priest . . ."

And so they did. Within two weeks I got the insurance on two children out of them. Then I held forth on insurance for the elderly: cost of funerals and so on. The old woman was willing to pay for her husband, Jack the Scológ . . . I came down to the other sister, Caitríona. She was on her own in the house.

"Look," says I, "these forms were filled in by the woman up there, for her two children and the old man. I told her I was coming in here on my way down, but she made me promise not to . . ."

"What did she say? What did she say?" says Caitríona.

"Ah, I wouldn't like to be talking about it," says I. "You're neighbours . . ."

"Neighbours! We're sisters," she says. "Didn't you know that? . . . You're a stranger. Yes indeed, sisters. But even if we are, may no corpse go to the graveyard ahead of her! What did she say?"

"Ah, it's difficult to talk about," says I. "Only for my tongue was too long I wouldn't have mentioned it at all."

"What did she say?" says she. "Out of this house you will not go till you tell me."

"Have it your way," says I. "She said I'd only be wasting my time coming in here; that you couldn't afford to pay insurance in this house . . ."

"The pussface! The bitch! . . ." says she. "It would be a sorry day indeed that we wouldn't be able to pay it as well as Nell. And we will pay it. You'll see that we'll pay it . . ."

Her son and his wife came in. The arguing began. Herself trying to take out insurance on two of the children; the married couple bitterly opposing her. "I'm in a hurry," I said. "I'll leave you to it. Maybe you'll have a definite word for me the day after tomorrow: I'll be going back up to Nell's again. She told me to come back and that she'll take out insurance on the old man who's living on his own up there . . ."

"Tomás Inside!" says she. "Ababúna! Tomás Inside. Another of her schemes to get his land away from us. Could we take out insurance on him? . . . I'll pay for it myself out of my half-guinea of a pension . . ."

It was truly the Battle of the Sheaves[11] now. They began to spin around each other all over the house as if they were dancing a three-hand reel. The son and his wife would have liked to break my neck outside on the street. But Caitríona protected me and kept me inside till the papers were filled out . . . And filled out they were. She had to have her way in the end. It was the greatest danger I was ever in during all my time in insurance.

That's how I fooled Caitríona. I couldn't help it. Tricks of the trade . . .

—That's a damned lie! That's a damned lie! You didn't fool me! If you did, you fooled Nell too . . .

—Nell never mentioned yourself or Tomás Inside. The tricks of the trade, Caitríona dear . . .

—Hey, Muraed . . . Do you hear me? . . . I'll explode! . . .

---

11. The "battle" in which nearly all of the Fianna were killed by the sheaves of corn they were busily binding and throwing back over their heads, inadvertently killing one another in the process. A little fellow of the underworld called Tufty Mouth (Cab an Dosáin) was the sole reaper!

. . . That same Peadar the Pub is a stiff-lipped fellow too. Even though I went against the current in voting for him, he never thanked me for it or anything. If he was any way civil he could have easily spoken to me and said: "Caitríona Pháidín, I'm grateful to you for giving me your vote. You were a woman of courage, to defy all the Fifteen-Shilling crowd. We did well against Nóra Filthy-Feet . . ." But he didn't. He should have ignored the fact—especially during an election—that I'm still without a cross.

I should have told Siúán the Shop a long time ago that I'm going to get the cross. Why should I be concerned about her? It's ages since I was at the mercy of her credit. I might as well tell her, now that the excitement of the Election is over . . .

Hi, Siúán. Siúán the Shop . . . Are you there? . . . Siúán, are you there? . . . Do you hear me, you Pound crowd? . . . You can't all be asleep? . . . I'm looking for Siúán the Shop . . . It's me, Caitriona Pháidín, Seán Thomáis Uí Loideáin's wife. Siúán, I'm getting a cross of Island limestone put up over me in a . . . in a very short time. A cross like the one on Peadar the Pub, and railings round my grave like there are on yours, Siúán . . .

Don't be annoying you—is that what you said, Siúán? I thought you'd be pleased to hear about it, Siúán . . . You don't want to have anything to do with the Fifteen-Shilling people from now on? I voted for Peadar the Pub, Siúán. I drew the wrath of all the Fifteen-Shilling crowd down on me by doing so . . . You'd prefer to do without my vote? Ababúna! You'd prefer to do without my vote! . . . Propriety forbids the people in the Pound Plot to talk to Fifteen-Shilling people! Now, what do you know? . . . I can wear my tongue out talking, you say, but you won't pay any heed to me . . . You're not willing to talk to a chatterbox like me any more? . . . A chatterbox, Siúán! You're not willing to talk to a chatterbox like me any more! . . .

Have it your way so, you wretch. You'll speak to me a long time before I'll say a word to you again. You've no cause to be stuck-up, if you only knew it! . . . Just because you had a little shop above ground, and were destroying the country with your clogs . . . I know well what's irritating you, you wretch! I voted for Peadar the Pub in the election. I wish I hadn't! Yourself and himself begrudge me a cross and railings as fine as the ones on yourselves. I'll be as good as you then . . .

That wretch Siúán. By Dad, how the world has changed . . .

—. . . "Tomás Inside was there with his britches to-orn
        But aid was fo-orth-coming on either si-ide . . ."

—. . . Nóra! Nóra Sheáinín! . . .

—Hoy! *How are tricks?* Are you over election exhaustion yet? I feel a bit worn-out myself.

—You'll forgive me, Nóra . . .

—Arrah, Peadar dear, why wouldn't I? A word to the wise is sufficient. There was a rumpus—a *stink*, as people of culture would say—between us, but that doesn't matter. "For the small-minded, to forgive a wrong is a heroic deed. For the noble-minded it is only a passing need," as Jinks said in *Sunset Tresses. Honest* . . .

—Ababúna! Peadar the Pub is talking to Nóra Sheáinín again, even though he vowed and he swore during the Election that he'd never speak another word to her. Oh, what's the use in talking! . . .

What was it he called her? . . . Bitch and harlot and hussy! Nóirín Filthy-Feet. Nóirín of the Sailors. The Drunkard from Mangy Field of the Puddles and Ducks. He said she was drinking secretly in his snug; that she often had to be carried home; that she began to sing at the top of her voice when Tiúnaí Mhicil Tiúnaí's funeral was passing his door; that she robbed a cattle-jobber[12] from down the country inside in his parlour; that she drank porter from the black butler the Earl used to keep; that she began to throw bottles when she was drunk; that she brought Seán Choilm's big puck goat into the shop in a drunken bout, got it in behind the counter, perched it up on top of

---

12. One who goes from fair to fair and from farm to farm buying up cattle in small lots, to sell to bigger dealers.

a tapped half-barrel and started combing its beard and plying it with porter; that she used to be hugging Tomás Inside . . .

But what's this he used to call her? . . . Isn't it awful I can't remember? . . . That's it, upon my soul! A *So-an'-so.* I must ask the Master, if he ever gets back to being his old self again, what a *So-an'-so* is.

He called her a *So-an'-so,* then, and he'd call her worse if he could think of it. After all that, he's talking to her as friendly as if there'd never been a cross word between them. And he wouldn't even thank me for voting for him . . .

Just because I don't have a cross over me . . . If that's the reason. Or maybe it's because Nóra used to leave a lot of drink-money with him above ground. Neither Peadar the Pub nor any other Peadar would have much of a pub if they depended on my custom. He knows very well he'd have neither cross nor credit here only for Nóra of the Pints and her likes . . . I was never a drunkard . . . And all the same, it's many a time I was tempted by his window.

—. . . Indeed, Peadar. The cultural people all voted for me, and the Fifteen-Shilling people too, apart from Caitriona Pháidín, and God help us, that jade has neither culture nor upbringing. I'd rather do without Caitríona's vote, although it still would have been mine, were it not for one reason. Caitríona voted for you, Peadar, because she was worried about the goods she left unpaid for in your shop. *Honest!*

—That's a damned lie, you *So-an'-so!* I died not leaving a penny of debt any more than the bird in the sky, thanks be to the Eternal Father. You bitch. "The goods she left unpaid for . . ."!

Hello, Muraed! Hello, Muraed! . . . Did you hear what porter-swigging Nóirín said? I'll explode! I'll explode! . . .

Interlude Five

THE BONE-FERTILISING OF THE CLAY

1

I am the Trump of the Graveyard! Let my voice be heard! It must be heard . . .

Here in the graveyard the shuttle is in perpetual motion: weaving blackness over whiteness, ugliness over beauty, weft of green scum, mildew, mould, slime and mist-coloured lichen over the entwined golden plaits of silken tresses. The coarse veil of indifference and negligence is being woven from the golden threads of sunlight, from the silver tissue of moonlight, from the jewel-studded mantle of fame, and from the soft down of irretentive memory. For this weaver's material is the smooth, ductile clay. His loom is the withered rubbish out of which arose the dreams of the one who hitched his chariot to the brightest star in the zenith, or who plucked a cluster of the most forbidden fruit from the deepest darkness. Anxiety of dream, sheer radiance of unattainable beauty, longing of tormented desire, these are the usual fulling-waters of this ancient weaver.

Above ground everything is dressed in the cloak of everlasting youth. Every shower miraculously creates a multitude of mushrooms in the grass. Opium poppies cover meadow and field like a dream of the goddess of growth. The mouth of the corn is smudged with gold from constant kissing of the sun. The waterfall's voice is drowsy as it pours its cascade into the salmon's parched beak. The parent wren hops happily under the dock leaves, watching over the fluttering leaps of its fledgling. The forager puts to sea with a song on his lips that is full of the vigour of tide, wind and sun. The young maid, skimming the dew by the first ray of sunlight, searches for the elf with the inexhaustible purse, that she might dress herself in the bright clothes and the jewels and precious stones her heart yearns for.

But some sorcerer has scorched the green apparel of the trees with his wicked wand. The golden crest of the rainbow has been clipped by the shears of the east wind. The rosy flush of consumption has appeared in the sunset sky. The milk is thickening in the cow's teat as she seeks shelter in a nook of the stone wall. The dumbness of inexpressible grief is in the voices of the young men weaning lambs up yonder on the moor. The stack-builder descends from his well-thatched cornstack and slaps his hands under his armpits, because black boils of bad matter are heaping up in the northern sky and caravans of noisy greylag geese head hurriedly southwards . . .

For the graveyard exacts its tithe from the living . . .

I am the Trump of the Graveyard. Let my voice be heard! It must be heard . . .

2

. . . Who are you? . . . What sort of old carcass are they shoving down on top of me now? . . . My son's wife for sure. But no. You're a man. You're not a Loideáin anyhow. You're fair-haired. None of the Loideáin were fair. Dark-haired they were. As black as the berry. Nor my own people either, except for Nell, that pussface . . .

You're one of Pádraig Labhráis's. I should recognize you so. Are you Pádraig Labhráis's second lad or the third? . . . The third lad . . . You're only nineteen . . . a bit young indeed to be starting this caper, son . . . Nine months you were ailing . . . Consumption. That's the killer! This cemetery is fat with it.

You were to go to England only for you were struck down . . . You were all set to go, you say . . . The young men and women of Donagh's Village left last week . . . And of Mangy Field! . . . May they not return, then! . . . True for you, my son. I believe there's great money to be made there . . .

You tell me you heard nothing about a cross to go over me.

There's no talk of it now . . . Not even a word, you say . . . He brought it up when he was in to see you. What did he say? Don't be embarrassed to tell me, my son. Indeed, you should know yourself I have no love or liking for Big Brian . . . The Sive's Rocks people have all gone to England! Indeed, son, weren't that same crowd wandering labourers and hired hands every day of their lives . . . Only for you were struck down you'd have gone too . . . to earn money. It's a bit late for you now to be talking of earning money . . . But what did Big Brian say? Why don't you spit it out? . . . "That dolt of a woman doesn't deserve a cross," he said. "Her breed aren't accustomed to crosses. Pádraig Chaitríona—a man who can't afford to give his children a bite to eat—talking about putting up a cross of Island limestone!" He said that? He still bears a grudge against me . . .

You tell me Big Brian was in Dublin. In Dublin! . . . That ugly streak of misery, up in Dublin! . . . He saw the man stuck on top of the pillar of stone![1] A pity the man and the pillar of stone didn't fall down on the ugly streak's stupid grin! . . . Great porter there, he said? May the devil take it past his ugly stopped-up nose! . . . Fine women in Dublin! It's an awful pity he didn't go there long ago when I had to refuse him twice. The Dublin women would be very impressed by his flat feet and his slouched shoulders . . . He saw the wild animals! There was no wilder or uglier animal there than himself, not wishing to demean him! . . . And the judge praised him to the skies? A witless judge he was, then! . . . "You're a wonderful old man voluntarily to travel such a distance at your age, in order to help the court," says he. A witless judge he was, if it wasn't obvious to him that he was helping his daughter and her husband, the ugly streak of misery! . . .

You'd think a young man like you wouldn't be so silly, and yet you'll make a Seáinín Liam and a Bríd Terry of yourself if you keep going. I was hoping you'd tell me about the court case, and you told me about the Glen of the Pasture crowd going to England. Let them go to England! Good riddance to the Glen of the Pasture crowd! The beggars wouldn't come to my funeral . . .

---

1. Nelson's Pillar, blown up by an Irish republican faction in 1966.

Ababúna! So Nell's son got eight hundred pounds . . . in spite of being on the wrong side of the road. Are you sure? Maybe pussface Nell added five or six hundred to it . . . Oh, it was in the paper! You read it yourself in the paper. Six weeks ago . . . in *The Galwayman.* Arrah, nobody should heed that paper . . . it was in *The Reporter* and *The Irishman* as well! . . . And there's nothing wrong with him, you say . . . He has thrown away the crutches altogether now . . . He's doing all sorts of work again . . . And three doctors swore for him that he was in bad health. Good God! Oh, a witless judge he was. Was he told that he was on the wrong side of the road? 'Twas the priest fixed it. Who else! . . .

She gave the priest fifty pounds for Masses? So well she might, the pussface. Her son is in good health and she has a fistful of money . . . She also gave him ten pounds to say Masses for my soul! . . . She handed it to the priest in Pádraig's presence, you say . . . Oh, that pussface's Mass money wouldn't do me any good, son . . .

The Wood of the Lake crowd went to England five weeks ago. Well now! It must be a great asset to England to have the Wood of the Lake hooligans over there . . . they wouldn't come to a person's funeral half as fast . . . Hold on! Don't go till you tell me more! . . . Jack the Scológ isn't well? Easily known. The St. John's Gospel. He'll be here any day now. Nell and Big Brian's daughter prepared that potion for him. They'll collect insurance money on him . . .

There's a road being built up to Nell's house! Ababúna! I thought devil a road would ever be built up into that rugged wilderness . . . This new crowd she voted for got it for her, you say. How well the pussface knew who to vote for! A corner of a field of ours is to be given over for the road? Ababúna! That's the field—Flagstone Height. There's no other field of ours by the path up to Nell's . . . My Pádraig has given away a corner of Flagstone Height! What! I knew since I departed that Pádraig was too easy-going for that pussface . . . The priest visited the spot. One of Nell's little tricks . . . So the priest laid out the boundary . . . That's the day Nell gave him the money for the Masses for me. God above, there are no flies on that one! It was a trick to get room for the road. There was no room for a road without going into our Flagstone Height. You think Pádraig got paid for the field? No matter. He shouldn't have let her have it. How I wish I'd lived a few more years even!... So that's what Big Brian said: "Oh musha musha, Nell paying out money for a bald tail-end of a shitty old flagstone field, where there's nothing but stones breeding more stones!... If Pádraig Chaitríona had the slightest spark of common sense he'd dig some sort of hole for that one's prickly old bones... up on Flagstone Height... and he'd have plenty of tombstones there without the Island limestone... to keep Seáinín Liam and Bríd Terry... away from the hedgehog..." Oh, the ugly streak! The ugly streak of misery!...

Here we go again: "If only I were in England! If only I were in England!" Did I stop you going?.... "All the West Headland crowd went over there six weeks ago." I don't give a tinker's curse where the sun may set on the West Headland crowd. There are a couple of those loudmouths here in the cemetery and they're no great credit to the place...

You tell me you didn't hear anything about my sister Baba's will ... Nothing at all... How would you, and you so mad keen on going to England?... that's all you heard about Tomás Inside, that he's still in his shack... He comes into our house now every time he goes for the pension. Good man! That's good news... He sometimes gives the pension book to my son's wife, to collect it for him? Good man! He's not as limber as he used to be... Oh, he gives the book to Nell and Big Brian's Mag too! Huh!...

Little Cáit has a bad back, you tell me. May the woman to stretch her be no nearer than the graveyard clay!... Bid Shorcha is very crippled? She's another one of them! She wouldn't come to keen me, the sponger!...

You weren't interested in anything else but going to England ... You'd have gone to England two months ago, seeing that the scroungers from Woody Hillside were going! Nobody who ever followed the example of the Woody Hillside scroungers was the better for it. My son's wife is still sickly, of course...

God save us!... She was fighting with Big Brian's daughter...

with Big Brian's Mag! . . . fighting with her! . . . She went up to Nell's, and into her house, and caught Big Brian's daughter by the hair of the head? You're not serious! . . . Oh, it wasn't Little Cáit at all who said that Máirín's college clothes were bought from Cheap Jack! What was Bríd Terry on about so, the slut? . . . Oh, it was Big Brian's daughter who first said it to Little Cáit! It's in her nature to talk out of turn, the daughter of that streak of misery. And my son's wife pulled her hair, in her own house . . . She knocked her to the floor! I thought she didn't have the spunk, Nóirín Filthy-Feet's daughter! . . .

She threw Nell in the fire? She threw Nell in the fire! Good for her! My life on her! Good man! Good man! You're sure now she threw Nell in the fire? . . . Nell went to save Big Brian's daughter, and my son's wife threw her in the fire! May God spare her health, then! Good man! Good on you, my son. That's the first news to lift my heart out of this cold lump of clay.

They were at one another's throat till Pádraig went up in the evening and brought his wife down home! May God forgive him for not leaving them at it! . . .

Arrah, we're better off rid of the Middle Mountain crowd. A pack of hungry savages! They won't leave a bite uneaten in England. But my son's wife and Big Brian's Mag will be going to law now . . .

They won't? Why not? Faith then, if she'd gone to Brightcity and engaged Mannion the Counsellor to sue for libel she'd put a good hole in Nell's money. She might take five or six hundred pounds off her . . . Nell brought the priest in to make the peace! She would . . . So that's what Pádraig said about them: "Let nobody heed the scolding of women." It was Nell put him up to saying that. She knows I'm gone, the toothless bitch! . . .

What's that you said? That my son's wife is very industrious now . . . She's a hard worker since the fight . . . She has no disease or distress now! That's a hell of a wonder, then! And I was sure she'd be here any minute . . . She's up with the lark, you say . . . In the field and on the bog . . . She's raising piglets again! Good man! They had three or four calves at the last fair! Good man! It's a joy to listen to you, son!

. . . And you heard your mother say she saw their yard littered with chickens! I wonder how many clutches they hatched this year? . . . Of course you're not to blame for not knowing that, son . . .

You tell me Pádraig's doing well too. It'll be a long time before he beats Nell and her eight hundred pounds all the same. The judge they had was a witless judge. But if my son's wife keeps on at the present rate, and when Máirín becomes a schoolmistress . . .

That's right, my son! Pádraig was penniless . . . What did he say? What did Big Brian say? . . . That since Pádraig couldn't pay his rent he should give someone a mortgage on his fistful of clay and his fistful of a wife, and go over to England to earn some money . . . A fistful of clay, is that what the streak of misery called the big holding? "But it's a good job that dolt of a mother of his isn't alive to give him bad advice," he says. The streak of misery! The streak of misery! The streak . . .

Where have you gone, young man? Where are you? . . . They've carried you off from me . . .

3

—. . . You don't know, my good man, why the Conamara region is as rugged and bare and shallow-soiled as it is . . .

—Patience, Cóilí. Patience. The Ice Age . . .

—Oh, stop it! The Ice Age my foot! Not at all, but the Curse of Cromwell.[2] The time God sent the Devil to Hell it very nearly failed Him. This is where he fell down out of Heaven. Michael the Archangel and himself spent a whole summer wrestling with one another. They ripped up the countryside from deep down in the ground . . .

—That's right, Cóilí. Caitríona showed me the print of his hoof up there on Nell's land . . .

—Shut your mouth, you little brat . . .

—You're insulting the faith. You're a heretic . . .

—I don't know how the brawl would have ended if the Devil's

---

2. A garbled and parodic version of widely known folklore about Oliver Cromwell.

shoes hadn't begun to fall apart. It was Cromwell made them for him. Cromwell was a cobbler beyond in London, England. The shoes fell off him completely out in Galway Bay. One of them broke in two halves. Those are the three Aran Islands ever since. But even though the Angel of Pride was in a predicament for want of his shoes I swear to the devil he pushed Michael back again as far as Shellig[3] Michael. That's an island to the west, off Carna. Then he let an almighty roar out of him for Cromwell to come over and mend the shoes for him. I don't know how the brawl would have ended if the shoes had been mended . . .

Over comes Cromwell to Connacht. Over come the Irishmen following him, and no wonder, because they were always and ever against the Devil. Five miles south of Oughterard, in a place they call the Holes of Laban's House,[4] is where Michael met them, and him still fleeing from the Devil . . . "Stand your ground, you rascal," they said, "and we'll give the Devil a good kicking in the old pants." That's where he was sent to Hell, in Sulphur Lake. That's where Sulphur River[5] rises, that flows eastwards through Oughterard. Sulphur is the proper name of the Devil in Old Irish, and Sulphuric is his wife's name . . .

Between the jigs and the reels, what do you think but Cromwell got clear away from them to Aran, and he has stayed there ever since. Aran was holy till then . . .

—But Cóilí, Cóilí, allow me to speak. I am a writer . . .

—. . . The devil pierce yourself and the *Golden Stars!* . . .

—. . . Faith then, as you say, all the good turf sods were stolen from us . . .

---

3. What looks like a typing error is in fact a play on words. *Seilg* (Shellig) means "pursuit," and Seilg Mhichíl (Shellig Michael) means Pursuit of Michael. As St. Michael is being pursued by the Devil between Conamara and the Aran Islands the author invents his own island, Seilg Mhichíl (Shellig Michael), which looks like and sounds like the real Skellig Michael (Sceilg Mhichíl) off the Kerry coast, famous for its ancient monastic settlement of beehive huts. *Sceilg* means a steep rock.

4. *Poill Tí Lábáin* in the original. The caves are actually north of Oughterard.

5. Abhainn Ruibhe in Oughterard, east Conamara.

—You talking about stealing, Road-End Man, when you'd steal the egg from the heron, and the heron as well. It was my bad luck that my turf bank bordered on yours, and the only spreading place for my turf was beside yours. You used to draw up your cart or your donkey and creels to the open end of your own turf stack but it was from mine you filled your load. Do you remember the morning I caught you? The day was just dawning. I'd told you the previous night I was going to the fair with pigs. You told me you were going to the fair too . . .

And the day I caught your wife. I saw her going to the bog in broad daylight. I knew there would be nobody up there because they were all down cutting seaweed in the strand during the spring ebb.[6] That's where I should have been too, but I knew by the look of your wife she was intent on theft. I crawled on my belly ever so slowly up by the back of the Ridge till I came upon her just as she was tightening the rope on the load, right in the opening of my turf stack . . . "No matter how far the fox goes, he's caught in the end," says I . . .

"I'll have the law on you," says she. "You have no right to accost a woman in a lonely place like this. I'll swear on oath against you. You'll be transported . . ."

—You talking about stealing, Road-End Man, and you'd steal the honey from the hive. You sold every sod of your own turf. Not a sod to call your own from All Saints' Day and still you had a roaring fire in the kitchen, and in the parlour, and in the rooms upstairs . . . I was visiting in your house one night. I recognised the turf I'd brought from the bog myself the day before. "Upon my soul, as you say, there's neither fire nor flame in that turf," says you. "It should be better than that . . . the best sods have all been stolen from us . . ."

—You're talking about stealing, and you'd steal the shroud off a corpse. You stole the drift-weed[7] I collected from off the island. "Since we can't bring all this ashore on our backs or with the horse,"

---

6. One of the very low tides that occur once a fortnight, exposing a wide area of the shore.

7. *Feamainn ghaoithe*, loose floating seaweed brought to land by an onshore wind.

says I to the wife, "we'd better tie strings[8] to the stems to show that we've claimed it. It wouldn't cost this crowd up at Road-End a thought to take it tomorrow morning when the tide casts it up."

"Surely to God they wouldn't go stealing drift-weed," says the wife.

"God grant you sense," said I. "If you had it spread out on your own field they'd take it, never mind anywhere else."

The next morning on my way from the top of the village I met your daughter in the Deep Hollow, and she had a load of seaweed on her donkey.

— Oh, that temptress my eldest son is keeping company with!

— I recognised my drift-weed immediately, even though some of the strings were taken off the stems. "In Colm's Cove you collected that," I said.

"In the Middle Cove," said she.

"Indeed it was not," said I, "but in Colm's Cove. Seaweed from the island would never come into the Middle Cove with the wind due south and a springtide running. That's my seaweed. If you have any scruples you'll lay down that load and let me have it . . ."

"I'll have the law on you for attacking me like this in a lonely place," she said. "I'll swear on oath against you. You'll be transported . . ."

— You stole my little lump-hammer. I saw you with it when you were building the back kitchen . . .

— You stole my sickle . . .

— You stole the rope I left outside . . .

— You stole the scallops[9] I left ready pointed in the barn after my two days' hard work cutting them in Banishment Wood . . . I knew my own two notches on each scallop . . .

— Faith then, a small heap of periwinkles was stolen from me. I had them in bags at the top of the boreen. "Faith then," says I to the

---

8. Seaweed, timbers, and other goods thrown up on the shore would be claimed by tying a string to them or putting a stone on them.

9. Sharpened sticks used to pin down thatch on a roof.

young lad, "if we gather that much every week till next November we'll have the best part of the price of a colt." There were seven fine fat bagfuls of them. The next morning I went down to meet the Periwinkle Man. He looked at them. "This bag is a couple of stone short," says he. He was right. It had been opened and a couple of stone stolen out of it the night before. It's best to tell the truth: I had my doubts about Caitríona Pháidín . . .

—Ababúna! . . .

—I did indeed. She had a great liking for periwinkles. I've heard people say they're great for the heart. But I didn't know at the time that I had a bad heart, God help us! But I wrenched my . . .

—You old sourpuss! Don't believe him . . .

—Listen, Seáinín Liam, usen't I see my own father. The poor man, he'd drink tea at all hours of the day. The devil a penny of his pension I ever saw in the house, Seáinín, nor did I know where he put it. But there was plenty of tea to be had at the time, and he used to buy a pound and a half or two pounds of it every Friday. Siúán the Shop told me he often bought as much as two and a half pounds. "Might as well enjoy it while it lasts," he always used to say, the poor man.

Every Friday Caitríona would lie in wait for him on his way home, and she'd spirit him into her house. He was easily led like that, the poor man. "You'll have a cup of tea," she'd say.

"Indeed I will," he'd say. "There's two pounds of it there. Might as well enjoy it while it lasts."

He'd go over the whole story again and again at home with me. He was simple like that, the poor man. So the tea was made. And tea was made twice, maybe. But no more than a half pound of all that tea was ever brought home to me. May God forbid that I'd tell a lie about him, Seáinín! . . .

"I bought two pounds," he'd always say. "Unless I lost it! See if there's any hole in them pockets. Maybe I left some of it behind me in Caitríona Pháidín's. I'll get it the next day. And even if I don't, what harm? Might as well enjoy it while it lasts. Caitríona's household can knock back an awful amount of tea, God bless them! . . ." He was simple like that, the poor man . . .

—That's a damned lie, you slut! Didn't he have me robbed trying to keep him in tea! Running over to my house at every stroke of a clock or watch, because you had him poisoned, Bríd Terry, with your spotty potatoes and salt-water dip, you beggarwoman you. Don't believe her . . .

—Peace and quiet is all I want! Peace and quiet! Spare me the lash of your tongue, Caitríona. I don't deserve all your snarling. Peace and quiet! Peace and quiet!

—I'll tell you the truth now, Bríd Terry. We had the Rape Field sown the same year and we had heaps of old potatoes left. It was out towards the end of May. Micil and myself were on the bog every day that dawned for the previous two weeks. We'd have been there that particular day too only for Micil was bringing up a lock of dry seaweed from the shore until dinner-time. He went into the barn after his dinner to get an armful of straw to put in the donkey's straddle, since he was going to spend the rest of the day on the bog. "You'd think, Cite," he says, "the heap of old potatoes out there in the barn wouldn't have gone down so much. I wouldn't mind but the pigs have been sold for the past two weeks."

"Faith then, Micil," says I, "I didn't set right foot or left in that barn for the past three weeks. I had no call to. The children bring in the potatoes for the meal."

"We should have kept it locked since we started going to the bog," says he. "Anybody could get in there during the day, when we're not at home and the children are at school."

"They could indeed, Micil, or during the night," says I.

"It's shutting the stable door after the horse has bolted," says Micil.

Out I went myself to the barn on the spur of the moment, Bríd. I looked at the potatoes.

"Faith then, Micil," says I when I came in. "It's shutting the stable door after the horse has bolted, right enough. There was a fine heap of potatoes there two weeks ago, but it's shrunk to nothing now. There's not near enough left to keep us going till the new potatoes. Would you have any clue, Micil, who's stealing them?"

"I'll go to the bog," says Micil. "Let you go up to Meadow Height, Cite, pretending you're going to the bog like you do every day, and come down into the stony hollows at the back, and lie down and hide in the sallies."[10]

So I did that, Bríd. I lay down in the sallies, turning the heel on a stocking and keeping an eye out on the barn. I was a long time there, and I think I was on the verge of falling asleep when I heard a noise at the barn door. I jumped through the low gap in the wall. There she was, Bríd, and what you might call a fine hump of spuds on her back . . .

"You may as well take them with you and sell them to Siúán the Shop, as you did with your own all year," says I. "You haven't a potato to put in your mouth since May Day now. I wouldn't mind one year, but that's your carry-on every year."

"I had to give them to Tomás Inside," says she. "His own lot failed."

"Failed! Because he didn't look after them," I said. "He didn't earth them up and he didn't weed them or put a squirt of spray on them . . ."

"I humbly implore you not to tell anyone, Cite," says she, "and I'll make it up to you. I wouldn't mind who'd hear about it so long as that pussface Nell doesn't get wind of it."

"Very well, Caitríona," says I, "I won't tell."

And by the oak of this coffin, I didn't, Bríd . . .

—Listen, Shitty Cite of the ash-potatoes, I always had lashings of potatoes of my own, thanks be to God . . .

—. . . Dotie! Dotie! She left Tomás Inside penniless. I often met him in the village. "By the docks, I haven't a red cent left that she hasn't stolen from me, Nóra," he'd say. *Honest*, he would. I used to give him the price of a few glasses of whiskey, Dotie. *Honest*. He was to be pitied, the creature, and his tongue like parched flowers in a pot . . .

---

10. Thin stems of pollarded willows, cultivated for basket-making.

But what am I talking about, Dotie? Didn't my own daughter play the same trick? It was here I found out about it . . . She did it to my son in Mangy Field straight away after my death. Himself and the wife were going to a fair in Brightcity. My daughter offered to come over and look after the house till they came home. She gathered up everything of value in the house and threw them into a big chest. She had the horse and cart outside. She told four or five young lads who were there to put the chest onto the cart. They didn't know a thing in the world about it. She threw them the price of a drink. "It's my mother's chest," says she. "She left it to me." *Honest,* that's what she said. She brought it off home with her. *Honest,* Dotie. It was a fine chest of the old-fashioned Irish style. It was as strong as iron. And lovely looking as well. Utility and beauty combined, Dotie . . . Not to mention the money's worth that was in it! Silver spoons and knives. A silver toilette set I had myself when I was in Brightcity. Valuable books bound in calfskin. Sheets, blankets, sacking, wrappers . . . If Caitríona Pháidín had been able to mind them properly she wouldn't have been laid out in a dirty shroud . . .

Exactly, Dotie! That's the chest Caitríona is forever talking about . . .

—Silver knives and spoons in Mangy Field of the Ducks! Oh, Holy Mother of God! Don't believe her! Don't believe her! The *So-an'-so.* Muraed! Muraed! Did you hear what Mangy Nóirín said? . . . and Seáinín Liam . . . and Bríd Terry . . . and Cite . . . I'll explode! I'll explode . . .

4

—. . . A little white-faced mare. She was the best . . .

—A little mare you had. A colt we have . . .

—A little white-faced mare, indeed. At St. Bartholomew's Fair I bought her . . .

—After Christmas we bought that colt of ours.

—A little white-faced mare. A ton and a half was no bother to her . . .

—A fine big colt we have, God bless her! We were building a new stable for her . . .

—. . . "Golden Apple" won: a hundred to one.

—Galway won. They beat Kerry . . .

—"Golden Apple" won, I tell you.

—You're confused, like that eejit who's forever arguing that Kerry won. Galway won, I tell you . . .

—But there was no "Galway" in the big three o'clock race.

—There was no "Golden Apple" on the team that won the football final in 1941. Concannon, you meant to say, maybe . . .

—. . . "Tom-á-ás Inside was there . . ."

—. . . There are seventeen houses in my village and every single vote in them going to Éamon de Valera . . .

—Seventeen houses! And yet not a shot was fired at a Black-and-Tan[11] in your village! The devil as much as a single shot. Not as much as a shot, or even the sound of a shot.

—Mind you, they laid an ambush. Late on a dark night. They wounded Glutton's donkey that was getting into Curraoin's Roadside Field.

—I remember it well. I twisted my ankle . . .

—. . . You're one of Pádraig Labhráis's? . . . The third lad. You used to come to school to me. You were a fine sturdy lad. With a head of fair hair. Brown eyes. Glowing cheeks. You were a splendid handballer . . . So the Wood of the Lake crowd have gone off to England . . . The Schoolmistress is in the best of form, you tell me! Aha! Billyboy the Post is very ill . . . very ill . . .

—He is, Master. Rheumatism, they say. He was reported for giving the letters to the first person he'd meet, and he had to start bringing them to the houses again . . .

—That's the stuff for him! The scoundrel! . . .

—He was caught in a downpour on his way to the mountain

---

11. An undisciplined force of British soldiers, named from their mixed uniforms, that terrorised parts of Ireland during the War of Independence.

homesteads. He got an awful drenching . . . When he got home he took to his bed . . .

—Good enough for him! The beggar! The thief! The . . .

—He had great talk of going off to England, Master, before he was struck down . . .

—Going to England! Going to England! . . . Out with it. Don't be shy . . .

—People say, Master, that he wasn't in great health since he got married . . .

—Oh, the intruder! The greedy little grabber! . . .

—She didn't want him to go, herself. The time I was ready to go, she was talking to my father about it, and she said that if Billyboy went away there was nothing in store for her but death . . .

—The harlot . . .

—She brought three doctors from Dublin to see him, Master . . .

—With my money! She wouldn't bring a doctor to see me, the hussy . . . arse in the bracken . . .

—De grâce, Master!

—. . . "Tomás Inside was there with an urge to ma-a-rry . . ."

—I had no intention of getting married. I'd have gone to England only for I got ill. The Donagh's Village crowd and the Mangy Field crowd had gone . . .

—And Glen of the Pasture and Wood of the Lake. I know as well as yourself who's gone. But is there any old fogey getting married? . . .

—Tomás Inside has great talk of getting married.

—Talk of it is all he'll do, the useless yoke. Who else?

—The Red-haired Policeman, to a nurse from Brightcity. The Small Master too . . .

—The Small Master, indeed? Schoolteachers seem to be in a devil of a rush to marry. They must be expecting another pay rise . . .

—They'd be better off not to, sometimes. You heard the Big Master yourself just now. But who's the fair lady?

—A young woman from Brightcity. A fine-looking woman, indeed! The day I was getting my photograph taken for going to England I saw the two of them together. They went into the Western Hotel.

—What shape of a woman was she?

—A tall slender woman. With fair hair in plaits . . .

—A ring in her ear?

—Yes . . .

—Dark eyes?

—The devil do I know what sort of eyes she had. It wasn't her I was worrying about . . .

—A bright smile?

—She was smiling at the Small Master right enough. But she wasn't smiling at me . . .

—Did you hear where she's living?

—I didn't. But I think she works in Barry's Betting Office, if there is such a place. The Wood of the Lake Master and the priest's sister are getting married next month. They say he'll get the new school.

—The woman with the trousers?

—That's her.

—Isn't it a wonder she'd marry him?

—Why? Isn't he a fine handsome man, and he doesn't touch a drop.

—But even so. It seems to me that a trousers-woman wouldn't be content to marry just any man. They'd be choosier than other women . . .

—Arrah, have an ounce of sense! My own son is married in England to a Frenchwoman, and you wouldn't know what in the world she's saying, any more than that babbler buried over here. Wouldn't she be choosier than a trousers-woman . . .

—Never mind your Frenchwoman! My son is married in England to an *Eyetalian*.

What do you think of that?

—Yourself and your *Eyetalian*. My son is married in England to a *black!* What do you think of that, now?

—A *black!* My son is married in England to a Jewess. It's not every man a Jewess would be willing to marry . . .

—It's not every man would marry her. A fellow would have an aversion to her . . .

—A fellow would have much more of an aversion to the woman who's married to your son. A *black*. Ugh!

—The big boss is to be married to a woman from Glen of the Pasture. That young fellow of Seáinín Liam's has finished the stable, and they say he's on the lookout for a wife. He was refused when he asked for Road-End's daughter.

—Road-End, who spent every day of his life stealing my turf . . .

—And mine . . .

—And my lump-hammer . . .

—Oh, the devil pierce her! Trying to get in on my big holding . . .

—She's the one who threatened to have the law on me over my drift-weed. Seáinín Liam's son wouldn't marry that one, would he?

—She's good enough for him. What the devil did Seáinín Liam ever have? Periwinkles. What the devil does he have now? Periwinkles . . .

—Faith then, periwinkles were not to be sneezed at, so they weren't. Myself and the young fellow earned the best part of the price of a colt on them. We have more than what you people say we have: we have a fine big colt and a stable that only needs a roof. I told him when he'd have finished the stable to look out for a little rump of a girl for himself . . .

—The young fellow was refused in the house on the hill too, and for the Red's daughter in Donagh's Village, and for the Little Carpenter's daughter in Mangy Field . . .

—There's no go in that young fellow. Did he say that we'd earned the best part of the price of a colt on the periwinkles; that we'd just finished building a new stable, and that we bought a fine big colt after Christmas? He'll never settle down, I'm afraid. Only for I died so suddenly myself . . .

—Listen, Seáinín Liam, the Red of Donagh's Village is my first cousin. He was damn right to refuse your son. I refused you yourself for my daughter. Do you remember the time you came asking for her?

—I didn't have a colt or a stable that time.

—You sound so full of self-importance the way you talk about the Red of Donagh's Village, by the way. You'd think he was the Earl himself, and didn't my father refuse him about a wife! "Do you think, Red," said my father, "that I'd send my daughter to Donagh's Village to live on nettles and the chirping of grasshoppers?"

—Your father refused the Red! My mother refused your father about a wife! "There's two score pounds and a cow coming with my daughter," says she, "and by my soul it's not on the flea-infested hillocks of your village I'm going to settle herself or her two score pounds."

—Your mother refused him about a wife! Your mother! Her father tried to pawn her off on me, but I wouldn't marry her. She was purblind. She had a mole under her ear. Fifteen pounds was all the dowry she had. I wouldn't marry her . . .

—I wouldn't marry Big Brian. He asked for me . . .

—Arrah, I wouldn't marry Big Brian either. He asked for me twice.

—Nor would I. He asked for me three times. By the oak of this coffin, he did. He damn near failed to get any wife at all. Caitríona Pháidín would have gladly married him, the time Jack the Scológ left her there, but he didn't come asking for her . . .

—Ababúna! Cite of the lies! The ash-potatoes hag . . .

—. . . *Honest*, Dotie. The place wasn't good enough at all. There'd be no fear of me settling my daughter there, and six score pounds of a dowry with her, only for it would have grieved me too much to keep her from him. There was always that streak of romance in me, and I wouldn't have the heart to let paltry worldly considerations become an insuperable obstacle to their pitiable love. *Honest*. Only for that, Dotie, do you think I'd let my daughter, or my six score pounds, in on Caitríona Pháidín's few measly pockets of land? . . .

—You mangy bitch! You *So-an'-so!* Don't believe her! Don't believe her! Muraed! Muraed! . . . Do you hear what Nóra Filthy-Feet is saying? And Cite of the lies? . . . I'll explode!

5

—. . . Do you think it's the War of the Two Foreigners?

—. . . A bad bottle the murderer gave me . . .

—. . . I had two score pints and two in my belly, and not a drop less, when I was tying Tomáisín . . .

—. . . It's well I remember it. I twisted my ankle . . .

—"Zee dog is sinking." *Qu'est-ce que c'est que* "zee dog" . . . *Qu'est-ce que c'est que* "zee-dog"? Zee dog. Zee dog.

—Bow wow! Bow wow!

—*Un chien, n'est-ce pas?* Zee dog. Bow wow! Zee dog.

—The dog. The dog. The dog, you numskull!

—"Zee dog is sinking." *Le chien pense, n'est-ce pas?* "Zee dog is sinking." *Mais non!* "Zee dog is sinking."

—How would a dog be sinking, you numskull? Maybe he was thinking, or drinking, or even stinking. But it wasn't sinking. Sinking! The devil a dog I ever saw sinking.

—Zee dog is sinking.

—The dog is thinking. The dog is thinking.

—"Zee dog is sinking." "Sinking: t . . . h . . . i . . . n . . . k . . . i . . . n . . . g"! "Sinking." *Ce sont les mots qui se trouvent dans mon livre.* "Zee dog is sinking."

—If it's sinking let it sink. The devil a thing we can do about it, or about whoever put it in the book either. Maybe it went drinking, and then it started sinking on account of the hangover and the empty pockets . . .

—*Je ne comprends pas. Après quelques leçons peut-être* . . . "Zee white cat is on zee stool." "*Cat*": *qu'est-ce qu'il veut dire?* "Cat"? "Cat"?

—Me-ow! Me-ow!

—Miaou! Miaou! *Chat! N'est-ce pas? Chat.*

—Yes, what else?

—"Zee mat is small. Zee 'at is tall. Zee 'at is tall. Pól 'as a tall 'at . . ."

—You're a liar! I never had a tall hat. You could hardly say I even had a low one! Do you think I'm a bishop or something?

—*Je ne comprends pas.* "Pól is old . . ."

—You're a liar. I was young enough. I would only have been twenty-eight this next Feast of Saints Peter and Paul.

—*Je ne comprends pas.* "Pól is not drinking."

—He's not drinking now, because he doesn't get the chance, but he drank all he had before this, and that wasn't much.

—*Je ne comprends pas.*

—*Au revoir! Au revoir! De grâce! De grâce! . . .*

—The devil a word of Irish he'll ever learn.

—He wouldn't be long picking it up, all the same. We had an Irish learner staying with us the year I died. The devil a word in the whole wide world he had, but learning out of those little books like your man there. He'd be in the kitchen every morning an hour before I got up and he'd have the whole house topsy-turvy: "This is a cat. This is a sack. The cat is on the sack. This is a dog. This is a stool. The dog is on the stool." That was his rigmarole all day long. He had my mother demented. "For God's sake, Pól, take that fellow with you over to the field," she said to myself. I was mowing a meadow by the boreen down to the shore at the time. I took him off with me. We were barely there when it was time to come back for our dinner, because he read the *lesson* to everyone we met on the way.

Back we went after dinner. I began giving him little words like "scythe," "grass," "wall," "cock," little words like that. The day was very sultry, and he was having great difficulty getting his tongue round the words. He spat out a few thick spits. He asked me how I'd say "pint" in Irish. "Pionta," says I.

"Pionta," says he, and he gave me the nod . . . The two of us went over by the shore to Peadar the Pub's. He stood me two pints. Back we came to the field. I gave him another word. "Pionta," says he. "Pionta," says I. Over we went again. Two more pints. Back to the field again. I gave him another word. Over again. Back again. Over and back like that all day long. Me giving him a word for each pint, and he giving me a pint for each word . . .

—. . . I fell off a stack of oats, indeed . . .

—. . . Do you think I grew in a cabbage patch, that I was never at the pictures? . . .

—An old fellow like you?

—An old fellow like me? I wasn't always old, you know!

—They're really lovely. I saw beautiful things at the pictures. Houses like the Earl's house . . .

—I saw a fine cross there, and I'd say it was made out of Island limestone . . .

—I saw lots of trousers-women . . .

—And *black* women . . .

—And people of culture, nightclubs, quays, tall ships under sail and mariners with skins of every colour. *Honest* . . .

—And the odd ugly streak of misery . . .

—And women with sweet malicious smiles, like Siúán the Shop when she'd be refusing you cigarettes . . .

—And women with wily intentions, like Peadar the Pub's daughter, waiting inside the door to play the parlour trick on some poor unsuspecting customer . . .

—You'd see fine big colts, faith . . .

—And football matches. But I swear to God Concannon would make curds and whey of the backside of any of those footballers . . .

—You wouldn't see any drift-weed at all at the pictures . . .

—Or two thatchers on opposite sides of a house . . .

—Or nettles like there were in Donagh's Village . . .

—Or flea-ridden hillocks like there were in your own village . . .

—I'd prefer Mae West myself to any of them. If I got a new lease of life my only wish would be to see her again. She'd be a great woman to handle a colt, I'd say. Myself and the young fellow were in Brightcity the night before the fair. We had a few pints. "That's enough now," says I. "If we overdo it we could easily put a hole in the price of the colt." "It's too early to go to bed yet," says he. "Come on to the pictures." "I was never at the pictures," said I. "What harm?" said he. "Mae West will be on tonight." "Faith then, if that's the case, I'll go."

In we went. A woman came on. A fine big woman, faith, and she began to smile at me. I began to smile back at her. "Is that her?" said I. "Arrah, not at all!" said the young fellow. Soon another fine stump came on. She placed a hand on her hip. She tilted herself to one side and began to smile at us all. We all began to smile back at her.

"That's her now," said the young fellow.

"Look at that!" said I. "She'd be a great one to handle a colt, I'd say. As soon as the stable is finished a young fellow like you could do worse than find a young little rump of a woman for himself. But I wouldn't advise you to have anything to do with the likes of her. She'd be good at handling the colt alright, but . . ."

"But what!" said the young fellow . . .

A stout little man came on then, like that paunchy fowler who comes to Jack the Scológ's, and he was talking to the two women. He began to wave his arms wildly in the air. Another stumpy little man came out. The spitting image of that gent who comes fishing to Nell Pháidín's—Lord Cockton. Mae West said something to him. Indeed, the young fellow told me what it was, but for the life of me I can't think of it now . . .

The stout little man's cheeks puffed up as if he had a balloon in his mouth and he put the palms of his hands against his ribs. He was very fat and out of breath. I'd say he was a man who had a weak heart, God help us! . . .

—. . . Only once, Cite. That's as often I was ever at the pictures. I'd much rather see them again than to know what life held in store for me. It was the time my daughter who's married in Brightcity was having a baby. I spent a week there minding her. She was convalescing at this stage. Her husband came in from work one evening. He had his dinner, and dressed himself.

"Were you ever at the pictures, Bríd Terry?" said he.

"What are they?" said I.

"There are all sorts of pictures shown in a place up there," said he.

"In the church?" said I.

"Not at all," he said, "the pictures."

"Pictures of Jesus Christ and the Virgin Mary, and St. Patrick and

St. Joseph?" said I. "Not at all," he said, "foreign countries and wild animals and peculiar people." "Foreign countries and wild animals and peculiar people," said I. "Upon my soul, I won't go near them at all. How do I know, the Lord between us and all harm! . . ."

"You have the mind of a peasant," he said, in stitches laughing at me. "They're only pictures. They can't harm you." "Wild animals and peculiar people," says I. "Who knows what might happen?"

"There'll be a picture about America on tonight," says he.

"America," says I. "I wonder would I see my own dear Bríd and Nóirín—God be with them!—and Anna Liam . . ."

"You'll see people like them," he said. "You'll see America."

And of course I did. There never were such wonders! A pity I can't describe them! That wretched fire destroyed my memory completely! But I can assure you, Cite, everything was as clear to me as if I had been over there beside them. There was an old woman there cleaning the door with a cloth, with a grimace like Caitríona Pháidín's face when she'd see Nell and Jack the Scológ going past her up home from the fair . . .

—Ababúna!

—And there was a fine spacious room there, Cite, with a *round-table* like the one you gave the pound to Caitríona to buy, that she never paid back . . .

—That's a damn lie . . .

—And there was a silver teapot like the one in Nell's, sitting on top of it. And a man in black clothes with golden buttons opened the door. I thought it was the Red-haired Policeman, till I remembered they were in America. Another man came in wearing what looked like a postman's cap, and the man of the house and himself began to argue. The man with the golden buttons and himself caught the man of the house and threw him down the stairs. I thought he'd be a heap of bones because there were three or four flights of stairs below. Then they threw him out the door on top of his head and he nearly upended the old woman. *Honest to God*, Cite, I felt sorry for her. Her head was in a tizzy.

Then the man of the house looked back and waved his fist at the man who threw him out. I thought it was the Big Master—the same snub nose and slit eyes—and that it was Billyboy the Post who threw him out, till I remembered they were in America. I knew that whatever about the Big Master being in America that Billyboy the Post couldn't be there, with the post to be delivered every day . . .

—The ruffian! The lecher! The . . .

—This man who you'd take for Billyboy went up the stairs again to the room, and there was a woman there wearing black clothes with flower prints.

"That's the Schoolmistress, if I'm not dreaming," says I to myself. But then I remembered that they were in America and that the Schoolmistress was teaching school at home a few days before that . . .

—The trollop . . .

—De grâce, Master . . . Now, Dotie . . .

—The man with the golden buttons opened the door again. Another woman came in who had a snub nose and a fur coat just like the one Baba Pháidín had when she was home from America, till she had to get rid of it on account of all the smudges of soot in Caitríona's . . .

—That's a damn lie, you slut . . .

—. . . Oh! A smashing picture, Dotie! Honest! There was excitement and consternation. If only you saw that part where Eustasia said to Mrs Crookshank:

"My dear," she said. "It's no use going on arguing about it. Harry and I are married. We were married in a Registry Office on Sixth Avenue this morning. Of course, my dear, Bob is still there . . ."

And she shrugged her shoulders triumphantly. Oh! It's an awful pity you didn't see Mrs. Crookshank's face, Dotie, when she was left completely speechless. I couldn't help thinking—if the cultural comparison may be excused!—of what Nell Pháidín said to Caitríona: "We'll leave Big Brian to you, Kay."

—You mangy bitch! You So-an'-so . . . Muraed! Muraed! Do you hear me? Do you hear the nit-infested Filthy-Feet, and Bríd Terry? I'll explode! I'll explode! . . .

6

And Nell won her case against the lorry driver! Even though her son was on the wrong side of the road. He can't have been a very bright judge. That slut Bríd Terry was wrong when she said the law would take the last penny off her. And she got eight hundred pounds after all that! The priest, who else? And the pussface had the nerve to go offering up Masses for my soul . . .

There's a road being built up to her house. A road that couldn't be built if my Pádraig wasn't such a simpleton. She's playing on him now, just as she played on Jack the Scológ with the St. John's Gospel. If I were alive . . .

Not the wind of a word about the cross now. And what that ugly streak of misery said: "That harridan is not worthy of a cross." Has he no fear of God or the Virgin Mary! And him nearly a hundred years old! May his visit to Dublin do him no good! . . .

They have forgotten about me above ground. That's the way, God help us! I thought Pádraig wouldn't go back on his word. That is if that young fellow picked up the story right? He probably didn't. He was too keen on going to England . . .

If my Pádraig only knew how I'm being treated in the graveyard clay! I'm like a hare cornered by the hounds. Betrayed and flayed by Seáinín Liam, by Cite, by Bríd Terry, by them all. Trying to hold my own with the lot of them. And not a single soul to stand up for me. I won't be able to stand it. I'll explode . . .

That pup, Nóra Filthy-Feet, is inciting them all . . .

Her daughter has changed completely. I was sure she'd be here a long time ago. She's a great woman. I'm happy now that Pádraig married her. I must tell the truth. I am indeed. I'd forgive her everything herself and her mother ever did to me, for having thrown Nell on her back in the fire, and for pulling every lock of hair and every bit of skin and every strip of clothes off Big Brian's daughter. And she broke the delph. She overturned the churn Big Brian's daughter and Nell were making butter in. She jumped on top of a brood of young chickens on the floor. She grabbed the silver teapot Nell had on show on top of the dresser and made a pancake of it against the wall. And she threw the clock Baba gave the pussface out through the window. That's what the young fellow said . . .

She's a great woman. I wish I hadn't been so hard on her. To throw Nell on her back in the fire! That's a thing I never had the guts to do . . .

And she's left her sickness behind her now. Raising hens and pigs and calves. If she lives she'll make money . . .

But to throw Nell on her back in the fire! Her head of fair hair got a scorching. I forgot to ask the young fellow if her fair hair was scorched. I'd give everything I ever yearned for to see her throwing Nell in the fire. A pity I wasn't alive!

I'd shake her hand, I'd kiss her, I'd clap her on the back, I'd send for one of the golden bottles from Peadar the Pub's window, we'd drink one another's health, I'd offer a prayer for the soul of her mother and I'd see to it that her next girl-child would be christened Nóra. But what's wrong with me? There's a Nóra there already!

Upon my soul, I'll call Nóra Sheáinín, I'll tell her about the job her daughter did and how she's a great worker now, and I'll tell her I'm delighted that she's married to my son . . .

But what will Muraed, Cite, Bríd Terry and the rest of them say? That I used to revile her, that I used to call her a bitch and Nóra Filthy-Feet; that I wouldn't vote for her in the Election . . .

They'll say that. They'll also say—and it's true for them—that she told lies about me: that she said I robbed Tomás Inside, that her daughter got six score pounds of a dowry . . .

But let them. I'd forgive her anything on account of her daughter throwing Nell on her back in the fire . . .

Nóra . . . Hey! Nóra . . . Nóra dear . . . I'm Caitríona Pháidín . . . Nóra . . . Nóra dear . . . Did you hear the news from the land above? About your daughter . . .

What's that, Nóra? What did you say? Good God above! That you have no time to listen to silly rubbish from the world above! . . . You involved yourself with filth in the Election, and all you got for it was the seal of the clay! By God! . . . You can't be bothered listening to my story . . . About sordid affairs! You'll spend all your time from now on with . . . with . . . with . . . what did you call it? . . . with culture . . . You haven't time to listen to my story as it has nothing to do with . . . with culture. Holy Son of God tonight! Nóra Filthy . . . Nóra Filthy-Feet from Mangy Field talking about . . . about culture . . .

Will you repeat that mouthful of English, when it's as rare as a cat with a straddle to have English in Mangy Field. Say it again . . .

—*"Art is long and Time is fleeting."*

—*"Fleet! Fleet!"* The *Fleet* is the big bead on your rosary. *Fleet* and sailors. Oh! Mother of Mercy tonight, I must have little respect for myself to be talking to you at all, you *So-an'-so* . . .

Interlude Six

THE KNEADING OF THE CLAY

1

I am the Trump of the Graveyard! Let my voice be heard! It must be heard . . . Here in the graveyard is the autocratic policeman that is darkness. His baton is the melancholy that will not be broken by the sweet smile of a maiden. His bolt is the bolt of insensibility that will not be loosened by the glitter of gold or the smooth words of authority. His eye is the shadow of misfortune across the path through the wood. His judgement is the harsh judgement that no sword of a knight at arms will thwart on the sod of death.

Above ground Brightness is dressed in his suit of valour. He wears a mantle of sunshine with buttons of roses, hem of sea song, seam of birdsong, tassels of butterfly wings and a belt of stars from the Milky Way. His shield is made of bridal veils. His sword of light is made of children's toys. His reward of valour is the corn stem that is ripening at the ears, the cloud that is impregnated by the virgin morning sun, the fair maiden whose eyes are alight with love's young dream . . .

But the sap is drying in the tree. The golden voice of the thrush is turning to copper. The rose is fading. The black rust that blunts, rots and decays is infesting the sword edge of the knight.

Darkness is overcoming brightness. The graveyard demands its due . . . I am the Trump of the Graveyard. Let my voice be heard! It must be heard . . .

—Who have I here? Máirtín Pockface, upon my word! It was time for you to come! I'm a long time here and I was the same age as you . . . Yes, I'm that same woman, Caitríona Pháidín . . .

Bedsores is what you had, you tell me . . .

—Caitríona, dear, the bed was very hard. Very hard indeed on my poor buttocks, Caitríona. My back was completely blistered. There wasn't a shred of skin left on my thighs and I had an old injury in my groin. It was no wonder, Caitríona, dear, after being bedridden for nine months. I couldn't twist or turn. My son used to come in, Caitríona, and turn me over on my other thigh. "I can't give my body a proper stretch," I'd say. "It's a long time to be bedridden," I'd say. "A long time laid up never lied,"[1] he'd say. Caitríona, dear, the bed was awfully hard on my poor buttocks . . .

—Your buttocks were well able for it, Máirtín Pockface. You had some surplus there . . . If you had bedsores it's all the better for getting used to the boards here . . . Bid Shorcha, you said. She's still above ground. Rather her there than here. Not wishing to demean her, but she was an ugly sight above ground and I don't think this place would improve her looks much either . . . You and Bid were vying with each other to see which of you would live longest, you say? Yes, indeed. Yes. That's how it goes, Máirtín Pockface . . . And she buried you before her! Those things can't be helped, Máirtín dear. Bad luck to her, but isn't she long-lived! She should have died long ago, if she had any shame . . . That's true, Máirtín, it's a great wonder she didn't get bedsores, she was so fond of the bed. She was sick every day of her life except on funeral days. All the other days she'd be hoarse with a cold. But there'd be nothing wrong with her voice on a funeral day. "Only for my being throaty," she'd say after the funeral, "I'd be the one to keen him . . ." The brazen scold! Drawing pensions and half-

---

1. *Ní dhearna luí fada riamh bréag* (a long time laid up never lied) is an old saying, meaning that a long spell of being confined to bed ends in death.

crowns still, and heaping them into her son's wife's apron. As long as she keeps putting money in the apron her son's wife won't let a bedsore near her, I'm telling you! There'll be butter rubbed on that one's thighs and buttocks . . . She doesn't keen anybody now, you say. The spouter! . . . Red-haired Tom is laid up. He's another one . . . The hovel didn't fall in on Tomás Inside yet, you say . . . Ababúna! Nell put in a table for him . . . and a dresser . . . and a bed. A bed, even! She wouldn't put a bed in for anybody only for her ill-gotten money. Oh! A stupid judge . . . Afraid he'd get bedsores in the old bed. Afraid she wouldn't get his land, Máirtín Pockface . . .

Big Brian, you say? That fellow will never die till a jar of paraffin is poured over him and a match put to him. That's the truth, Máirtín Pockface. That ugly streak of misery won't get bedsores . . . He'll die all of a sudden. True for you. All of a sudden, indeed. May his heap of bones steer clear of us here! . . .

What's that? . . . Another bad illness in Lower Hillside! That's nothing new to them, not wishing to demean them. They're going to be a great asset to this graveyard, indeed! They'll fatten it and deafen it . . .

Our Baba is laid up in America! Had Dad! . . . What do you mean! Bedsores on that one, Máirtín Pockface! She has thighs twice as fat as yours. And she can afford to keep a soft bed under her, unlike you, Máirtín Pockface . . . Have an ounce of sense, my good man . . . You think because you felt your own old bed hard that every bed is hard . . . May God give you sense, there are soft beds in America for anybody with money . . . You didn't hear if she wrote home? You didn't hear if Nell was with the priest recently? . . . You may be sure she was, Máirtín. She'll gobble up the will by hook or by crook . . . The priest is writing for her? Who else!

Of course, that schoolmaster who's writing for our crowd is no use . . . He has no learning, Máirtín. True for you. Things are not too bad if he doesn't tell the priest about it . . . The priest and the schoolmaster often go strolling together, you say . . . The new road up to Nell's is nearly finished. Oh, wasn't that little fool of a son of mine unfortunate when he let her have Flagstone Height! . . .

Nell is talking of building a slate-roofed house? A slate-roofed house! May she not live to enjoy her slate-roofed house, then, the cocky bitch! Unless she's got some of the will already? That crowd in Wood of the Lake got a share before their brother died at all . . . But, of course, she had the money from the court. She'll be buried in the Pound Plot now, for certain . . .

Jack is still ailing. The poor thing! Oh, didn't Nell and that lanky lump of a daughter of Big Brian's play a trick on him with the St. John's Gospel! You didn't hear about the St. John's Gospel! Of course you didn't! You don't think they'd tell you about it! . . .

Pádraig's wife up at cockcrow every morning! Good for her! . . . Lots of calves on Pádraig's land, did you say? . . . The wife has taken everything over from Pádraig! She does the selling and buying herself now. Look at that now! And me thinking she'd be here any day! You wouldn't know anything about a child, of course? . . . You had enough on your mind. Bedsores . . . Easily known you're new here, to be talking like that, Máirtín Pockface. Don't you know that everyone must have some cause of death, and bedsores are no worse than any other cause.

Ababúna! You heard that plans for my cross have been abandoned! . . . Is that what you heard? . . . Now, Máirtín Pockface, maybe that's not what you heard, and you picked up the story wrong on account of your bedsores . . . You heard it was abandoned . . . That Nell was talking to Pádraig about the cross . . . You don't know, for fear of telling a lie, what she said to him. Now, Máirtín Pockface, none of your "fear of telling a lie." "Fear of telling a lie!" Nell would have no fear of telling a lie about you if it suited her . . . God blast yourself and your old bed! You won't be seeing that bed any more. Tell the story straight out. You don't know how the story went! You had bedsores! Listen here a moment now. Maybe Nell said something like this to my Pádraig: "Faith then, Pádraig dear, you have enough calls on you without a cross . . ." Oh, Nóra Sheáinín's daughter said that! Pádraig's wife said that! . . . "We'll be well off in the world before we go buying crosses . . . many a person as good as her is without a cross . . . She should be thankful to be buried in a cemetery, even, the way things are nowadays." She would say that! The Filthy-Feet Pullet! But she learned it all from Nell. May no corpse come into the graveyard ahead of her! . . . Pádraig won't pay any heed to them . . .

Pádraig's daughter is at home . . . Máirín at home! Are you sure she's not on holidays from school? . . . She failed at school. She failed! . . . She's not going to be a schoolmistress at all . . . Oh, bad scran to her! Bad scran to her! . . .

Nóra Sheáinín's grandson from Mangy Field has gone off . . . On a ship out of Brightcity . . . He got a job on board . . . He's taking after his granny if he's fond of the sailors . . .

Say that again . . . Say it again . . . That Nell's grandson is going to be a priest. The son of Big Brian's daughter going to be a priest! A priest! That cocky little blackguard going to be a priest . . . That he's gone to a seminary . . . that he wore the soutane at home . . . And the collar . . . And a huge great big Prayer Book under his oxter.[2] That he was reading his office going up and down the new road at Flagstone Height! You'd think he wouldn't become a priest straight off like that . . . Oh, he's not a priest yet, he's only going to college. The devil a priest they might ever make of him, Máirtín Pockface . . .

Yes, what did Big Brian say? . . . Don't be mumbling your words but speak up . . . You don't like to, you say! You don't like to . . . On account of Big Brian being related to me by marriage! He's not related to me. He's related to that cocky sister of mine. Out with it . . . "My daughter has money to spend on making priests." "To spend on priests." The streak of misery! . . . Out with it, and to hell with you! Hurry up or they'll have carried you off with them again. Surely you don't think I'm going to let you into this grave, a man who's infested with bedsores for the past nine months . . . "Unlike Caitríona Pháidín's son . . ." Out with the rest of it, Pockface . . . "who hadn't enough to put a little rag of a college petticoat on his daughter . . ." Brian the wretch! Oh, Brian the wretch! . . .

The devil flay you! You're mumbling again. Nell sings "Eleanor of the Secrets" going up the new road every day! Clear off, you raw-

---

2. Under his arm; *ascaill* is the Irish for armpit.

arsed Pockface. You seldom brought good news, nor did any of your kind. . . .

3

—. . . Do you think this is the War of the Two Foreigners? . . .

—. . . Me giving the Gaelic Enthusiast a word for each pint and he giving me a pint for each word . . .

Over and back again the following day. The third day he brought the car to rest his bottom in. The journey over and back was tiring us.

"Pól, dear," said my mother to myself that evening, "the hay should be reasonably dry by now."

"Arrah, how could it be dry, mother dear?" said I. "It's impossible to dry that weedy old hay . . ."

I was two weeks at it before I made meadow cocks of it. I let it out[3] of the cocks again, then turned it, gave it another turn, and then top-turned it.

That's how it was when the sudden shower came, as the two of us were in Peadar the Pub's. I had to let it all out again then to give it some more sun. Then I cleared the ditches, knocked down the stone walls and built them up again. I cut the grass margins, the ferns and the briars. I made gullies. We spent the best part of a month in the field altogether, except that we were over and back to Peadar the Pub's in the motor car.

I never saw a decenter man. And he was no dimwit either. He took between twenty and thirty Irish words from me every day. He had lashings of money. A high-ranking job with the Government . . .

But one day, when he went over without me, Peadar the Pub's daughter brought him into the parlour and hoodwinked him . . .

I missed him terribly. A week after he left I was laid low with the sickness that killed me . . . But, Postmistress . . . Hey! Postmistress . . . how did you know he hadn't paid for his lodging? You opened the letter my mother sent up after him to the Government . . .

---

3. Spread it to dry.

—How did you know, Postmistress, that An Gúm wouldn't accept my collection of poems, *The Yellow Stars?* . . .

—Indeed, you don't deserve any sympathy. They'd be published long ago if you took my advice and wrote from the bottom of the page up. But look at me, my short story "The Setting Sun" was rejected by *The Irishman*, and the Postmistress knew about it . . .

—And the Postmistress knew about the advice I gave Concannon about maiming the Kerry team, in the letter I sent him two days after the semi-final . . .

—How did you know, Postmistress, what I wrote to the judge about the One-Ear Breed the time I went to law with them?

—And, Postmistress, how did your daughter, who's postmistress herself now, know before I knew it myself, that I wouldn't be allowed into England, and that T.B. was the reason? . . .

—You opened a letter Caitríona Pháidín sent to Mannion the Counsellor about Tomás Inside. The whole world knew what was in it:

"We'll bring him to Brightcity in a motor car. We'll make him drunk. If you had a few good-looking girls in the office to excite him, maybe he'd sign over the land to us. He's very fond of the girls when he's merry . . ."

—Ababúna! . . .

—You opened letters a lady in a bookie's office in Brightcity used to send to the Small Master. You'd have the tips for the horses before he got them . . .

—You opened a letter Caitríona Pháidín sent to Big Brian offering to marry him . . .

—Ababúna-búna-búna! That I'd marry Brian the wretch . . .

—Indeed, Postmistress, I had no reason to be grateful to you. You always had the kettle on the boil in the back room. You opened a letter my son wrote to me from England telling me he married a Jewess. The whole country knew about it, and we never said a word about it. Why would we? . . .

—You opened a letter my son wrote to me from England to say he married a *black*. The whole country knew about it while we didn't mention it to anybody . . .

—I wrote a letter to Éamon de Valera, advising him on the sort of proclamation he should send out to the People of Ireland. You kept it in the post office. It was an awful shame . . .

—All the love letters Pádraig Chaitríona wrote to my daughter, you opened them beforehand. I myself never opened one of them without seeing where you had torn it. *Honest!* They reminded me of the letters I used to get years before. I got the postman to deliver them into my own hand. Foreign fragrance. Foreign paper. Foreign writing. Foreign stamps. Foreign postmarks that were poetry in themselves: Marseilles, Port Said, Singapore, Honolulu, Batavia, San Francisco . . . Sun. Oranges. Blue seas. Golden complexions. Coral islands. Gold-embroidered mantles. Ivory teeth. Lips that were aflame . . . I'd press them to my heart. I'd kiss them with my lips. I'd shed a salt tear on them . . . I'd open them. I'd take out the *billet doux*. And then, Postmistress, I'd see your clumsy, greasy fingermark on them. *Ugh!*

—You opened the letter I sent home to my wife, when I was working on the turf[4] in Kildare. There were nine pounds in it. You kept them . . .

—Why wouldn't I? Why didn't you register it? . . .

—Don't you think the oldest resident of the graveyard should have something to say? Permission to speak. Permission . . .

—Indeed, Postmistress, I have no reason to thank yourself or your daughter, or Billyboy the Post who used to give you a hand in the back room. After I came back from London there wasn't a letter I got from there you didn't open. There was an *affaire de coeur*, as Nóra Sheáinín would say. You told the whole country about it. The priest and the Schoolmistress—my wife—heard about it . . .

—That's defamation, Master. If I were above ground I'd have the law on you . . .

—The time Baba wrote to me from America about the will, that chatterbox Nell was able to tell Pádraig what she had to say:

---

4. A government scheme of employment in cutting and distributing turf during World War II.

"I haven't made my will yet. I hope I don't meet with an accidental death, as you imagined I might in your letter . . ."

You opened it, mangy buttocks. You took a backhander from Nell.

—Not at all, Caitríona Pháidín. The letter about the will wasn't the one I opened at all; it was the letter O'Brien the Attorney in Brightcity sent you, threatening to sue you within seven days if you didn't pay Holland and Company for the *roundtable* you bought five or six years previously . . .

—Ababúna! Don't believe her, the mangy little bitch! Muraed! Muraed! . . . Did you hear what the Postmistress said? I'll explode! I'll explode . . .

4

—. . . I'll tell you a story now, my good man:

"Columkille[5] was in Aran the time St. Paul came to visit him there. Paul wanted to have the whole Island to himself.

"'I'll open a pawnshop,' said Paul.

"'Faith then, you will not,' said Columkille, 'but I'm telling you now in plain Irish you'll have to clear off.'

"Then he spoke to him in the ancient legal language of Féne.[6] He spoke to him in Latin. He spoke to him in Greek. He spoke to him in baby-language. He spoke to him in Esperanto. Columkille knew the seven languages of the Holy Ghost. He was the only one to be left that gift by the other apostles when they died . . .

"'*Very well*,' said Columkille, 'if you won't clear off, in pursuance of the powers invested in me, we'll solve the problem thus. You'll go to East Aran and I'll go to the West End of the island at Bungowla. Each of us will say Mass at sunrise tomorrow. We'll then walk towards

---

5. A parody of a folktale well known in Conamara as well as the Aran Islands, usually told as concerning Sts. Enda and Brickan dividing the largest of the three Aran Islands between them.

6. The dominant Celtic race element in ancient Ireland.

each other, and each of us can have as much of the island as he has walked by the time we meet.'

"'It's a bargain,' said Paul, in Yiddish. Columkille said Mass and then he walked towards East Aran, which accounts for the old saying, 'to come on you from the northwest' . . ."

—But, Cóilí, Seán Chite in Donagh's Village used to say that Columkille didn't say Mass at all . . .

—Seán Chite said that! Seán Chite is a heretic . . .

—Seán Chite should mind what he's saying! Didn't God—praise be to Him forever!—give a revelation there and then. The sun was up when Columkille was saying Mass. It set again then, and God kept it set till Columkille had walked the island to East Aran. That's when St. Paul saw it rising for the first time! . . .

"'Clear off now and be quick about it, you Jew-man,' said Columkille. 'I'll leave a castration mark on you, on your way back to the Wailing Wall: I'll give you a horsewhipping like the one Christ gave you out of the Temple. Have you no shame at all! I wouldn't mind but you're so slithery and greasy looking! . . .'

"That's why no Jew ever settled on Aran since . . ."

—The way I used to hear that story, Cóilí, from old people in our own village, was: the time the two Patricks[7]—Old Patrick, alias Cothraighe, alias Calprainnovetch, and Young Patrick—were travelling all over Ireland, trying to convert the country . . .

—The two Patricks. That's heresy . . .

—. . . There was such a day, Peadar the Pub. Don't deny it . . .

—. . . Master, dear, the bed was very hard. Very hard indeed under my poor buttocks, Master . . .

—I was bedridden for only a month myself, Máirtín Pockface, and I felt it hard enough . . .

—My back was completely blistered, Master. There wasn't a shred of skin on my thighs . . .

—The devil a shred then, Máirtín, you poor thing . . .

---

7. There is a theory that two saints of the name of Patrick evangelized Ireland.

—The devil a shred, indeed, Master, dear, and there was an old injury in my groin. The bed was . . .

—Let us forget the bed now till some other time. Tell me this now, Máirtín Pockface, how is . . . ?

—The Schoolmistress, Master. In the bloom of youth, so she is. Earning her salary in the school every day, Master, and caring for Billyboy from night till morning. She slips over from the school twice a day to see him, and they say she gets very little sleep, the creature, sitting on the edge of the bed and plying him with medicinal draughts . . .

—The hussy . . .

—Did you hear, Master, that she brought three doctors from Dublin to see him? Our own doctor comes to see him every day, but I'd say, Master, the same Billyboy has had it. He's lying down for so long now that he must have bedsores . . .

—May his lying be long and without relief! The thirty-seven diseases of the Ark on him! Hardening of the tubes and stoppage on him! Graveyard club-foot and crossed bowel on him! May the pangs of labour consume him! May the Yellow Plague consume him! May the Plague of Lazarus consume him! May the Lamentations of Job consume him! May swine-fever consume him! May his arse be knotted! May cattle-pine, bog lameness,[8] warbles, wireworm, haw and staggers consume him! May the squelching of Keelin daughter of Olltár consume him! May the Hag of Beare's diseases of old age consume him! Blinding without light on him, and the blinding of Ossian on top of that! May the itch of the Prophet's women consume him! Swelling of knees on him! The red tracks of a tail-band[9] on him! The sting of fleas on him! . . .

—Bedsores are the worst of them all, Master dear . . .

—May bedsores consume him too, Máirtín Pockface.

—She does the Stations of the Cross for him, day and night, Master, and a visit to St. Ina's Well once a week. She made the pil-

---

8. Aphosphorosis. Phosphate deficiency causing lameness in cattle.

9. A strap passing under a horse's or donkey's tail.

grimage to Knock Shrine for him this year, the pilgrimage to Croagh Patrick, to St. Columkille's Well, to St. Mary's Well, to St. Augustine's Well, to St. Enda's Well, to St. Bernan's Well, to St. Callen's Well, to St. Mac Dara's Well, to St. Bodkin's Well, to Conderg's Bed, to St. Brigid's Well, to the Lake of the Saints and to Lough Derg . . .

—A pity I'm not alive! I'd empty St. Brickan's Well[10] against the thief, against the . . .

—She told me, Master, only for the shaky state of the world, she'd go to Lourdes.

"Lough Derg[11] is worse than any of them, Máirtín Pockface," she said. "My feet were bleeding for three days. But I wouldn't mind all the suffering if it did poor Billyboy some good. I'd crawl on my hands and knees from here to . . ."

—The hussy . . .

—"I was broken-hearted after the Big Master," she said . . .

—Oh, the hussy . . . If you only knew, Máirtín Pockface! But you wouldn't understand. It would be no use telling you . . .

—Well, the way it is, Master, the bed was so hard . . .

—To hell with yourself and your bed, give it a rest! . . . Oh, the things that hussy said to me, Máirtín! . . .

—Faith then, I suppose so, Master . . .

—The two of us seated below by the Creek. The gentle lapping of the tide licking the flat rock at our feet. A young seagull encouraged by his father and mother on his first flutterings, like a shy bride making her way to the altar. Shadows of nightfall fumbling at the feet of the setting sun on the wave crests, like a blindfolded child groping to "tip" the other children. The plashing of the oars of a currach on its return from the fishing-ground. Holding her in my arms, Máirtín. A lock of her abundant tresses brushing against my cheek. Her arms around my neck. I reciting poetry:

---

10. To empty the water out of Tobar Bhriocáin in Ros Muc was regarded as a way of putting a curse on someone.

11. The penitential rituals associated with the pilgrimage to Lough Derg in Donegal are very severe.

"Glen Masan:
White its stalks of tall wild garlic.
Uneasy was our sleep
Above the long-maned firth of Masan.

"'If ever you come, love, come discreetly.
Come to the door that makes no creaking.
If my father asks me who are your people,
I'll tell him you are the wind in the treetops.'"

Either that or telling her love-stories, Máirtín . . .

—I know what you mean, Master . . .

—The Sons of Uisneach, Diarmuid and Gráinne, Tristan and Isolde, Strong Thomas Costelloe and Fair Oonagh McDermot Ogue, Carol O'Daly and Eleanor of the Secrets, *The Red-Hot Kiss*, *The Powder-puff* . . .

—I know what you mean, Master . . .

—I bought a motor car, Máirtín, for the sole purpose of taking her out. I could ill afford it but I didn't begrudge it to her, all the same. We went together to films in Brightcity, to dances in Wood of the Oxen, to teachers' meetings . . .

—Indeed you did, and you went the Mountain Road, Master. One day when I was fetching a cartload of turf, your car was by the roadside at the Steep Hillock and the two of you were over in the glen . . .

—We'll forget about that till some other time, Máirtín Pock-face . . .

—Faith then, I remember the day I got the form for the pension. Nobody in the house knew from the soles of the devil what it was. "The Big Master is our man," says I. I went as far as Peadar the Pub's and I stayed there till the pupils had gone home. Over I went then. When I got to the school gate there wasn't a grunt or a groan from inside. "I left it too late," said I, letting on to be mannerly. "He's gone home." I looked in through the window. Faith then, begging your pardon, Master, you were screwing her inside . . .

—I was not, I was not, Máirtín Pockface.

—Faith then, you were, Master, there's nothing better than the truth . . .

—Had Dad, Master!

—You should be ashamed of yourself, Master.

—Who would think it, Bríd?

—Our children were going to school to him, Cite . . .

—If the priest had caught him, Siúán . . .

—It was Pentecost Monday, Máirtín Pockface. I had the day off. "You should come to Ross Harbour," said I to her, after lunch. "The outing will do you good." Off we went. That night in Ross Harbour I thought, Máirtín Pockface, I got to know the secret of her heart more than ever before . . . The long summer's day was losing its light at long last. The pair of us were leaning on a rock, looking at the stars glittering in the sea . . .

—I know what you mean, Master . . .

—Looking at the candles being lit in houses on the headlands across the bay. Looking at the phosphorescence on the seaweed left by the receding tide. Looking at the Milky Way like bright sparkling dust out beyond the mouth of Galway Bay. That night, Máirtín Pockface, I felt I was part of the stars and of the lights, of the phosphorescence, of the Milky Way and of the fragrant sighing of sea and air . . .

—I know what you mean, Master. That's how it was, I suppose . . .

—She told me, Máirtín Pockface, that her love for me was deeper than the sea; that it was more sincere and more certain than sunrise or sunset; that it was more constant than the ebbing or the flowing tide, than the stars or the hills, because it was there before tide, star or hill. She told me her love for me was eternity itself . . .

—She did, Master . . .

—She did, Máirtín Pockface. She did, upon my word!

. . . But hold on. I was on my death-bed, Máirtín Pockface. She came in after doing the Stations of the Cross and she sat on the edge of the bed. She took my hand. She said if anything should happen to me that her life after me would not be life at all, and that her death would not be death to her if we both would die together. She swore and she promised, whether she lived for a long time or for short, that she'd spend it in mourning. She swore and she promised she'd never marry again . . .

—She did now, Master . . .

—By God she did, Máirtín Pockface! And after all that, see how the serpent was in her heart. I was only a year under the sod—a short miserable year compared to the eternity she promised me—and she was making promises to another man, with another man's kisses on her mouth, and another man's love in her heart. Me, her first love and husband, under the cold sods, and she in the arms of Billyboy the Post . . .

—In the arms of Billyboy the Post, then, Master! I saw them myself . . . There are many things one should turn a blind eye to, Master . . .

—And now he's in my bed, and she giving him full and plenty, tending to him night and morning, going on pilgrimages for him, sending to Dublin for three doctors . . . Had she brought even one doctor from Dublin to me, I would have recovered . . .

—Would you believe what she said to me about you, Master? I called on her with a little bag of potatoes a week after you were buried. We spoke about you. "The Big Master is a great loss," said I, "and the poor man had no cause to die. If he had gone to bed with that cold, minded himself, drank a few whiskeys, and sent for the doctor when it first came on . . ." "Do you know what it is, Máirtín Pockface?" she said. I'll never forget the words she said, Master. "Do you know what it is, Máirtín Pockface, all the physicians of the Fianna wouldn't cure the Big Master. He was too good for this life . . ." Yes indeed, Master, and she said another thing I never heard before. It's probably some old saying, Master. "He whom the gods love, dies young . . ."

—The hussy! The hussy! The promiscuous little hussy . . .

—*De grâce*, Master. Watch your language. Don't make a Caitríona Pháidín of yourself. The curate came in to her one day. He was new in the place. He didn't know where Nell's house was. "Nell, the bitch," said Caitríona. *Honest!* . . .

—You Filthy-Feet damsel! You *So-an'-so!* . . . Muraed! . . .

—. . . He had Big Brian pestered every Friday when he was collecting the pension. "You'd better take out a bit of insurance on yourself soon, Briany," the scoundrel would say. "Any day now you'll be going the County Clare Way[12] . . ."

—"There isn't a thing in creation that creeping little scrounger wouldn't take insurance on," said Big Brian to me one Friday in the post office, "except Nell Pháidín's little dog, that has a habit of sniffing around in Caitríona's house whenever it passes up the boreen."

—I was over there collecting the pension with Brian the day he was buried.

"The Insurance Man didn't live long himself," said I.

"That's him gone west now, the windbag," said Brian, "and if he goes up above, he'll have the Man Above demented, droning on about that accident long ago, and trying to get him to insure his *property* of saints and angels against sparks from the Man Below. If the Man Below gets him, he'll have him demented, pestering him to insure his few embers against the water-cocks of the Man Above. The best thing for both of them to do with the cheeky little leech would be to play Tomás Inside's trick: every time he gets annoyed at Nell's cattle coming onto his patch of land, he turns them in to Caitríona's land, and Caitríona's cattle in to Nell's land . . ."

—Did you hear what he said when Road-End Man died? "By cripes, lads, St. Peter had better watch his keys now, or this new tenant of his will walk off with them . . ."

—Arrah, that's nothing compared to what he said to Tomás Inside when Caitríona died:

"Tomás, you snow-white angel," said he, "yourself and Nell and Baba and Nóra Sheáinín's daughter will be visiting the harness-maker often, to get your broken wings mended, if God grants you to be on the same roost as herself. I myself have a very slim chance of get-

---

12. Euphemism for dying.

ting any wings at all, I'd say. Caitríona wouldn't consider my *valuation* high enough. But, by Dad, Tomás, you blessed dove, your wings would be quite safe if I managed to get any little lobster hole of a lodging near her ..."

—Ababúna! Brian the wretch near me! God forbid tonight! Oh, what would I do? ...

—What the Postmistress said about my death was—that she didn't manage to open a single letter for days, as she had to attend to so many telegrams ...

—My death was in the newspaper ...

—My death was in two newspapers ...

—Listen to this account from the *Reporter* about my death:

"He was a member of a well-known old local family. He played a prominent part in the national movement. He was a personal friend of Éamon de Valera's ..."

—This is the account that was in the *Irishman* about me:

"He came from a family that was well-respected in the locality. He joined Fianna Éireann[13] as a child, and afterwards the Irish Volunteers.[14] He was a close friend of Arthur Griffith's ..."

—... And Cóilí recited "The Tale of the Pullet that Laid on the Dung-heap" at your wake too.

—You're a liar! What a story to tell at any decent wake! ...

—Wasn't I listening to him! ...

—You're a liar! You were not ...

—... A row at your wake! A row where there was nobody but two old-age pensioners!

—And one of them as deaf as Tomás Inside, whenever Caitríona suggested he should come with her to see Mannion the Counsellor about the land.

—Yes indeed, and not a vessel in the house that wasn't filled with holy water.

---

13. A nationalistic youth movement on the lines of the Boy Scouts.
14. A military organisation dedicated to the fight for Irish independence.

—There was a row at my wake . . .

—There was. Tomás Inside took exception to Big Brian telling him: "You've thrown back so much of Éamon of the Hill Field's 'fresh milk' since you came in, Tomás, you should have enough for a churning by now."

—I had two half-barrels at my wake . . .

—I had three half-barrels at my wake . . .

—You had indeed, Caitríona, three half-barrels at your wake. That's the God's honest truth, Caitríona. You had three—three fine big ones—and a splash of the waterworks of Éamon of the Hill Field as well . . . Old and all as I was, I drank twelve mugfuls of it myself. To tell you the truth, Caitríona, I wouldn't have dreamed of taking that much if I'd known my heart was faulty. I said to myself, Caitríona, when I saw the lashings of porter: "This man would be better off buying a colt than making those loudmouths drunk . . ."

—You sourpuss! . . .

—They were nothing else. Some of them were stretched like hulks in everybody's way. Peadar Nell fell into the bed you were laid out on, Caitríona. His injured leg couldn't prop him up . . .

—The dirty sponger!

—That was nothing, till Bríd Terry's son and Cite's son began to trounce one another, and they broke the *roundtable* before they could be separated . . .

—Ababúna! . . .

—I went to separate them. Faith then, if I'd known the heart was faulty . . .

—. . . Indeed, it seemed to me you were laid out in a very common way, unless there was something wrong with my eyes . . .

—There must be something wrong with your eyes if you didn't see the two crosses on my breast . . .

—There were two crosses and the Scapular Mantle on me . . .

—Whatever was or was not on me, Cite, there wasn't a dirty sheet on me as there was on Caitríona . . .

—Ababúna! Don't believe that little slut . . .

—. . . Your coffin was made by the little carpenter in Mangy Field. He made another one for Nóra Sheáinín and it was like a bird-trap . . .

—You had a carpenter-made coffin yourself as well . . .

—If I had, it wasn't made by the Mangy Field botcher, but by a carpenter who served his full apprenticeship. He had his certificate from the *Tech.*[15] . . .

—My coffin cost ten pounds . . .

—I thought you had one of the eight-pound coffins like the one Caitríona had . . .

—You liar! you dolt! I had the best coffin in Tadhg's . . .

—It was Little Cáit laid me out . . .

—It was Little Cáit laid me out too, and Bid Shorcha keened me . . .

—Indeed, she keened you badly. There's some stoppage in Bid's throat that doesn't dissolve till she has her seventh glass. That's when she starts singing *"Let Erin Remember"* . . .

—I think Caitríona Pháidín wasn't keened at all, unless her son's wife and Nell did a bout of it . . .

—. . . Six pounds, five shillings is all the altar-money that was collected at your funeral . . .

—I had ten pounds of altar-money.

—Hold on now till I see how much was collected at mine: 20 by 10 plus 19, equals 190 . . . plus 20, equals 210 shillings . . . equals 10 pounds, 10 shillings. Isn't that right, Master? . . .

—Peadar the Pub had a big altar collection . . .

—And Nóra Sheáinín . . .

—Faith then, there was a big collection of altar-money at Nóra Sheáinín's funeral. There would have been a big collection at my funeral too but nobody knew about it, I went off so suddenly. The heart, God help us! If only I'd been bedridden for a long time with bedsores . . .

---

15. Technical or vocational school.

—I would have had an even fourteen pounds, only for a dud shilling in the collection. It was only a halfpenny wrapped in silver cigarette paper. It was Big Brian noticed it when he felt the pig on the halfpenny. He says it was Caitríona put it there. Many is the bad shilling like that she left on altars. She wanted to be on every altar, which she couldn't afford, the poor woman . . .

—You scrawny little liar . . .

—Oh, I forgive you, Caitríona. I wouldn't mind at all, only for the priest: "They'll be leaving their old teeth on the table for me soon," he said.

—It was "Pól" here and "Pól" there from yourself and your daughter, Peadar the Pub, the time she played the parlour trick on the Gaelic Enthusiast. But there was no mention of Pól when it was time for you to put a shilling on my altar . . .

—I tied Tomáisín, although I'd drunk two score pints and two, and still not a single one of that household came to my funeral, though they're living in the same village as me. They hardly put a shilling on my altar. They all had a cold, they said. That was all the thanks I got, even though he'd grabbed the hatchet. Can you imagine, if he had to be tied again? . . .

—I didn't have a big funeral. The people of Donagh's Village had gone to England, and the people of Mangy Field, Sive's Rocks . . .

—. . . What do you think of Caitríona Pháidín, Cite, who didn't set foot in my house from the moment my father died till he was put in the coffin, after all the pounds of his tea she drank . . .

—Those were the days she went to Mannion the Counsellor about Tomás Inside's land . . .

—Do you hear that slut Bríd Terry, and mangy Cite of the Ash-Potatoes?

—Three times I had to put my hand over the mouth of that old empty-head over there, when he was trying to sing "Mártan Sheáin Mhóir Had a Daughter" at your funeral, Curraoin.

—The whole country was at our funeral, newspaper people and photographers and . . .

—For a very good reason! You people were killed by the *mine*. If you had died in the old bed as I did, there'd be very few newspaper people there . . .

—There was *bien de monde* at the funeral *à moi. Le Ministre de France* came from Dublin and he laid a *couronne mortuaire* on my grave . . .

—There was a representative from Éamon de Valera at my funeral and the tricolour on my coffin . . .

—There was a telegram from Arthur Griffith at my funeral and shots were fired over my grave . . .

—You're a liar!

—You are the liar! I was the First Lieutenant of the First Company of the First Battalion of the First Brigade . . .

—You're a liar!

—God help us, forever and ever! Pity they didn't bring my heap of clay out east of Brightcity . . .

—The Big Butcher from Brightcity came to my funeral. He had respect for me, and his father had respect for my father. He often told me that he himself had respect for me on account of his father having respect for my father . . .

—The doctor came to my funeral. That was hardly any wonder, of course. My sister Kate has two sons doctors in America . . .

—You've just said it! It was hardly any wonder. It would have been totally shameful if he didn't come to your funeral, after all the money you left him over the years. Twisting your ankle at all times of day and night . . .

—The Big Master and the Schoolmistress were at my funeral . . .

—The Big Master and the Schoolmistress and the Red-haired Policeman were at my funeral . . .

—The Big Master and the Schoolmistress and the Red-haired Policeman and the priest's sister were at my funeral . . .

—The priest's sister! Was she wearing the trousers?

—It's a wonder Mannion the Counsellor didn't come to Caitríona Pháidín's funeral . . .

—A wonder indeed, or the priest's sister . . .

DEIRFIÚR AN tSAGAIRT

—Or even the Red-haired Policeman . . .

—Checking dog licences in Donagh's Village he was that day . . .

—No dog would live on the flea-bitten hillocks of your village . . .

—. . . "Tomás Inside was there, grinning and jolly,
For it was Nell would marry him since Caty was
dead . . ."

—I assure you, Caitríona Pháidín, if it cost me my life's blood I'd be at your funeral. I owed it to Caitríona Pháidín to come to her funeral, even if it was on my two knees. But devil a word I heard about it till the night you were buried . . .

—A right blatherer you are, Sweet-talking Stiofán. Are you here long? I didn't know you had arrived. The epidemic . . .

—. . . There was a big crowd at my funeral. The Parish Priest, the Curate, the Lake Side Curate, a Franciscan and two Religious Brothers from Brightcity, the Wood of the Lake Master and School-mistress, the West Side Master and Schoolmistress, the Sive's Rocks Master, the Little Glen Master and the Sub-Mistress. The Assistant in Kill . . .

—There was indeed, Master dear, and Billyboy the Post. To give him his due, he was most obliging that day. He tightened the bolts on the coffin and he was under the coffin leaving the house, and he lowered it into the grave. Faith, to give him his due, he was willing and able. He stripped off his jacket there and grabbed a shovel . . .

—The thief! The lusty lout!

—. . . There were five cars at my funeral . . .

—The car belonging to that clown in Wood of the Lake, who got the legacy, got stuck in the middle of the road and your funeral was delayed for an hour . . .

—There were as many as thirty cars at Peadar the Pub's funeral. There were two hearses under him . . .

—Faith then, as you say, there was a hearse under me as well. The old lady wouldn't be happy till she got one: "His poor guts would get too much of a shaking on people's shoulders or an old cart," she said . . .

—It was easy for her, Road-End Man, with my turf . . .

—And with my seaweed wrack.

—. . . With such an abundance of drink at Caitriona Pháidín's funeral, there weren't enough people fit to carry her coffin to the church. And even they began shouting and fighting among themselves. The corpse had to be set down twice, with the state they were in. Indeed it had: on the bare road . . .

—Ababúna!

—I'm telling you the bare truth, Caitríona dear. There were only six of us from Walsh's Pub onward. The rest went into Walsh's or they dropped out along the way. We thought we'd have to put women under the corpse . . .

—Ababúna! Don't believe him, the sourpuss . . .

—That's the honest truth, Caitríona. You were very heavy. You weren't long bedridden or suffering from bedsores.

"The two old men will have to go under her," said Peadar Nell when we reached the Sive's Rocks Boreen. We were glad to have the old men, Caitríona. Peadar Nell himself was on crutches and Cite's son and Bríd Terry's son were snapping at one another again: each of them trying to blame the other for breaking the *roundtable* the night before. There's nothing better than the truth, Caitríona dear. Faith, I wouldn't have shouldered your coffin myself, nor would I have accompanied you one foot of the way, had I known at the time that the heart was so faulty . . .

—Bloated on periwinkle soup you were, you snarling sourpuss . . .

—"She wants to act the stubborn mule even now. My soul from the devil, whether she likes it or not, she's going to the chapel and to the grave," said Big Brian, as himself and myself and Cite's son went under you, to carry you up the path to the chapel . . .

"Devil a word of a lie you said, father-in-law," said Peadar Nell, as he threw away the crutches and thrust himself under you . . .

—Ababúna forever and ever! The son of the pussface under me! Big Brian under me! The bearded streak of misery. Of course the coffin was lopsided if that flat-footed round-shouldered slouch was under me. Ababúna búna! . . . Big Brian! Nell's son! Muraed!

Muraed! . . . If I'd known, Muraed, I'd explode. I'd explode there and then . . .

6

—. . . And do you tell me you can't insure colts?

—An insurance agent like myself wouldn't do it, Seáinín.

—You'd think you wouldn't be taking any risk at all on a fine young colt. It would be a great help, if anything should happen to it, to get a fistful of money . . .

—I nearly got a fistful myself, Seáinín, in the crossword competition in the *Sunday News*. Five hundred pounds . . .

—Five hundred pounds! . . .

—Yes, indeed, Seáinín. I was only one letter out . . .

—I see . . .

—What they wanted was a four-letter word beginning with "j." The clue said the meaning of the word was "prison."

—I see.

—I immediately thought of the word "gaol," but that begins with "g" . . .

—I see.

—"That's not it," says I. I spent a long time deliberating and hesitating. In the end I put down "jaol" . . .

—I see.

—And do you know, when the solution came out in the paper, the word was "jail"! Bad luck forever to the simplified spelling,[16] Seáinín! If I had a gun handy I'd have done away with myself. That had a lot to do with shortening my life.

—I see what you mean now . . .

—. . . By the oak of this coffin, Sweet-talking Stiofán, I gave Caitríona the pound . . .

—. . . She had that sweet smile on her face . . .

—That sweet smile proved unfortunate for the Small Master!

---

16. Spelling reform of the Irish language, 1948.

But for the grace of God he'll end up like the Big Master. There's a jinx on that school of ours that the masters are unlucky with their wives . . .

—. . . The advice I sent in a letter to Concannon after he won the All-Ireland semi-final for Galway:

"Concannon, my friend," says I, "if you can't hit the ball in the final against Kerry, hit something else! There must be a levelling of conditions. The referee will be on the side of Kerry anyhow. You're the man to do it. You have the strength and the skill. Every time you hit something I'll raise three shouts of triumph for you . . ."

—. . . Hitler is my darling! When he comes over to England! . . . I think he'll shovel that same England down to hell altogether: he'll sweep away that scuttering bloated pig of an England like the donkey that was carried away by the wind: he'll place million-ton mines under her navel . . .

—May God save us! . . .

—Faith then, England is not to be condemned. There's great employment there. What would the youth of Donagh's Village do without her, or the people of Mangy Field, or Sive's Rocks? . . .

—Or this old gadfly over here who has a patch of land at the top of the village that can't be beaten for fattening cattle . . .

—. . . *Après la fuite de Dunkerque et le bouleversement de Juin 1940, Monsieur Churchill a dit qu'il retournerait pour libérer la France, la terre sacrée* . . .

—. . . You shouldn't allow any black heretic to insult your religion like that, Peadar. Oh, Lord, I wish it had been me! I'd question him like this, Peadar: "Do you even know there is a God? Of course, you're like a cow or a calf, or like . . . or like a puppy." All a dog worries about is filling his belly. A dog would eat meat on a Friday[17] too, so he would. Oh, he wouldn't have the least aversion to it. But, all the same, it's not every dog would do it . . . I had a bit of meat left over at home once. "I'll put it aside till Saturday," says I. "Tomorrow is 'avoid-the-joint' day." After dinner-time on Friday I was coming in from the

---

17. It was customary for Catholics to abstain from eating meat on a Friday.

garden with a handful of potatoes when I saw the Protestant Minister passing by, on his way up the mountain after fowl. "You would, you black heretic," said I. "You'll not even let Friday pass without fresh meat. You're like a cow or a calf . . . or like a puppy." When I went in with my handful of potatoes, the staple was off the dresser door. Every scrap of the meat was gone! "A cat or a dog for certain," said I. "When I catch hold of you, you won't get away with it. To go eating meat on a Friday. It serves me right, for not putting them out and closing the door after me!" I found them at the back of the house. The Minister's dog was gobbling the meat and my own dog barking at him, trying to stop him. I grabbed the pitchfork. "Easily known whose dog you are," says I, "eating meat on a Friday." I tried to bury the pitchfork up to the handle in him. The dirty thing managed to escape. I offered the meat to our own dog. May God forgive me! I shouldn't be tempting him. He wouldn't go next or near it. Devil a bit of him. Now, what do you think! He knew it wasn't right . . . Why didn't you tell him that, Peadar, and not allow him to insult your religion. Lord, if I'd been there! . . .

—How could I? The Minister's dog never stole a bit of meat off me . . .

—But the Spanish eat meat every Friday of their life, and they are Catholics.

—That's a lie, you windbag!

—The Pope gave them permission . . .

—That's a lie. You're a black heretic . . .

—. . . Do you tell me that, Master dear? If they'd rubbed me with—what's this you call it, Master?—methylated spirits—in time, I'd have no bedsores. Oh, Master dear, I had nobody to give me proper care. Dimwits. You can't beat the learning after all. Methylated spirits. Pity I didn't know about that! It comes in a bottle, you say. By Dad, Master, they must be the bottles the Schoolmistress buys from Peadar the Pub's daughter. I was told she buys an awful lot of them. For Billyboy . . .

—Not them, Máirtín Pockface. They'd never be in a pub. She's drinking, the hussy. Drinking for certain. Or else Billyboy is drinking. Or the pair of them. What a way to spend good money, Máirtín Pockface . . .

—I assure you, Máirtín Pockface, even if it cost me my life's blood, I would have been at your funeral. I owed it to you to come to your funeral, Máirtín Pockface, if I had to go there on my knees . . .

—Muraed! Muraed! . . . Do you hear Sweet-talking Stiofán babbling again? He'd turn your stomach. Hey, Muraed! Do you hear me? Hey, Muraed . . . You're not paying much heed recently. Do you hear me, Muraed? . . . It was time for you to speak . . . I was talking about that babbler, Sweet-talking Stiofán. I didn't know he had arrived at all till very recently. They're a very unmannerly bunch here, Muraed. They wouldn't tell a person anything. See how they kept the news about Sweet-talking Stiofán from me . . .

Oh, I know that Máirtín Pockface has arrived, Muraed. I was talking to him. They tried to bury him on top of me . . .

True for you, Muraed: if a person has a cross over him, it's easy to identify the grave. It won't be too long now till my own cross is ready, but they say the Island limestone is being used up: that it's difficult to get a proper headstone for a cross there. Máirtín Pockface says you have to curry favour to get a stone there at all now. But he told me my own cross is being speeded up all the same . . .

You say he didn't, Muraed . . . There's so much limestone on the island that it will never be used up! Now, Muraed, that sort of dishonesty will get you nowhere. Why would I tell a lie about the good man? Neither he nor I has been conniving in the land of lies, since we were stacked away in this haggard . . .

You say my son's wife said that, Muraed: "We'll be very well off in life before we start buying crosses." I see, faith. You were listening at back doors again, Muraed, as you were in the Land Above . . . Now Muraed, it's no use denying it. You used to listen at back doors. The tale you told Dotie and Nóra Sheáinín here about my life, where else did you get it but at my back door?

Oh, you were listening to me talking to myself going the road! . . . and behind the wall when I was working in the field! Well, Muraed, isn't it as decent to listen at the back door as it is to listen in the road-way and behind the wall . . .

Listen here to me, Muraed! Why has everyone in the graveyard turned against me? Why don't they get someone else to chew the cud over? It's because . . .

It's not because of having no cross over me, you say! What else? What else, so?

The people of the cemetery didn't like me since I refused to co-operate! How do you mean, I didn't co-operate, Muraed? . . .

I see, now. I voted against Nóra Sheáinín! Don't you know in your heart and soul, Muraed, that I couldn't do anything else. That scruffy Filthy-Feet. That godsend to sailors, that *So-an'-so* . . .

She was the Fifteen-Shilling joint-candidate after all, you say. And you didn't mind filthy feet or ducks or sailors or drinking behind closed doors, or being a *So-an'-so*, Muraed . . .

What did you say the Master called me? . . . "*Scab*." He called me "*Scab*" for voting against the Fifteen-Shilling crowd, Muraed. But I didn't vote against the Fifteen-Shilling crowd. I voted against Nóra fat-arse Sheáinín. You know yourself that our people above ground always voted the same way. Nell is the one who changed. It was Nell, the pussface, who was disloyal. She voted for this new crowd because she got a road built to her house . . .

The Master called me that too. Say it again, Muraed . . . "*Bowsie!*"[18] "*Bowsie*," Muraed! . . . because I spoke to Siúán the Shop even though she'd insulted me before that! Good God! I never spoke to her, Muraed. She spoke to me, Muraed. I'll tell the Master that. I will indeed, I'll tell him out straight. "Caitríona," she said, "Caitríona Pháidín, do you hear me?" she said. "I'm thankful to you for giving us your vote. You were a courageous woman . . ."

I didn't even pretend, Muraed, to hear the tight-arse. If I'd answered her at all I'd have said to her: "You stuck-up wench, I didn't vote for you or for Peadar the Pub or for the Pound crowd, I voted against that *So-an'-so*, Nóra Sheáinín . . ."

---

18. Dublin slang for blackguard.

He said I was a *turncoat* for having spoken to Nóra Sheáinín . . . trying to make up to her . . . after vilifying her ever since I came into the graveyard . . . Good God Almighty, Muraed! That I spoke to Nóra Sheáinín! . . . What's that, Muraed? . . . He called me that. The Master! He must have meant Nóra Sheáinín, Muraed. Who else! . . .

He called me a *So-an'-so*, Muraed? A *So-an'-so!* I'll explode. I'll explode! I'll explode . . .

Interlude Seven

THE MOULDING OF THE CLAY

1

I am the Trump of the Graveyard. Let my voice be heard! It must be heard . . .

Here in the graveyard is the parchment whose obscure words are the web of mankind's dreams; whose faded ink is mankind's defiant struggle; whose withered leaves are the ages of mankind's vanity . . .

Above ground, land, sea and sky are a fresh, ornate manuscript. Every hedge is a majestic curve. Every boreen is a streamline of colour. Every field of corn is a golden letter. Every sunlit hilltop and winding land-locked bay with its white sails is a compound sentence of beauty. Each cloud is a glorious dot of lenition[1] on the purple capital letters of peak-tops. The rainbow is an apostrophe between the wonderful hemisphere of the sky and the wonderful hemisphere of the earth. For this scribe's task is to publish the gospel of beauty on the parchment of land, sea and sky . . .

But already the deciduous trees on the mountain summit are a gapped sentence. The cliff on the steep seashore is a dark full stop. Out there on the horizon the half-formed letter ends in a blot of ink . . .

The colour is drying on the brush and the scribe's hand feels writer's cramp . . .

---

1. In the old Irish script, a dot placed over a consonant, indicating a softening of the sound.

The graveyard demands its due . . . I am the Trump of the Grave-yard. Let my voice be heard! It must be heard . . .

2

—. . . Who are you? . . . Who are you, I say? . . . Are you deaf or what? Or dumb . . . Who are you? . . . The devil take your rotten soul, who are you? . . .

—I don't know . . .

—By the testimony of the blenny![2] Red-haired Tom! Why are you making strange, Tom? I'm Caitríona Pháidín . . .

—Caitríona Pháidín. You're Caitríona Pháidín. Now, then. Caitríona Pháidín. Caitríona Pháidín, then . . .

—Yes, Caitríona Pháidín. You don't have to make the Tale of the Yellow Calf[3] about it. How are they up there?

—How are they up there? Up there. Up there indeed . . .

—Why can't you answer a person who speaks to you, Red-haired Tom? How are they up there?

—Some of them well. Some of them unwell . . .

—A fine bringer of news you are! Who's well and who's unwell?

—It's a wise man could say, Caitríona. It's a wise man could say, Caitríona. It's a wise man could say who's well and who's unwell. It's a wise man, faith . . .

—Since you lived in the next village, don't you know whether our Pádraig and his wife and Jack the Scológ are well or unwell? . . .

—Faith then, I was in the next village, Caitríona. In the next village, sure enough. Not a word of a lie but I was in the next village, indeed . . .

—Have a bit of gumption, I tell you. You don't have to be shy here, any more than you were above ground. Who's well and who's unwell? . . .

---

2. A small shore fish.
3. A long drawn-out story.

—Little Cáit and Bid Shorcha are often ill. Faith then, they could even be bad enough . . .

—A fine story you have! I don't remember a time they weren't ill, except when there were corpses to be laid out or keened. It's high time for them to be unwell at this stage. Are they at death's door? . . . Do you hear? Are Bid Shorcha and Little Cáit at death's door? . . .

—Some people say they'll pull through. Others say they won't. It's a wise man could say . . .

—And Jack the Scológ? . . . Jack the Scológ, I said? How is he? . . . Have you got rheumatism in your tongue? . . .

—Jack the Scológ. Jack the Scológ, now. Yes indeed, Jack the Scológ. Some say he's unwell. Some say he's unwell, for certain. He could be. He could indeed . . . But many a thing is said that hasn't a grain of truth in it. Many a thing, faith. He's probably not unwell at all . . .

—Will you not quit your tomfoolery and tell me if Jack the Scológ is confined to bed . . .

—I don't know, Caitríona. I don't know, faith. Unless I tell you a lie . . .

—"Unless you tell me a lie!" As if it would be your first lie! How fares Nell? . . . How fares the pussface Nell?

—Nell. Yes indeed. Nell, Nell indeed. Nell and Jack the Scológ. Nell Pháidín . . .

—Yes, yes. Nell Pháidín. I asked you how she's faring . . .

—Some say she's unwell. Some say she's unwell, for certain . . .

—But is she? Or is it more of her tricks? . . .

—Some say she is. They do, definitely. She could be, faith. She could be, without a doubt. But many a thing is said . . .

—Confound your toothless gob! You must have heard if Nell is able to go in and out of the house, or if she's confined to bed . . .

—Confined to bed. She could be, faith. Faith then, she could be . . .

—Suffering Jesus! . . . Listen to me, Red-haired Tom. How is our Baba who's in America?

—Your Baba who's in America. Baba Pháidín. She's in America, sure enough. Baba Pháidín is in America, so she is . . .

—But how is she?

—I don't know. Faith then, I don't, Caitríona . . .

—It's the devil's own business if you didn't hear something about her. That she was unwell, maybe . . .

—Some say she's unwell. They do, for sure. She could be . . .

—Who says it? . . .

—Faith, unless I tell you a lie, Caitríona, I don't know. I don't indeed. Maybe there's nothing wrong with her . . .

—Who'll get her money? . . . Who'll get Baba's money?

—Baba Pháidín's money? . . .

—Yes, what else? Baba's money . . . Who'll get Baba's money? . . .

—The devil do I know, Caitríona . . .

—Did she make a will? Did our Baba make a will yet? Aren't you damned heedless! . . .

—Musha, I don't know that, Caitríona. It's a wise man could say . . .

—But what do the people of our village say about it, or the people of your own village? . . . Did they say Pádraig will get it? Or that Nell will get it?

—Some say Nell will get it. Some say Pádraig will get it. Many a thing is said without a grain of truth in it. Many a thing, indeed. I don't know myself which of them will get it. It's a wise man could say . . .

—You wordless toothless booby! Everybody so far made some sense, till you arrived! How fares Tomás Inside? . . . Tomás Inside. Do you hear me?

—I do, Caitríona. I hear that, for sure. Tomás Inside. Faith then, there is such a person, so there is, for sure. Not a word of a lie but Tomás Inside exists . . .

—Where is he now?

—In your village, Caitríona. Where else? In your village, definitely. I thought you knew well where he was, Caitríona. He was in your village all his life, I think, or am I right?

—Warbles on your stupid grin! What I asked you is where is he now? . . . Where's Tomás Inside now?

—Devil do I know, unless I tell you a lie, where he is now, Caitríona. If I knew what time of day it was, but I don't. I don't, indeed. He could be . . .

—But before you died where was he?

—In your village, Caitríona. He used to be in your village for certain. In your village, indeed.

—But which house? . . .

—Faith then, I don't know that, Caitríona . . .

—But you know if he left his own house on account of the leaking roof or something . . .

—Some say he's in Nell's house. Some say he's in Pádraig's house. Many a thing is said that . . .

—But he's not in his own house? . . . Do you hear? Tomás Inside is not in his own house? . . .

—Tomás Inside in his own house? In his own house . . . Tomás Inside in his own house. Faith then, he could well be, indeed. He could indeed. Only a wise person would say . . .

—You silly blabberer, for that's what you are, Red-haired Tom! Who has Tomás Inside's land?

—Tomás Inside's land? Faith then, he has land. Tomás Inside has land, definitely. Tomás Inside indeed has land. He has land . . .

—But who has his land now? Does Tomás himself still have it, or does our Pádraig have it, or does Nell have it? . . .

—Pádraig, Nell, Tomás Inside? Yes now, Pádraig, Nell . . .

—On the devil's tracks to hell with you, and tell me who has Tomás Inside's land! . . .

—Some say Pádraig has it. Some say Nell has it. Many a thing is said without a grain . . .

—But you are sure that Tomás Inside himself doesn't have the land? . . . You are sure, Red-haired Tom, that Tomás Inside himself doesn't have the land? . . .

—Tomás Inside himself, if he has the land? Faith then, he could have, so he could. It's a wise man could say who has Tomás Inside's land . . .

—You useless shit! What a present I got: Red-haired Tom! A heap of disease! It was the epidemic brought you here. Only for that you wouldn't come till you'd rot. Indeed, nobody would murder you on account of your tongue, anyhow! What an asset to the graveyard, you red-haired rubbish! Be off! Ugh! . . .

3

—. . . I fell off a stack of oats . . .

—. . . A white-faced mare . . .

—. . . May the devil take yourself and your useless verses! Can't you see I have enough on my mind, not knowing if my old lady at home might give the holding to the eldest son . . .

—. . . I had a patch of ground at the top of the village . . .

—. . . "Mártan Sheáin Mhóir had a daughter,
And she was as broad as any man . . ."

—. . . *Monsieur Churchill a dit qu'il retournerait pour libérer la France, la terre sacrée. Mon ami, the French Gaullistes and les Américains and les Anglais* will capture *la France.* That is *promis by Messieurs Churchill et Roosevelt . . .* That is a *prophétie . . . Prophétie . . .* Prophecy, *je crois en Irlandais . . .*

—"Foretelling" is what we call it on the fair plains of East Galway. That is the correct Old Irish . . .

—Oh! Listen to her again! . . .

—It was prophesied that the glen would be as high as the hill.[4] I remember the time when the people were afraid not to touch their hat to the Earl's bailiffs and stewards, not to mention the Earl himself. Nowadays, it's the people who expect the Earl to touch his hat

---

4. From a collection of obscure prophesies attributed to St. Columkille and widely circulated in books and by word of mouth.

to them. Upon my soul, I myself saw him one day bowing to Nell Pháidín.

—The pussface! The cocky little lump! She used to give him socks and chickens for nothing, to get the road built for her. There were no flies on that one. She knew it would benefit himself too, for the fowling . . .

—I saw him one day bowing to Nóra Sheáinín . . .

—The Earl is a cultured person. *Honest* . . .

—*Honest*, your rump, you Mangy-Feet Nóirín . . .

—. . . The "malicious egg" was in the prophecy. That was the *mine* that killed us . . .

—. . . That an *Antichrist* would come before the end of the world and that three parts of the people would convert to him. I really think we're close to it now. And the state the world is in: people on the dole gobbling meat on Friday as ravenously as any black heretic . . .

—. . . Before the end of the world comes, that there'll be a miller somewhere down the country with two heels on one of his feet. He'll be called Peadar Risteard. I've often heard it said. I was talking to the Small Master, shortly after he came to our school. I mentioned it to him. "Faith then," he said, "that man lives where I come from." He told me the name of the place too, if only I could remember it. Somewhere down the country, anyhow. "He does, upon my soul," he said. "I know him well, and there isn't a word of a lie in that story: he has two heels on one of his feet. He's a miller, and he's called Peadar Risteard . . ."

—. . . That everybody would have to dip his bread in the sweat of his own brow. And don't they?

—Not at all! Look at Billyboy the Post dipping it in the Big Master's sweat, and do you think Nell Pháidín's son, who managed to come by hundreds of pounds, is dipping it in his own sweat? And Tomás Inside is forever dipping it in the sweat of Caitríona Pháidín and Nell. Very soon now Nell will be dipping her bread in Baba's sweat . . .

—Ababúna! May she not live to see it! . . .

—. . . That a man called the Devil-Air[5] would rule over Ireland. And doesn't he?

—Arrah, that's not Columkille's prophecy you have at all . . .

—You're a liar! It is Columkille's prophecy I have . . .

—Don't believe Columkille's prophecy unless you get the right book. Only one book is true . . .

—That's the one I have: *The True Prophecies of Saint Columkille.*

—Hold on now. Allow me to speak. I'm a writer. *The True Prophecies of Saint Columkille* was a book written to deceive the public . . .

—You're a liar, you old puff-ball!

—He is indeed, and a barefaced liar!

—I'm a writer . . .

—If you had written as much as would cover the whole sky and more, you're telling lies. A holy man like Columkille to go writing a book to deceive the public! . . .

—Exactly! A holy man. You're insulting the faith. You're a heretic. No wonder there's an *Antichrist* close at hand indeed. Do you even know there's a God?

—The oldest inhabitant of the graveyard here. Permission to speak . . .

—Only one man has the true prophecy of Columkille now: Seán Chite in Donagh's Village . . .

—What a coincidence! Your own first cousin . . .

—The Redman in Donagh's Village has it too . . .

—It seems the prophets migrated to the nettly groves of Donagh's Village, and it's now their Holy Ground . . .

—At least the true prophecy of Columkille is to be found there, which can't be said of the flea-ridden hillocks of your village . . .

—Liam in our village is a great prophet. I'd spend my whole life listening to him. His prophecy makes great sense to me, and some of it has already come true . . .

---

5. *Dúil Aeir,* air as one of the four elements, in the original; sounding like "de Valera."

—The false prophecy of Liam of Sive's Rocks.

—Not a false prophecy at all. It is the unadulterated prophecy of Columkille, the last prophecy he made. But Liam often used to say that only a third of it would come true, as Columkille left two-thirds of his prophecy false . . .

—You're a liar! A holy man like Columkille . . .

—Oh! Don't be surprised if you see an *Antichrist* approaching any minute now!

—Have a bit of sense, yourself and your Columkille! In our village we have the prophecy of the Mischievous Elf . . .

—We have the prophecy of Conán in our village . . .

—The prophecy of the Son of Murrough Sock on Hole is the one we have in our village . . .

—I heard the prophecy of Cathal Buí from a man from West Headland . . .

—A man from our village had the prophecy of Knotted Bottom. He's in America . . .

—A man from our village had the prophecy of Malachi of the Songs. He married in Lakeside. He used to say that Malachi was a holy man. He lived in Joyce Country[6] . . .

—My mother's brother had the prophecy of O'Doogan. "O'Doogan's Rule" he called it . . .

—There's a man still living in our village who has the prophecy of Dean Swift . . .

—. . . That there would be "a road over every gully and English spoken in every shanty." And there is! Nóra Sheáinín from Mangy Field has plenty of English, and there isn't a gully into Nell Pháidín's now without a bridge over it . . .

—. . . That "the Romans" would marry heretics. And didn't the children of those people over here marry an *Eyetalian*, a Jew and a *black!* . . .

—Look out for yourselves now! It won't be too long till you see

---

6. Mountainous region on the northeast of Conamara, settled in medieval times by the Norman-Welsh Joyces.

an *Antichrist.* Marrying heretics . . . Do they even know there is a God? . . .

—My son knows as well as you do that there's a God, even though he married an *Eyetalian* . . .

—. . . That the old man would be turned three times in the bed . . .

—It's a pity, my dear, that I wasn't turned now and again. If I had been, my poor buttocks wouldn't be so blistered . . .

—. . . That Galway would win the All-Ireland in 1941 . . .

—In 1941? Some other year, maybe? . . .

—Not at all. Not at all. Why some other year? 1941. What else! Do you want to contradict the prophecy?

—This is the War of the Two Foreigners. It was in the prophecy: "On the sixteenth year Ireland will be red with gore . . ." And isn't it so, this year? There was a war in Dublin and in East Galway at Easter . . .

—Wake up, man. That's thirty years ago, or very near it . . .

—What do you mean, thirty years ago? The fighting was at Easter and I died around the Feast of Our Lady . . .

—Wake up, man. You'd think you came here just this year . . .

—He's right about the sixteenth year . . .

—Arrah, listen to me, Pádraig Labhráis's son. Have an ounce of sense. Columkille never said that . . .

—If he didn't, Red Brian said it. The prophecy of Red Brian is what he has. My uncle has it too:

> "On the sixteenth year after the thirty
> Ireland will be red in its gore.
> And on the seventeenth year the women will ask:
> 'Alas, where did all the men go'"?

The women of Donagh's Village, Mangy Field, Sive's Rocks, Glen of the Pasture, Wood of the Lake and Old Wood are asking that already. How do you think they'll be in another few years, when there won't be even one man left?

I heard my uncle say it was in Red Brian's prophecy that a woman and her daughter would be standing on the Wood of the Lake bridge and that they'd see a man approaching from the east. He would be a *black* but they would find no fault with that. They would both lunge at him like dogs and they would grab him. The man would be full of fear. But the two women would attack one another then, each of them saying he was hers. The man would manage to get away in the heel of the hunt. That's the time the men'll be scarce!

—It's no wonder, when they're marrying *Eyetalians*, Jews and *blacks* . . .

—Since the news reached home every man is off to England. I reckon that the "autumn of the faint women," as my uncle called it, is quite close now. The women of Mangy Field won't be able to get men to marry them, nor will the women of Donagh's Village or Sive's Rocks. Isn't that the reason I wanted so much to go to England my-self: the women would tear me apart between them . . . I'd be like Billyboy the Post . . .

—Listen here, son of Pádraig Labhráis, yourself and your uncle have brought the women of Ireland into disrepute . . .

—Doesn't the Big Master do that every minute of the day!

—Listen here, son of Pádraig Labhráis, yourself and your uncle have insulted the faith. Black heretics . . .

—Everybody says those who are leaving the country are the best of men. The reason for that, I think, is that we're approaching the *Antichrist* and the end of the world, and if it happens that the road down to hell is in this part of the country there will be no end to the number of *blackguards* visiting us from Brightcity, from Dublin, and of course from all over England. I fear for our sisters . . .

—Hold your tongue you, Pádraig Labhráis's brat! . . .

—Hold your tongue, you brat! . . .

—Arrah, I think it won't be long now till England will be shovelled away to hell altogether. Hitler . . .

—It's in the prophecy of Caitríona Pháidín that her son's wife will be here on her next childbirth . . .

—Ababúna!

—I'd believe in prophecies myself. I wouldn't like any misunder-standing about this. I don't say I believe in any particular prophecy, but I can see that people could have that gift. There are gifts that material science knows nothing about because they cannot be demonstrated by experiment. The poet is the same as the prophet in many ways. "Vates" is what the Romans called the poet: a person who would have a vision or an insight. I discussed that point in the "Guiding Star" in my poetry collection, *The Golden Stars* . . .

—May the devil pierce you! The only thing you ever did above ground was your useless verses . . .

—Hold your tongue, you brat. It would be hard for you to do any good above ground, when your father and mother didn't nurture any good in you. They allowed you to stay in the house, herding the embers and daydreaming, while they killed themselves working . . .

—. . . The way it was promised in the prophecy is that the Foreigners would come ashore in the West Headland, and would drive on eastwards . . .

—There'll be plenty of men then for the women of Mangy Field, Donagh's Village and Sive's Rocks . . .

—You're insulting the faith . . .

—A big General in charge of them will go down to the river at Wood of the Lake bridge to water his horse. An Irishman will shoot at him and the horse will be killed . . .

—That big General will immediately go looking for another horse! Do you think if he should see a fine big colt he would take it away with him? . . .

—This is the War of the Two Foreigners. I was up in the boghollow footing turf[7] when Peaits Sheáinín came up to me. "Did you hear the news?" says he.

"Devil the news," says I.

"The Kaiser attacked the poor Belgies yesterday," says he.

"They're much to be pitied," says I. "Do you think it's the War of the Two Foreigners?"

---

7. Putting sods of turf leaning against one another and across one another on the turf bank to dry after being cut.

—Wake up, man. That war ended a long time ago . . .

—. . . The Big Master said the other day this must be the World War, as the women are so fickle . . .

—Tomás Inside said it too. "By the docks, dear," he said, "it's the end of the world, the way people have lost their good nature. Look at my little shack full of leaks . . ."

—When the Insurance Man got started here there wasn't a house he went into without saying it was the War of the Prophecy.

"Now or never," he used to say, "you must take out a bit of insurance on yourself. There's no fear of them killing someone who's insured, for if they did they'd have to pay out too much money at the end of the War. All you have to do is to carry your insurance paper with you at all times, and to show it if . . ."

—Oh! Didn't the little good-for-nothing fool me . . .

—Tricks of the trade . . .

—Caitríona herself said the other day it must be the War of the Territories. "The Island limestone is used up," she said, "and it was in the prophecy that when the Island limestone was used up you'd be very close to the end of the world."

—Ababúna! The Island limestone. The Island limestone. The Island limestone! I'll explode! . . .

4

—. . . Patience, Cóilí. Patience . . .

—Allow me to finish my story, my good man:

"I laid an egg! I laid an egg! Red hot on the dunghill . . ."

—Yes, Cóilí. Even though there's no artistry in it, I think it has some deep and obscure meaning. Stories of this type always do. You know what Frazer said in *The Golden Bough* . . . I beg your pardon, Cóilí. I forgot you weren't able to read . . . Now Cóilí, allow me to speak . . . Cóilí, allow me to speak. I'm a writer . . .

—. . . *Honest*, Dotie. Máirín failed. If she had taken after me or after my daughter she wouldn't have failed. But she took after the Páidín clan and the Loideáin. The nuns in the convent completely failed to drive anything into her head. Would you believe, Dotie, that she began to call her teachers "pussface" and "bitch"!... *Honest Engine*, Dotie. It was impossible to stop her using rude words. What would you expect, after listening to them since she was born, in the same house as Caitríona Pháidín ...

—Ababúna! Nóirín ...

—Let on you don't hear her at all, Dotie dear. Don't you see for yourself now that Máirín was "destined to be afflicted," as Blinks says in *The Red-Hot Kiss*... You're right, Dotie. He's a cousin of Máirín's. It's no wonder he's going to be a priest, Dotie. He was surrounded by a good deal of culture since he was born. The priest used to call to the house every time he came fowling. Fowlers and hunters from Brightcity and Dublin and from England came there regularly too. Of course, Nell is his grandmother and he's still with her. Nell is a cultured woman ...

—Oh!... Oh!...

—His mother, Big Brian's daughter, was in America, and she met cultured people there. America is a great place for culture, Dotie. The grandfather, Big Brian, used to visit the house from time to time, and though you wouldn't think it, Dotie, Big Brian is a cultured man in his own way ... He is as you say he is, Dotie, but at least he had enough culture not to marry Caitríona Pháidín. *Honest...*

—Oh!... Oh!... You honeycomb of fleas ...

—Let on you don't hear her at all, Nóra ...

—*Yep*, Dotie ... Nevertheless, isn't it amazing how different two families can be!... My grandson in Mangy Field is another first cousin of Máirín's: the young man the Big Master talks about. He got to be a ship's petty officer, Dotie. Lucky him! Marseilles, Port Said, Singapore, Batavia, Honolulu, San Francisco... Sun. Oranges. Blue seas ...

—But it's very dangerous at sea since the war began ...

—"The valiant youth doesn't measure the blind leap of danger," as Frix said in *Two Men and a Powder-puff*. Happy, happy the life of the sailor, Dotie. Beautiful romantic clothes on him that are every woman's heart's desire.

—I told you before, Nóra, I'm an old-fashioned rustic myself...

—Romance, Dotie. Romance... I fell head-over-heels in love with him, Dotie. *Honest!* But don't say a word about it. You know, Dotie dear, that you're my friend. Caitríona Pháidín would love to have something to gossip about. Having no culture herself she'd have a very unsophisticated attitude to a matter like that...

—Let on you don't hear her at all, Nóra...

—*Yep*, Dotie. I fell head-over-heels in love with him, Dotie. He was like a brand-new statue of bronze with life breathed into it. The pupil of his eye was like the sparkle of a star in a mountain lake on a frosty night. His hair was like black silk... But his lips, Dotie. His lips... They were on fire. On fire, Dotie. Burning from *The Red-Hot Kiss* itself...

And the stories he told me about foreign countries and ports. About turbulent seas and the driven storm blowing white foam to the topsails. About bright sandy estuaries in the recesses of wooded headlands. About snow-covered, windswept peaks. About sun-drenched pastures on the margins of gloomy forests... About foreign birds, strange fishes and wild animals. About tribes that have stones for money, and about other tribes that wage war to capture spouses...

—That's cultured enough, Nóra...

—About tribes that worship the devil, and about gods that go courting milkmaids...

—That's cultured too, Nóra...

—And about adventures he had himself in Marseilles, Port Said, Singapore...

—Cultural adventures, I suppose...

—Oh! I'd give him the last drop of my heart's blood, Dotie! I'd go with him as bondmaid to Marseilles, to Port Said, to Singapore...

—You stabbed one another after all that...

—We had only known one another briefly at the time. An ordinary true-lovers' *tiff*, Dotie. That was all. He was sitting by my side on the sofa. "You are beautiful, my Nóróg," he said. "Your tresses are more luminous than the sunrise on the snow-capped peaks of Iceland." *Honest*, he did, Dotie. "Your eyes are more sparkling, my

Nóróg," he said, "than the Northern Star appearing over the horizon to the mariner as he crosses the Equator." *Honest, he did, Dotie.* "Your countenance is more beautiful, my Nóróg," he said, "than white-crested waves on the smooth strands of Hawaii." *Honest, he did, Dotie.* "Your slender body is more stately, my Nóróg," he said, "than a palm-tree by the rampart of a seraglio in Java." *Honest, he did, Dotie.* "Your snow-white body is more delicate," he said, "than the lighthouse that guides the mariners to the port of Brightcity and that beckons me to the loving embrace of my fair Nóróg." *Honest, he did, Dotie. He embraced me, Dotie. His lips were aflame . . . Aflame . . .*

"Your well-formed legs are more shapely, my Nóróg," he said, "than the silver bridge of the moon over San Francisco Bay."

He made a grab at the calf of my leg . . .

—He made a grab at the calf of your leg, Nóróg. Now for you! . . .

—*Honest, he did, Dotie. "De grâce,"* said I. "Don't be grabbing my calves." "The curves of your calves are prettier, my Nóróg," he said, "than a whirl of seagulls in the wake of a ship." *He grabbed my calf again. "De grâce,"* said I, "leave my calves alone." "The calves of your legs are more beautiful, my Nóróg," he said, "than the Milky Way, thrown on its back in the raging seas of the south." *"De grâce,"* I said, "you'll have to leave the calves of my legs alone." *I grabbed a book I'd been reading from the window ledge and I smacked him on the wrist with the edge of it . . .*

—But you told me, Nóróg, that you took a pot-hook to him, like I did myself . . .

—Dotie! Dotie! . . .

—But that's what you told me, Nóra . . .

—*De grâce,* Dotie . . .

—And that he drew a knife, Nóróg, and made a sudden lunge to stab you; and then he apologised and said it was the custom in his country to grab another person's calves as a sign of friendship . . .

—*De grâce,* Dotie. *De grâce . . .*

—That you made it up again then, and that every time his ship reached Brightcity he wouldn't take his finger off his nose till he came as far as you . . .

—*De grâce*, Dotie. "Finger off his nose." Very uncultured . . .

—But that's exactly the way you put it yourself, Nóróg. And you said he used to write to you from San Francisco, Honolulu, Batavia, Singapore, Port Said and Marseilles. And that you were down in the dumps for a long time when you got no letter from him, till a sailor told you he was laid low after being stabbed with a knife in a *bistro* in Marseilles . . .

—Ugh! Ugh! Dotie. You know how sensitive I am. It would upset me greatly if anybody should hear that story. *Honest*, it would, Dotie. You are my friend, Dotie. What you said a while ago would give me a terrible reputation. That he would draw a knife! That I would do something so uncultured as taking a pot-hook to somebody! Ugh!

—That's what you told me a good while ago, Nóróg, but you didn't have as much culture then as you have now . . .

—*Hum*, Dotie. It would take a rustic like Caitríona Pháidín to do a thing like that. You heard Muraed Phroinsiais say it was boiling water she took to Big Brian. She must be a right harridan. *Honest!* . . .

—It's a terrible shame he didn't bury the knife to the hilt in you, you sailors' leavings. Where was it you said he sat down beside you? Oh, Lord God, the unfortunate man had no mind to do what was good for him. Easily known he'd be stabbed in the end if he sat down with the Filthy-Feet Breed. He had a fine present parting from you, indeed: a cargo of nits . . .

—Let on you don't hear her at all, Nóróg . . .

—. . . Now, Red-haired Tom, for God's sake listen to me. I'm yelling at you for the past hour and you're paying no more heed to me than if I were frogspawn. Why don't you have confidence in me? Weren't we the closest of acquaintances above ground? . . .

—The closest of acquaintances, Master. The closest . . .

—Tell me this, Red-haired Tom. Is Billyboy the Post unwell? . . .

—Billyboy the Post? Billyboy the Post, now. Billyboy the Post. Billyboy the Post, indeed. Faith, there is such a man, Master. Billyboy the Post definitely exists . . .

—Arrah, may the devils and the demons and the thirty-seven million devils that were present at Alexander Borgia's death-bed take

Billyboy the Post to hell with them! Don't I know he exists! Do you think, Red-haired Tom, I don't know Billyboy the Post exists. Is he unwell, the blubber-lipped little lout? . . .

—Some people say he is, Master. Some people say he's not. Many a thing is said without a grain of truth in it. But he could be unwell. He could, faith. He could, surely. It's a wise man . . .

—I humbly ask you, Red-haired Tom, to tell me if Billyboy the Post is unwell . . .

—Oh! He could be, Master. He could be, indeed. He could be, Master. He could, surely. Musha, devil do I know . . .

—I implore you, in the name of the age-old custom of neighbourly gossip, to tell me if Billyboy the Post is unwell . . . Good man, Red-haired Tom . . . I'll love you forever, Red-haired Tom . . . You're my golden apple, Red-haired Tom, but tell me is Billyboy the Post unwell, or is he likely to die soon?

—It's a wise man . . .

—I implore you, Red-haired Tom, as a man who was espoused to a woman—as I was myself—to tell me if Billyboy the Post is unwell . . .

—He could be . . .

—My earthly store, white of my eye, my life's help, Red-haired Tom! . . . Do you believe in private property at all? . . . In the name of everybody's duty to sustain the natural foundation of marriage, I implore you, Red-haired Tom, to tell me if Billyboy the Post is unwell . . .

—If I told anything, Master, I'd tell it to yourself as soon as to anyone else, but I won't tell anything. One should keep one's mouth shut in a place like this, Master. It's not a place to be indiscreet. Graves have holes . . .

—My seven cries of curses on you, tonight and tomorrow and a year from tomorrow, you Communist, you Fascist, you Nazi, you heretic, you red-haired *Antichrist*, you right mouthful of vulgar-blood, you putrid dregs of rustic table attendants, you remnant of disease, you leavings of fly, maggot and earthworm, you lifeless wretch who frightened death himself till he had to put a bad sickness on you, you worthless creature, you useless boor, you red ruffian . . .

—*De grâce*, Master. Control yourself. Remember you're a cultured Christian gentleman. If you keep on like this you'll soon be able to keep up a sparring match with that hooligan, Caitríona Pháidín...

—Master, Master, answer her. You have the education, Master. Answer her. Answer Nóirín...

—Let on you don't hear the *So-an'-so* at all, Master...

—*So-an'-so! So-an'-so!* Nóirín Sheáinín calling me a *So-an'-so!* I'll explode! I'll...

5

—...A bad bottle, then. A bad bottle. A bad bottle...

—...Another time I saw the two of them on the roof of the house: Pádraig Chaitríona and Peadar Nell...

—Do you think I don't know?...

—...Indeed, Bríd Terry, if it cost me my life's blood, I'd be at your funeral. I owed it to come to Bríd's...

—Sweet-talking Stiofán blabbering again, or is that him at all? Our Lady knows I have difficulty in hearing any news story here. That earthworm, God blast it! Nowhere would suit it but to go into my earhole! Straight over from Muraed Phroinsiais's grave it came. That grave is riddled with earthworms. Muraed was used to that, of course. She had a filthy abode above ground too. Dirt on the floors piled high as a ship's mast, and a coating of filth on every bit of furniture under her roof. No wonder she's in her element in the clay now. Not to mention herself. You could grow potatoes in her ears, and she never cleaned her shoes going to Mass. You'd recognize the daubs of yellow soil from the swallow hole outside her house, that she left in her trail all the way up the chapel. And she wouldn't rest till she'd cock herself up beside the altar in front of Siúán the Shop and Nell—the little bitch. If Muraed had married Big Brian the pair of them would have been well matched. He never washed himself either, unless the midwife washed him. They say cleanliness is a virtue, but I wonder. Filthy people thrive too. I kept a clean house every day of my life. There wasn't a Saturday night in the year that I didn't wash and scrub everything within the four walls of the house. Even when I wasn't able to stand up I'd still do it. And all I gained by it was to shorten my life.

What's this? What sort of commotion is this? Blocked and all as my ears are, they can hear that much at least . . . Another corpse. The epidemic . . . The coffin is only an old hen-box. That's all it is. They'd throw any old tinker down on top of me now . . .

Who are you? . . . On the devil's tracks to hell with you and speak up! My ears are stuffed . . . They said to bury you in this grave beside your mother? I don't recognize your voice, then. But you're a woman. A young woman . . . You were only twenty-two. I'm afraid you must have gone astray on the "sod of bewilderment."[8] If you could turn your shroud inside out, maybe you'd find your way. My daughters are dead this long while . . . Why don't you speak up and tell me who you are! . . . Do I need any spiritual assistance? What sort of spiritual assistance are you talking about? . . . What's spiritual assistance? . . .

Big Colm's daughter? Big Brian is your uncle! It's very unwise of you to try and gate-crash your way into the same grave as me. I have too many of your ilk all around me here as I am. I'm not even distantly related to you. Go down to your mother down there. I heard her whining a short time ago. It was coming home from her funeral that I first caught what killed me. A desperate downpour of a day it was . . .

Ugh! Keep away from me! The Lower Hillside epidemic.[9] Keep away, or God help you. Your uncle Big Brian's house was an inhospitable place to call on.

What's that you said, now? . . . You know only too well how inhospitable it was! . . . You fell out with him? . . . You didn't go near his house for the past year? You were none the worse for that, sister dear . . . You may say that again, sister dear. Isn't that what I said a while ago? Devil a drop of water that fellow splashed on himself since he

---

8. The "stray sod," a patch of ground said to make you lose your way if you tread on it. The remedy was to turn your coat inside out.

9. "Typhus Outbreak in Spiddal . . . Dr Charles McConn, acting County Medical Officer[,] . . . is striving to subdue the outbreak . . ." (*Irish Times,* 14 November 1942).

was born . . . By japers, you could be telling me the truth: that your father was a clean man. You wouldn't recognise a trace of him in that other streak of misery? Your father took after his mother! He was a mild-mannered man? . . . You went to Big Brian a year ago? . . . You asked him if you could give him spiritual assistance? Oh, you were badly employed offering that ugly streak of misery any sort of assistance! . . . Ah, it was for the Legion of Mary[10] you visited him! . . . True for you, devil a Family Rosary he said since he was born . . . That's what he said to you? . . . That he wouldn't accept any spiritual assistance from you! . . . He told you the Legion was full of jennets! That man has no fear of God or the Virgin Mary . . .

The streak of misery is ailing at last. The devil take him, it's about time for him . . . Is that what he said: "I think I'll take a *tour* back there any day now . . . And I'll guarantee you this much, there'll be ructions in those holes back there . . . If Páidín's mule . . ." You're certain he didn't finish what he was saying . . .

Haven't I told you already I don't want . . . what's this you call it? . . . spiritual assistance. . . Nell's talking about building a new slated house? . . . They're breaking rocks for it. Ababúna! That's what the little hunchback said: that they had to do it, now that the new road was built up as far as the door. Oh, the little crupper! . . . "that there'd be a priest in the house soon, if God spares the people." Oh, the bitch! . . . Her legs are giving up? It would serve her right if she was never able to walk the new road . . . The things you don't know now, you'll know all about them in a week's time. But they were all scared to come to the house to you.

What's that you said? . . . That Jack the Scológ was very ill. That's the fatal illness now. The St. John's Gospel. Nell and Big Brian's daughter will get another lump of money . . . You didn't hear anything about the St. John's Gospel . . . You didn't know that Jack needed spiritual assistance. He needs all the assistance he can get now, the poor man . . .

---

10. A lay Catholic organization founded in 1921.

Beartla Blackleg was anointed . . . Little Cáit and Bid Shorcha are poorly, you say . . . They don't stir out of the house at all now. They won't be stretching or keening any more stiffs from now on, so . . .

They put up the cross over Máirtín Pockface the other day . . . and over Red-haired Tom too. Of course, that red good-for-nothing is no length at all here . . . That's what you heard: that Nell advised Pádraig not to put a cross of Island limestone over me . . . You'll know all about it in a week's time. Thanks very much! . . . Oh, you may be sure, sister dear, that it's true. She would say that—the bitch—and Big Brian's daughter and Nóra Sheáinín's daughter urging her on . . . Big Brian said that: "If I were Pádraig, I'd give that babbling little hag her fill of Island limestone . . . I'd dig her up out of yonder hole . . . I'd whisk her into the Island . . . I'd cock her up on the highest pinnacle of stone there . . . like the man on the Big Stone in Dublin . . ." Oh, indeed, it isn't the word of the Lord that's on his lips even though death has him on a halter . . . I tell you I don't want any spiritual assistance . . .

Nóra Sheáinín's daughter, Nell and Big Brian's daughter talking again? Easily known. Arrah, devil the fight was ever there, just that little prattler of Pádraig Labhráis's telling lies . . . True for you, sister dear. The Battle of the Hornless Cows.[11] Tinkers, the whole lot of them . . . You'll know more in a week's time . . .

A letter must have come so? . . . She didn't say who she'd leave the money to . . . Oh, she wrote to Pádraig too . . . Wasn't she the meddlesome stump to go writing to Big Brian's house where she has no kith or kin . . . She said for certain that she was poorly . . . And that she had made her will. Had Dad! . . . And that she'd ordered a tomb in Boston graveyard. A tomb! Like the Earl has. A tomb over our Baba. Bad luck to her, couldn't she make do with something more modest than a tomb! . . . She put money in a bank for the tomb to be perpetually maintained. By God, now . . . And money for Masses! Two and a half thousand pounds for Masses! Two and a half thousand pounds! The will isn't worth much now. Big Brian's family in America will pilfer

---

11. A fight in which no one is hurt.

BRIAIN MÓR

the rest of it. Couldn't suit me better. Nell's share must be tiny now. She won't be singing "Eleanor of the Secrets" any more, going up past our house . . .

You think Pádraig didn't write back to Baba. He's gone to the devil if he didn't! . . . Will you stop annoying me about how you'll know more in a week's time! What use is it to me what you'll know in a week's time? . . . The Small Master doesn't write letters for anybody now . . . Too busy . . . What did you say he was doing? . . . Studying form. That's very strange talk indeed . . . Betting on racehorses. Oh, you're not serious! He doesn't do a tap in school except reading about them . . . The priest has turned against him. My God, I thought the pair of them went for walks together. Or was that not true? One shouldn't believe a word you hear in this place . . . He gave a sermon about him . . . Of course, everybody would know who he was talking about, without mentioning his name or surname . . . "Wasting their time and their money on gambling, and going around with drunkard women in Brightcity," he said . . . "I heard of a man from this parish who drank forty-two pints, but little gluttons of women who can guzzle a small barrel of brandy without having to powder their noses afterwards . . ." By Dad, if he'd known about Nóra Sheáinín! . . . There's talk that he'll get rid of the Small Master . . . Oh, here we go again! You'll know more in a week's time . . . You'll know things in a week's time, alright, my sister oh! . . .

Ababúna! The Small Master forgot to post the American letters he wrote for Pádraig . . . Ó Céidigh's wife found them in old clothes he left behind when he moved into new lodgings . . . Ababúna! She told Nell all that was in the letters . . .

Pádraig has some sort of jinx on him: why didn't he take the letters himself and post them? Do you think that I'd ever leave my letters behind me with the Small Master, or with the Big Master? Schoolmasters are a strange lot. It was always obvious to me that they had more on their minds than my letters. When the Big Master was writing for me didn't I see him going like a weaver's shuttle from table to window to try and glimpse the Schoolmistress going along the road! . . .

The Schoolmistress wouldn't write a letter for anybody either, you say? . . . Too busy looking after Billyboy, the thieving hussy! Oh, if only Pádraig had taken my advice and gone in to Mannion the Counsellor he wouldn't have to depend on anybody. That's the man who wouldn't be long writing a powerful letter for seven shillings and sixpence. But Nóra Sheáinín's daughter would be loath to part with as much as a penny . . . You heard Pádraig was half-hearted enough about the will? . . . That's more of Nell's deception. Surely you don't think she has scruples about deceiving my son when she's deceiving her own husband . . . "That Pádraig was alright since Bessy died." Big Brian would say that . . . Will you leave off about your spiritual assistance! . . .

Máirín is to go back to college again? She'll get on fine this time. Oh! She wasn't sent home at all the last time; she came home of her own accord! The creature was homesick? You don't know what she's going to be? . . . A schoolmistress, I suppose . . . That's all you heard about her? . . .

Pádraig has a lot of cattle on the land. More power to him! . . .

Tomás Inside has moved out of his own house? . . . The leaking roof shifted him . . . It should have shifted him a long time ago. That's what he said: "By the docks, the drop was hitting me between my gob and my eye, no matter where in the house I moved the bed to. I think I'll go rubbing shoulders with the gentry for the rest of my life" . . . He came to Pádraig's house for two nights and then moved permanently into Nell's? The land is left to Nell, so . . . You don't know whether he signed it over to her or not. Only Mannion the Counsellor would know that! . . . It's of no damn interest what you'll know more exactly in a week's time! It's what you know now! . . . Tomás Inside said that: "Nell was much more good-natured than Caitríona. I prefer to stay in Nell's where I'll be rubbing shoulders with the gentry. None of the gentry go near Caitríona's." Tomás Inside's blenny-head will make a fine sight indeed for gentry! . . . "The gentry have the best of tobacco and they have fine women around them." That little pussface will soon give him his bellyful of women. If she feels any ailment coming on she'll get the St. John's Gospel from the priest and make Tomás Inside hit the road. A pity there isn't some good soul above ground to alert the poor unfortunate! How the world has changed! Tomás Inside the grinner rubbing shoulders with the gentry . . .

Lord Cockton came fishing to Nell's place every day this year. He was able to bring the car up to her door . . . The priest brings the car to her door too . . . Ababúna! Lord Cockton brought that bedraggled head out in the car . . . Brought her to Headland Harbour to take the air. He has little respect for his car, putting bitches like her into it . . .

The priest's sister was up there fowling too. Was she wearing trousers or a dress, then? . . . Trousers . . . Herself and Lord Cockton were fowling together. Isn't it a wonder the priest wouldn't stop them! I suppose the same Lord Cockton is a black heretic. There was a lot of talk that she was going to marry the Wood of the Lake schoolmaster . . . Oh! Here we go! You'll know exactly in a week's time! We'll have to get you permission to go back up above again for a week . . .

You think the marriage has been abandoned? I thought the Wood of the Lake master was a decent man and that he didn't touch a drop . . . What did you say? My ears are stuffed . . . That she's keeping company with Road-End's son? That the priest's sister is keeping company with Road-End's son! By God, it's a funny world! . . .

Road-End's son warned Lord Cockton: not to go fowling with her any more unless he himself was there with them. . . Seáinín Liam's son heard him say that to him . . .

What's this? Where are you? . . . They're carrying you off . . . They know now this isn't your grave . . . God speed you, my friend! Even though you're related to Big Brian you can speak pleasantly to a person. Not like that useless lump, Red-haired Tom . . .

6

—. . . Me giving a word for each pint to the Gaelic Enthusiast . . .

—. . . The Big Butcher often told me he had great regard for me on account of the regard his father had for my father . . .

—. . . And me down to my last shilling . . .

—I wonder is the Small Master down to his last shilling now . . .

—. . . "I laid an egg! I laid an egg! . . ."

—*C'est l'histoire des poules, n'est-ce pas?*

—. . . *Honest*, Dotie. My mind is extremely sluggish this past while. I am as much in need of culture as the head of corn is in need of sunlight. But there's no culture at all here now. It's a crying shame for the Big Master. When a person comes to the graveyard he should leave the futile pettiness of life above behind him and use his time to develop his mind. I often tell the Master that but it's no use. He can't talk of anything now but the Schoolmistress and Billyboy the Post. Something has to be done to rescue him. *Honest*, Dotie. We don't have that many cultured people that we can afford to do without any one of them. He must be prevented from imitating Caitríona Pháidín's scolding. Words like "bitch" and "hussy" and "snot-face" are forever on his lips now. Caitríona is a bad influence on him. That one belongs down in the Wastelands of the Half-Guinea . . .

—Mangy Nóirín . . .

—Let on you don't hear her at all, Nóróg . . .

—*Yep*, Dotie. I mean to go ahead on my own and found a cultural society. I think a lot can be done to improve the minds of the people here and to give breadth and scope to their cultural feelings. A wide range of subjects will be discussed, from political matters to communications, economics, science, learning, education, and so on. But they'll be discussed in a proper and academic manner, irrespective of sex, race or religion. No one who's accepted into the society will be hindered from expressing their views, and the only qualification for membership will be a love of culture . . .

—Do you think it was the yeast of culture germinating in me that made me take up the pot-hook and strike . . .

—*De grâce*, Dotie. "God forgives the big sins, but it is we who cannot forgive ourselves the little sins," as Eustasia said to Mrs. Crookshank when they were fighting over Harry. We'll aim to broadcast information about other aspects of life—foreign affairs in particular—and by so doing give various groups of people an understanding of each other. We'll have debates regularly, lectures, *soirées*,

Question Time, Symposium, a Prestigious Periodical, Colloquium, Discussion, Summer School, Weekends, and Information Please for the Half-Guinea Regions. This society will be a great asset to the cause of wide-ranging culture and peace. This type of society is called a Rotary. Cultured people such as the Earl are involved with the Rotary . . .

—And sailors . . .

—Let on you don't hear her at all, Nóróg . . .

—*Yep*, Dotie. I will. But that's a good example of the sort of opinion that has to be obliterated by the shining light of the Rotary. Caitríona is not the only one who has a mind like that. If she were, one wouldn't mind, but the perception is quite common. Sailors are an interesting group. Only a narrow uncultivated mind would criticize them . . .

—Only for those knives they have, Nóróg . . .

—*De grâce*, Dotie. That's another perception that has to be abolished . . .

—Who else will be in Rotary, Nóróg?

—I'm not exactly sure yet. Yourself, Dotie. The Big Master. Peadar the Pub. Siúán the Shop . . .

—The poet . . .

—The devil pierce him, the cheeky brat . . .

—. . . But you haven't read *The Golden Stars*, Nóróg?

—*No infernal odds, old man!* You won't be accepted. *Honest!* You are *decadent! . . .*

—Bríd Terry should be admitted. She was at the pictures in Brightcity once . . .

—Faith then, I was there myself with the young fellow, the time we bought the colt . . .

—Hold on now. I'm a writer . . .

—You can't be admitted. If you're admitted we'll rip the graveyard apart. You insulted Columkille.

—. . . It's no use reading it. I won't listen to your *Setting of the Sun. Honest!* I won't . . . It's no use pressing me: I won't listen. I have a very liberal mind, but nevertheless a certain level of decorum has to be maintained . . . I'm a woman . . . I won't. *Honest!* . . . You won't be admitted. Your work is Joycean . . . You won't change my mind. I'll not listen to *The Setting of the Sun*. You have a low-down mind to have written a thing like that . . . You're working on *The Dream of the Dinosaur* . . . I won't listen. *The Dream of the Dinosaur*. A right Joycean galoot.[12] You're a very low specimen of humanity . . . You won't be admitted till you learn every word of the *Sixty-One Sermons* off by heart . . .

—I propose that the Frenchman be admitted. He's an enthusiastic Gael. He's flat out learning the language . . .

—He's writing a thesis on the canine dental consonants in the Half-Guinea dialect. He says their gums are blunt enough by now to have a learned study carried out on their sounds . . .

—The Institute thinks he has learned too much Irish—of the kind that has not been dead for the prescribed period—and as there's a suspicion that a few of his words are "Revival Irish," he has to unlearn every syllable before he's qualified to carry out the study properly.

—He also intends to collect and preserve all the lost folklore so that future generations of Gaelcorpses will know what sort of life there was in the republic of Gaelcorpses in the past. He says there isn't a traditional storyteller the like of Cóilí to be found this side of Russia now, and there will not be his like again.[13] He thinks it will be easy to make a Folklore Museum of the Graveyard and that there will be no difficulty in getting a grant for doing that . . .

—Oh! But wasn't that fat fellow fighting against Hitler . . .

—Let him be admitted . . .

—Thank you all, *mes amis! Merci beaucoup* . . .

---

12. Ó Cadhain overheard this, on a bus in Dublin, when *Cré na Cille* was being serialised in the *Irish Press:* "This Ó Cadhain fellow. A right galoot if ever there was one. A Joycean smutmonger."

13. An often imitated and parodied phrase from *An tOileánach*, translated as *The Islandman*, Tomás Ó Criomhthain's account of life on the Great Blasket Island, Kerry.

—Hitler is against Rotary . . .

—If he is, then to hell with yourselves and your Rotary! . . .

—. . . A man who drank forty-two pints! Indeed, you would not be admitted, or in Alcoholics Anonymous, or in Mount Mellary.[14] Nowhere but in "Drunkards Limited" . . .

—Faith then, I drank two score pints and two! . . .

—But Nóra Sheáinín used to drink twice that much on the sly . . .

—Shut your mouth, you little brat!

—Of course it's not possible that you'd accept any of the One-Ear Breed. If you do, you'll be stabbed . . .

—. . . How could you be admitted to Rotary when you don't know your tables? . . .

—But I do. Listen. Twelve ones are twelve. Twelve twos . . .

—. . . How could you be accepted: a man who killed himself going to see Concannon? That was a very uncultured death . . .

—The bookseller will be admitted. He handled thousands of books . . .

—And the Insurance Agent. He used to do Crossword Puzzles . . .

—And Sweet-talking Stiofán. He was a good funeral-goer . . .

—. . . Why wouldn't you be accepted? Isn't your son married to a *black*! The *blacks* are a cultured people.

—At least, they're more cultured than the *Eyetalians* that son of yours is married into . . .

—Caitríona Pháidín should be admitted. She has a *roundtable* at home . . .

—As well as Nóra Sheáinín's chest . . .

—She knew Mannion the Counsellor well . . .

—And her son's daughter is going to be a schoolmistress . . .

—Big Colm's daughter should be admitted. She was in the Legion of Mary. She gives spiritual assistance to people . . .

—Easily known, with all her gossip! She hasn't stopped talking since she cast anchor here . . .

—You're insulting . . .

---

14. A Cistercian Abbey in Co. Waterford.

—If that's the way, the Postmistress should be admitted. She was information and exploration officer in the Legion of Mary, and she can't but have culture after all she has read . . .

—And Cite. Her son was a lance-corporal in the Legion, and she had a Credit Corporation herself . . .

—And Road-End. His old lady put a hearse under him for fear his poor bowels would be shaken . . .

—Upon my soul, then, as you say . . .

—Everybody in Road-End's house was in the Legion . . .

—And his son is going out with the priest's sister . . .

—His whole household stole my turf . . .

—And my lump-hammer . . .

—You're insulting the faith. You're black heretics . . .

—. . . You'll be accepted. The Big Butcher was at your funeral, wasn't he? . . .

—Tomás Inside would be a good Rotary man. He's a friend of culture.

—And Big Brian. He was in Dublin . . .

—And Nell Pháidín. She meets many Rotary people. Lord Cockton . . .

—Permission to speak. Permission . . .

—Seáinín Liam will give the first lecture to Rotary. "My Heart" . . .

—Cite then: "Money-lending" . . .

—Dotie: "The Fair Plains of East Galway" . . .

—Máirtín Pockface: "Bedsores" . . .

—The Big Master then: "Billyboy the Post" . . .

—This fellow over here: "The Direct Method for Twisting Ankles" . . .

—Caitríona Pháidín: "Big Brian's Beauty" . . .

—Oh! Flat-footed, miserable Brian . . .

—Red-haired Tom then . . .

—I'll say nothing. I won't indeed. Nothing . . .

—. . . You'll give a lecture on the prophets of Donagh's Village . . .

—And you, on the flea-bitten hillocks of your own village . . .

—. . . *Honest*, Dotie, there was never a day that I wasn't keen on culture. Whoever told you I took it up here is prejudiced, I assure you. When I was in Brightcity as a young girl, I was no sooner home from the convent and finished with my dinner than I was out again in search of cultural activity. That's when I met the sailor . . .

—You never told me, Nóra, that you were attending the convent . . .

—*De grâce*, Dotie. I often told you, but you have forgotten. You understand I was putting the finishing touches to my education in Brightcity, and I was lodging with a relation of mine, a widow-woman called Corish . . .

—You're a damned liar, Nóirín Filthy-Feet. She was no relation of yours. You were in service with her. It was a great wonder she allowed yourself and your stock of fleas into her house at all. But the very minute she found out you were hanging around with sailors she whipped you home with a nettle to your buttocks, to Mangy Field of the Ducks, of the Puddles, of the Fleas and of the Filthy Feet. I wouldn't mind, but to say she was going to school in Brightcity . . .

—Don't let on you hear her at all . . .

—*My goodness me*, Dotie, that strap isn't entitled to talk at all. Lying there without a cross or inscription over her, like a letter posted with no address . . .

—Be thankful to that idiot of a brother of yours, Nóirín . . .

—Your son is at home and he can't afford to pay the insurance you took out on Tomás Inside. And the very moment Tomás found out, he left your house and went to Nell . . .

—Oh! Oh! . . .

—Whether it's O or P, that's the truth. Your son Pádraig has let his land to Nell, and all the cattle on your holding now are Nell's rent-cattle . . .

—Oh! Oh! Oh! . . .

—If he goes on much longer the way he is, he'll have to sell the land. A man is hardly worthy of a wife if he can't afford to keep her. I gave him my daughter as I didn't want to be a hindrance to pitiable love. That was the only reason he got her. I was always romantic.

But romance or whatever, if I'd realized what I was doing and knew exactly where she was going . . .

—. . . What's that? . . . You're a corpse . . . A new corpse . . . I won't have any dealing with you in this grave. A corpse's grave is his castle. There's respect here for the right of private property . . .

—. . . Be off with you! By the oak of this coffin, you'll not come down on top of me. I'm going to join Rotary . . .

—. . . Peace is what I want, not company. I'm going to join Rotary . . .

—. . . You'd hurt me. I've already got bedsores . . .

—. . . My heart is faulty . . .

—. . . Be off with you out of this grave. I'll not tell you a thing. Graves have holes. Wouldn't you think you'd easily recognise all of us? We have crosses over us. Even so, they dug your grave too far over towards mine. The drink! Get over there to Caitríona Pháidín. Over to Caitríona! . . .

—She has a great welcome for every new corpse. She'll give you plenty of gossip . . .

—It's down on top of her they throw anybody they can't find a place for in the graveyard . . .

—You must have trodden on the stray sod, not to have gone over to her. There's no cross over her . . .

—And she won't be accepted in Rotary . . .

—Red-haired Tom! Red-haired Tom! Muraed! Cite! Bríd Terry! Máirtín Pockface! Seáinín Liam! Red-haired Tom! Red-haired Tom has got his speech back! I'll explode!

Interlude Eight

THE FIRING OF THE CLAY

1

I am the Trump of the Graveyard. Let my voice be heard. It must be heard . . .

The ploughed red earth is unwelcoming to its lining of ice. The kernel of the clay has an acid-sour taste. For this is the meadow of tears . . .

The new suit of Spring is being fashioned for the surface of the earth. The gentle small stalks of late corn and the faint green smile that is springing up all over the bare clay are the basting thread in this suit. The rays of sunlight—like refined gold on the epaulettes of the clouds—are its hems. Its buttons are the clusters of primroses in the welcoming arms of hedgerows, in the recesses of every fence and in the shade of every crag. Its lining is the love-song of the lark, coming to the ploughman from the vault of the firmament through the light April haze, and the thicket that has become a gentle harp with the coupling song of blackbirds. The joyful gambolling of the boy who received the reward for finding a newborn lamb on the rugged uplands, and the cheerful tune of the boatman peaking his sail in the welcoming weft of the wavelets, are the seams of hope that stitch the transient beauty of eye and of heart to eternal glory, which is the reverse side of this perishable tunic of land, sea and sky . . .

But the strands the tailor is threading through the eye of his needle are now a pallid rainbow. The scissors of the gale are severing the buttons. The cloth is being chewed up by the smooth-cutting sickle. The golden hem is fraying in the field where the grain is falling from the head . . .

The fairy whirlwind reaps havoc in the haggard, sweeping off every ear of corn, wisp of hay and flake of chaff left over from last year's harvest.

There is a tremor in the milking girl's song as she returns from the summer pasture. She knows the cattle will soon be removed to the old milking place by the homestead . . .

Because Spring and Summer have slunk furtively away. They have been hoarded by the squirrel in its hovel beneath the tree. They have disappeared on the wings of swallows and sunshine . . .

I am the Trump of the Graveyard. Let my voice be heard! It must be heard . . .

2

—. . . "Hoh-roh, my Mary,[1] your wares and your bags and belts,
   And my Stack-of-Barley La-ady . . ."

—What's this? Beartla Blackleg, upon my word, and he singing away to himself. You're welcome, Beartla!

—"Hoh-roh, my Mary, your wares and your bags and belts . . ."

—Upon my soul, 'tis fine and cheerful you are, my good Blackleg friend . . .

—*Bloody tear and 'ounds,*[2] who have I here?

—Caitríona. Caitríona Pháidín . . .

—*Bloody tear and 'ounds*, Caitríona. We're going to be neighbours again so . . .

—They're not burying you in the right grave, Beartla.

—*Bloody tear and 'ounds*, Caitríona, sure it doesn't matter to a person where his heap of old bones is thrown. "Hoh-roh, my Mary . . ."

---

1. A happy, light-hearted song.
2. Thought to be a garbled version of "By Christ's Bloody Tears and Wounds."

—It seems death didn't upset you too much, Beartla. What was your cause of death?

—*Bloody tear and 'ounds*, Caitríona, haven't you heard that the steed can't keep its speed forever, as Big Brian said about . . .

—Oh! The boastful scold!

—Devil the cause at all, but lying down with no life left. *Bloody tear and 'ounds*, but isn't that cause enough! "Hoh-roh . . ."

—How are they blooming up there, Beartla? . . .

—*Bloody tear and 'ounds*, Caitríona, just as you've always seen them. Gaining one and losing one and one in between. Isn't that how it is and that's how it has to be, like a gun being loaded and then being fired, as Big Brian said . . .

—Oh! Faith then, he's the gunner, alright . . .

—He hasn't stirred out, Caitríona, since he went to see Red-haired Tom after Tom was anointed.[3] He was grief-stricken after Tom . . .

—They were well matched, the red-haired sourpuss and the snotty streak of misery . . .

—I was listening to him that night giving Tom advice up in the room. "*Bloody tear and 'ounds*," he said, "if you should take a *tour* over there, Red-haired Tom, and if you should meet herself in your travels, take care you don't tell her anything. Unless she's greatly changed she'll be looking for gossip . . ."

—But who is "herself," Beartla?

—*Bloody tear and 'ounds*, Caitríona, it wouldn't be right or proper for me to answer a question like that . . .

—Oh! Beartla, for the love of God, don't make a Red-haired Tom of yourself. That's how he's going on ever since he came into the graveyard clay . . .

—*Bloody tear and 'ounds*, if there's going to be trouble let there be trouble. Yourself. Who else, Caitríona?

—Myself, Beartla? Me looking for gossip! He's a damned liar.

---

3. Given Extreme Unction (or the Last Rites) by the priest, in expectation of death.

That man's big mouth will keep getting him into trouble till death puts its latch-pin in his tongue . . .

—I'd say that won't be too long now, Caitríona.

—The devil's welcome to him . . .

—*Bloody tear and 'ounds*, don't you know he's a dying man when he didn't have the courage to go to Jack the Scológ's funeral! . . .

—Ababúna búna! Jack the Scológ's funeral! Jack the Scológ's funeral! Jack! Jack! Spouting lies you are, son of Blackleg . . .

—*Bloody tear and 'ounds*, isn't he here for the past three weeks!

—Alas! and woe forever! Jack the Scológ here that long and Muraed and the others didn't tell me. Oh! This place has been turned upside-down by Nóirín Filthy-Feet, Beartla. Guess what she's planning now? . . . Rotary! . . .

—*Bloody tear and 'ounds*, Rotary! "Hoh-roh, my Mary, your wares and your bags . . ."

—Jack the Scológ! Jack the Scológ! Jack the Scológ is here! Easily known he wouldn't live long. The St. John's Gospel . . .

—*Bloody tear and 'ounds*, the St. John's Gospel, Caitríona! . . .

—The St. John's Gospel, wheedled out of the priest by that pussface, what else? Jack the Scológ! Jack the Scológ! Jack the Scológ in the graveyard for the past three weeks and I didn't know. Those boobies here wouldn't tell a person anything, especially since that cursed Election. Seáinín Liam the dullard and Bríd Terry the strap and Red-haired Tom the sourpuss would all have been bundled down in the one grave with me. Jack! Jack the Scológ . . .

—*Bloody tear and 'ounds*, Caitríona, sure it doesn't matter to a person—unless he wants to be silly about it!—who's going to share a grave with him. "Hoh-roh, my Mary . . ."

—I'll bet Nell was at her boastful best the day of the funeral! Showing off and capers, and not the slightest bit of pity for the poor creature who was laid out. She buried him in the Pound Plot, of course? . . .

—In a grave beside Siúán the Shop . . .

—That slut, Siúán the Shop. Poor Jack has a bad article beside him. That sharp-tongued jade will slander him. But what would mathaired Nell care but to throw him down in any old hole . . .

—*Bloody tear and 'ounds*, Caitríona, didn't she get a dry pound grave for him beside Siúán the Shop and Peadar the Pub; didn't she put a hearse under him; wasn't there plenty of everything at the wake and funeral, except that she didn't let anyone fall down drunk; wasn't there a High Mass for him, as there was for Peadar the Pub and for Siúán the Shop; four or five priests singing, and the Earl above on the gallery with Lord Cockton and that other fowler who comes there . . .

Bloody tear and 'ounds, what else could she have done? . . .

—She's still very fond of the priests and the Lords. But I'll wager any bet she didn't shed as much as a tear for the poor man. Arrah, herself and Big Brian's daughter didn't give a damn but to get the poor creature out of the house, out of their way . . .

—*Bloody tear and 'ounds*, Caitríona, herself and Big Brian's daughter keened him tearfully. And everybody says they never heard a finer outburst from Bid Shorcha . . .

—Bid Shorcha! I thought that sponger was confined to her bed now . . .

—*Bloody tear and 'ounds*, she is too! Didn't Big Brian say about herself and Little Cáit and Billyboy the Post: "The priest has rubbed so much oil on those three," he said, "that there won't be a drop left for us when we need it . . ."

—Indeed, that streak of misery Brian doesn't deserve any oil! And Bid Shorcha came to Nell? . . .

—*Bloody tear and 'ounds*, didn't Nell send a motor car to fetch herself and Little Cáit! But Cáit decided to walk . . .

—The scent of the corpse, what else? . . .

—"*Bloody tear and 'ounds*," she said, as she was laying Jack out, "if I were to go on the bier-poles tomorrow myself I couldn't but come, seeing who sent for me."

—Bid Shorcha the sponger! Little Cáit the grinner! They went to Nell but they wouldn't come to decent people at all. I wouldn't begrudge it to Jack the Scológ, the poor creature, only for that other dishevelled little bitch. Jack the Scológ! Jack . . .

—It won't be long till somebody will have to keen Bid Shorcha herself. *Bloody tear and 'ounds*, didn't she fall on her way home from

Jack's funeral and didn't they have to send the motor car back to the house with her again . . .

—Drunk! As she often was . . .

—She took ill. She didn't get up since. "Hoh-roh, my Mary, your wares and your bags and belts . . ."

—Has Nell herself any notion of coming here?

—She says she's not well. But *bloody tear and 'ounds* for a story, she came to see me, and I think I never saw her looking so young.

—That's because she's delighted she got Jack shifted. Jack! Jack . . .

—*Bloody tear and 'ounds*, Caitríona, isn't it easy for her, with a motor car under her backside to go wherever she wants . . .

—In Lord Cockton's motor car. Hasn't she little decency or shame, to be off gallivanting! Jack the Scológ . . .

—*Bloody tear and 'ounds*, she doesn't have to, Caitríona. She has a car of her own!

—A car of her own?

—The only regret I had about leaving life was that I didn't get a ride in it. Herself and Peadar had promised to bring me anywhere in the county I wanted, but *bloody tear and 'ounds*, I lay back with no life left! . . .

—Ababúna! It can't be that the motor car is her own, Son of Blackleg! . . .

—Her own and her son Peadar's. *Bloody tear and 'ounds*, Caitríona, didn't you hear she bought a car for Peadar?

—Oh! She didn't! She didn't, Beartla Blackleg . . .

—*Bloody tear and 'ounds*, Caitríona, she did. He's not fit for hard work on account of his leg. He'll never put much strain on it, even though you wouldn't notice any lameness in his step. He's earning great money with the motor car, bringing people places in a hurry.

—I suppose there's no end to the noise she makes with it going past our house. Amn't I lucky I'm not alive, Beartla . . .

—*Bloody tear and 'ounds*, and she wears a hat any day she travels far from home! . . .

—Oh! Beartla! Beartla Blackleg! A hat . . .

—A hat as fancy as the Earl's wife wears . . .

—I'm absolutely convinced, Beartla, that she has charmed some of the money out of Baba . . .

—*Bloody tear and 'ounds*, Caitríona, of course she has, and for the past four months! Two thousand pounds!

—Two thousand pounds! Two thousand pounds, Beartla Blackleg! . . .

—Two thousand pounds, Caitríona! *Bloody tear and 'ounds*, isn't that how she bought the motor car, and isn't she going to put a grand big window into the church! . . .

—She has good reason to be thankful to the priest. But I'd have sworn on the book, Beartla, that Baba wouldn't take her claws off her money till she died! . . .

—*Bloody tear and 'ounds*, isn't she dead a long while! Nell got a thousand before she died, and another thousand since. She has some odd hundreds to get yet, and she'll hand them in to the bank down there to be spent on the fellow who's going to be a priest . . .

—Ababúna! What my Pádraig will get won't cover the palm of his hand . . .

—Some people say he'll get a lot, but that he won't get as much as Nell. *Bloody tear and 'ounds*, he's so easy-going that he doesn't query it! . . .

—He's been deluded by Nell.

—"Hoh-roh, my Mary, your wares and your bags and belts . . ."

—Oh! Good God Almighty! Baba's will. Poor Jack, like a burnt stick, thrown out in the refuse, and her son kept alive by St. John's Gospel. A new road up to her house. Her son's son going to be a priest. The pussface building a slate-roofed house. A motor car. Tomás Inside's land. Jack . . .

—*Bloody tear and 'ounds*, Caitríona, nobody has Tomás Inside's land.

—But isn't he staying in Nell's?

—*Bloody tear and 'ounds*, he is not, not for a long time. He's in your Pádraig's house, and Pádraig's cattle are on his land. He didn't like the gentry who frequented Nell's. "By the docks, they're not half as generous as they're made out to be," he told Pádraig. "I wasn't able to sleep a wink up there. Motor cars roaring outside from night till morn; chopping and hammering and blasting from morn till night. Aren't they badly off with their slate-roofed houses! By the docks, look at me, and not a dry spot for the bed in my cabin, where the drop wouldn't hit me between my gob and my eye . . ."

— The devil a word of a lie he said about the slate-roofed houses . . .

— Baba left him two hundred pounds in her will, and *bloody tear and 'ounds*, of course he didn't take his snout out of the drink since. Nell's house is too far up from the pubs for him . . .

— The useless yoke, Tomás Inside . . .

— Useless yoke indeed. That's the honest truth, Caitríona. Useless yoke indeed. *Bloody tear and 'ounds*, didn't I often say it myself, that he was a useless yoke. Any man who left Nell's house in a huff because he wasn't allowed into the motor car . . .

— But Beartla, wasn't he just as good as the rabble who were allowed into it? . . .

— *Bloody tear and 'ounds*, Caitríona, when Nell first got the motor car he hardly got out of it at all. Taking the air around the countryside with that silly grin on his face every day — to Brightcity, to Lakeside, to Headland Harbour — himself and Big Brian . . .

— The streak of misery . . .

— *Bloody tear and 'ounds*, Peadar Nell couldn't sit into the car without the two of them sitting in by his thigh. He was trying to earn a bit of money, and it didn't suit him to have those old scarecrows making their nest in his car. Some say it was the cause of Big Brian's failing health — being banned from the car. At least it was around that time he began to keep to the house . . .

— The wrath of Friday's King[4] on him, but wasn't it time for him! Blundering Brian was a fine sight in a motor car!

— *Bloody tear and 'ounds*, Caitríona, wasn't he as fine a sight in a motor car as Tomás Inside! Road-End's son hired Peadar Nell one night to bring himself and the priest's sister to a dance in Brightcity. Tomás Inside had just come home from Peadar the Pub's, and *bloody*

---

4. Jesus.

tear and 'ounds, what do you think he did but sit into the motor car! "I'll go to the dance too," he said. "By the docks, there'll be fine-looking women there."

— The old grimacer . . .

— He was smoking tobacco for all he was worth, and *bloody tear and 'ounds* didn't he throw out a huge gob of spittle! No great remarks were passed, Caitríona, but I heard that Big Brian said afterwards that the priest's sister had to change her trousers before going to the dance . . .

— That was coming to her, the shameless little slut, for getting into nosey Nell's motor car . . .

— Peadar Nell told Tomás to go in home. "By the docks, I won't," he said . . .

— May God grant him his life and health! . . .

— Big Brian's daughter told him to go in . . . "By the docks, I'll go to the dance," he said.

— He did right, not to heed ugly Brian's daughter . . .

— *Bloody tear and 'ounds,* didn't Road-End's son grab him by the arse and throw him out head over heels on the road, and give him two good "salamanders"[5] of kicks! *Bloody tear and 'ounds,* didn't he go down to your Pádraig's house, there and then, and he's sheltering there ever since . . .

— That left Nell in a pretty fix! He'll leave the land outright to Pádraig now.

— *Bloody tear and 'ounds,* Caitríona, nobody knows who Tomás Inside will leave his patch of land to. When they were going around in the motor car together Big Brian used to be at him to sign it over to his daughter, but to no avail!

— That's the stuff for that streak of misery Brian and for mathaired Nell! You didn't hear anything about a cross, Beartla?

— Crosses. *Bloody tear and 'ounds,* there's talk of nothing else in the townlands. Seáinín Liam's cross, Bríd Terry's cross, Red-haired Tom's cross, Jack the Scológ's cross that's not finished yet . . . *Bloody*

---

5. Resounding blows.

tear and 'ounds, Caitríona, what does it matter beneath the horns of the moon whether a person has a cross or not! "Hoh-roh, my Mary..."

—You won't say that, Beartla, when you've spent a while here listening to Nóra Sheáinín. You'd think she was the Earl's mother. But you didn't hear that Pádraig was to put a cross over me soon?

—Nell and himself are often away in the motor car, since Jack the Scológ was buried. Business about crosses, or wills...

—Oh! He won't do what's good for him, going around with that sleeky pussface...

—*Bloody tear and 'ounds*, Caitríona, isn't he thriving, God bless the man! He never had as many cattle on his land. He sold two batches of pigs very recently: huge big pigs with hams as hot as loaves from the oven. *Bloody tear and 'ounds*, aren't two children of his going to college...

—Two?

—Two. Yes. The eldest girl and the one after that...

—May God spare them!...

—And the one after that again will be going in the autumn, they say. *Bloody tear and 'ounds*, isn't that what Big Brian said!... "Hoh-roh, my Mary, your wares and your bags..."

—What did the streak of misery Brian say?

—"Hoh-roh, my Mary, your wares and your bags and belts..."

—But what did he say, Beartla?

—*Bloody tear and 'ounds*, that was a slip of the tongue, Caitríona! "Hoh-roh..."

—But what harm, Beartla. You know I won't be able to throw it back in his face. The blessings of God on you, Beartla, and tell me. It'll do me good...

—*Bloody tear and 'ounds*, it won't do you any good, Caitríona, any good at all. "Hoh-roh, my Mary..."

—It'll do me good, Beartla. You wouldn't believe the good a bit of news does a person here. The people of this graveyard wouldn't tell you anything, not even if it brought them back to life again. Jack the Scológ, for example, who's in the graveyard for the past three weeks. Jack the Scológ! Jack...

—"Hoh-roh, my Mary . . ."

—Ah, tell me. Good man, Beartla Blackleg! . . . Quickly now. Those people up above us will soon find out this is the wrong grave . . .

—*Bloody tear and 'ounds*, Caitríona, it doesn't make any difference to a person which grave his old bones are thrown into . . .

—Ah! tell me, Beartla, what Brian the Blubberer said . . .

—If there's going to be trouble, let there be trouble, Caitríona: "Everything's going well for Pádraig," he said, "since he left that little bess of a mother of his in that hole back there. A long, long time ago he should have turned a pot upside-down on her, put a red ember under it and have her die like a cat in the smoke . . ."

—They've swept you off again, Beartla Blackleg! . . . Jack the Scológ! Jack the Scológ! . . . Jack the Scológ! . . .

3

—. . . My heart turned to dust when the *Graf Spee*[6] was sent to the bottom. I was here a week from that day . . .

—The *mine* barely managed to kill us. Only for that, Murcháin would have robbed the Five of Trumps . . .

—. . . To stab me through the edge of my liver. The foul blow was always the hallmark of the One-Ear Breed . . .

—. . . A cold I caught from sweat and sleeping in the open, the time I cycled to Dublin to see Concannon . . .

—. . . I fell off a stack of oats and broke my thigh . . .

—A pity you didn't break your tongue as well! . . .

—Wasn't it a long way up your legs brought you, on a stack of oats!

—I'll bet you won't fall off a stack of oats again. You may be sure you won't . . .

—Only for you fell off a stack of oats you'd die some other way. A horse would kick you; or your legs would give up . . .

—Or your man would give you a bad bottle . . .

---

6. German cruiser damaged in battle and then scuttled, 1939.

—Or you wouldn't get enough to eat from your son's wife, on account of losing the pension for having money in the bank.

—You may be sure you'd die in any case . . .

—Falling is a bad thing . . .

—If you'd fallen in the fire as I did . . .

—The heart . . .

—Bedsores. If methylated spirits had been rubbed on me . . .

—You cowardly Siúán! You were the cause of my death. For the want of *fags* . . .

—Your coffee, you ugly Siúán . . .

—Faith then, as you said, the cause of death I had was . . .

—*Bloody tear and 'ounds,* I had no cause of death at all but stretched out, with no life left . . .

—The cause of death the Big Master had was . . .

—Piteous love. He thought if he died the Schoolmistress wouldn't consider life worth living without him . . .

—No, he thought he'd be doing Billyboy the Post an injustice if he stayed alive any longer . . .

—Not at all, it was Caitríona put a curse on him after he wrote a letter to Baba for her. "May no corpse go into the graveyard before that fellow in there!" she said. "Going from table to window . . ."

—The cause of death Jack the Scológ had was that Nell shifted him with the St. John's Gospel . . .

—Shut your mouth, you little brat!

—'Tis true for him. 'Tis true for him. The little bitch got the St. John's Gospel from the priest . . .

—. . . Shame is what caused your death. Your son having married a *black* in England . . .

—It would be twice as shameful if he had married an *Eyetalian* as your son did. From that day on, you drank no drop of the milk of good health. I saw you going the road one day. "That man is a goner," says I to myself. "Rigor mortis is setting in already. Once the news came that his son had married an *Eyetalian* he began to go downhill. Pure shame. And little wonder . . ."

—. . . Heartbreak is what the East-Side-of-the-Village Man felt about our losing the English market . . .

—. . . That fellow was disgruntled, after spending a whole month without managing to twist his ankle . . .

—Big Brian said that Curraoin died of regret that he didn't manage to make two halves of Glutton's donkey by splitting it with the adze along the cross on its back, when he found it in his field of oats . . .

—I thought it was Road-End's donkey . . .

—May the devil pierce him, it was Road-End's donkey, but I'd much prefer if it was his daughter instead of the donkey! . . .

—Big Colm's daughter died of . . .

—The Lower Hillside epidemic . . .

—No fear of that. But once the epidemic hit her nobody but the doctor came near the house, so she couldn't hear any rumours . . .

—You're insulting the faith. You're a black heretic . . .

—. . . The Insurance Man was only one letter short of winning the Crossword. That's what hastened his death . . .

—Red-haired Tom's cause of death was the length of his tongue . . .

—What cause did I have? What cause did I have, is it? What cause did I have? It's a wise man could say . . .

—Sweet-talking Stiofán died of regret that he didn't hear about Caitríona Pháidín's funeral . . .

—. . . Faith then, as you say, the cause of death I had was the intestines . . .

—. . . Oh! Do you hear him? The intestines indeed! The intestines! Oh! It was God's revenge that you died, Road-End Man. You stole my turf . . .

—. . . Upset that he wasn't appointed Chief Inquisitor . . .

—. . . God's revenge, Peadar the Pub. You were watering the whiskey . . .

—I was robbed in your house, Peadar the Pub . . .

—And so was I . . .

—. . . God's justice, Glutton. Drinking two score and two pints . . .

—"Nobody can ever say that I'm a windbag," said I. "Getting between that raging madman and the hatchet! Not only had I not made an Act of Contrition, but I was only on the second *bar* of the Creed when the little girl came over to the house for me. I'm telling you, Tomáisín's family, you may thank your lucky stars I had two score pints and two inside me . . ."

—. . . It was God's revenge on you, Insurance Man, for tricking Caitríona Pháidín and Tomás Inside . . .

—Ababúna! He did not. He did not . . .

—True for you, Caitríona. I did and I didn't. The tricks of the trade . . .

—. . . Because An Gúm wouldn't accept my collection of poems *The Golden Stars* . . .

—You're better dead than alive, you impudent brat. There on your own in the house by the hearth, praying to the ashes. "Oh, Sacred Ashes! . . . Oh, congealed blood that was spilled to broil my vitals in the embers! . . ."

—He's a black heretic . . .

—. . . The *Irishman* was unwilling to publish *The Setting Sun*. Nobody in the six townlands would listen to me read it . . .

—God's justice for certain! You said Columkille made a prophecy to lead the people astray . . .

—. . . It's no wonder you died. I heard the doctor say that nobody could stay healthy in those nettly groves of Donagh's Village . . .

—The priest told me that nineteen families used to pay him on the flea-bitten hillocks of your village twenty years ago, but now . . .

—Jack the Scológ's funeral was the cause of my death. I got up off my bed to go and keen him. I collapsed on my way home. I began to perspire. The perspiration was pouring off me from then till the time I expired . . .

—Jack the Scológ's funeral was the cause of my death too. I began to swell up after it . . .

—Ababúna! It was no wonder, the way you stuffed that shameless stomach of yours. Tell me, Bid Shorcha the sponger, how long have you been here, and you, Little Cáit the grinner? . . .

—*Bloody tear and 'ounds*, Caitríona, they were nearly neck and neck with myself coming here. I had six days' start on Bid Shorcha, and ten days on Little Cáit.

—That'll teach them to stay in their beds the next time! Why did they want to go to mat-haired Nell? Curiosity. They wouldn't come to decent people half as willingly . . .

—There'll be nobody left now to stretch or keen Tomás Inside or Nell Pháidín . . .

—Oh! Isn't it great to have the pussface in a fix! . . .

—. . . It was God's vengeance for certain that was the cause of Caitríona Pháidín's death. *Honest*. . .

—You're a damned liar, Nóirín . . .

—He wreaked vengeance on her for robbing Tomás Inside, and for stealing Bríd Terry's father's tea, Cite's potatoes and Seáinín Liam's periwinkles . . .

—Not at all, Nóra Sheáinín, it was the St. John's Gospel that Nell got from the priest for your daughter. They sent Caitríona to her death instead of her. Only for that, your daughter would have been here on that childbirth. She was sickly all her life till Caitríona died. But then she began to thrive . . .

—Ababúna búna! The devil a word of a lie you're saying! By the book, it never crossed my mind!

—. . . The death I'd give Siúán the Shop is to make her drink her own coffee . . .

—. . . To wear her own *clogs*.

—The death I'd give you, Glutton, is to make you drink pints of porter till it came out your nostrils, your eyes, your ears, under your nails, in your armpits, under your eyebrows, between your toes, in the hollows at the back of your knees, in your elbows, in the roots of your hair, till you'd sweat the seven perspirations of porter . . .

—. . . The most fitting death for you would be to be let live to see Kerry beat Galway in the All-Ireland final of 1941, with "The Rose of Tralee" being played on Concannon's backside . . .

—. . . The death I'd give you and every single one of your treacherous One-Ear Breed, is to make you . . .

—To make them shout "Up de Valera" . . .

—. . . No, but the death I'd give Road-End Man . . .

—To leave him to me till I'd ram one of my thatching scallops down his throat, into his gullet and through that gut of his . . .

—To leave him to me till I'd crack him with the lump-hammer he stole from me . . .

—I would gladly and promptly cut the head off him with my reaping hook . . .

—No more gladly than I would hang him with my rope . . .

—. . . Peadar the Pub? Drown him in his own worthless watered whiskey . . .

—. . . Pól? Make him wait with parched throat for the Gaelic Enthusiast to finish reading the "lesson" . . .

—. . . May the devil pierce himself and his trivial verses! Not to give that impudent brat, that good-for-nothing, anything to eat but his own "Sacred Ashes" . . .

—The death Caitríona would give to Nóra Sheáinín would be to make her disinfect herself, especially her feet . . .

—Shut your mouth, you brat . . .

—. . . The writer, is it? He insulted Columkille, the measly pup. To be compelled to make as many pilgrimages as the Schoolmistress makes for Billyboy the Post . . .

—To make him stuff *Sixty-One Sermons* down his throat . . .

—To make him recant in public his heresy and his insult to Columkille; to make him humbly ask forgiveness for all he has ever written; for all the young innocent maidens led astray by his evil writings; for the many married couples he drove apart; for all the happy families he split up; for being the precursor of the *Antichrist*. Then to excommunicate him and then burn him at the stake. Nothing less would teach heretics a lesson . . .

—. . . The death the Big Master would give to Billyboy . . .

—The thieving scoundrel! The death I'd give that cocky lout . . .

—. . . The Postmistress! To keep her from reading anybody else's letters but her very own for a week . . .

—'Tis true for you. A week without gossip caused Big Colm's daughter's death . . .

—They say the Schoolmistress said the Big Master's cause of death was . . .

—That he was too good for this world . . .

—Faith then, she did. I'll never forget what she said. "Whom the gods love . . ."

—Oh! The harlot! The draggle-haired slut! The cocksnout!

—*De grâce*, Master. You're behaving like Caitríona!

—. . . Don't you remember that I am the oldest inhabitant of the graveyard! Permission to speak . . .

—. . . Little Cáit! To keep her away from corpses . . .

—You must be joking! Even the Afrika Korps couldn't do that, once she got their scent . . .

—The death Big Brian would give to Caitríona Pháidín . . .

—The thieving cat's death under the pot! . . .

—To make her stand outside her own house; Nell in her flowery hat going past in her motor car; a little crescent of a smile on her face as she looks in at Caitríona, and Nell blowing the horn for all she's worth . . .

—Oh! Leave me alone! Leave me alone! I'd explode . . .

—Isn't that what I said!

—I'd explode! I'd explode!

4

—. . . "Would you come ho-ome along with me:
    There's roo-oom beneath my shaw-awl,
    And indeed, my Jack . . ."

—*Écoutez-moi, mes amis. Les études celtiques.* We'll have a *Colloquium* now.

—A *Colloquium*, lads! Hey! Bríd Terry, Sweet-talking Stiofán, Máirtín Pockface! A *Colloquium* . . .

—A *Colloquium*, Red-haired Tom! . . .

—I'll say nothing. Nothing . . .

—Isn't it a pity Tomás Inside isn't here! He'd be a good man for a *Colloquium* . . .

—The result of my findings concerning the dialect of the Half Guinea. I'm afraid this will not be a proper *Colloquium*. The only language a *Colloquium* can be properly held in cannot be spoken fast enough by me or by you people . . .

—Fast enough?

—Fast, *mes amis*. The first qualification for a *Colloquium* is speed. I have to say, my Irish friends, that I'm greatly disappointed by my research . . .

—Musha, God help us, you poor thing! . . .

—*Mes amis*, it's not possible to carry out learned research into a language spoken by a great number of people, such as English or Russian . . .

—I've a great suspicion he's a black heretic . . .

—It's only possible—and only worthwhile—to carry out research into a dialect known to two persons, or three at most. There should be three senile dribbles accompanying every word.

—. . . There was such a day, Peadar the Pub. Don't deny it . . .

—It's not worth researching a person's speech unless the words come out astride one another . . .

—. . . Eight into eight, that's one. Eight into sixteen, that's two . . .

—. . . This *Colloquium* is a heaven-sent opportunity for me to read *The Setting Sun* . . .

—*Pas du tout!* This is a *Colloquium convenable* . . .

—I won't listen to *The Setting Sun*. I won't. *Honest!* . . .

—Hold on now, my good Frenchman! I'll tell you a story . . .

—*Écoutez, Monsieur* Cóilí. This is a *Colloquium*. Not a University lecture on Irish Literature . . .

—I'll tell you a story. Upon my soul I will![7] "The Kitten That

---

7. The following passage in the text involves elaborate wordplay in Irish, French, and Breton, a language Máirtín Ó Cadhain studied.

Committed an Impropriety on the White Sheets of All of Conn's[8] Half of Ireland . . ."

—. . . "Mártan Sheáin Mhóir had a daughter
And she was as broad as . . ."

—. . . "At the Wattle Ford[9] of Merriment he met Moghchat of the round fat thighs. 'Don't go any further,' said the Moghchat. 'I have just returned from Wattle Ford, after having committed that little impropriety on all the white sheets there. From now on it will be called Wattle Ford of Black Pool. I left this fine conspicuous piece of mischief—the Eiscir Riada[10]—in my tracks coming down, and before that I committed a little smear of mischief on the fine sheets all over Mogh's Half of Ireland'" . . . Mogh's Half, my good friend, from Moghchat: big cat in Old Irish . . .

—*Ce n'est pas vrai!* Mathchat is the word. Matou.[11] Mathshlua. Mathghamhain.

—*Gast*[12] was the word for a female cat in proper Old Irish . . .

—*Mais non!* Gaiste, a loop, a noose, a snare, a trap, a battery of guns, a convenience. "Oh, gast of gasts in the gast of gasts I am,"[13] said Knotted Bottom, as his cloak was being ripped off . . .

Modern Breton: *gast:* a woman who has a stall of holy objects, in order to collect money for the poor at *pardon* in Leon.[14] In the dia-

---

8. Conn, Mogh: mythical heroes who divided Ireland between them.

9. Áth Cliath, the ancient name of Dublin. The word Dublin comes from Dubh Linn (black pool).

10. An esker or ridge of glacial deposits that runs nearly all the way across Ireland and provided a convenient way across the bogs; it also was the boundary between the two halves of Ireland.

11. French for male cat (tomcat).

12. "Gast" is Breton for prostitute/whore. The Irish word "gaiste" means snare.

13. From the Breton expletive "Gast ar c'hast," which means "whore of whores," used for emphasis to show astonishment or disbelief (. . . in the gast of a gast I am: in the snare of a whore I am).

14. Modern Breton: *gast:* a woman who has a stall of holy objects—a humorously deliberate and false etymology of the word "gast." The pardon was a local reli-

lect of Gwened[15] . . . I'd have to consult my notes about that, Cóilí. But the *thèse* is right: Old Irish: *Gast*; S muted before T; *Gât*: Cat: *Pangur Bán:*[16] *Paintéar: Panther:* Big Smart Fat-Cat of Learning . . .

—Hold on now, my good friend, and I'll tell you how the cloak was ripped off Knotted Bottom . . .

—Cóilí, Seán Chite in our village says it was how he lost it . . .

—Seán Chite in your village! It's not often a man of your village said anything decent . . .

—. . . By the oak of this coffin, Little Cáit, I gave Caitríona Pháidín the pound . . .

—. . . A big fur coat on her, Red-haired Tom, like the one Baba Pháidín used to wear, till she had to throw it away after all the smuts that fell on it in Caitríona's . . .

—You're a damned liar, Bríd Terry . . .

—Peace and quiet is what I want. Stop abusing me, Caitríona . . .

—. . . Can I give you any spiritual help, Sweet-talking Stiofán?

—. . . Billyboy the Post, Master? *Bloody tear and 'ounds*, if a person is going to die he's going to die. If Billyboy's to die, *Bloody tear and 'ounds*, Master, he'll stretch out, with no life left . . .

—. . . Didn't the little colt die!

—Didn't the little mare die!

—It's many a day since that happened, but Beartla Blackleg told me the little colt died only recently . . .

—It's many a day since I had her, indeed. She was great! I bought her at St. Bartholomew's Fair. It was no bother to her to carry a ton and a half against any hill. Two years exactly I had her . . .

—As soon as Beartla Blackleg told me the colt died, I said: "Soaking rain killed it. The young fellow hadn't finished putting the roof

---

gious festival, like the Irish "pattern," in Leon in northwest Brittany, a region renowned for its priests and piety.

15. Gwened is the name of the town and diocese of Vannes in southeast Brittany (not to be confused with Gwynedd in Wales).

16. Pangur Bán, name of a cat in a celebrated medieval Irish poem.

on the stable, and he left the colt too long in the open." *"Bloody tear and 'ounds,* that wasn't it at all," he said . . .

—It was around the Feast of St. Bartholomew, of all the days in the year. I was moving the little mare down to the New Field by the house. She had the upper half of the village picked bare. I met Nell and Peadar Nell at the Meadow Height, on their way up home. "Would you have a match?" says Peadar. "By Dad, I might have," says I. "Where are you going with the little mare, God bless her?"[17] he said. "I'm moving her down to the New Field," said I . . .

—"Wireworm so," says I. *"Bloody tear and 'ounds,* not at all," said Beartla Blackleg . . .

—"She's a beautiful little mare, God bless yourself and herself," said Nell. "She would be," said Peadar, "only for her condition." "Condition!" said I. "'Tis no bother to her to carry a ton and a half against any hill . . ."

—"Coughing," said I. *"Bloody tear and 'ounds,* coughing!" said Beartla. "Not at all . . ."

—"Have you any notion," said Peadar, "of bringing her to the St. Bartholomew Fair, God bless her?" "Musha, I don't rightly know," said I. "I'm between two minds. I'm reluctant to part with her. She's a great little mare. But I don't have much fodder this winter."

—"Worms," said I. *"Bloody tear and 'ounds,"* said Son of Blackleg . . .

—"How much would you be asking for her, God bless her?" said Nell. "Musha, if I took her to the fair I'd ask for twenty-three pounds," said I. "Get away, yourself and your twenty-three pounds!" said Peadar, and he took himself off up the boreen. "Would you accept sixteen pounds?" said Nell. "Indeed then, Nell, I would not," said I. "Seventeen pounds," she said. "Get away with your seventeen pounds!" said Peadar. "Come on!" The mother took herself off after him, but she kept looking back at the little white-faced mare . . .

---

17. To speak of an animal (or a person) without adding God's blessing was held to put the evil eye on it, that is, to bring it bad luck.

—"What do you mean, worms?" he said. *"Bloody tear and 'ounds,* she had no more worms in her than I had! Didn't they open her up! . . ."

—Caitríona Pháidín came over from her own Little Fields of Haws. "What did that pussface have to say?" she said. "She offered me seventeen pounds for the white-faced mare," said I. "Faith, I'd let her have her for twenty, or for nineteen, even. I'd give her to her for a pound cheaper than I would to a man from outside the village. It would brighten my heart to see her going past me every day. I'd say, from the way she fancied her, herself or her son will be down to me again before morning. They won't let me take her to the fair."

"Arrah, that pussface!" said Caitríona. "She'll destroy your white-faced mare going up those steep rocky paths. If she buys her indeed, may she have no luck with her! . . ."

—"Devil do I know what cause of death the colt would have so," said I. "It wouldn't have been a weak heart, would it? . . ."

—Faith then, she said that, Seáinín Liam. "Go to the fair," she said, "with your white-faced mare, and get the right price for her, and don't heed that pussface's sweet talk . . ."

—*"Bloody tear and 'ounds,"* said Son of Blackleg. "What cause of death would it have but to lie down and die? . . ."

—"Go off to the fair with your white-faced mare," said Caitríona again. I would never have noticed that she didn't say "God bless her," only for the wild way she was glaring at the mare . . .

—'Tis a great blow for the poor young fellow that the colt is gone. He'll have plenty to do to get a wife now.

—That evening the mare was puffing and coughing. The following morning with the lark Peadar Nell landed down to me. The two of us went over to the New Field. She was an awful loss, Seáinín Liam! She was stretched out there from ear to tail and not a stir out of her.

—Exactly as the colt was . . .

—"That is so," said I. "The evil eye."

—Indeed then, they say that Caitríona had the evil eye. I wouldn't buy a colt while she was alive . . .

—Ababúna! It was pussface Nell put the evil eye on her.

—She went past me without saying "God bless you," and before I had two more handfuls of oats on the stack I fell off it . . .

—Faith then, she didn't say "God bless you" to me, and I twisted my ankle the same day . . .

—Of course, the Big Master didn't have a day's health since he wrote the letter for her. A curse . . .

—She can't have put the evil eye on Mannion the Counsellor, for he's still alive . . .

—Don't believe them, Jack! Jack the Scológ! . . .

—. . . Did you not hear, Cite, that Tomás Inside migrated yet again? . . . He did indeed, two weeks ago . . .

—Ababúna!

—He wasn't able to get a wink of sleep in Pádraig Chaitríona's with the grunting of pigs from night till morn. The sow had piglets and they were brought into the house. "Didn't they have a great need of sows!" he said. "Look at me who never had a sow! I'll go up to the house where there's no grunting of pigs and where I'll have slates over my head." On his way up to Nell's he chased Pádraig's cattle off his patch of land . . .

—. . . The cocky old fool, the same Tomás Inside . . .

—. . . It would be much more of a shame to you, as you say, if your son had married an *Eyetalian*. Those *blacks* are very gentle. Didn't you see the *black* who was butler to the Earl long ago?

—Faith then, that same *black* could be quite short-tempered too . . .

—Sometimes, as you say, he could be quite short-tempered. Well, I don't know what my young man at home is going to do, may God guide him to do what's good for him. The priest's sister asked him to marry her. They're keeping company for a while now . . .

—Isn't that what happened to my son in England too! He was keeping company with this *black* for a good while, and she asked him to marry her. What do you think, but didn't the little fool go off and marry her!

—By Cripes, as you say, that's how it goes. Foolish lads. I heard my old woman at home was delighted with Nancy—I think Nancy is her name—but if I were alive I'd say to him: "Look out for yourself, now. What's that little girl able for in a country household? Do you think she could spread a bank of turf or carry a creel of seaweed? . . ."

—Isn't that exactly what I wrote to my son in England! "Wasn't it the fine heifer you married," said I. "If you ever come home, what good-looking specimens you'll have on a halter coming into the country: a *blackeen*, and a clutch of young *blackeens* running round the village. Your reputation will go all over Ireland. People would come from near and far to look at them. Don't you know she won't be able to forage on land or on strand. Devil a bit of seaweed or turf was ever seen where that one came from . . ."

—There's no accounting for foolishness, as you say. There was no getting our fellow to listen to advice. He was always . . . what's this Nóra Sheáinín called it? . . .

—A coxcomb? . . . A *bowsie?* . . . A blackguard?

—Faith then, he was not. He wasn't a blackguard, anyhow. I brought him up a well-mannered, honest lad, even if I say so myself. Why can't I think of how Nóra Sheáinín put it? . . .

—Adonis! . . .

—Faith then, as you say, that's the way. Nancy brought him off to Brightcity and he put a wedding ring on her finger. It warmed the cockles of my old woman's heart . . .

—And my old woman was overjoyed too! She thought a *negress* was some sort of a grand *lady* until I told her she had the same colour skin as the Earl's butler. When she heard that, the priest had to be sent for . . .

—That's how it goes, as you say. The priest was trying to get Nancy to marry the Wood of the Lake schoolmaster, but faith then, she told him out straight, without putting a tooth in it, that she wouldn't marry him. "That miserable nonentity is already married to the school," she said, "and what would he want to marry me for, then? I don't like the Wood of the Lake schoolmaster," she said. "Sure, there's no pep in him! He's an impotent old thing . . ."

—My son was an impotent thing, in any case. Wasn't he hard up to go and marry a *black* in London, where there's as many people as there is in the whole of Ireland . . . I heard she has hair as curly as an otter . . .

—Foolishness, as you say. "I won't marry that impotent thing from Wood of the Lake," said Nancy. "Road-End's son has a motorbike. He's a fowler, an angler, a fiddler, and a top-class dancer. He's an eyeful when he dresses up. He offered to shoot Lord Cockton if he saw him in my company again. His house is as bright as a villa—a villa she said, on my soul!—it's so well furnished and ornamental. It clears the clothes-moths out of my heart to go in there . . ."

—It's easy for you to boast about your ornamental house, Road-End Man. Ornamental . . .

—Thanks to my drift-weed . . .

—. . . *Honest*, Dotie. Every word of what I told you was the truth. Caitríona Pháidín never paid for anything: the *roundtable*, or Cite's pound . . .

—You're a damned liar . . .

—And her son is like that too, Dotie. Her coffin is still to be paid for in Tadhg's, and the drink for her wake and funeral in Siúán the Shop's . . .

—You're a damned liar, Nóirín . . .

—Doesn't her son get demands for them every second day. *Honest*. That's why Peadar the Pub and Siúán the Shop are so annoyed with her here.

—Ababúna, Nóirín, Nóirín . . .

—Not the least little bit of her burial expenses has been paid, Dotie, except that my son from Mangy Field paid for the tobacco and snuff . . .

—Oh! Nóirín, you guiding light of mariners! Don't believe her, Jack the Scológ . . .

—God would punish us . . .

—Nell paid for her grave here too, out of pure shame . . .

—Oh! The pussface, she did not, she did not. Don't believe Rotten Thighs from Mangy Field! Don't believe her, Jack! I'll explode! I'll explode! I'll explode! . . .

—... It was I laid you all out, my dear neighbours . . .

—You were great, Little Cáit, to give you your due . . .

—I never accepted a pound, shilling or penny from anyone. The Earl sent for me the time his mother died. When I had finished with her, "How much will you charge?" he said. "You'll get whatever you ask for . . ."

—You'd be sent to prison for the rest of your life, Little Cáit, if you had as much as tried to lay a finger on her, or even go near the room she was laid out in . . .

—It was I laid out Peadar the Pub . . .

—It was not, Little Cáit, it was two nurses from Brightcity, in uniforms and white caps. People said they were nuns . . .

—It was I laid out the Frenchman . . .

—If you had laid a hand on him, Little Cáit, you'd be sent to prison for contravening Ireland's neutrality in time of war . . .

—It was I laid out Siúán the Shop . . .

—That's a damned lie. My daughters wouldn't allow you one nostril's ration of air in the room I was laid out in. Why would they? For you to go pawing me! . . .

—Even the viewing of Siúán's corpse was rationed, Cáit . . .

—The Big Master . . .

—Indeed it was not you, Little Cáit. I was working over there next to his house, in our own Roadside Field. Billyboy the Post called me:

"Your man is for the stray letters office," he said. You and I, Little Cáit, were in through the door at the exact same moment. We went upstairs and said a blast of prayers with the Schoolmistress and Billyboy.

"The poor Master has expired," said the Schoolmistress, with a lump in her throat. "Easily known. He was too good for this life."

—Oh! The hussy! . . .

—You went over, Little Cáit, and stretched out your hand to put your thumbs on his eyelids. The Schoolmistress stopped you. "I'll do all that's to be done with the Big Master, the poor man," she said.

—Oh! The cocky little bitch!

—Now, Master, remember that Máirtín Pockface saw you in the school . . .

—Faith then, there's nothing better than the truth, Master . . .

—"Let you go down to the kitchen and rest yourself, Little Cáit," she said. She told myself and Billyboy to go for food and drink and tobacco. "Don't spare anything," she said to Billyboy. "I don't begrudge it to the Big Master, the poor man . . ."

—With my own money! Oh!

—When we came back you were still in the kitchen, Little Cáit. Billyboy went up to the Schoolmistress who was snivelling upstairs . . .

—Oh! The beggar! The frisky little lout!

—When he came down you spoke to him, Little Cáit. "That poor creature up there must be exhausted," you said. "I'll go up and help her wash him." "Rest yourself there, Little Cáit," said Billyboy. "The Schoolmistress is so grief-stricken for the Big Master that she's better off on her own for a while," he said. He grabbed a razor out of a press and I held the strop for him to sharpen it.

—My own razor and strop! They were kept in the top of the press. How well he knew where to find them, the thief . . .

—You were darting around the kitchen, Little Cáit, like a dog with fleas . . .

—As busy as Nóra Sheáinín when she'd come over to Caitríona's . . .

—Shut your mouth, you little brat . . .

—"I must go upstairs and keep him propped up on his side while you're shaving his cheeks," you said. "The Schoolmistress will do that," said Billyboy. "You can rest yourself there, Little Cáit . . ."

—Oh! The mangy pair! . . .

—Don't heed him, Big Master. It was I who laid you out. And a fine-looking corpse you were, God bless you! That's what I said to the Schoolmistress when we had you decked out. "He's a credit to you, Mistress," said I. "He made a fine-looking corpse, may the Lord have mercy on him, but that was to be expected: a fine man like the Big Master . . ."

—Faith then, Cáit, it wouldn't matter how the likes of us would be laid out, but it seems to me you'd be too rough and ready to go pawing a schoolmaster . . .

—. . . Five days I spent watching over you, East-Side-of-the-Village Man; up and down to your house to see you: up and down to the Little Height to look over at your house to see if there was any sign of your death. Raving in your sleep you were, and the only complaint out of you was about a patch of land at the top of the village that was the best ever for fattening cattle. It seemed to me you'd much prefer not to go at all if you couldn't take it with you . . .

—And so much blather out of the gadfly about the English market . . .

—. . . It was I who laid you out indeed, Curraoin, and still and all, you were very reluctant to be off. You definitely went through the death-throes. Every time I was about to put the thumbs on you, you'd wake up again. Your wife felt your pulse. "He's expired, may the Lord have mercy on him!" she said.

"Musha, may his soul have calm and fair sailing!" said Big Brian, who had just come in. "He got his passage money at last. By Dad, I thought he wouldn't sail without taking Road-End's daughter on board with him."

"May his bed be bright in Heaven tonight!" I said myself, and I ordered a tub of water to be prepared. Didn't you wake back up at that very moment! "Take care that Tom gets the big holding," you said. "I'd rather see it swept away by the wind than the eldest son to have it, unless he marries some woman other than Road-End's daughter . . ." You woke up again: "If the eldest son gets the land from you," you said to your wife, "the devil mend me but my ghost will have you by the tail of your shirt by day and by night! Isn't it a pity I didn't go to an attorney and make a sound will! . . ."

You woke up the third time: "That spade Tomáisín's daughter took away with her, the time of the early potatoes, let one of you go and get it back, since they didn't have the decency to return it themselves. May the devil pierce them! Be sure you issue a *summons* on Glutton for letting his donkeys into our oats. If you don't get satisfaction in court, the next time you catch them inside our wall, drive horseshoe nails through their hooves. May the devil pierce himself and his donkeys! Don't be too lax or lazy to get up before dawn and keep an eye on your turf, and if you should catch Road-End Man . . ."

—I thought it was the old woman who was stealing it . . .

—They were all as bad as each other, himself and his old woman and their four children.

—. . . You were about to surrender your soul when I came in. I knelt down as the litany was being recited. Even at that stage you were still murmuring. "Jack, Jack, Jack," you kept saying. "How well the poor thing remembers Jack the Scológ," I said to Nell Pháidín, who was on her knees beside me. "But the two were always great friends." "God grant you a bit of sense, Little Cáit," said Nell, "'*Black, black, black*' is what he's saying! The son . . ."

—I heard, Cáit, that the last warning Caitríona Pháidín gave to her son was . . .

—To bury her in the Pound Plot . . .

—To put a cross of Island limestone over her . . .

—Ababúna!

—To go to Mannion the Counsellor and get him to write a powerful letter about Baba's will . . .

—To let Tomás Inside's house fall down . . .

—To poison Nell . . .

—Ababúna! Don't believe him, Jack . . .

—If Nóra Sheáinín's daughter didn't die on her next childbirth, to divorce her . . .

—You're insulting the faith, you little brat. The *Antichrist* will soon be here . . .

—. . . Oh! There was pandemonium all over the village straight away:

"He fell off a stack of oats."

"He fell off a stack of oats."

"Your man fell off a stack of oats."

Up I went to the house to you immediately. I was certain I'd find a brand-new corpse waiting for me there. What did I get instead but yourself there like a lazy lump, telling everyone how your left foot slipped.

—Upon my soul, Cáit, I broke my thigh in two halves.

—What good was that to me? I thought I'd have a brand new corpse waiting for me . . .

—But I died, Cáit . . .

—. . . I never saw a big lazy lump in a bed as restless as you were. You had one leg on the floor . . .

—I knew, Cáit, that I was dying, and I tried to get up and go to the murderer and kill him. "Drink two spoonfuls from this bottle . . ."

—*Bloody tear and 'ounds*, for a story . . .

—. . . I probed your throat. "Where's the bone that choked her?" said I. "The doctor took it out," said your sister. "May the Lord's mercy be no less for that!" said I. "Nobody should stuff themselves. If that woman hadn't been so greedy in eating her food we wouldn't be laying her out now . . ."

"She hadn't tasted a bit of meat since the Feast of St. Martin,"[18] said your sister . . .

—*Bloody tear and 'ounds*, didn't Big Brian say she'd still be alive and kicking today if she hadn't chased Caitríona Pháidín's dog out of the house before dinner-time? "He was so wild with hunger," he said, "he'd have easily gone down her windpipe and got up the bone . . ."

—Oh! Brian the scold!

—. . . It was summer, and the perspiration was congealed in your skin. "He couldn't but smell of sweat," said my mother. "My poor child was a foolish boy, and it shows on him now. Putting himself

---

18. The 11th of November. There was a custom of spilling blood in honour of St. Martin, which involved killing a fowl or animal and making the sign of the cross with the blood on each forehead and door. This meant that even the very poor ate meat at least once a year.

through that ordeal of going to Dublin on an old bike, and sleeping in the open the same night! I hope God won't hold it against him . . ."

—Oh! If I'd been alive a month from that day I'd have seen Concannon beating Kerry . . .

—In 1941, is it? If it is . . .

—. . . You gave myself and Muraed Phroinsiais grey hair. We scrubbed and scrubbed and scrubbed you, but to no avail. "These spots are not dirt at all," said I to Muraed at last. "There are five or six of them," said Muraed. "They're emblems that have to do with Hitler," said your daughter. Amn't I the forgetful one now that I can't remember what she called them . . .

—Tattoo.

—*Swastika* . . .

—That's the very word, by all that's holy. We'd wasted three pots of boiling water on you, four pounds of soap, two boxes of Rinso, a lump of Monkey Brand, two buckets of sand, but they wouldn't come out. I wouldn't mind, but you didn't show the least bit of gratitude after all the trouble you put us to . . .

—I'd have put you to more trouble, only for the *Graf Spee*, for I would have branded every little bulge of my body. Hitler was worthy of that much.

—"Arrah! bad luck to him! Leave them," said Muraed. "He can't be let go in the condition he's in," said I. "Isn't he as pockmarked as a stray letter! Put another pot of water on the fire, in the name of God."

Big Brian happened to come in at that very moment. "It seems to me," he said, "that you two want to scald the poor fellow like a dead pig . . ."

—Oh! He was the right scald himself, and an ugly scald he was!

—. . . No more than the fellow a while ago, I was exhausted washing you. There wasn't the least lump of your body that wasn't covered with ink. "This fellow is like a man who has been left soaking in a tub of ink," said I. "He might as well have been," said your sister. "The ink is what killed him. Sucking it into his lungs from morn till night and from night till morn . . ."

—Writer's cramp he had, according to himself . . .

—Whatever he had, he brought it on himself. He was a black heretic. He shouldn't be allowed into consecrated ground at all. It's a wonder God didn't make an example of him . . .

—. . . I got the whiff of it as soon as I walked into the room to you. "Was there porter or something like that spilled here?" said I to Curraoin's wife. "Not that I know of," she said.

—And no wonder: a man who used to drink two score and two pints . . .

—There wasn't a drop in my belly the day I died. Devil as much as a drop, then! . . .

—That's the truth you're saying. There was not. That was one of Little Cáit's tricks, the grinner. Expecting a drink she was, when she said that to Curraoin's wife . . .

—. . . That was what was wrong with me, Little Cáit. Siúán the Shop's coffee. It rotted my intestines . . .

—. . . Your legs were as brittle as rotted wood, with black lumps on them, and creaking like a cow with bog lameness . . .

—Siúán the Shop's *clogs*, of course . . .

—I suppose you couldn't get a scent as far away as Mangy Field, Little Cáit. If you'd seen Nóra Sheáinín's feet, who never wore *clogs*! That is if Caitríona is to be believed, of course . . .

—Shut your mouth, you little brat . . .

—. . . The very moment I reached the door I got the smell of ash-potatoes, Cite. "Put those ash-potatoes away," said I, "till the dead person is dressed." "There are no potatoes in the ashes," said Micil. "And I wish there had been none since morning either. Too many ash-potatoes she ate. They were too heavy on the stomach. They made a rock in her belly . . ."

—*Bloody tear and 'ounds* for a story. Cite just lay back, with no life left . . .

—. . . They had left you too long and let your body grow cold. There you were, a stiff lump, and four of us working on you to no avail. "Let somebody go and get your man's lump-hammer," said Big Brian, "and you'll see how I'll stretch his knees for him . . ." "*Bloody tear and 'ounds,*" said the son of Blackleg, "didn't Road-End Man steal it from him! . . ."

—It was he who stole it, indeed. A lovely lump-hammer . . .

—. . . The creel of potatoes you brought from the Common Field had left its print on the broad of your back, Seáinín Liam . . .

—When I was easing it off me inside in the house, the strap handle slipped and it came down lopsided. I gave my side a little wrench. The dresser began to dance. The clock went from the wall to the chimney, the chimney went to the doorway, the colt that was straight in front of me in the House Field rose in the air and went down the boreen and over the road. "The colt!" said I, and I made for the door to go after it. The heart . . .

—I got the smell of the bed off you immediately, Máirtín Pockface . . .

—Faith then, the bedsores were what finished me off . . .

—. . . It gives me no satisfaction to publicise this, poet, but you were covered in a coat of dirt from the top of your head to the tips of your toes . . .

—. . . His "Sacred Ashes." The devil pierce him, the impudent brat! He never washed himself . . .

—Myself and your aunt stripped it off you, till you had only a spot left on your thigh. We couldn't get that off. "The dirt is stuck to him like barnacles here," said I to your aunt. "Plenty of boiling water and sand." Your mother had gone out looking for winding-sheets. She came in at that very moment. "That's a mole," she said. "Every time my dear boy got a fit of poetry he used to scratch himself there and the words would come with great difficulty . . ."

—He was a fatty, he was a softy, he was a lump of lard. We were put to the pin of our collar to carry him here at all.

—I never saw a corpse whose eyes were more difficult to close than Road-End Man. I had a thumb on one eye, and his old lady had her thumb on the other, but no sooner I'd have my side closed than the old lady's side would open . . .

—To see if there was any lump-hammer going a-begging . . .

—Or any drift-weed . . .

—I never got as fragrant a smell as was off the Postmistress . . .

—The smell of the drugs she used for opening letters and sealing them again. The back room was like a chemist's shop . . .

—Not at all! The kettle was O.K. for that. Fragrances for the bath-tub. I took a bath just before I died . . .

—That's true, Postmistress. There was no need to wash your corpse at all . . .

—You don't know whether it was necessary or not, Little Cáit. Gosh! If you'd as much as touched my corpse the Minister for Posts and Telegraphs would have the law on you . . .

—. . . Whoever laid you out, I'd say he got the smell of the nettles of Donagh's Village off you . . .

—Even that was better than what was off you . . .

—I never saw a cleaner corpse than Jack the Scológ's. Rigor mortis never even touched him. He was like a flower. You'd think his skin was silk. You'd think he had just laid down for a rest . . . Not only that, but every stitch of clothes about him was as pure white as that "flour"[19] that was sprinkled on the Earl at the door of the church on his wedding morning! Of course, they wouldn't be allowed in Nell Pháidín's house if they were any other way . . .

—The pussface! The cheeky busybody!

—They say, Cáit, that Caitríona's corpse wasn't . . .

—Caitríona's corpse! That one! I was sent for, but I wouldn't go next or near her corpse . . .

—Ababúna!

—It would turn my stomach . . .

—Ababúna! Little Cáit, the grinner! Little Cáit, the grinner! I'll explode! I'll explode! . . .

6

. . . There isn't a God above or he'll punish that pair for it! It was easily known! I had no violent pain. The doctor said the kidneys

---

19. Confetti.

wouldn't kill me for some time. But that pussface Nell coaxed the St. John's Gospel from the priest for Nóra Sheáinín's daughter, and they bought me a single ticket to this lodging, as they did for Jack the Scológ, the poor man. Wasn't it plain to a stump of bog-deal[20] that if there hadn't been some skulduggery going on Nóra Sheáinín's daughter would have been here on her next *blast* of childbirth. Instead of that, the pain and sickness left her completely . . .

And of course there were no flies on that pussface! She knew that as long as I had the least puff of breath in my body I'd keep tit for tat with her about Baba's will and Tomás Inside's land. But she can hoodwink Pádraig to her heart's content . . .

Two thousand pounds. A slate-roofed house. A motor car. A hat . . . Son of Blackleg said Pádraig would get a fistful of money, but what good is that when the whole will isn't going to him! God blast that one over beyond, I wish she'd left every shiny halfpenny belonging to her to priests! . . .

Twenty-three pounds of altar-money for Jack the Scológ. And she never let a shilling out of her own house to any funeral! . . . High Mass. Priests. The Earl. Lord Cockton. Four half-barrels of porter. Whiskey. Cold meat . . . And how well the little schemer thought of lighting twelve candles over him in the chapel! To be one up on me. What else? I wouldn't begrudge poor Jack anything, but it was just to show off the pussface did it. It was easy for her—with the old hag's easy money.

Jack the Scológ wouldn't sing a song the other day. He has completely lost heart. No wonder, having spent his life with that bitch. And all the respect she had for him in the end was to get St. John's Gospel to put him to death! . . .

When I told him that the other day he never said a word except "God would punish us . . ." I'd say he's in a red rash of anger by now on account of how she treated him . . . And the little fool didn't notice it at all himself. He was always and ever without guile. Otherwise he'd have realized that stiff-jointed little Nell was playing on him when

---

20. Timber from ancient forests, found in bogs.

she asked him to marry him. "I have Jack," she said. "We'll leave Big Brian to you, Caitríona" . . . But I'm closer to Jack now than she is. I can speak to him whenever I want to . . .

Only for Pádraig heeded Nóra Sheáinín's daughter I'd be buried in the Pound Plot beside him. That sharp-tongued Siúán the Shop is beside him now. She'll give me a bad name. She has told him a bellyful of lies about me already. That's why he's so reluctant. I wouldn't mind but the fair maid of the Filthy Feet is trying to coax him into her Rotary! And Bid Shorcha and Little Cáit are forever whining about his funeral. You'd think the poor man was responsible for their death. Not only that, but they're showering praises to the clay-top on the pussface who got them up out of their beds . . .

Muraed Phroinsiais and Ash-Potatoes Cite have cramps in their tongues praising Nell too, and so have Bríd Terry and Seáinín Liam, the Useless Red-head and Máirtín Pockface. But they won't open their mouth to me because I won't praise her. No. Not as much as a word. You'd think it was unlucky to speak to me. It would be great if a person would fight manfully and openly with you . . . This graveyard is worse now than the places the Frenchman was talking about the other day: Belsen, Buchenwald and Dachau . . .

—. . . Had I been alive, indeed, I'd have been at your funeral, Jack the Scológ. I owed it to . . .

—. . . Hold on now, my good man. Did you ever hear what nickname Conán[21] had for Oscar? . . .

—By the oak of this coffin, Bid Shorcha, I gave Caitríona the pound, and I never saw as much as a penny of it . . .

—Spouting lies you are, you little scabby arse! Muraed! Muraed! Did you hear what the Hag of the Ash-Potatoes said again, Muraed? Muraed, I say! Hello, Muraed! Why don't you answer me? . . . Muraed, I say! . . . You won't speak? I'm a prattler, you say! . . . I thrive on stirring up quarrels! . . . There was peace and quiet in the graveyard clay till I arrived, you say! How shameless of you, Muraed, to ruin a person's reputation like that! . . . I have the place like the Feast

---

21. Conán, Oscar: mythical members of the Fianna.

of Bricriú with my lies! Now, is that so, Muraed! You didn't have to travel far from your own creek to find liars. I never peddled gossip or lies, thanks be to God! . . .

Hello, Muraed! Do you hear me? Your own kind were the liars . . . You'll take no heed of my impertinence from now on, you say! Impertinence, oh! It's the blatant truth! Hello, Muraed! Muraed! . . . Devil the talking, then! Hello, Muraed! . . . Why don't you wake up your tongue?

Hello, Little Cáit! . . . Little Cáit! . . . This isn't very neighbourly, Little Cáit . . . Seáinín Liam! . . . Do you hear me, Seáinín Liam? . . . Devil as much as a word! . . .

Hello, Bríd Terry! . . . Bríd Terry! . . . Tell me, Bríd Terry, what did I ever do to upset you?

Máirtín Pockface! . . . Máirtín Pockface! . . . Cite! . . . Cite! . . . This is Caitríona. Caitríona Pháidín . . . Cite, I say!

Jack! Jack! . . . Jack the Scológ! . . . Hello, Jack the Scológ, it's me, Caitríona Pháidín . . . You Pound Plot People, call Jack the Scológ! Tell him Caitríona Pháidín is calling him! Jack, I say! . . . Siúán the Shop, Siúán! May God bless you Siúán, and call Jack the Scológ! . . . He's beside you there . . . Siúán! . . . Jack! . . . Jack! Jack! . . . I'll explode, explode, I'll explode, I'll explode . . .

Interlude Nine

THE SMOOTHING OF THE CLAY

1

—Sky, sea and land are mine . . .

—Mine are the hind side, the down side, the internal side, the least side. Only the peripheries and the accidents are yours . . .

—Glowing sun, shining moon, sparkling star are mine . . .

—Mine are the mysterious depths of every cavern, the rugged bottom of every abyss, the dark heart of every stone, the unknown innards of every clay, the hidden ducts of every flower . . .

—Southerly aspect, brightness, love, red of rose and the maiden's loving laugh are mine . . .

—Mine are northerly aspect, darkness, gloom, root system that sends growth to rose leaf, and arterial system that brings the gangrenous blood of depression to erupt on the smiling cheek . . .

—Egg, pollen, seed, produce are mine . . .

—Mine are . . .

2

—. . . *Monsieur Churchill a dit qu'il retournerait pour libérer la France. Vous comprenez, mon ami?* . . .

—He's losing his Irish again fast, since he joined the higher learning . . .

—. . . I fell off a stack of oats, Sweet-talking Stiofán . . .

—. . . With my own two ears I heard "Haw Haw"[1] promise that the *Graf* Spee would be revenged . . .

—. . . The Big Butcher came to my funeral, Soft-spoken Stiofán . . .

—. . . Hitler himself, his very own self, will come over to England and with his own two hands he'll stuff a little bomb about the size of a loaf of bread down those well-filled trousers of Churchill's . . .

—. . . Administering spiritual assistance to people is what I do. If you think you need spiritual assistance at any time . . .

—I will not, I'm telling you. And I'm warning you in time, Big Colm's daughter, to leave the black heretics here to me, and not to poke your nose into the business in any way, or upon my soul . . .

—. . . The Lord between us and all harm, if England is isolated like that, where will the people find a market? You have no land at the top of the village . . .

—. . . *Mon ami*, the United Nations, England, *les États Unis, la Russe, et les Français Libres* are defending human rights against . . . *quel est le mot?* . . . Against the barbarism *des Boches nazifiés*. I've already told you about the concentration camps. Belsen . . .

—Nell Pháidín is on Churchill's side. Fowlers and anglers from England, of course . . .

—She was always treacherous, the little bitch! *Up Hitler! Up Hitler! Up Hitler!* Do you think if he comes over he'll raze her new house to the ground?

—The Postmistress is on Hitler's side too. She says the Postmistress is a most important executive in Germany and that if she suspects anybody it's part of her duty to read that person's letters . . .

—Billyboy the Post is on Hitler's side too. He says . . .

—Oh, the dishevelled little upstart! What would you expect? Of course, that fellow has no belief in private wealth or the traditional living standards aspired to in Western Europe. He's a Communist, a non-traditionalist, a revolutionary, an *Antichrist*, a blackguardly little

---

1. Nickname of William Joyce, who broadcast Nazi propaganda to Britain and Ireland and was executed as a traitor in Wandsworth Prison, 1946.

fart, an evil spirit just like Hitler himself. Up Churchill! . . . Shut your cocky mouth, Nóra Sheáinín! You're a disgrace to womanhood! To say that dirty knobnose is a romantic . . .

—Well said there, Master! Let the Fair Darling of the Filthy Feet have it hot and heavy now! . . .

—Red-haired Tom says about Tomás Inside . . .

—Tomás Inside? What side is Tomás Inside on? It's a wise man would say what side Tomás Inside is . . .

—. . . Do you think I don't know that? . . .

—Nobody would rightly know it but someone from the same village as them . . . Tomás Inside was as fond of that burrow of a hovel of his as a king would be of his throne.

—By the docks, dear, didn't they let my cabin fall in on top of me in the end! . . .

—Ababúna! Tomás Inside is here! . . .

—The leak from the roof was hitting me between the gob and the eye, no matter where in the house I put the bed. They let me down badly. They did, dear. Caitríona had a lazybones of a son and Nell had another lazybones of a son, and weren't they the bad relatives that wouldn't put a little strip of thatch on my cabin! . . .

—Tomás Inside buried in the Fifteen-Shilling Plot, Cite! . . .

—Yes indeed, Bríd, Tomás Inside in the Fifteen-Shilling Plot! . . .

—The least they could do was to bury him in the Fifteen-Shilling Plot. They have his patch of land, and they'll get a fistful of money from the insurance.

—But Nóra Sheáinín says Pádraig didn't keep up the insurance payments after his mother's death.

—She's a damned liar! The Filthy-Feet slut! . . .

—Even if he did keep up the payments the Insurance won't compensate him for what he's spent on Tomás. All Caitríona's prayers for his death were no more than a goat's puff to Tomás. We'll ask the Insurance Man . . .

—Are you long here, Tomás Inside?

—By the docks, I'm only barely landed here, Caitríona dear. I never had an ache or a pain, and isn't it odd that I died all the same. I died just as if I had. What the doctor told me was . . .

—What the doctor told you is no use to you now. Nell buried you before herself . . .

—She's convalescing, Caitríona. Convalescing. She spent three weeks or a month in bed, but she's completely recovered now . . .

—Of course she is, the bitch! . . .

—And look at me, Caitríona, who never had an ache or a pain, and isn't it odd that I died all the same . . .

—Did you think you'd live forever?

—By the docks, Caitríona, I think the priest wasn't at all pleased with me, so he wasn't. The day he was visiting Nell he passed me by in the boreen as I was on my way over to Peadar the Pub for a grain of tobacco . . .

—The tobacco in Peadar the Pub's is better than anywhere else . . .

—It is, Caitríona dear, and a halfpenny cheaper. "Faith then, this poor woman up here is feeble enough, priest," says I . . .

—You windbag! . . .

—"It doesn't look as if she's well," says he. "She's been confined to bed a long time. Where are you wandering off to now, Tomás Inside?" says he. "I'm going over for a grain of tobacco, priest," says I. "I heard, Tomás Inside," says he, "that you've taken a fancy to this place over here; that you don't take your head out of the drink at all . . ."

—Oh, the pussface told him. She was always treacherous . . .

—"By the docks, I take the odd drop, priest, the same as anyone else," says I. "A drop is one thing, Tomás Inside," says he, "but I'm told that one of these nights you'll be found dead on the way home." "There isn't a thing wrong with me, priest," says I. "I never had an ache or a pain, thanks be to God, and of course now I have the new road under my feet right up to Nell's door."

—Hitler will destroy that road again, with the help of God!

—"My advice to you, and it's for your own good, Tomás Inside," says he, "keep away from that place over there as much as you can, and give up your drinking bouts. They're not good for you at this stage of your life. And this crowd up here have enough to do without having to go out every night to bring you home . . ."

—Good God above, that cocky little bitch has him under her thumb. She won't have Hitler under her thumb that easily . . .

—"By the docks, don't they have a motor car, priest!" says I. "If they have, Tomás Inside," says he, "petrol is not to be found in bog-holes. Look at me, having to go round on my bicycle! I'm also told, Tomás Inside," says he, "that you're like the change trolley in a shop, shuttling back and forth between the two houses. You'd think, Tomás Inside," says he, "that you'd have a little spark of sense at this stage of your life and settle in one house or the other. I wish you godspeed, Tomás Inside," says he, "and don't let my advice go in one ear and out the other." "If that's the way things are," says I to myself, "I won't be troubling them with bringing me home every night from now on. There are far too many priests around that house up here. Themselves and their priests! . . ."

—Devil a word of a lie you said, Tomás Inside . . .

—"I'll go down to Pádraig Chaitríona's where I'll have peace and quiet," says I. I turned down the little boreen by the Cliff, in case I'd find any of Nell's cattle on my patch of land. I didn't. The stone walls had fallen down in a few places. "I'll tell Pádraig Chaitríona to come up in the morning and build up the walls, and to put his cattle in on my patch of land," says I to myself . . .

—You were perfectly right, Tomás Inside . . .

—I came back to the head of the boreen again, and I started off down towards Pádraig's house. By the docks, you won't believe it, but all of a sudden I couldn't walk as much as a step, or talk as much as a word. One half of me was dead and the other half alive. I never had an ache or a pain, Caitríona, and isn't it strange that I died all the same! . . .

—To burst like a bicycle tube by the side of the road! Nell is the thorn that did for you, you unfortunate little fellow!

—I didn't die by the side of the road, my dear. Peadar Nell came by at that very moment and whisked me up to his house in the motor car. I'd have died in your house only for that, Caitríona. But I was in bed in Nell's house before I got my speech back, and then I thought it would be rude to ask them to bring me down to Pádraig's house.

—There wasn't a day of your life you didn't do something stupid, Tomás Inside . . .

—I only lived for ten days or so. My speech was coming and going. Faith then, I think the priest was no help to me. I never had an ache or a pain . . .

—You never gave yourself cause, you lazybones . . .

—By the docks, Caitríona dear, I used to do heavy bouts of work. Faith then, I had a hard life . . .

—Faith then, if you did, Tomás Inside, it wasn't from being useful. You had a hard life on account of your drinking and your contrariness . . .

—Faith then, to be honest about it, Caitríona, I suppose I did have a hangover on the odd Saturday, after the Friday . . .

—Faith then you did, Tomás Inside, and every Saturday, and every Sunday, and every Monday, and a good many Tuesdays and Wednesdays too . . .

—You always have your tongue at the ready, Caitríona. I always said that Nell was much more kind-hearted than you . . .

—You windbag! . . .

—Faith then, I did, Caitríona. "The devil a bit of looking after me would Caitríona do but to spite Nell," I used to say. You should see the care Nell gave me when I was laid low, Caitríona. Two doctors . . .

—For herself she got them, Tomás Inside. Ho-ho, there are no flies on that little pest! . . .

—It was for me, indeed, she got them, Caitríona. The very moment I was brought into the house to her, she got up off her bed to attend to me . . .

—She got up off her bed! . . .

—Faith then she did, Caitríona, and she stayed up . . .

—Oh, you simpleton! You simpleton! She played a trick on you! She played a trick on you! Sure you never had an ache or a pain, Tomás Inside . . .

—The devil an ache or a pain then, Caitríona, and isn't it odd that I died the same as a person who had. By the docks, I think the priest was no help to me . . .

—You can swear on the book that he wasn't, Tomás Inside. That cocky little one coaxed the St. John's Gospel from him that evening, and sent you packing instead of herself, as she did to Jack the Scológ . . .

—Do you think so, Caitríona? . . .

—Isn't it obvious to yourself, Tomás Inside! A woman who was on the flat of her back for a month, rising up like a butterfly like that! You were courting disaster by ever going near that bitch at any time. Had you stayed in my Pádraig's house you'd be alive and well today. But what did you do with your patch of land? . . .

—Musha, Caitríona dear, I left it to the two of them: to Pádraig and to Nell . . .

—You left them a half each, you useless lout! . . .

—By the docks, I didn't, dear. I did not, or anything of the sort. I used to say to myself like this, Caitríona, whenever I got my speech back: "If it were much bigger than it is, I wouldn't begrudge the whole lot of it to either of them. It's not worth making halves of it. Big Brian always used to say it wasn't worth dividing . . ."

—Of course he'd say that, hoping you'd leave it all to his own daughter . . .

—"I'll have to leave it to Pádraig Chaitríona," says I to myself like that. "I'd have left it to him anyhow, if I had managed to reach his house before I collapsed. But Nell was always kind-hearted. I couldn't but leave it to her, seeing that I died in her house . . ."

—Oh, you useless fool! You useless fool! . . .

—The priest was there, writing down what I said, whenever I found my speech: "Make two halves of it, Tomás Inside," he said. "Either that or leave it to one of the two houses."

—Why the devil, Tomás Inside, couldn't you do a bit better than that! Why didn't you do the decent thing and go in to Mannion the Counsellor in Brightcity?

—By the docks, Caitríona, I only got my speech back now and

again, and faith then, a person would need frost-nails[2] in his tongue to go splitting words with Mannion the Counsellor. Apart from that, Caitríona, I never felt much like visiting the same Mannion . . . Your Pádraig was there: "I don't want it," he said. "I've already got plenty of my own."

—Oh, the little fool! I knew that Nell would hoodwink him. He's lost without me . . .

—Isn't that what Big Brian said! . . .

—Brian blubber-lips! . . .

—Indeed then, Caitríona, he sent for the motor car and came over to visit me . . .

—To help Nell get your patch of land. If not, it wasn't for your sake, Tomás Inside. He sent over for the motor car! He was a fine sight in a motor car! A beard like rolls of unspun wool. Buckteeth. Slouched shoulders. Stopped-up nose. Club-foot. Crusted with filth. He never washed himself . . .

—"If the go-between who's laid to rest back there were here," says he, "I'd say it wouldn't be you, priest, but Mannion the Counsellor would be escorting Milord Inside past the gander . . ." Nell put her hand over his mouth. The priest pushed him out the door of the room . . . "We don't want your land either, Tomás Inside," says Nell . . .

—She's a damned liar, the cocky little scrounger! Why wouldn't she want it? . . .

—"I'll leave the patch of land to Pádraig Chaitríona and to Nell Sheáinín," says I when I got my speech back. "I won't begrudge it to you." "There's neither rhyme nor reason to what you're saying, Tomás Inside," says the priest. "It would end in wrangling and law, were it not for the good sense of these decent people . . ."

—Decent people! Oh! . . .

—I couldn't speak a word from then on, Caitríona. Devil an ache or a pain I ever had, and isn't it odd that I died! . . .

—You're no great asset, alive or dead, you stupid little fool!

---

2. Nails in horseshoes, or in the sole of a boot, to prevent slipping.

—Listen Tomás! *That's the dote!* That *tiff* with Caitríona won't make . . .

—By the docks, *tiff?*

—That scolding will only *vulgarise* your mind. I must establish a relationship with you. I am the cultural relations officer of the graveyard. I'll give you lectures on the "Art of Living."

—By the docks, the "Art of Living" . . . ?

—A perceptive group of us here felt we had a duty to our fellow corpses, and we founded a Rotary . . .

—What do you want a Rotary for? Look at me! . . .

—Exactly, *Thomas.* Look at you! You're a romantic roebuck, Tomás. You always were. But romance must have the stilts of culture under its feet, to raise it up out of the wild sod, and to make it the coercive King Stork of the Twentieth Century, graduating to the high sunlit groves of Cupid, as Mrs. Crookshank said to Harry . . .

—Hold on there now, my good Nóra. I'll relate to you what Gambolling Naked said to Knotted Bottom in the "Ripping of the Mantle" . . .

—Culture, *Thomas.*

—By the docks, this can't be Nóirín Sheáinín from Mangy Field I have here! . . . I wonder will I begin to speak like that in the graveyard clay. Indeed then, Nóra, you had fine homely talk in the old days! . . .

—Nóróg dear, don't let on you hear him at all.

—Gug-goog, Dotie! Gug-goog! We'll have a cosy little conversation after a while. Between ourselves, so to speak. A nice friendly chat between ourselves, you know. Gug-goog!

—I always had culture, Tomás, but you weren't able to appreciate it. That was obvious to me in the first *affaire de coeur* I ever had with you. Only for that maybe I could have incited you a little. Ugh! A man without culture! A mate should be a companion. I'll give you a lecture, with the help of the writer and the poet, on platonic love . . .

—I'll have nothing to do with you, Nóra Sheáinín. Indeed then, I won't! . . .

—That's my darling, Tomás Inside! . . .

—I used to rub shoulders with the big shots in Nell Sheáinín's...

—You useless little fool!...

—Oh! Them foreign ones are great fun, Caitríona. A big yellow stump was fishing with Lord Cockton this year, and she'd smoke all the *fags* that were ever made. She would, and so would the priest's sister. She keeps them in big boxes in her trousers pocket. She has Road-End's son robbed supplying her. Good enough for him, the blackguard. But I must say she's lovely herself. I sat into the motor car beside her. "Gug-goog, Nancy," says I...

—Your mind, Tomás, *dote*, is raw and lumpy clay, but I will mix it, mould it, fire it and polish it, until it's a beautiful vessel of culture.

—I'll have nothing whatever to do with you, Nóra Sheáinín. Nothing at all. I got enough of you. I couldn't put a foot inside Peadar the Pub's but you'd be in at my heels, sponging drink. Many is the fine pint I bought for you, not begrudging it to you!...

—Nóróg dear, don't let on...

—Good on you there, Tomás! God grant you life and health! Let her have it now, hot and heavy; let Nóirín Filthy Feet have it. Going around sponging! Were you in Peadar the Pub's, Tomás Inside, the day she made the billy-goat drunk?... The blessings of God on you, and tell the graveyard about that!...

3

—... I keened you all, my family oh! Woe is me, alas and woe! I keened you all, my family oh!...

—You had a fine tearful wail, Bid Shorcha, to give you your due...

—... Woe is me, alas and woe! You fell off that dreadful stack, my woe!...

—You'd think, listening to you all, that he fell off an aeroplane! He only fell off a stack of oats! Sure, that wouldn't kill anybody but a person who was half-dead already. If he drank the bottle I drank!...

—Woe is me, alas and woe! You drank that awful bottle, my darling oh!...

—You've so much talk about your bottle. If you drank two score pints and two as I did . . .

—Woe is me, alas and woe! You won't drink another pint, never ever oh! And many's the big pint went down your sluice-gate oh!

—Arrah, you've bored an auger-hole in the clay of my ear with your two score pints and two! If you inhaled as many barrels of ink into your lungs as the Writer did . . .

—Woe is me, alas and woe! My fine writer forever more laid low!

—God bless us and save us forever oh! . . .

—Sentimentality again! . . .

—I keened you, Dotie! Darling Dotie oh! Wasn't it far away from your native clay you met your death, my woe! my woe! Alas, my great sorrow and my seven torments, they drove you west without much knowledge! You were cast away from your relations and home! You met your death by the raging foam! Your bones will be laid . . .

—In the barren clay of nettles and sandy seaweed . . .

—I keened you all, my family oh! . . . My darling oh! My darling oh! . . . Never, no more, will he write, my woe! . . .

—That's no loss! A cursed heretic! . . .

—. . . I keened you, musha. I did indeed. Woe is me forever oh! A fine fertile patch at the top of the village! He'll never set foot there for harvest or tillage.

—Did you say, Bid, there was no better land for fattening cattle?

—Faith then, you did, Bid Shorcha. I was listening to you. And then you began to sing "The Lament of the Ejected Irish Peasant" . . .

—. . . I keened you too! I keened you too! Woe is me, alas and woe! He'll rise in the saddle no more, no more, on a white-faced colt, no! never oh! . . .

—Oh! Caitríona Pháidín laid her evil eye on it! . . .

—That's a damned lie! It was Nell . . .

—. . . I cried my head dry over you, Big Master, oh! Woe is me forever oh! The Big Master dying in his prime, my woe! . . .

—Now, Bid Shorcha, you didn't keen the Big Master at all, at all. I should know, for I was there helping Billyboy the Post to put the lid on the coffin . . .

—The blackguard! . . .

—The Schoolmistress was sobbing. You took her hand, Bid Shorcha, and began to clear your throat. "I don't know," says Billyboy the Post, "which of the two of you—you Bid Shorcha, or the Schoolmistress—has the least sense . . ."

—Oh! The thief!

—"Out you go, and down the stairs with all of you whose address is not in the Kingdom Beyond, till I put the lid on the coffin," says Billyboy. They all went downstairs except you, Bid Shorcha. "But the poor Big Master must be keened," you said to the Schoolmistress. "He well deserved it, the poor man," said the Schoolmistress . . .

—Oh, the hussy! . . .

—"Keening or no keening," says Billyboy, "unless you get downstairs out of my way, Bid Shorcha, he won't make it in time for today's delivery." You came down to the bottom of the stairs then, Bid Shorcha, and you were snivelling. Billyboy was making the world of noise upstairs, driving in screws and tightening them. "He'll never leave that coffin after Billyboy is finished with him," said Big Brian. "If as many screws were put into Mannion the Counsellor's tongue, Caitríona would have gone to another solicitor about Baba's will . . ."

—Ababúna! The blundering streak of misery! . . .

—At that same moment, Billyboy came out at the top of the stairs. "In under him now, four of you," says he.

—I remember it well. I twisted my ankle . . .

—"It's not proper to let the Big Master out of the house without shedding a tear over him," you said, Bid Shorcha, and you went back up the stairs again. Billyboy stopped you. "He'll have to go to the graveyard," said Billyboy. "It's no use nursing him here any longer . . ."

—Oh, the arrogant little squirt! . . .

—"Faith then, it's no use nursing him," said Big Brian, "unless you're going to put him in pickle! . . ."

—You keened me, Bid Shorcha, and I wasn't grateful to you for it, nor half grateful, nor grateful at all. Oh, indeed you made enough commotion over me, but you were shooting at the hen when you should have been shooting at the fox. You didn't say a word about the

Irish Republic or about the treacherous One-Ear Breed who stabbed me because I fought for it . . .

—I said that the people were thankful . . .

—That's a lie; you did not! . . .

—Bid Shorcha had nothing to do with politics, no more than myself . . .

—You spineless coward, under the bed you were when Éamon de Valera was risking his life . . .

—You were no good when you keened me, Bid Shorcha, because you didn't say out loud in front of everybody that it was Siúán the Shop's coffee that killed me . . .

—And that Peadar the Pub's daughter robbed me . . .

—And me . . .

—You didn't say a thing when you were keening me, about Road-End Man stealing my turf . . .

—Or my drift-weed . . .

—Or that the man down here died on account of his son marrying a *black* . . .

—I think that man was right a while ago when he said that Bid Shorcha had nothing to do with politics . . .

—. . . I'd have keened you better only for my voice was hoarse that day. I'd keened three others already that same week . . .

—Faith then, it wasn't hoarseness at all, but drink . . . Speechless from drink you were. When you tried to begin "Let Erin Remember," as you usually did, it was "Will Ye No' Come Back Again?" came out . . .

—Indeed it was not, but "Some Day I'll Go Back across the Sea to Ireland" . . .

—I'd have gone to keen you, Beartla Blackleg, but I wasn't able to get up out of bed at the time . . .

—*Bloody tear and 'ounds*, Bid Shorcha, what does it matter to a person whether he's keened or not! "Hoh-roh, Mary . . ."

—Why, Bid Shorcha, didn't you come and keen Caitríona Pháidín, when you were sent for?

—Yes, why didn't you come and keen Caitríona?

—But you went to Nell's, although you had to get up out of your bed . . .

—I couldn't bear to refuse Nell, and she sent her motor car to my door to collect me . . .

—Hitler will take the motor car off her . . .

—I would have keened you, Caitríona, without a word of a lie, but I didn't want to be competing with the other three: Nell, Nóra Sheáinín's daughter, and Big Brian's daughter. They were whining . . .

—Nell! Nóra Sheáinín's daughter! Big Brian's daughter! The three who got the St. John's Gospel from the priest in order to kill me! I'll explode! I'll explode! I'll explode! . . .

4

—. . . Jack! Jack! Jack the Scológ! . . .

—. . . Gug-goog, Dotie! Gug-goog! We'll have a cosy little chat now . . .

—. . . What would you say, Red-haired Tom, about a man whose son married a *black*? I think he's a heretic himself, as well as the son . . .

—Indeed, that could be so, so it could . . .

—The sins of the children are avenged on the fathers . . .

—Some say they are. Some say they're not . . .

—Wouldn't you say, Red-haired Tom, that any man who drank two score pints and two is a heretic?

—Two score pints and two. Two score pints and two, then. Two score pints and two . . .

—Faith then, I did . . .

—Tomás Inside rubbed shoulders with heretics . . .

—Tomás Inside. Tomás Inside, then. It's a wise man would say what Tomás Inside is . . .

—Faith then, I'm not so sure about the Big Master either, Red-haired Tom. I've been observing him for a while now. I'll say nothing till I see . . .

—A person should keep his mouth shut in a place like this. Graves have huge big holes . . .

—I have my doubts about Caitríona Pháidín too. She swore to me she was a better Catholic than Nell, but if it turns out that she had the evil eye . . .

—Some say she had. Some say . . .

—You're a liar, you dumb redhead . . .

—. . . By the docks, don't you know well, Master dear, that he'll die. Look at me who never had an ache or a pain, and isn't it a wonder that I died all the same! I died the same as a man who had . . .

—But do you really think, Tomás, that he'll die? . . .

—Don't you know well, Master, that he'll soon have a dock growing in his ear!

—Do you think so, Tomás?

—Don't worry, Master. He'll die, my friend. Look at me! . . .

—If only God would grant it, the skinny little squirt . . .

—Ah, musha Master, she's lovely, herself . . .

—Oh! The harlot! . . .

—Do you need any spiritual assistance, Master? . . .

—I do not. I do not, I tell you. Leave me alone! Leave me alone or I'll have the skin off your ears! . . .

—By the docks, Master dear, didn't I hear that she used to have cottiers[3] in the kitchen, and you upstairs on your deathbed . . .

—*Qu'est-ce que c'est que* cottiers? What sort of things are cottiers? . . .

—Tomás Inside is not a cottier, because he had a nice patch of land. Nor is East-Side-of-the-Village Man either. He had a patch at the top of the village that couldn't be beaten for fattening cattle. But Billyboy the Post was a cottier. The only land he had was the garden of the Master's house . . .

—Billyboy used to be inside with her, indeed, Master. I heard

---

3. A cottier (*pailitéara*) is a landless person, one renting land for eleven months of the year only, and so unable to claim to own it.

that no matter how fierce the day was he'd come to inquire about you . . .

—Oh, the blackguard! The sweet-toothed cock-of-the-roost!

—Ah, musha, Master, there is no denying the truth when all is said and done. The Schoolmistress is lovely. Myself and herself used to be together in Peadar the Pub's. If only Billyboy wasn't sticking his scissor-nose in everywhere, while he was still able to do his rounds! I met her at the Steep Hillock on the Mountain Road a few months after you were buried. "Gug-goog, Schoolmistress," says I. "Gug-goog, Tomás Inside," says she. We didn't have a chance for a cosy little chat because Billyboy the Post was heading down towards us on his bicycle after delivering letters . . .

—. . . They say that unless the first form is filled in properly it's easy to strike you off the *dole*.[4] The Wood of the Lake Master filled mine in for me the first time ever the *dole* came out. He wrote something in red ink right across the form. Long life to him, the *dole* was never taken off me since! . . .

—Faith then, it was taken off me. The Big Master filled it in for me. All he did was to draw a stroke of his pen across the form. It wasn't red ink he used either . . .

—The Big Master, the poor man, used to be bad-tempered thinking of the Schoolmistress. Didn't you hear how he used to keep looking out the window while he was writing letters for Caitríona! . . .

—May she do him no good, the same Schoolmistress, couldn't he fill in a *dole* form properly for a person! . . .

—I always got eight shillings. The Red-haired Policeman did it for me . . .

—For a good reason. He was screwing your daughter in the nettly groves of Donagh's Village . . .

—I was done out of the *dole* completely. Somebody wrote in to say I had money in the bank . . .

—God bless your innocence, my friend! Some people envy any

---

4. Social Welfare Assistance for the unemployed.

improvement in their neighbour's circumstances. Don't you see Nell Pháidín's son, who used to get the *dole* throughout the year, as his land wasn't valued over two pounds, and Caitríona did him out of it . . .

—He didn't deserve it! He didn't deserve it! He had money in a bank and was getting fifteen shillings of *dole* permanently. It served the pussface right!

—Faith then, as you say, I had a big *dole* . . .

—You had a big *dole*, indeed, Road-End Man . . .

—A storm never blew but you were the better for it, Road-End Man. The little stray sheep would always end up with you . . .

—The little wooden plank washed ashore in the Middle Harbour would always end up with you . . .

—And the drift-weed . . .

—And the turf . . .

—And the scallops for thatching . . .

—Anything left lying around the Earl's house always ended up with you . . .

—Even the wooden leg of the Earl's little black servant, didn't it end up with you? I saw a pullet of yours laying an egg in its thigh, and you used its foot on Caitríona's chimney cap . . .

—Even the priest's sister who went around in her little trousers whistling and yawning, she ended up with your son . . .

—Oh, do you hear the tailor boasting? You made a white home-spun jacket for me, and a bus would get lost inside it . . .

—You made trousers for Jack the Scológ and no one in the country could get his feet down them but Tomás Inside . . .

—God would punish us . . .

—By the docks, dear, my feet went down them nice and sprightly . . .

—Didn't you all know well that's what would happen, when you brought your cloth to the Breed of the One-Ear Tailor who stabbed me! . . .

—Arrah, you shouldn't be talking, Mangy Field Carpenter! Wasn't the whole country able to look in at Nóra Sheáinín through the coffin you made for her . . .

—She was the first of the Filthy-Feet Breed to go into any sort of wooden coffin at all . . .

—She'd be better off, Caitríona, without that particular one. It was as flimsy as the chimneys Road-End Man used to make . . .

—What could I do about your chimneys when you wouldn't pay me?

—I paid you . . .

—As you say, you paid me, but for everyone who did, there were four who didn't . . .

—I paid you too, you crook, and you did my chimney more harm than good . . .

—You paid me, as you say, but there was another house in the village where I fixed a chimney shortly before that, and the devil a word, good or bad, I've heard about my money since.

—Was that a reason for making a botch of my chimney, you crook? . . .

—But I told you to make a chimney-brush . . .

—And I did. And I scrubbed it clean from top to bottom, but you'd made a botch of it . . .

—I didn't know, as you say, who would pay me and who wouldn't. A woman from the village came up to me. "We're having the priest," she said. "The chimney is always puffing whenever there's an east wind. If there happened to be an east wind the day we'd have the priest I'd be mortified. Nell's chimney draws on all winds." "I'll stop it puffing on an east wind, as you say," says I. I reshaped the top. "You'll see for yourself now," says I, "that it won't be puffing on the east wind, as you say. I'll go easy on you, as you say, as you're a neighbour and all that. One pound and five shillings." "You'll get it next fairday, with the help of God," says she. The fairday came and went, but I didn't get my one pound, five shillings. Oh, the devil a word, good or bad, did I hear about my money from Caitríona . . ."

—Isn't that what I told you, Dotie, that Caitríona never paid for anything! *Honest!*

—Why should I pay that crook—Road-End Man—for fixing a few little boards on the chimney top to beckon the wind to them!

Even though the wind was from the west it was never as short of breath as it was the day the priest came. It would draw the child off the hearth on a west wind before that. When Road-End Man was finished with it, it wouldn't draw at all on any wind but the east wind. I offered to pay him if it would draw on every wind like Nell's chimney. But he wouldn't touch it any more. Nell, the pussface, gave him a backhander . . .

—That's the truth, Caitríona. Road-End Man would accept a backhander.

—Any man who stole my seaweed.

—Now, to be fair, Caitríona, it wasn't Road-End Man, bad and all as he was, who was responsible for your chimney, but Nell who got the St. John's Gospel from the priest for her own chimney . . .

—And sent the smoke over to Caitríona's, as she tried to do with Big Brian . . .

—Oh! Oh! I'll explode! I'll explode!

5

—. . . I could have had the law on him for poisoning me. "Take two spoons of this bottle before going to bed, and again in the morning while fasting," said the murderer. Oh! Fasting didn't come into it! I had just lain down in the bed . . .

—*Bloody tear and 'ounds*, didn't you lie down and die! . . .

—"Ha!" said he to me, as soon as he saw my tongue. "Siúán the Shop's coffee . . ."

—"I never had an ache or a pain, my friend," says I to him one day he was in Peadar the Pub's. "Even if you didn't, Tomás Inside," says he, "you're drinking too much porter. Porter doesn't suit a man of your age. The odd small whiskey would be much better for you." "By the docks, my friend, isn't that what I used to drink all the time before now," said I. "But it's too scarce and too dear now." "Peadar the Pub's daughter here will give you the odd half-one," says he. And indeed she did, and gave me all I asked for, but from the second drink on she charged me four fourpenny bits, and from the sixth one on, eighteen pence. The doctor Nell brought from Brightcity to see me said it was the whiskey shortened my life, but myself and Caitríona were of the opinion it was the priest . . .

—God would punish us for speaking ill of our neighbour . . .

—What he told the Big Master was: "You're too good for this life . . ."

—Shut your mouth, you little prattler! . . .

—The doctor in the hospital put the bottle under my nose while I was stretched on the table. "What's that, doctor?" said I. "A knick-knack," said he . . .

—*Bloody tear and 'ounds* for a story, it would be a decent thing for a person to lie down on his bed and die, as Big Brian said, instead of lying down on a hospital table and not getting up again, as cut up as the *free beef* [5] from the Sive's Rocks butcher.

—. . . "The flaw is up here," says I, "in there in the pit of my stomach." "Faith then, it's not up there," said he, "but down below here, in the feet. Take off your boots and socks." "There's no need for that, doctor," said I. "The flaw is up above. In there in the pit of my stomach." He had no interest whatsoever in the pit of my stomach. "Take off your boots and socks," he said. "There mightn't be any need for that, doctor," said I. "There's nothing wrong with me down there . . ."

"If you don't take off your boots and socks, and be quick about it," he said, "I'll put you where they'll be taken off you . . . You could hardly have avoided contracting something," says he. "Did you wash those feet of yours since you were born?" "Down by the shore, doctor, last summer twelve months . . ."

—Constipated I was. I was permanently bunged up. It's not something you'd like to talk about. "I don't like telling you, doctor," said I. "It's not a decent subject."

—That's how it goes, as you say. I awoke and sat up in bed. The

---

5. Beef distributed by the Irish Government among the poor people of the west of Ireland during the economic war with England in the 1930s, when the cattle trade with England was seriously disrupted.

man from Menlo[6] was in the bed next to me, as he had been all along. "I thought they weren't going to open you up for another two days," says I . . . "Hey, wake up," says I . . . "and don't be lying there like a sand bag." "Let him be," said the nurse to me. "When you were brought down to the salting room his intestines became homesick. They got knotted up all of a sudden and he had to be sent for salting too. They didn't put as much sugar on the knife for him as they did for you. That's why he hasn't woken up yet." These *nurses* are a little indelicate, as you say.

—"Decency!" says he. "Arrah! what?" says he. "Decency with me! Did you kill a man, or what?" "The cross of Christ on us, doctor!" said I. "I did not!" "What's wrong with you so?" says he. "Out with it." "Musha, it's not a decent subject," I said. "Constipated I am . . ."

—Constipated, as you say. I didn't get my appetite back for four or five days. "Hot oven bread," said I to the *nurse.* "Arrah, to hell with you!" says she. "Do you think I have nothing to do but get hot oven bread for you?" That's how the likes of them are, as you say. I asked the doctor for hot oven bread the following morning. "This decent man must get hot oven bread from now on," said he to the *nurse.* Faith then, he did. The devil a word she could say . . .

—. . . "My ankle is twisted," said I . . .

—"Constipated I am." "Constipated," said he. "Begging your pardon, doctor, yes," said I. "Bunged up in my body." "Oh, if that's all that's wrong with you!" says he. "I'll cure that. I'll make up a good bottle for you." He mixed some white stuff with some red stuff. "This will wipe your slate clean," said he . . .

—. . . "The poor Belgies are much to be pitied," says I to Paitseach Sheáinín. "I wonder is this the War of the Two Foreigners? . . ."

—Wake up man. That war is over for the past thirty years . . .

—He said that, as you say. "You'd better make sure she gets cold bread for me," said the Menlo Man to him. "What's this?" said the doctor. "Isn't the bread here cold enough for anybody?" "But hot

---

6. Mionlach, a partly Irish-speaking village on the eastern outskirts of Galway City.

bread is what I'm getting," said the Menlo Man. "Oh, I remember you now," said the doctor. "You gave a standing order for hot oven bread when you came in. The bread here was too cold for you." He was grinding his teeth with rage. That's how the likes of them are, as you say. "Not a bite of hot bread will touch my lips," said the Menlo Man. "I'm paying my way here and I must get whatever suits me," he said. Upon my soul he did. He was adamant. "But you thought cold bread didn't suit you when you came in," said the doctor. "You're the one who should be doctor here!" "I believe a person's stomach plays nasty tricks once it's opened," said the Menlo Man . . .

— . . . "It is. It's my ankle that's twisted," says I.

— "This will wipe your slate clean, indeed," he said. "The blessings of God on you, doctor!" said I. "This is a great bottle," he said. "The components are expensive. Would you believe how much the full of that white bottle cost me in Brightcity?" "Quite a penny, I'd say, doctor," said I. "Two pounds, five shillings," said he.

— Faith then, that's how it is, as you say. From that day on I couldn't stomach cold bread, and it was like gall to the Menlo Man to be offered a bit of hot bread. If I was handed every penny I was ever owed for repairing chimneys I couldn't touch the pipe since, after being so fond of it before that. And would you believe that the Menlo Man is now burning turf banks of tobacco, a man who never put a pipe in his mouth before going into hospital! . . .

— "Everything is gold since this ridiculous war began," said he, "and I wouldn't mind if things were available, even." "Oh! Doctor," said I, "the people are in a bad way. If it continues we won't be able to survive at all, but for the grace of God . . ."

— Faith then, the people are in a bad way, as you say. "My intestines are completely scoured," said the Menlo Man to me, as we were strolling up and down outside, a few days before we were sent home. "My intestines feel like trousers that are too tight for me, or something. After eating two mouthfuls I feel stuffed. Look at me now! . . . My poor belly is as prickly as a coil of barbed wire," he said. He was a huge big mountain of a man. He was head and shoulders over me, and powerfully built as well. "Be damned to it, as you say," says

I, "but I feel my own intestines are not the best either. All the food in the hospital wouldn't fill them. They gulp everything, as if they were a few sizes too big for me. If I make the slightest move, they're like a cow's udder, going from side to side . . ."

—. . . The Big Butcher often told me that he had respect for me on account of the respect his father had for my father . . .

—"Seven shillings and sixpence this bottle will cost you," says he. "It's the very best." "The blessings of God on you, doctor!" said I. "Only for you, I don't know what the people would do at all. I don't, faith. You're great for the man in distress. There's nothing lazy or laggardly about you . . ."

—The man in distress, as you say. From then on, myself and the Menlo Man would write to one another every week. He'd say in every one of his letters that his appetite had changed completely. He'd complain that he couldn't bear to taste a potato or meat or cabbage now. He'd give the air above him and the earth beneath him for tea and fish, things I had come to detest, myself, now. But, as you say, you never saw anything more baffling. I had never been fond of meat or cabbage, but since being in hospital I would eat them half-cooked straight out of the pot with my bare hands. And potatoes as well. I'd eat potatoes three times a day if I got them . . .

—. . . "Your old ankle is twisted again," he said. "By Galen's[7] windy plexus and by the umbilical cord of the Fianna's physician, if you come in to me again with your shitty old ankle . . ."

—"Seven shillings and sixpence," he said. "I don't begrudge you seven shillings and sixpence," said I. "I'll give it to you as soon as the bottle does me good . . ."

—Does you good, as you say. But nothing would do me any good. The intestines were still insatiable. Potatoes, meat and cabbage for my breakfast, dinner and supper. "These sooty old chimneys are whetting your appetite," said the old lady. "The soot is forming a coat-

---

7. Roman physician and philosopher who practised dissection and wrote treatises on anatomy.

ing on your intestine." "Not at all," says I, "but 'tis how my intestines are insatiable . . ."

—Arrah, my dear man, he jumped up, he smashed the bottle on the floor . . .

—Faith then, if I jumped like that, as you say, my intestines would start going to and fro, and they wouldn't stop for half an hour. I told the Irish-language learner who was lodging with us that summer I died. He was a trainee doctor. He'd get his credentials the following year. He quizzed me up and he quizzed me down about the way I was operated on. "Yourself and the Menlo Man were together on the table," he said . . .

—. . . *Qu'il retournerait pour libérer la France . . .*

—He made smithereens of the bottle on the floor. He kicked the shelf and knocked all that was on it. "Only for I'd lose my doctor's licence, I'd make you eat those broken bottles," he said. And over he goes to Peadar the Pub's . . .

—*Bloody tear and 'ounds* for a story, weren't you lucky! If you'd drunk that poison bottle, you'd lie back in your bed like the man a while ago . . .

—He would indeed lie back, as you say. "Your intestines are insatiable since," said the young doctor. "And you have the Menlo Man's appetite. The doctors and nurses were tipsy that day after the dress-dance the night before!" he said. "That's how the likes of them are, as you say," says I. "Oh, not a doubt about it," said he, "but when they were putting the intestines back into the two of you, they put the Menlo Man's into you and yours into the Menlo Man. That's why you gave up the tobacco . . ."

—But you didn't give up the thieving, Road-End Man. It was after they opened you up that you stole my drift-weed . . .

—And my little lump-hammer . . .

—Take care that he didn't steal the intestines from the Menlo Man! . . .

—If he found them hanging loose at all . . .

—All he said to me is that I had been stabbed through the edge of my liver. "You've been stabbed through the edge of your liver," he said, "and that's all there's to it." "The treacherous One-Ear Breed!" said I. "On behalf of my sliced-up liver I implore you, doctor! You'll swear against them as best you can. They'll be hanged . . ."

—Caitríona went over to him. "What's wrong with you now?" he said. "Nell was here the other day," she said. "Do you think, doctor, will what she's complaining of kill her? The blessings of God on you, doctor!" says she. "People tell me you have poison. I'll share Baba's will with you! Nobody will ever know about it if you drop the least little bit into the next one and tell her it's the best of bottles: two spoons before she goes to bed and again on an empty stomach . . ."

—But Nell could have the law on her and on the doctor then . . .

—Ababúna! Didn't the doctor admit to me that day . . .

—. . . And I never saw my pound from that day till the day I died . . .

—. . . That the little bitch asked him to poison me. He didn't say it straight out, but . . .

—. . . But listen, Siúán, did she ever return your silver teapot?

—. . . I could easily know from the way the doctor spoke that day . . . Cite of the Ash-Potatoes! Don't believe her, Jack! Jack the Scológ, don't believe mangy Cite!

—God would punish us, Caitríona, for saying anything . . .

—I'll explode! I'll explode! I'll explode! . . .

6

—. . . Faith then, as you say, I fixed the chimney for her at the same time . . .

—. . . By the docks, my friend, not begrudging it to her, but she wheedled some money out of me, my friend, and it was the time of the *roundtable* too. What did she want a *roundtable* for? Look at me! . . .

—You little good-for-nothing! When did you have a penny? . . .

—. . . Shame on us, Curraoin, that we let the English market go! I had a patch of land . . .

—By the docks, there wasn't a sweeter bit of land from the stairs of Heaven down than that patch of mine. There wasn't, my friend. But towards the end there was no will to walk or to work left in me, what with running after Nell's and Caitríona's cattle every minute, trying to keep them off it. They are the two who fleeced me, not that I begrudge it to them!

—Oh! See how my big holding is going to rack and ruin! Glutton's donkey and Road-End's donkey and cattle are picking it bare every day and every night. The eldest son is keeping steady company with Road-End's daughter, even though she's under some spell since the day she was born not to pass my turf stack . . .

—*Bloody tear and 'ounds*, didn't she tell Big Brian there was a stoat's nest in her own stack!

—Oh, the devil pierce her! She has cast some sort of spell or bewilderment on my eldest son. She had a camera and she used to take pictures of herself dressed in those flimsy little rags. The Son of Blackleg thinks my old lady at home is more inclined now to make the second son hit the road and give the big holding to the eldest one. The devil take me, if she does . . . !

—. . . Exercise: A donkey would lay bare four square perches of common pasturage in the course of one night. The question is now, Curraoin, how many times would four square perches go into the seventeen acres of my holding: 17 multiplied by 4, multiplied by 40 . . .

—. . . *Honest*, Dotie, there wasn't a spark of romance in Caitríona. It was the house and land she was after. Hoping to rob some of the gentry who used to frequent the place. You may be sure it wasn't for love of Jack the Scológ . . .

—Don't believe her, Jack. Don't believe Mangy Calves Sheáinín! . . .

—God would punish us for saying anything . . .

—. . . It was failing her to get a man at all, Dotie. Big Brian told me that she was like a cold you couldn't get rid of! No sooner had you spat her out of your mouth than she was in again through your nose . . .

—Oh! Jack, don't believe her! Good Heavens tonight! Big Brian! . . .

—. . . *Honest*, Dotie. Not a night went by that she wouldn't come over the old path from her own village, to be there before him in the boreen when he was going visiting . . .

—Oh, Mother of God above! The streak of misery!

—. . . She asked him to marry her, two or three times . . .

—Big Brian! To marry Big Brian! . . .

—. . . *Honest*, Dotie.

—Gug-goog, Dotie!

—Gug-goog, Tomás Inside!

—*Honest to Heavens*, Dotie! It's not refined to be shouting "Gug-goog" like that all over the graveyard. What will the Pound people say? It's a bad example to the Half-Guinea crowd. Say "Okeedoh." But why bother to answer the old brute at all? . . .

—Unrequited love, Nóróg . . .

—. . . Big Brian, Jack! Big Brian of the stuffed-up nose, slouched shoulders, buckteeth, beard. Big Brian who never washed . . .

—God would punish us, Caitríona . . .

—. . . I tell you that life wouldn't be half as bad if there were no women . . .

—Didn't you hear the story Cóilí had the other day! The servant-girl tempted the Pope, and Rory McHugh O'Flaherty—a holy man who was here long ago—had to go over straight away to tell the Pope to watch himself. Riding on the Devil's back he went to Rome . . .

—Look at that drunkard of a woman in Brightcity who's threatening law on the Small Master if he leaves her for another one . . .

—Road-End Man would say that the women are worse than the men. The priest's sister asked his son to marry her . . .

—The Big Master himself says so . . .

—Oh, the women are always to blame! . . .

—The women are always to blame, Bríd Terry?

—Oh, didn't I see the state of those floozies in the pictures! . . .

—Faith then, you did, and so did I, Bríd. When Mae West was smiling at us, didn't I say to the young fellow: "I wouldn't advise you to have anything to do with the likes of her," says I. "She'd be good handling a colt all right, but . . ."

—Listen, Seáinín Liam, the women are nothing but a rainbow on its hunkers, as the old proverb says.

—Well, by Dad, an old codger like you giving out about women, and you never in all your life had anything to do with women, unless you saw them going the road! How the devil would you know? . . .

—I do know, then. A man told me a long time ago. An old man who was very old . . .

—The women are a hundred times worse. They are indeed, my friend. By the docks . . .

—Oh, don't annoy me! Look at that eldest son of mine who wouldn't give up Road-End's daughter although I'd let him have the big holding! The devil pierce . . .

—And the son of the man over there who married a *black* . . .

—I'm a woman, and I'd take the part of the women if I could find it in me to do so. But all you have to do is to listen to Caitríona Pháidín driving Jack the Scológ to distraction day in day out . . .

—Faith then, Caitríona isn't the only woman in the graveyard who has her tongue cocked at the Scológ's fair son . . .

—I never saw a woman as bad as that one. Do you know what she said to him the other day, that Nell deceived him when she asked him to marry her. Isn't she the shameless one . . .

—By the oak of this coffin, what I heard her say was: "The pack of women here are jealous that you talk to me, Jack," says she. "But be very stern indeed with them, like a good man!" . . . Whatever shame she ever had she left above ground . . .

—"Muraed Phroinsiais," says she to me, "the barb has been removed from my heart, and since Jack arrived I feel the time flying by as fast as a night of music." "Have you auctioned off every last stitch of shame, Caitríona?" says I to her . . .

—Did you hear, Muraed, what she said to me? "Bríd Terry," she said, "isn't it great revenge on the pussface! 'Jack is mine. Jack is mine.' She hasn't got Jack under her little rag of a shawl now, Bríd Terry . . ."

—I'll speak to Jack the Scológ. And you'd speak to him too, you slut, if he'd speak to you. It's not for want of trying on your part that he doesn't speak to you, you little tight-arse . . .

—Spare me the lash of your tongue, Caitríona. Peace and quiet is what I want . . .

—More power to you, Caitríona! They badly need a dressing down like that! You'd think from this flock of women here that there's no other man in the graveyard but Son of Scológ! I wouldn't mind if they weren't married women . . .

—But the Big Master admitted the other day that death dissolves marriage vows . . .

—What does he have against Billyboy the Post so?

—He said that: Death dissolves marriage vows! I was right to have my suspicions about him. He's a heretic for certain . . .

—Will you hold on till you hear the full story! If Caitríona had only said that much I wouldn't mind . . . "Bríd Terry," she said, "there's . . ." Decency forbids me to repeat what she said, with all the men listening . . .

—Whisper it, Bríd . . .

—Whisper it to me, Bríd! . . .

—To me, Bríd! . . .

—I'll tell it to Nóra . . . Now, what do you think of that, Nóra? . . .

—*Upon my word!* I'm *shocked!* Who would ever think it of Jack! . . .

—I think we should warn Jack, on account of Nell not being here . . .

—I'll speak to him . . .

—You don't have the discretion a woman should have . . .

—Do you need any spiritual advice, Jack the Scológ?

—It's very interfering of you, Big Colm's daughter, to be poking your nose into the matter at all, and women here three times your age . . .

—Hey, Jack the Scológ! Jack the Scológ! . . . this is Muraed Phroinsiais . . . I have some advice to give you . . . After a while. You'll sing a little song first, Jack . . .

—Do, please, Jack . . .

—The blessings of God on you, Jack, do!

—Jack, you can't be discourteous to me. Bríd Terry here . . .

—*Honest*, Jack, that new refrain: *Bunga Bunga Bunga*[8] . . .

—*Bunga Bunga Bunga!* By the docks, *Bunga Bunga Bunga*, Son of Scológ! . . .

—You won't refuse me, Jack. Siúán the Shop here . . .

—May God forgive you all! . . . Why don't you leave me alone! . . . I've told you already that I won't sing a song.

—Oh Jack, my dearest Jack, this shoal of women are as voracious and persistent as porpoises after a sturgeon. Tell them, Jack, as you used to tell us long ago on the bogs, when we were young girls throwing clods at you: "I thought the fowling season didn't open this early in the year . . ."

—God would punish us for saying anything untoward, Caitríona. But I implore God and His Blessed Mother to get the women of this graveyard off my back . . .

—Nóirín Filthy Feet, lying Cite, smiling Siúán, Bríd Terry. Oh, Jack sweetheart, I know these women better than you do. You were always far off from them, up there in the wilderness of the marsh. And I'm longer here than you are. Take care not to pay any attention to them! I wouldn't mind, but asking you for songs!

—Every minute, Caitríona. But God would punish us for saying anything about our neighbour . . .

—These women would say about Good God Himself, Jack, that he came looking for a pound of money off them and didn't pay it back! Oh, I've suffered life with themselves and their lies! Hey, Jack . . . You've been promising me for a long time, but you might as well sing a song now . . .

—Don't ask me to, Caitríona . . .

—Just one verse, Jack! Just one verse! . . .

—Some other time, Caitríona. Some other time . . .

—Now, Jack. Now . . .

---

8. A vaguely risqué slang phrase, recorded from 1910 perhaps in connection with African dance.

NEIL PHAIDIN

—How do I know my own old woman isn't in the throes of death at home?

—Oh, if that's all you're worried about, Jack! She's only complaining of rheumatism and that won't bring her corpse to the graveyard for another twenty years!

—She's not keeping well, Caitríona . . .

—She had no pain or sickness, Jack. May her corpse stay far from this graveyard! Sing the song. Like a good man, my dear little Jack! . . .

—She was a good woman, Caitríona, every day of her life, and I'm not telling you that just because she's your sister . . .

—It doesn't matter a jot what sisters do in this life, Jack. But sing the song . . .

—I don't like to refuse you, Caitríona, but it's no use going on at me. It's strange the way things happen, Caitríona dear. The night before I was married, I was in the room in your house and a bunch of people were urging me to sing a song. Bríd Terry was there and Cite and Muraed Phroinsiais. May God forgive me for saying anything to anybody, but those three were going on at me very hard. My voice was as screechy as the lid of an old chest from singing songs for them all night. "Jack will never sing another song," said Nell, jokingly, while sitting in my lap . . . "unless I ask him to . . ." Would you believe, Caitríona, that those were the words going through my head the following morning when I was on my knees at the altar-rails before the priest? May God not punish me for it! It was an awful sin for me! But it's strange the way things are, Caitríona. Every time I've been asked to sing a song ever since, that was the first thing I thought of! . . .

—Ababúna búna búna! Oh, Jack! Jack the Scológ! I'll explode! I'll explode!

Interlude Ten

THE WHITE CLAY

1

—It's hard for him to go . . .

—It's a fair exchange for him . . .

—It's painful for him . . .

—It's a fair exchange for him . . .

—It's dark for him . . .

—It's a fair exchange for him . . .

—It's dangerous for him . . .

—It's a fair exchange for him . . .

—But . . .

—It's a fair exchange for him . . .

2

—By the docks, you couldn't hear Oscar's flail[1] up there, with all the hammering and the blasting. You could not, my friend . . .

—Was there any letter from young Brian? . . .

—Arrah! God bless your sense, my friend! Indeed, a young man who's going to be a priest has more to do than writing letters to those swamp-holes up there. Making more journeys for postmen . . .

—Nell spent a while in bed, Tomás? . . .

—Rheumatism, my friend. Rheumatism. She got out of bed the evening I was laid low . . .

---

1. The legendary Oscar, grandson of Fionn, fought the demons in Hell with his flail.

—She was always a kind woman, Tomás . . .

—I've always said, Jack, that she was more good-hearted than Caitríona . . .

—God would punish us for saying anything about our neighbour, Tomás . . .

—By the docks, don't the neighbours have stinging tongues too, my friend! Only for she was more good-natured, she wouldn't have offered to pay for Caitríona's cross, and for putting three of Pádraig's children through college. For that matter, aren't they getting very grand, with their college education. Look at me! . . .

—There wasn't a penny she ever laid hand on that she didn't put to good use, Tomás . . .

—That's true for you, my friend. Didn't I often say to myself that if it were Nóra Sheáinín got that legacy, she wouldn't be sober any day of the year . . .

—God would punish us for saying anything about our neighbour, Tomás. Not as much as a "don't be silly" ever came between myself and Nell . . .

—By the docks, didn't she cry a trunkful of big white handkerchiefs after you. She did indeed, my friend. Not to speak of all the Masses she offered up for your soul! People say she gave our own priest two hundred pounds into his hand in one go, not to mention all she sent to holy priests all over the country . . .

—*Bloody tear and 'ounds,* didn't Big Brian say: "If the priests don't place Son of Scológ on the high ladder, and give him a good push in the bottom onto that loft up there, I don't know what it takes . . ."

—By the docks, Son of Blackleg, you don't know the half of it! You couldn't hear a finger in your ear up there, with all their talk about Masses. Masses for Jack's soul, for Baba's soul, for Caitríona's soul . . .

—Mercy shared is not mercy spared, Tomás . . .

—That's exactly what Nell used to say. "Aren't you offering up an awful lot of Masses for the soul of Caitríona," I used to say to her, like that. "Good against evil, Tomás Inside," she'd say . . .

—God would punish us for saying anything about our neighbour, Tomás. Poor Caitríona can't help it. The poor creature is tormented for want of a cross . . .

—By the docks, my friend. You couldn't hear a finger in your ear up there, with all their chattering about crosses. Caitríona's cross was ready and paid for, but when you died Nell and Pádraig said they'd leave Caitríona's cross until hers and yours could be put up together . . .

—*Bloody tear and 'ounds*, didn't Big Brian say it was no wonder the world was in a mess, with all that fine money wasted on old stones . . .

—By the docks, Son of Blackleg, you didn't hear the half of it. Damned if I know if all that chatter about crosses did me any good at all. Crosses from morning till sunset and from night till morning. A person couldn't enjoy his drop of porter in peace without crosses being dragged in. A man couldn't walk his patch of land without imagining crosses in every field. I took myself off down to Pádraig Chaitríona's, where there wasn't half as much talk about crosses. Aren't they getting very grand . . .

—. . . *Qu'il retournerait pour libérer la France* . . .

—. . . Over again. Back again. Not a day passed that I didn't drink twenty pints at least . . .

—God help yourself and your twenty pints! I drank two score pints and two . . .

—Faith then, my friend, the doctor Nell brought from Brightcity to see me said it was Peadar the Pub's whiskey hastened my death. He did indeed, my friend. "Faith then, my friend," said I, "it was the doctor told me to drink it." "What doctor?" he said. "Our own doctor, God spare him!' said I. "Faith then, he did, my friend. Peadar the Pub's daughter was listening to him. If you don't believe me, go in to her on your way over. I'm not blaming the doctor at all, my friend. I'd been drinking it all my life and it never did me any harm. By my soul I blame the priest, my friend. By the docks, I think he was no help at all to me . . ."

—Could I give you any spiritual assistance, Tomás Inside? . . .

—Gug-goog, Big Colm's daughter. Gug-goog! A cosy little conversation . . .

—Seeing as it failed the priest . . .

—It did not fail the priest. Nothing fails the priest. You're a heretic . . .

—. . . By the oak of this coffin, Jack the Scológ, I gave the pound to . . .

—God would punish us, Cite . . .

—. . . Legacies! Only for Baba Pháidín's legacy, Tomás Inside wouldn't have got his walking-papers so soon . . .

—He can blame himself! The drink would remain where it was, only that Tomás brought his little belly the length of it. A legacy brought no misfortune on Nell. She bought a motor car with it and a hat with peacock's feathers . . .

—Oh! Oh! . . .

—We've seen all this before, of course! It was legacies kept the people of Donagh's Village alive down the ages. It wasn't nettles anyway. We've seen women who were down on their uppers today, all dressed up in hats and frills tomorrow. Signs on them: the hens would soon be laying in the hats . . .

—The people of Donagh's Village had the persistence to travel to the very hunkers of the sun, to the boundary wall of hell itself, in search of legacies. If the wretches of your village left their hillocks, they'd be homesick for the fleas . . .

—What do you say to the man from our village who was buried with as little as a shilling! . . .

—A man from our village was buried with much more than a shilling, but it would have been a happy day for him if he hadn't. He was a fine down-to-earth fellow till he got the big money. Neither God nor man has seen him since except standing around on every corner with his stupid face bashed in. Isn't that so? I'll bet you've never seen him without his face bashed in . . .

—Having your face bashed in is not too bad, but look at that young fellow from Sive's Rocks—a relation of my own—who got a small fortune, and nothing would do him but to go and break his neck. That's the only way to put it: the devil another thing in the world would please him but to go and break his neck . . .

—Oh, look at that greasy clown from Wood of the Lake! Some old hag in America left him a few thousand. Siúán the Shop's tea-ration had barely settled in his paunch when he was up in Dublin buying a monster of a motor car. He met a flimsy little thing straying around up there, and didn't he bring her home with him! She wasn't long with him, though. The rattle of the car was upsetting her stomach. And she went back to straying around up there again. The motor car was nicknamed Knotted Bottom. May I not leave this spot if he could get it to move an inch without having to call out a gang of louts from the end of some boreen to push it!

—Didn't I twist my ankle! . . .

—The gang would push it to the nearest pub. It would stay there till day-break, and then they'd push it back again. Its wheels and body finished up at Road-End. It had an almighty horn! . . .

—So has Nell Pháidín's motor car . . .

—Going up and down past Caitríona's house . . .

—Ababúna! . . .

—Faith then, for a legacy car, it trundles along fairly merrily . . .

—Maybe, with the help of God, Hitler will be here soon . . .

—Not a glint of the Woody Hillside legacy ever came out of Mannion the Counsellor's Office. He told me so, the day I was in with him to bring the law on Road-End Man about my little lump-hammer . . .

—. . . "The bottom will fall out of Wall Street, as happened before," he said, with his eye sneaking over to the hatchet. "It will fall out of its groove and I'll lose another legacy as I did before . . ."

"The devil would I care, Tomáisín," says Caitríona who was present, "if it fell like mud out of it, as long as it fell like thunder out of Nell's legacy too . . ."

—Road-End's old woman got a dodgy legacy . . .

—That's what left her with the fancy house . . .

—Oh no, it was not; it was my turf . . .

—I brought off a great insurance *coup* there at the time. Road-End Man himself and his eldest daughter . . .

—I sold a full set of *The Complete Carpenter and Mechanic* to his son . . .

—Faith then, as you say . . .

—Your man over here had got a legacy the time Peadar the Pub's daughter brought him into the parlour . . .

—The Big Master got a legacy . . .

—Billyboy won't be short of doctors so . . .

—Oh, the thief! The tufted prickle-stick![2] . . .

—. . . You're a liar! It wasn't over a legacy that the One-Ear meat-carver stabbed me . . .

—. . . That fellow couldn't afford to pay for forty-two pints! A man who had so little land that only the hind legs of his donkey could fit on it! The two front legs had to be on Curraoin's land beside it . . . That was him! Pushing the motor car for the Wood of the Lake eejit is how he got it . . .

—Curraoin too, it was a legacy left him the big holding, where his eldest son wants to bring in Road-End's daughter . . .

—Oh! The devil pierce her! I swear to God, if the old woman at home lets her in! . . .

—Road-End's daughter is insured . . .

—. . . If that's how things are, Caitríona was lucky she didn't get the legacy. If she had . . .

—She'd build two slate-roofed houses . . .

—She'd buy two motor cars . . .

—She'd put two crosses over herself . . .

—And two hats . . .

—You'd never know but she might even wear trousers . . .

—*Bloody tear and 'ounds*, didn't Big Brian say, when his own

---

2. Tufted prickle-stick: *an briogadáinín bobailíneach*, derogatory phrase invented by Ó Cadhain.

daughter's son went to college to be a priest: "If that ruminating bess back there were alive," he said, "she wouldn't stop till she'd make her Pádraig put aside his wife and become a priest himself . . ."

—If you tell me, Caitríona, how much money there was in the legacy, I'll tot up the interest for you:

$$\text{Interest} = \frac{\text{Principal} \times \text{Time} \times \text{Rate}}{100}$$

Isn't that right, Master? . . .

—It would be enough anyway to repay Cite's pound . . .

—And Road-End Man for the chimney . . .

—And Nóra Sheáinín for the silver spoons and knives . . .

—Oh, Holy Mother of God! Silver spoons in Mangy Field! Silver spoons! Oh, Jack! Jack the Scológ! Silver spoons in Mangy Field! I'll explode! I'll explode! . . .

3

—. . . She said that, Master? . . .

—She did, Máirtín Pockface. She told me . . .

—. . . "The flaw is up above," says I . . .

—. . . "By the devil," said Caitríona, "it's a fine pig for scalding . . ."

—. . . "Mártan Sheáin Mhóir had a daughter . . ."

—When will she marry again, do you think? . . .

—Musha, Cite, neighbour, I don't know . . .

—She can easily get a man, of course, if she intends to get married again. She's a strong, active woman, God bless her! . . .

—That's true for you, Muraed, neighbour! . . .

—If she didn't say anything about it when she saw you were dying . . .

—She didn't, Bríd . . .

—Maybe the Small Master would marry her . . .

—Or the Wood of the Lake Master, since the priest's sister has jilted him . . .

—You're a *dote*, Billyboy. *Honest!* Tell us if the Schoolmistress had any talk of getting married again . . .

—Oh! Is that really him, the blackguard, the ruffian, the lustful little letter-bag? Oh! Where is the ruffian? . . .

—This is a fine welcome into graveyard clay . . .

—By the docks, Master, don't you remember I told you? Didn't he die! . . .

—Ha! Where is he? . . .

—Now, Master, neighbour, calm down! Calm down! We were good neighbours above ground. Did I ever open a letter of yours? . . . Oh, Master dear, don't lie! . . . Oh, Master, if that is so, I didn't do it . . . The Postmistress could do whatever she pleased, but don't accuse me of something I didn't do, Master . . . Oh, that's definitely a lie, Master! I didn't give a letter of yours to anybody, I went straight to your house and handed it piping hot out of the bag into the palm of your hand. I'll have you know, Master, it's not every postman would do that! . . .

Oh, Master, Master, may God forgive you! It was not to see your wife that I came so promptly with the post. Oh, God forbid, Master, that such a thought would enter my mind! . . . Oh, Master, neighbour, don't say that! Don't tell a lie about her. She's on the dark road of lies, and you're on the bright road of truth . . .

Believe you me, Master, neighbour, I was very sorry about your death. You were a decent man to call in to. And you were worth listening to, Master. You had a fine flow of words about the affairs of life . . . Oh, Master, don't say things like that! . . . Oh, Master! . . .

Not a day went by that I didn't sympathise with herself on your death . . . Oh, my dear neighbour, will you for God's sake stop that sort of talk! "It's a great pity about the Big Master," I used to say. "It's not the same house at all, since he left. Believe me, Schoolmistress, I'm very sorry for you . . ."

. . . Patience, Master! Patience, Master! Can't you listen to what I'm saying! "Billy the Post," the poor thing used to say, "I know that. He was very fond of you . . ." . . . Aw! now, Master! Take it easy, Master! "I did my best for him, Billy, but he was beyond the doctors' skill . . ."

Oh, Master dear! My dear, dear Master! . . . "It's like this, Billy, the Master was too good . . ."

. . . Aw! Master, don't make a show of yourself in front of the neighbours! Remember, Master, you are the Sergeant-Major of learning, and you have to set a good example . . . Patience, Master! Oh, Master, you have me skinned and flayed. It's a fine welcome into the graveyard clay!

—Do you need any spiritual assistance, Billyboy the Post? . . .

—Oh, the snouty lecher, he does . . .

—*De grâce*, Master! Control yourself. Billyboy is a very romantic person. *Honest* . . .

—You, yourself, Master, used to . . .

—Faith then, Master, I saw you! . . . In the school . . .

—It's no wonder our children marry heretics and *blacks* . . .

—. . . To make a long story short, Master, it was Whit Monday. I had the day off. I went west along the road to have a little walk for myself . . .

. . . Now, neighbour, what harm was there in going for a walk? Only once in a blue moon did I get a chance to lower the mainsail . . . It wasn't good for my health to walk east along the road, Master . . . Calm down! . . . When I was passing the gate of your house, she had the car out by the roadside. I pumped it up for her. What's the harm in that, Master? It was neighbourly co-operation . . . "May the Lord have mercy on the poor Big Master!" says I. "He was so proud of that car." "Billy," said the creature, "the Big Master wasn't destined to enjoy the comforts of this life. The poor Big Master was too good . . ." Oh, Master, it's not my fault! . . . But hold on a minute, Master! Hear me out . . .

"Sit in, Billy," she said. "You'll drive the car for me. I need an outing after being down in the dumps for the past while. Nobody could possibly think of scandal. You're an old friend of the family, Billy . . ." Control yourself, Master. Can't you see everybody is listening! I didn't think you were that sort of man at all! . . .

To make a long story short, Master, the place was deserted, apart from the two of us. If you've ever been to Promontory Pier at that time of day, Master, you know there's hardly a more beautiful spot on earth. The lights were being lit on the headlands and uplands across the bay. I felt, Master . . . Oh, for God's sake, Master, have a bit of decency! . . .

. . . To make a long story short, Master, she told me that her love for me was deeper than the sea . . . Oh, have patience, Master! Be patient! Ah, Master, I was certain you weren't that sort of person . . .

. . . "God be with this time four years ago!" she said. "Myself and the poor Big Master were here, looking at the lights and the stars and at the glimmering on the seaweed . . ." Oh, Master dear, you'll give yourself a bad name! Calm down! . . . "The poor Big Master," says I. "The Big Master," she said, "he was a great loss. But he was too good for . . ." Master, Master, neighbour, why don't you hear me out! . . .

"Whom the gods love, Billy," she said, "dies young. Musha, Billy, he was terribly fond of you . . ." What could I do, Master? . . .

—Now, Master! Máirtín Pockface saw . . .

—Faith then, you were screwing her, Master . . .

—. . . What would you do yourself, Master, if you were in my position there at Promontory Pier, and the two of you looking at the lights, at the stars, and at the glimmering? . . . Oh, calm down, Master! . . . To make a long story short, Master . . . Now, Master, neighbour . . . Oh, control your impatience, Master dear . . . Why are you turning nasty on me? I didn't deserve that from you . . .

To make a long story short, Master, she sent for three doctors from Dublin for me . . . I've never, in all my life, seen the likes of you, Master! Why are you taking it out on me, Master? Nobody who knew you above ground would believe you'd be going on like this . . .

"What happened to the Big Master won't happen to you if I can help it," she said . . . The blessings of God on you, Master dear, calm down. You'll disgrace yourself. And you a schoolmaster and all . . .

. . . To make a long story short, Master, I had a piercing pain in my side and kidneys. I got a little relief in the evening: relief before death. She sat on the side of the bed and held my hand . . . God bless us and save us! Will you look at the commotion he's making now! How could I control her? . . .

. . . To make a long story short, Master: "If it is fated that you should not recover, Billy," she said, "my life won't be life to me without you . . ." Oh, Master, don't be so vindictive . . . Even if she did marry again, would it be my fault? . . . Have patience, Master! . . .

. . . To make a long story short, Master, I was on the plank-bridge to eternity when she shouted in my ear: "I'll bury you decently, Billy," she said, "and whether my life is long or short after you . . ." Calm down, Master! Leave me in peace, for God's sake, Master! . . . But my peace is gone forever, I believe . . . Oh, if only she'd thought of burying me anywhere in the graveyard but stuck like a counterfoil to this lunatic. But she couldn't help it, the creature. She didn't know what she was doing . . . Oh, easy on now, easy on, Master!

—*Bloody tear and 'ounds* for a story, didn't Big Brian say when Billyboy took ill: "That little pipsqueak is for the clay soon," he said. "By gad, he'll be lucky to get a burial at all. If he were up in Dublin, he'd most certainly be shovelled into the rubbish bin. But your woman will make a clean sweep of it and bundle him down on top of the Big Master in that hole back there. The two will tear one another apart like two dogs with their tails tied together . . ."

—. . . My misfortune and affliction! . . . Big Brian was right . . . Two dogs with their tails tied together . . . Upon my soul, it was true for him! . . . Our tails were tied, Billyboy . . .

—It's true for you, Master . . .

—We were bounding about, wagging our tails and fawning, till we were trapped and consumed by the lights, by the stars, by the phosphorescence, by the vows. Oh! Billyboy, we mistook the glimmering light for the ever-burning candle . . .

—That is so true for you, Master . . .

—We thought we'd have the starry kingdom of heaven for a wedding present; that we'd drink at the harvest-home festival where the wine would never sicken you . . .

—*Oh my*, how romantic! . . .

—The whole lot of it, Billyboy my dear, was only a delusion, brought on by our own consuming egos . . . We were captured. Our agile tails were tied . . . Billyboy, my dear friend, she was only a female version of the Narrow-striped Kern[3] who played the trick that suited the moment. "I'm one day in Rathlin and another day in the Isle of Man . . ."

—"A day in Islay and a day in Cantyre," my dear Master and neighbour . . .

—Exactly, Billyboy my dear. That woman is not worth a biting word or a moment's worry. Billyboy, my dearest friend, she found two silly dogs who let themselves be captured and their tails tied . . .

—That is so true for you, my dear Master . . .

—Billyboy, my dear, our pleasant burden from now on, instead of being hard on our tails, is to be gentle and neighbourly with one another . . .

—Good man yourself, Master! Now you're talking, neighbour! Peace and quiet, Master. That's what matters most in the graveyard clay, Master: peace and quiet. If I'd known that she'd bury me cheek by jowl with you, I'd never have married her . . .

—I don't give a red curse what anybody does! No matter how she behaved, that was a hell of a mean, low-down thing for you to do, you blackguard, you thief, you ruffian! Into the gas chamber you should be shovelled, you windbag, you swine, you . . .

—Now, Master dear, calm down, calm down! . . .

4

—If I'd lived another while . . .

—It was a fair exchange for you . . .

—If I'd lived another while myself . . .

—It was a fair exchange for you . . .

—I'd be getting the pension on the following St. Patrick's Day . . .

—Another three months and I'd be in the new house . . .

---

3. *An Ceithearnach Caoilriabhach*, a trickster avatar of the sea-god Manannán, in Irish legends. This and other tales from *Silva Gadelica* (I–XXXI), edited from manuscripts and translated by Standish H. O'Grady, were used by Ó Cadhain in his Irish-language classes while he was interned in the Curragh Military Camp during the Second World War.

—God help us forever and ever! If I'd lived another while, maybe my heap of bones would have been brought back east of Brightcity . . .

—. . . I would have married in two weeks' time. But you stabbed me through the edge of my liver, you whetstone of murder. If I'd lived another while, I wouldn't have left a One-Ear Breed alive . . .

—I'd have taken the Woody Hillside land off my brother. Mannion the Counsellor told me I would . . .

—I thought I wouldn't die till I got even with Road-End Man about my seaweed . . .

—Oh! May the devil pierce him! If I'd lived another while, I'd go in to Mannion the Counsellor and make a secure will. Then I'd turf the eldest son out to hell and get a wife for the other son, Tom. Then I'd serve a summons on the porter-swilling Glutton about his donkeys, and if I got no satisfaction in court, I'd drive spikes through their hooves. Then I'd keep watch before daybreak till I caught the Road-End crowd in my turf stack, and I'd serve an almighty summons on them . . . And if I got no satisfaction in court, I'd get a few chunks of dynamite from the big boss. Then . . .

—I'd have the law on Peadar the Pub's daughter . . .

—*Bloody tear and 'ounds,* I'd get a fine pleasant ride in Nell Pháidín's motor car . . .

—I'd see *The Setting Sun* in print . . .

—If I'd lived another while, I'd rub . . . what was that name you had for it, Master? . . . yes, methylated spirits, on myself . . .

—By the oak of this coffin, I'd pursue Caitríona for my pound . . .

—God would punish us, Cite . . .

—I'd stamp my whole body like a love-letter with Hitler's emblems . . .

—The Postmistress said the other day that the Irish Folklore Commission and the Director of Statistics asked her for the records she kept, over forty-five years, of the number of little crosses in every letter. Fifteen was the Big Master's average number, and seven was how many Caitríona always put in her letters to Big Brian: one for his beard, one for his crooked shoulder . . .

—. . . Patience! Patience, Master dear! . . .

—. . . Don't believe him, Jack . . .

—I'd have gone to England to earn money and to see the West Headland crowd . . . I heard there's a plague of them on the streets of London now, with white jackets . . . and monocles . . .

—I'd travel the world: Marseilles, Port Said, Singapore, Batavia. *Honest* . . .

—*Qu'il retournerait pour libérer la France* . . .

—If I'd lived another while, you wouldn't have caused my death, you ugly Siúán. I'd take my ration cards elsewhere . . .

—. . . I'd have gone to your funeral, Billyboy the Post. I owed it to you to be at your funeral . . .

—I'd have keened you softly and sweetly, Billyboy . . .

—. . . I'd lay you out, Billyboy, as neatly as a lover would lay out his first love-letter . . .

—If I'd lived another while, I'd have asked her to bury me in another graveyard . . . Master, neighbour, calm down, calm down! But listen to me, Master! Two dogs with their tails tied . . .

—. . . I'd drink porter, of course, and a springtide of it . . .

—. . . The game would have been ours. I had the Nine and my partner had the fall of the play. Bad luck to the *mine*, if it didn't blow up at the wrong moment! . . .

—. . . I'd have the law on the murderer for giving me poison. "Take two spoonfuls . . ."

—So would I, even though I never cared for splitting hairs with Mannion the Counsellor. By the docks, my friend, I'd have the law on him nevertheless. He told me to turn to whiskey. He did, indeed, my friend. If I'd stayed on the porter I'd be alright. I never had an ache or a pain . . .

—. . . If I'd lived, I'd have had a bit of luck with the crossword some week. And of course I'd have great insurance coups in Jack the Scológ's. I'd put "Eternal Death to the Simplified Spelling" for my *nom-de-plume* on the next Sweepstake ticket . . .

—. . . "A Bright Smile Now, Nurse" is what I'd put . . .

—"Headland Harbour" is what Billyboy wrote . . .

—I'd go to the pictures again. *Honest to God*, I'd love to see that woman with the fur coat. It was an exact copy of the coat Baba Pháidín used to wear till the soot fell on it in Caitríona's . . .

—That's a damned lie, you slut! . . .

—Spare me the lash of your tongue, Caitríona. Peace and quiet is what I want. I didn't deserve your snarling . . .

—. . . If I'd lived another while! If I'd lived another while, then! What would I do? What would I do, then? Only a wise man would say . . .

—If I'd lived till the election meeting, I'd contradict Cosgrave. I'd tell him they were sent over as mere envoys, and that they exceeded their authority . . .

—I lived, thanks be to God, till I told de Valera up to his face that they were sent over as plenipotentiaries. I told him up to his face. I told him up to his face. I told him up . . .

—That's a damned lie, you did not! . . .

—I remember it well. I twisted my ankle . . .

—. . . If you had lived another while, you'd see all the young women of Donagh's Village smoking clay pipes. That's what they're doing since cigarettes got scarce. They say crushed dock leaves and nettles are great in clay pipes . . .

—If you lived to be as old as the Yew or the Hag of Beara,[4] you wouldn't see the last flea swatted on the hillocks of your own village . . .

—If the Postmistress had lived another while . . .

—She had no need to. Her daughter inherited her ways very well . . .

—If I'd lived another while . . .

—What would you need to live for? . . .

—I'd see the sod over you, for one thing . . .

—If Tomás Inside had lived?

—He'd migrate once again . . .

—He'd turn to the porter again . . .

---

4. An otherworldly woman, a Celtic deity in origin, who lived into extreme old age. Associated with the Beara Peninsula in west Cork.

—He'd chase Pádraig Chaitríona's cattle off his patch of land . . .

—Nell's cattle, more likely! . . .

—If Caitríona had lived . . .

—Oh, to have buried that pussface before her . . .

—If I'd lived, I'd administer spiritual assistance. If I'd lived another week, even, I'd have up-to-date information for Caitríona . . .

—Big Colm's daughter, you used to skip your Family Rosary in order to eavesdrop at closed doors, to see if the neighbours said theirs . . .

—. . . I'd go to Croke Park to see Concannon . . .

—Billyboy the Post saw your ghost there after the All-Ireland final and you whingeing and whining . . .

—. . . I'd have finished the stable during the fine weather, and the colt wouldn't have died . . .

—Oh, didn't everyone in the village see your ghost! . . .

—. . . I wouldn't believe there's any such thing as a ghost, Red-haired Tom . . .

—Some people would say there is. Some people would say there isn't. It's a wise man would . . .

—Oh, indeed, there are ghosts. God forbid that I'd lie about anybody, but I saw Curraoin chasing Glutton's donkeys and Road-End's cattle out of his oats, and him a year dead.

—The first cause of death for Billyboy the Post was when he saw the Big Master searching in the top of the press in his own kitchen, the day after he was buried . . .

—. . . Calm down, Master! Oh, calm down. Calm down! . . . I never shaved myself with your razor. I beg you as my friend and protector, Master, listen to me a minute! Two dogs . . .

—Road-End Man was seen . . .

—Faith then, as you say . . .

—Oh, he would be! Stealing my turf he was, for certain . . .

—Or lump-hammers . . .

—They say, God help us, there isn't a night that a phantom aeroplane isn't heard in the Middle Harbour since the Frenchman came down there . . .

—Arrah, that's a real aeroplane going to America from Ulster or from Shannon . . .

—Do you think I wouldn't recognize a real aeroplane! I heard it clearly, when I was gathering red seaweed there late at night . . .

—If the night was dark . . .

—Oh, don't be talking drivel! I swear by my soul it wasn't a real aeroplane! A real aeroplane is easily recognized . . .

—*Mes amis* . . .

—Permission to speak! Permission to speak, then!

—There are signs, all the same. The devil a bit of heed I ever gave to ghosts till I heard about Seán Mhaitiú who's buried here, down in the Half-Guinea Plot. It was his own son told me. This was before I came down through the hatch myself. He was up on the loft of lies at the time too, but he didn't tell a lie about his own father. His father's last request, when he was in the throes of death, was to bury him here in this graveyard beside the rest of his people. "I'll die peacefully," he said, "if you promise me that much." That West Headland crowd are lazy loafers. They put a bit of sod over him back there in the old cemetery near his house. But sometime during the following month the son was making cocks of dried seaweed on the shore. I heard this from his very own mouth. He saw the funeral coming out of the cemetery. He told me it was as clear—the coffin, the people and everything—as the armful of seaweed he was putting on the cock. They passed close to him. He recognized some of them, but he'd never divulge their names, he said. He was afraid at first, but when they'd passed over by the strand he plucked up a little courage. "No matter what God does to me," he said, "I'll follow them." And so he did, over by the shore, step by step, till they came into this graveyard and buried the corpse in the Half-Guinea Plot down there. He recognized the coffin. He wouldn't tell a lie about his own father . . .

—Where's Seán Mhaitiú? If he's here, nobody heard a squeak out of him . . .

—I don't have it from the Pope's own tooth, but that's what his son told me, and devil the lie he told about it . . .

—The dead didn't walk. Call the Half-Guinea crowd and they'll tell you whether he's there or not . . .

—Arrah, leave those loudmouths alone! . . .

—The devil a bit of me will leave them alone. Hey, you Half-Guinea lot! . . .

—. . . Bríd Mhaitiú is here . . .

—And Colm Mhaitiú . . .

—And Pádraig Mhaitiú . . .

—And Liam Mhaitiú . . .

—And Maitiú himself . . .

—. . . The West Headland cemetery is where Seán Mhaitiú is buried. He had married back there . . .

—He wouldn't tell a lie about his own father! . . .

—Changing places like that is not as easy as changing political parties. If it were, Dotie would be back on the fair plains of East Galway long ago . . .

—And the Frenchman . . . But maybe his ghost is all that's here of him . . .

—The story is no more strange than what Billyboy the Post told me: that Tomás Inside has been seen chasing cattle off his patch of land. Pádraig Chaitríona and Nell's son made two halves of it between them, but neither of them is happy. Pádraig's crowd and Nell's crowd see him every other week. The week one family sees him, the other one doesn't. Nell brought the priest to walk the land and they read a barrage of prayers and a few St. John's Gospels, he says.

—She would, the little bitch. I hope to God she'll never gain a mangy penny by it! My Pádraig has plenty of land without it . . .

—I heard, Caitríona, that you haven't given Jack the Scológ a bit of peace since you died . . .

—God would punish us . . .

—Nell told Tomás Inside that you won him over . . .

—Wasn't it Big Brian she used to be after?

—Oh! Jesus, Mary and Joseph! After Big Brian! . . .

—*Bloody tear and 'ounds*, didn't he say . . . "Hoh-roh, Mary, your wares and your bags and belts . . ."

—What did he say?

—What did he say, Son of Blackleg?

—What did he say, Beartla?

—The same Big Brian says mischievous things . . . "Hoh-roh, Mary . . ."

—What did he say, Beartla? . . .

—*Bloody tear and 'ounds*, it wouldn't do you any good, Caitríona . . .

—It would do me good, Beartla. Out with it . . .

—*That's the dote*, Bartly. Tell us . . .

—Oh! Do you hear that little sow of Seáinín's? Don't open your mouth about it, Beartla . . .

—*Be a dote*, Bartholomew. Tell it . . .

—Don't tell it, Beartla. Don't let it past your lips! . . .

—*Honest to Heavens*, you are *mean*, Bartly, if you don't tell it. Did he say that every time he opens his eyes her ghost is there in front of him? . . .

—If you tell it to Seáinín Robin's little sow, Beartla! . . .

—*Honest to God*, Bartly, you're *awfully mean!* All cultural relations with you should stop. *Let me see now.* Did he say that because he refused to marry her when she was alive, her ghost was now his fairy lover? . . .

—Ababúna! To be the fairy lover of that ugly looking blunderer! I'm warning you, Beartla! . . .

—*On the level*, Bartly. Did Caitríona's ghost tell him to shave himself, or to wash himself, or to go to a foot or shoulder specialist? . . .

—*Bloody tear and 'ounds*, Nóra! . . . *Bloody tear and 'ounds*, Caitríona! . . .

—For the life of you don't tell, Beartla! . . .

—*Honest to God*, Bartly! . . .

5

—. . . True for you, Jack the Scológ. God would punish anybody for saying I'd be a lover to that ugly streak of misery . . .

—...You fell off a stack of oats ... Did you ever hear of the Battle of the Sheaves? ... I'll tell you. "Cormac Mac Art[5] Mac Conn Mac Tréanmhór Ó Baoiscne was building a stack of oats one day in Tara of the Hosts. Tufty Mouth[6] was throwing the sheaves to him. The Seven Battalions of Learning and the Seven Battalions of Common-Learning and the Battalion of Minor Freemen came ..."

—... There's great talk of transferring him. A lot of talk ...

—But transferring him would be no satisfaction, unless he's dismissed, and killed or drowned, or hanged, or given the cat's death afterwards. This graveyard is bursting at the seams as a result of those mercenaries who are billeted on us, Billyboy. "Take two spoonfuls of this bottle," said the murderer ...

—Maybe, neighbour, he'll be dismissed. I think he might be, too, after the trouncing he gave to a man from Donagh's Village the other day for handing him a red ticket. But I don't think he'll be put to death ...

—Arrah, what's the use, so! That's what should be done to him: to smother him under a pot. Look at me, he gave me poison! ...

—By the docks, didn't he tell me to drink whiskey? He did indeed, my friend. The blackguard! I wouldn't mind but I never had an ache or a pain! ...

—Galway have a good football team this year, Billyboy? ...

—A great team entirely, neighbour. Everybody says that even if they played on crutches they'd win the All-Ireland. *Green Flag* said it the other day ...

—Concannon will make paste of backsides that day ...

—Concannon is only a substitute!

—A substitute! A substitute! What are you talking about so? They won't win! They won't win! They won't ...

---

5. High King of Ireland, ruling from Tara in Meath, according to legend.

6. *Cab an Dosáin*, the little fellow of the otherworld who was reaping the corn so fast in the Battle of the Sheaves that the Fianna nearly killed one another binding after him. Also associated with the buffoonish Conán Maol in legendary lore of Fionn's followers.

—They have great young players. The very best. They will win, neighbour. You'll see they'll win.

—Arrah, shut your mouth! What's the use in talking rubbish? I'm telling you your young players aren't worth a bullock's slime[7] without Concannon! I wouldn't mind but for all this "They'll win," "They'll win"! . . .

—Begging your pardon, neighbour, one would think you'd prefer them to be defeated with Concannon on the team than to win without him! A taste of revenge would be sweet, neighbour. Concannon was blamed by many in 1941. I never felt so cross as I did that day in Croke Park . . .

—That's the truth, Billyboy . . .

—Billyboy was always very obliging . . .

—It gladdened his heart to bring you good news . . .

—And even if it was bad news his grin was like a safety-belt . . .

—Who laid out Tomás Inside, Billyboy? . . .

—Nell and Big Brian's daughter and Tomáisín's wife did, Cáit . . .

—And who keened him, Billyboy? . . .

—Nell and the village women did, Bid. But yourself and Little Cáit were greatly missed. Everybody was saying: "May the Lord have mercy on Little Cáit, the poor thing, and Bid Shorcha, the creature! Weren't they great at stretching and keening a man! There won't be the likes of them again . . ."

—May God spare your health, Billyboy! . . .

—*Bloody tear and 'ounds*, what does it matter who stretches or keens a person! . . .

—. . . Hitler is still knocking soft eggs out of them, God bless him! . . .

—He's doing fairly well, neighbour, fairly well . . .

—What do you mean, fairly well! Shouldn't he be into England by now! . . .

---

7. Slime on a cow's rear is a sign she is in heat; a bullock's slime is therefore a nothing.

—Not at all, neighbour. But the British and the Yanks are back into French territory again . . .

—Arrah, what! You're spouting lies, Billyboy the Post! We're not making small-talk about sport now, you know . . .

—It's nine months now, neighbour, since I've been able to read a newspaper, and I don't know exactly how they're faring. At that time, everybody was saying that the British and the Yanks wouldn't be able to make a stand in France on D-Day . . .

—Arrah, Billyboy dear, why would they? And they were pitched to hell out into the sea again like a heap of dead blennies . . .

—Faith then, I suppose so, neighbour . . .

—And Hitler followed them this time—which he should have done at the time of Dunkirk—and he's into England by now! *Der Tag!* I think there's nothing left of England now . . .

—*Non! Non, mon ami! C'est la libération qu'on a promise. La libération! Les Gaullistes et Monsieur Churchill avaient raison . . .*

—Oh! You windbag, you stumbler, you blind fumbler . . .

—*C'est la libération! Vive la France! Vive la République Française! Vive la patrie! La patrie sacrée! Vive de Gaulle! . . .*

—Frenchman, my neighbour, did you hear about the newspaper report that you were awarded the Cross for your valour . . .

—*Ce n'est rien, mon ami. C'est sans importance. Ce qui compte, c'est la libération. Vive la France! La France! La France! La patrie sacrée! . . .*

—Oh, do you hear the racket the little scutterer is raising! He's worse than the Big Master . . .

—Musha, Billyboy, you didn't hear any talk of our getting the English market back? . . .

—Do you hear the gadfly again? . . .

—The English market will be fine, neighbour . . .

—Do you think it will, Billyboy? . . .

—It will, neighbour. Don't worry. I'm telling you the English market will be fine . . .

—May God save you, Billyboy! You've plucked the bitter thorn from my heart with those words. You seriously think it will be fine? I've a patch of land at the top of the village . . .

—. . . It has indeed been published, your book of poetry . . .

—*The Yellow Stars!* Oh! Billyboy, my dearest friend, you're not serious? . . .

—I didn't see it myself, but the Postmistress's daughter told me so . . . Don't worry, neighbour. Your own book will soon be published too . . .

—Do you think it will, Billyboy? . . .

—I'm certain it will, neighbour . . .

—You have secret information so, Billyboy? . . .

—Musha, I used to hear a little tattle, neighbour. I used to be very friendly with people here and there. The Postmistress's daughter . . . Oh! Master, calm down, calm down! . . .

—Have a bit more manners, Master! . . .

—There's great money to be earned in England still, Billyboy? . . .

—It's not as good as it was, neighbour. The food is awful. The Woody Hillside, Sive's Rocks and Donagh's Village crowd have come home . . .

—A holiday among the nobly bred nettles of Donagh's Village will do them good . . .

—. . . Your son, his wife and their two children are home . . .

—Ah! You're having me on, Billyboy! . . .

—God forbid, neighbour! By the holy little finger! . . .

—And the black wife is home with him? . . .

—She is, bedad, and the two children . . .

—Listen here to me, Billyboy. Tell me the honest truth. Are they as black as they say? As black as the Earl's little *black*? . . .

—Don't worry, neighbour. Far from it . . .

—Are they as black as Road-End Man after being up a sooty chimney? . . .

—By my soul, they are not, indeed . . .

—As black as the Big Tinker with the lumps on his face? . . .

—Don't worry, neighbour. Not that black, either . . .

—As black as Baba Pháidín's fur coat after Caitríona's house? . . .

—Shut your mouth, you little brat! . . .

—As black as Big Brian in a hangover sweat? . . .

—But when Big Brian went before the judge after being in the geyser-room in Dublin, he was as shiny-faced as any of the little saints in the chapel window . . .

—Big Brian in a hangover sweat. About as black as that, now . . .

—Oh! If that's the case, they're not *niggers* at all . . .

—The children are not nearly as black as the mother . . .

—Did they have to call the priest for the old lady? . . .

—Sure enough, neighbour, she was in a bad way. She didn't want to let them into the house at all. The people of the village gathered round, and some of them were more inclined to pelt them with stones and chase them off. But, to make a long story short, neighbour, they were brought to the priest and he sprinkled a dash of water from the font on them, and the old lady was happy then . . . She's very proud of them now. She brings them to Mass every Sunday . . .

—If that's the case, Billyboy, I don't mind being dead. I thought she'd lose heart and go to bits . . .

—Musha, have you any news of that young fellow of mine, Billyboy?

—Seáinín Liam, that young fellow of yours has a firm grip of what's good for him. He bought a colt the other day . . .

—That's great news, Billyboy. If he had a sturdy little girl now . . .

—Don't worry, Seáinín. From what I hear, he'll have that soon. A woman from West Headland who was in England. With plenty of money, I'm told. The Postmistress's daughter told me the Small Master is getting married one of these days . . . Yes. That one who's in Barry's Betting Office in Brightcity . . . The priest doesn't mention her at all now, neighbour. She took the pledge a while ago . . . Don't worry, neighbour. They still talk about that feat of yours. Some say you did it, and others say you'd have burst . . .

—Devil a burst, then, Billyboy! That's the God's honest truth. I drank two score pints and two . . .

—Do you think an *Antichrist* will come soon, Billyboy? . . .

—Don't worry, neighbour. I don't figure it will. I don't think it will. To make a long story short, I wouldn't say it will . . .

—Faith then I think, Billyboy, it won't be long now . . .

—That will all be fine, neighbour. You may be sure it will . . .

—Do many people need spiritual assistance, Billyboy, or do they say the Family Rosary?

—I've told you often enough, Big Colm's daughter, to leave matters of heresy to me . . .

—Would you think, Billyboy, the prophecy is coming true? . . .

—I would indeed, neighbour. That will all be . . .

—Would Seán Chite in Donagh's Village think it's coming true? . . .

—On my last trip to Donagh's Village, the village people—those who weren't in England—were gathered round Seán Chite in the shade of a clump of nettles in the middle of the houses, and him prophesying . . .

—Did he say that England would disappear into the air in a ball of fire and ashes?

—In a ball of fire and ashes! In a ball of fire and ashes! He said the clergy would be as hungry as the lay people. Hold on now . . . He said no distinction would be made between woman and man. Hold on now . . . Hold on now . . . He said the pint would cost tuppence again . . .

—To hell with your women! Did he say that England would disappear in a ball of fire? . . .

—He wasn't that far into it, neighbour. He had only reached where Knotted Bottom was woken up in the cellar and grabbed his sword to free Ireland. At that stage, I produced income tax notices about their legacies . . .

—Seán Chite is right. Every single word of it is coming true . . .

—. . . You say, Billyboy, that Éamon de Valera is winning . . .

—That's a damned lie! Billyboy said Dick Mulcahy[8] is winning . . .

---

8. Richard Mulcahy fought in the 1916 Rising and the War of Independence, and led the pro-Treaty forces in the Civil War.

—Éamon de Valera and Dick Mulcahy were at the chapel after Mass, a month ago. A Joint Meeting . . .

—A Joint Meeting?

—A Joint Meeting?

—By Dad! A Joint Meeting? . . .

—*Crikies!* A Joint Meeting? . . .

—A Joint Meeting about the emergency services . . .

—Éamon de Valera spoke about the Republic? . . .

—Dick Mulcahy spoke about the Treaty? . . .

—They didn't speak about the Republic or the Treaty . . . To make a long story short, they both made the same speech: thanking the people . . .

—Ah! I understand now, Billyboy! That was a trick of de Valera's to hoodwink the other crowd . . .

—That's a damned lie! Of course, every old stopped clock in this graveyard knows it was a plan of Dick Mulcahy's to make de Valera take the wrong turn. Wouldn't you agree with me, Billyboy? . . .

—Be careful, Billyboy! You've reached the age of sense and reason, and remember that it was our crowd gave you the pay rise and promotion. Remember you were only an "Assistant Rural Postman" . . .

—My Fellow-Irish People! I'm here today! . . .

—If you'd been here at the time of the Election . . .

—No more than myself, Billyboy has nothing to do with politics . . .

—You coward! Get back under the bed. . . .

—You spineless yoke!

—. . . Where are you, Pól? Your old friend was around here again this year . . .

—The Irish Language Enthusiast! You're not serious! . . .

—. . . He didn't go near Peadar the Pub's at all . . . He won't be hoodwinked there again, neighbour. Peadar the Pub's daughter isn't likely to hoodwink anybody any more, neighbour! Oh! There are plenty of reasons, neighbour! The Red-haired Policeman caught her one Sunday recently during second Mass. There wasn't one of that

Woody Hillside, Sive's Rocks and Donagh's Village lot home from England who wasn't in there drinking. People say it was the Irish Language Enthusiast told the police to go in. Your man has a very high-ranking job in the Government . . .

—She won't play the parlour trick any more . . .

—She robbed me . . .

—And me, too . . .

—Faith then, I wasn't thankful to her. I was not, dear. After the second half-glass of whiskey she charged me four fourpenny bits, and from the sixth one eighteen pence. By the docks, it was true for the doctor from Brightcity: it only suited the small intestine, while porter suited the large intestine. Too much whiskey caused the small intestine to burst and the large one shrivelled up with spleen. I had no pain . . .

—. . . She's lucky, neighbour, if the Sunday opening is all that'll be against her, but people say she watered the whiskey bottles . . .

—She'll lose the pub? . . .

—She might, neighbour, she might. But I wouldn't say so . . .

—What's the bloody use, so?

—Siúán the Shop's daughter will lose her trading licence for certain. She'll be tried in the Military Court . . . Black market tea. It was the sergeant caught her . . .

—The sergeant, then, even though she used to give him tea and cigarettes for nothing! . . .

—You were the cause of my death, my ugly Siúán! . . .

—. . . The One-Ear Breed, is it, neighbour? That youngest one of the tailor's was arrested in England . . .

—Well done, Billyboy! Well done! . . .

—He stabbed the Redman's son from Donagh's Village . . .

—Oh! The same ancestral kidney trick another One-Ear played on myself! He'll be hanged . . .

—They say he'll go to prison . . .

—He'll be hanged . . .

—They say, neighbour, that it's easy to hang a person in England right enough. But I don't think he'll be hanged, all the same. He'll get a few years in prison, maybe . . .

—A few years in prison! Arrah, to hell with yourself and your prison! If he's not hanged . . .

—They say the Postmistress's daughter will get a year and a half or a couple of years in prison too . . . Letters containing money, neighbour, but it was the Irish Language Enthusiast's letters that put the bloodhounds from Head Office onto her scent . . .

—*My goodness me!* After me spending twenty years teaching her . . .

—Faith then, Postmistress, believe you me, neighbour, I wouldn't like to see anything happen to your daughter . . . Take it easy, Master dear, calm down! . . . By the holy little finger, Master, I never opened a letter of yours! . . . Oh! She could have, Master, but I didn't help her! . . .

—That oldest son of mine, Billyboy, is he still keeping company with Road-End's daughter? . . .

—I'd say so, neighbour. Himself and Road-End's daughter will be at the next court. It's reported that your other son . . .

—Tom . . .

—Yes, Tom. It's reported that himself and Tomáisín's son caught them in your turf stack before daybreak . . .

—The second son and Tomáisín's son caught the oldest son stealing his own turf for that soot-stinking breed of Road-End's!

—All I know, neighbour, is that he's summoned to appear in court . . .

—Oh! May the devil pierce him with his front teeth! The nimble-fingered chimney-sweeps of Road-End are in a right sooty mess so!

—Your wife has served them with another summons, for putting their cattle on your land . . .

—Now, indeed! At the dead of night! Well done herself! She'll win too, you'll see! I wish the oldest one was cleared to hell out under the elements, and some excuse of a wife brought in on the big holding for the second son! I wonder, Billyboy, did Tomáisín's family ever return the spade they borrowed to dig their first meal of early potatoes? . . .

—I don't know that, neighbour . . . To make a long story short, neighbour, the Road-End crowd are getting a trouncing from the law at the moment. The other Sunday, the priest was like a man bitten by his lap dog. He got up before daybreak and caught some crowd stealing his turf. They say it's the Road-End crowd . . .

—The same crowd who were licking his eyebrows . . .

—. . . I don't think, neighbour, the priest would hold his umbrella between the Road-End crowd and the rain, ever since the son was given a six months' prison sentence . . .

—Road-End's son? . . .

—Road-End's son, seriously! You're spinning lies?

—And Road-End's old lady nearly got another six months' sentence, neighbour, for receiving stolen goods . . .

—My drift-weed for certain! . . .

—Not so, neighbour, but the contents of Lord Cockton's car, including fishing gear, a gun and all that sort of thing. He went into the Earl's at night and took dinner jackets, tennis trousers, gold watches and cigarette cases . . . And a few thousand cigarettes from Siúán the Shop's daughter, and sold them for threepence each to the young women of Donagh's Village. The clay pipes were killing them . . .

—It was good enough for Siúán the Shop's daughter! . . .

—And for the Earl! . . .

—And for the young women of Donagh's Village! . . .

—And for Road-End's son, the little blackguard. By the docks, dear, I don't begrudge him that much! He was a bit too ready with his boot . . .

—He stole the trousers from the priest's sister too, but there was nothing said about that. Seáinín Liam's son and some of the Woody Hillside young lads saw them on Road-End's daughter on the bog, but she wore a frock over them . . .

—The straddle-bag my eldest son is keeping company with? . . . Yes! She'll have her photograph taken in those trousers now, as more temptation for the eldest one . . .

—The priest's sister was upset when Road-End's son was sent to prison, Billyboy? . . .

—Arrah, don't you know well she was, Bríd!

—Bríd, neighbour, it didn't dampen her spirits in the least. "What use is a man in prison to me?" she said. "Road-End's son is a useless impotent little fellow . . ."

—She'll marry the Wood of the Lake Master now? . . .

—The Wood of the Lake Master is among her broken dolls for a good while now. At present she's with a Scotsman who's taking photographs in Woody Hillside. He wears short skirts . . .

—Now then! Short skirts. And tell me this, Billyboy, was she wearing the trousers when she was with him? . . .

—She wasn't, Bríd Terry, but a frock. The best trousers she had—the striped ones—were the ones Road-End's son stole . . .

—The trousers Tomás Inside spat on? . . .

—Now that you mention Tomás Inside, the Postmistress's daughter told me that Pádraig Chaitríona got . . . Patience now, Master! Have patience, Master! . . . Hold on there, Master! I never opened a letter of yours, Master . . . Listen to me, Master. Two dogs . . .

—Have a little decency, Master. What did she say about my Pádraig, Billyboy?

—That he got the insurance money on Tomás Inside, and that Nell got a nice fat sum on Jack . . .

—The blessings of God on you, Billyboy my friend! According to Nóra Sheáinín's mangy tongue, Pádraig didn't keep up the payments after I died! Ever since I came into the graveyard she's used me as a spittoon for every drool and dribble out of her lying mouth. Do you hear me, Seáinín's daughter, you sponger? May God reward you, Billyboy, and tell her that—tell that mangy daughter of Seáinín's—that Pádraig got . . .

6

—. . . God would punish us for saying a thing like that, Caitríona . . .

—But it's the truth, Jack . . .

—It's not, Caitríona. I had been ailing for years. She brought me to the best of doctors in Brightcity, every single one of them. I was told by an English doctor who used to come fishing up there to us eight years ago, how long I'd live, to the day. "You'll live," he said . . .

—. . . "Yes," says I. "My guts are tangled up . . ."

—. . . "Your ankle is twisted again," he said. "By Galen's windy plexus . . ."

—. . . Musha, you wouldn't believe, Caitríona, neighbour, how thankful I am to your Pádraig. Not a single Sunday passed but himself and his wife would come to look in on me . . .

—The Filthy-Feet breed . . .

—Musha, Caitríona, neighbour, there's no soil without weeds. Look at how the Big Master has changed! You wouldn't meet a nicer man on a pilgrimage to Knock Shrine . . .

—But don't you see the way herself and that dishevelled Nell treated me, Billyboy. They got the St. John's Gospel from the priest and bundled me down into this cupboard thirty years before my time. The same trick was played on poor Jack . . .

—God would punish us . . .

—Old wives' tales, Caitríona. If I were you I wouldn't believe it . . .

—You'd better believe it, Billyboy, even though it is an old wives' tale. The priest is able to . . .

—I believed that once, Caitríona, neighbour. I did indeed, though you wouldn't think it of me. But I asked a priest, Caitríona— a very learned priest—and do you know what he told me? He told me, Caitríona, what I should have known very well myself only for the old tale being rooted in my mind. "All the St. John's Gospels in the world wouldn't keep you alive, Billyboy the Post," he said, "when God wishes to send for you."

—I find it hard to believe, Billyboy . . .

—Another priest told my wife—the Schoolmistress—the same thing, Caitríona. A holy priest he was, Caitríona: a priest whose two eyes were aflame with holiness. The Schoolmistress had done every single pilgrimage in the whole of Ireland and Aran for me . . . Hold on there, Master dear! Hold on there! . . . Stop that commotion, now! What could I have done about what she did? . . . "It is right to make the pilgrimages," he said, "but we don't know when it's God's will to work a miracle . . ."

—But a pilgrimage is not the same thing as the St. John's Gospel, Billyboy . . .

—I know that, Caitríona, but wouldn't the St. John's Gospel be a miracle? And if God wants to keep a person alive, why should He have to make another person die instead of him? You don't think, Caitríona, neighbour, that He's as full of red tape as the Post Office? . . .

—*Bloody tear and 'ounds*, didn't Big Brian say . . .

—. . . Do you think it's the War of the Two Foreigners? says I . . .

—It's time you woke up, my friend!

—. . . It was my wife filled in the forms for Pádraig, Caitríona. Hold on, Master! Hold on! Very well, Master dear. She was your wife too . . . Have patience now, Master! Patience! Two dogs . . .

—. . . There was such a day, Peadar the Pub. Don't deny it . . .

—. . . Forms about the house, Caitríona. Isn't Pádraig building a slate-roofed house! . . . Yes, Caitríona, a two-storey house with bay windows, and a windmill on the hillock to supply the lighting . . . You should see the Government bull he bought, Caitríona!—ninety pounds. The cattle crowd are very thankful to him. All the bulls round the place were idlers.

—*Bloody tear and 'ounds*, didn't Big Brian say: "Since England put a stop to de Valera's cattle, and since the Slaughter of the Innocents, the bulls are so shy . . ."

—And he's thinking of getting a lorry for carrying turf. It's badly wanted in our area. There is no lorry since Peaidín's was taken off him . . . Five or six hundred pounds, neighbour . . .

—Five or six hundred pounds! A sum like that would leave a hole in anybody's pocket, Billyboy! Nearly as much as Nell got in the court case . . .

—It's not a hole in Pádraig's pocket, Caitríona, and especially since he got the legacy . . .

—But it was Nell got the fat notes all the same . . .

—*Bloody tear and 'ounds*, didn't Big Brian say that Pádraig Chaitríona wouldn't recognize a pound note any more than Tomás Inside would recognize the sweat of his own brow, or . . .

—Wouldn't you think, Billyboy, if there's a shower of banknotes blowing their way, that some one of them would think of paying back the pound I gave to Caitríona . . .

—You little mangy arse!

—. . . The Postmistress's daughter told me . . . Take it easy there, Master! . . . That's a damn lie, Master . . . I didn't open any letter . . .

—. . . Don't pay any heed to his rudeness, Nóra. Remember he was a non-commissioned officer in the Murder Machine[9] . . . I don't have time now to read you *The Setting Sun* again, Nóra. I'm too busy with my new draft of *The Piglet-Moon*. I got the idea from Cóilí. His grandfather was able to trace his family tree back to the moon. He'd spend three hours a night looking up at it, according to the ancient custom of our ancestors. With the coming of the new moon, his nostrils would produce three sorts of snot: one of gold, one of silver, and the old gaelic snot . . .

—. . . What she told me, Caitríona, was that Baba said you were her favourite of all the sisters she ever had, and that you'd be thankful to her, only for you died . . .

—I did my damnedest, Billyboy, but I failed to bury Nell before me . . .

—Musha, Caitríona, neighbour, it might be all for the best. Pádraig told myself and my . . . the Schoolmistress, that Nell left him a good few little extras that weren't due to him at all according to the will. She'd only accept the half of Tomás Inside's land from him, and believe you me when I tell you that hardly a Sunday goes by that the priest doesn't announce a Mass for the souls of yourself and Jack the Scológ . . .

—For the souls of myself and Jack the Scológ . . .

—*Bloody tear and 'ounds*, didn't Big Brian say . . .

---

9. Patrick Pearse's phrase for the official education system in Ireland under British rule.

—And of Baba, and . . .

—. . . "The best comparison I can think of for Páidín's daughters," he said, "are two scabby young dogs I saw observing a mule in the throes of death in Donagh's Village. One of them was barking, trying to keep the other one away. In the end it strained itself so much with yelping that it burst into a mush. As soon as the second dog saw he had the dead mule all to himself, what did he do but slink away and leave it there for the dead dog . . ."

—Angry that he'd dropped that stitch off his knitting needle! He thought his own family would coax every little pinch of the will to themselves! . . . For my own soul . . .

—Faith then, Caitríona, neighbour, himself and his daughter aren't fawning on Nell as much as they used to be . . .

—She won't be any the worse for that . . . for my own soul and for the soul of Jack the Scológ . . .

—He's between two minds as to whether he'll come or stay, Caitríona. He was anointed the other day . . .

—He won't do it any younger! He's twice my age . . .

—My . . . the Schoolmistress took a trip up to see him. Guess what message he sent down to me with her ? . . .

—A mouthful of bile, if he hasn't changed . . . For my soul . . .

—My poor uncle hasn't received any spiritual assistance since I was tending to him, or do you think, Billyboy, he says the Family Rosary? . . .

—*Bloody tear and 'ounds*, didn't he say . . .

—What he said to the Schoolmistress was: "You'll tell Billyboy the Post," he said, "if he hoists sail ahead of me, to tell them all back there I'll be easing my sails in their direction any minute. Let him tell Red-haired Tom that I'll knock the blockage out of his gut, in the event that he didn't heed my advice . . ."

—Neither she nor anyone else was any the wiser for anything I said, Billyboy. And I may tell you also that the graves are riddled with holes . . .

—. . . "Let him tell Son of Blackleg to strike up a verse of a song when he hears me coming . . ."

— "Hoh-roh, Mary, your wares and your bags and belts . . ."
   — "Mártan Sheáin Mhóir had a daughter
   And she was as broad as any man . . ."

— . . . "And let him tell that pint-swilling Glutton that I'll cut him in strips like a sally-rod for having his old wagon of a donkey permanently parked in my field of oats, since that wife of Curraoin's began her pilgrimages to the courts . . ."

— *Bloody tear and 'ounds*, Billyboy, finish it . . .

— . . . For my own soul and for . . .

— That's all he said, neighbour. Or if he did, my . . . the Schoolmistress didn't tell me . . .

— *Bloody tear and 'ounds*, what's the use of making a Red-haired Tom of yourself! If there's going to be ructions let there be ructions! "And let him tell my own darling Caitríona," he said, "that they had to send for the fire brigade's long hoses to extinguish me after the scalding I got in the geyser in Dublin, so I have no fear of her boiling water now . . ."

— Ababúna! Ababúna! Beartla Blackleg! Billyboy dear! Who's to know but that ugly . . . stop-nosed . . . blundering . . . slouch . . . might be stuffed down beside me . . . Oh, Billyboy dear, I don't believe he washed himself in Dublin . . . To bury him beside me! Ugh! Ugh! . . . The room . . . the grimace . . . "You can have Big Brian, Caitríona . . ." Oh! Billyboy, I'd explode, I'd explode, I'd explode . . .

— Oh, there's no danger, Caitríona, my neighbour. That will all be fine . . .

— But look at where they buried yourself, Billyboy . . .

— The poor creature didn't know what she was doing . . . Easy on, Master! Easy on! Don't worry, Caitríona. That hardy annual is still as healthy as ivy . . .

— His likes don't last long at all in the end. Holy Mother of God tonight. I would have less aversion to the Earl's little *black!* . . . What's this, Billyboy? Another corpse! Oh, woe forever, Billyboy my dearest friend, if it's him. Listen! . . .

— Hi, lads! Seán Chite from Donagh's Village has arrived . . .

—The place he's buried is . . .

—The great Prophecy Professor of the Western World is laid low and his prophetic skull laid at Beartla's feet . . .

—*Bloody tear and 'ounds*, what better pillow for his old skull?

—Seán Chite, what's your opinion of the world now, or do you think the prophecy is coming true? . . .

—I'll keen you now, Seán Chite, as befits your profession and fame . . . Alas and woe! Alas and woe! . . .

—. . . Arrah, to hell with it, Seán Chite! Quit your foolish talk about Redspot O'Donnell.[10] Will England be blasted to hell into the air in a squall of ashes in this war? Is that in your prophecy? Hi! Son of Blackleg, give him a crack of your clumsy foot on his prophetic skull . . .

—Oh! Billyboy, darling! . . . I won't rest easy in the graveyard clay . . .

—Don't be worried, Caitríona. The priest has ordered a brand-new map of the graveyard to be made. Road-End's old lady was complaining recently. "Weren't the soggy lumps from Sive's Rocks hard up for space," she said, "when they laid the legs of the corpse across the delicate guts of my old man . . ."

—Oh! That's the corpse that won't have a coffin or a sheet for long! See how he stole my little lump-hammer! . . .

—. . . Caitríona my dear, the cross will be put over you in any case . . .

—Oh! If only they would speed it up, Billyboy. If they'd speed it up before the old scold dies . . .

—It was worth waiting for, Caitríona. Everybody who saw it says it's beautiful. The priest himself went in right away to look at it, and

---

10. It had been prophesied that a leader by the name of Hugh O'Donnell, bearing a strawberry mark and known as "Ball Dearg (red spot) Ó Domhnaill" would defeat English oppression in Ireland. After the Battle of the Boyne in 1690 a man of that name and mark, a high-ranking officer in the Spanish Army, returned to Ireland, declared himself to be Ball Dearg Ó Domhnaill (Redspot O'Donnell), and set about fulfilling the prophesy.

the Small Master and my . . . the Schoolmistress, were in there the other Saturday, to scrutinize the inscription in Irish.

—Did you tell that, Billyboy, to Nóra Sheáinín and to Cite and to Red-haired Tom? . . . Oh! Billyboy dear, if it's not put over me . . .

—It will be, Caitríona. Don't be worried, neighbour. It's been ready for a long time, but they were waiting to put up yours and Jack the Scológ's together . . .

—My own cross and Jack the Scológ's cross going up together . . .

—And Tomás Inside's cross is what's causing the delay now . . .

—My own cross and Jack the Scológ's cross . . .

—Everybody says, Caitríona, that yours is nicer than Cite's cross, and Nóra Sheáinín's cross, and even Siúán the Shop's cross . . .

—My own cross and Jack the Scológ's cross . . .

—It's nicer than Jack the Scológ's cross, Caitríona. My . . . the Schoolmistress says she'd prefer it to Peadar the Pub's cross . . .

—It's of Island limestone so, Billyboy? . . .

—That's a thing I don't know, neighbour. In McCormack's in Brightcity it was bought, anyhow . . .

—*Bloody tear and 'ounds* for a story, how would that little pip-squeak know, and he laid up on the flat of his back this long while? . . .

—If it's not of Island limestone, Billyboy, it's not worth a blind nut to me . . .

—I thought the Island limestone was used up . . .

—Shut your mouth, you little brat! . . .

—It is of Island limestone! . . .

—It's not of Island limestone! . . .

—I'm telling you it's of Island limestone! . . .

—I'm telling you it's not of Island limestone! . . .

—They don't have crosses of Island limestone in McCormack's. In Moran's they have them . . .

—Oh, what are you talking about? Didn't Nóra Sheáinín's cross and Cite's cross come out of there, and aren't they of Island limestone! . . .

—And Bríd Terry's cross . . .

—And Siúán the Shop's cross . . .

—I heard sure enough, Caitríona, my neighbour, that the cross your Nell is putting on order for herself is of Island limestone . . .

—. . . The Big Butcher from Brightcity came to my funeral. He often told me that he had regard for me on account of the regard his father had for my father . . .

—. . . Nóra Sheáinín's cross is of Island limestone . . .

—. . . I was Twenty and I led with the Ace of Hearts . . .

—. . . Cite's cross . . .

—. . . *La Libération* . . .

—. . . Bríd Terry's cross . . . Siúán the Shop's cross . . .

—I was the first corpse into this graveyard. Don't you all think the oldest inhabitant should have something to say? Permission to speak, then! Permission to speak! . . .

—Allow him to speak! . . .

—Tear away! . . .

—. . . Nell's cross . . .

—Speak! . . .

—Speak now, you blockhead! . . .

—. . . Neither my cross nor yours, Jack the Scológ . . .

—. . . After all your bluster for the past thirty-one years, looking for permission to speak . . .

—. . . True for you, Master dear! Now you're talking! Two dogs . . .

—. . . is of Island limestone . . .

—. . . You have permission to speak now, but it seems you prefer to be deathly dumb . . .

—. . . Neither your cross nor mine is of Island limestone . . .

THE END

BIBLIOGRAPHY

Texts by Máirtín Ó Cadhain

1939. *Idir Shúgradh agus Dáiríre*. Dublin: Oifig an tSoláthair.

1948. *An Braon Broghach*. Dublin: Oifig an tSoláthair.

1949. *Cré na Cille: Aithris i ndeich n-eadarlúid*. Dublin: Sáirséal agus Dill.

1953. *Cois Caoláire*. Dublin: Sáirséal agus Dill.

1963. *Bás nó Beatha*. Dublin: Sáirséal agus Dill.

1964. *Irish above Politics*. Dublin: Press Cuchulainn.

1964. *Mr. Hill/Mr. Tara*. Dublin: N.p.

1964. *Cosnaítear an Creideamh-Chu[a]la Tú faoi Rath Cairn?* Drogheda: Clódóirí Dhroichead Átha.

1966. *An Aisling*. Dublin: Coiste Cuimhneacháin Náisiúnta.

1967. *An tSraith ar Lár*. Dublin: Sáirséal agus Dill.

1969. *Páipéir Bhána agus Páipéir Bhreaca*. Dublin: An Clóchomhar.

1970. *An tSraith dhá Tógáil*. Dublin: Sáirséal agus Dill.

1970. *Gluaiseacht na Gaeilge: Gluaiseacht ar Strae*. Dublin: Misneach.

1973. *As an nGéibheann: Litreacha chuig Tomás Bairéad*. Dublin: Sáirséal agus Dill.

1977. *An tSraith Tógtha*. Dublin: Sáirséal agus Dill.

1995. *Athnuachan*. Dublin: Coiscéim.

1999. *Tone: Inné agus Inniu*. Dublin: Coiscéim.

2002. *An Ghaeilge Bheo/Destined to Pass*. Dublin: Coiscéim.

2002. *Barbed Wire*. Dublin: Coiscéim.

Editions of *Cré na Cille*

1949. Sáirséal agus Dill (First Edition).

1965. Sáirséal agus Dill, An Dara Cló (Second Printing).

1970. Sáirséal agus Dill, An Tríú Cló (Third Printing).

1979. Sáirséal agus Dill, An Ceathrú Cló (Fourth Printing).

1996. Sáirséal Ó Marcaigh, editor Tomás de Bhaldraithe, An Dara hEagrán (Second Edition).

2007. Sáirséal Ó Marcaigh, editor Cathal Ó Háinle, An Tríú hEagrán (Third Edition).

2009. Cló Iar-Chonnacht, reproduction of 1965 edition, designated An Cló Seo (This Print).

Translations

Bammesberger, Alfred. 1984. *A Handbook of Irish: Twentieth-Century Irish Prose*, Vol. 3. Heidelberg: Universitätsverlag Winter.

Deane, Seamus (ed.). 1991. *The Field Day Anthology of Irish Writing*, Vol. 3. Derry: Field Day.

de Paor, Louis, Mike McCormack, and Lochlainn Ó Tuairisg. 2006. *Dhá Scéal/Two Stories*. Galway: Arlen House for the Cúirt International Festival of Literature.

Munch-Pedersen, Ole (trans.). 2000. *Kirkegardsjord: Genfortaelling i ti mellemspil*. Arhus: Husets.

Ní Allúráin, Eibhlín, and Maitiú Ó Néill (trans.). 1991. "*Cré na Cille*—Churchyard Clay." *Krino* 11:13–25. Corrandulla: Anna Livia Press.

Ó Tuairisc, Eoghan. 1981. *The Road to Brightcity: Short Stories*. Dublin: Poolbeg Press.

Rekdal, Jan Erik (trans.). 1995. *Kirkegardsjord: Gjenfortellinger i ti mellomspil*. Oslo: Gyldendal Norsk.

Titley, Alan (trans.). 2015. *The Dirty Dust: Cré na Cille*. New Haven: Yale University Press.

Trodden Keefe, Joan (trans.). 1984. "Churchyard Clay: A Translation of *Cré na Cille* by Máirtín Ó Cadhain, with Introduction and Notes." Ph.D. dissertation, University of California, Berkeley.

Secondary Literature

Bramsbäck, Birgit, and Martin Croghan (eds.). 1988. *Anglo-Irish and Irish Literature: Aspects of Language and Culture*, Vol. 2. Uppsala: Almqvist & Wiksell International.

Briody, Mícheál. 2009. "Is Fearr an tAighneas ná an tUaigneas: Máirtín Ó Cadhain agus Bailiú an Bhéaloidis." *Bliainiris* 9:7–49.

Cleary, Joe. 2007. *Literature, Partition and the Nation State: Culture and*

Conflict in Ireland, Israel and Palestine. Cambridge: Cambridge University Press.

Cló Iar-Chonnacht. 2009. *Sáirséal Ó Marcaigh (Sáirséal agus Dill): Catalóg agus Leabharliosta 1945–2009*. Indreabhán, Conamara: Cló Iar-Chonnacht.

Costigan, An tSiúr Bosco, and Seán Ó Curraoin. 1987. *De Ghlaschloich an Oileáin: Beatha agus Saothar Mháirtín Uí Chadhain*. Béal an Daingin: Cló Iar-Chonnachta.

Cronin, Michael. 2001. "It's time for *Cré na Cille* in English." *Irish Times*, 7 April 2001, B13.

Devine, Francis. 1992. "Obituary: Mattie O'Neill." *Saothar: Journal of the Irish Labour-History Society* 17:7–9.

Denvir, Gearóid. 1989. "Ó Chill go Cré." In *Léachtaí Uí Chadhain* 1:134–51.

———. 1987. *Cadhan Aonair: Saothar Liteartha Mháirtín Uí Chadhain*. Dublin: An Clóchomhar.

———. 1998. "Peacaí an Fhíréin: Smaointeachas Mháirtín Uí Chadhain." In *Criostalú: Aistí ar Shaothar Mháirtin Uí Chadhain*, ed. Cathal Ó Háinle, 53–86. Dublin: Coiscéim.

———. 2006. "Athchuairt ar *Cré na Cille*." *Léachtaí Cholm Cille* 16:178–218.

———. 2007. "*Cré na Cille*—Béal Beo nó Béal Marbh?" *Léachtaí Cholm Cille* 37:38–75.

———. 2008. Review of *Cré na Cille* (DVD 2007). *Estudios Irlandeses* 3 (2008): 222–25.

de Paor, Louis. 1987. "Ní Fhéadfadh sé a Inseacht don tSagart." *Irish Review* 2 (Autumn): 41–48.

———. 2006. "Ceist, Cé Léifidh Máirtín Ó Cadhain?" *Comhar* 66, no. 11 (November): 7–9.

Dobbins, Gregory. 2010. *Lazy Idle Schemers: Irish Modernism and the Cultural Politics of Idleness*. Dublin: Field Day.

Ferriter, Diarmaid. 2005. *The Transformation of Ireland 1900–2000*. London: Profile Books.

Greene, David. 1950. Review of *Cré na Cille*. *Irish Times*, 27 May 1950.

Handy, Amber, and Brian Ó Conchubhair. 2014. *The Language of Gender, Power and Agency in Celtic Studies*. Dublin: Arlen Books.

Kiberd, Declan. 1989. "Irish Literature and Irish History." In *The Oxford History of Ireland*, edited by R. F. Foster, 230–81. Oxford: Oxford University Press.

———. 1993. *Idir Dhá Chultúr*. Dublin: Coiscéim.

———. 2000. *Irish Classics*. London: Granta Books.

———. 2005. *The Irish Writer and the World*. Cambridge: Cambridge University Press.

Kilfeather, Siobhán. 2006. "The Gothic Novel." In *The Cambridge Companion to the Irish Novel*, edited by John Wilson Foster, 78–96. Cambridge: Cambridge University Press.

Mac Cóil, Liam. 1996. "Living Voices from the Grave." *Irish Times*, 28 December 1991, C9.

Mac Giollarnáth, Seán. 1954. *Conamara*. Dublin: Published for the Cultural Relations Committee of Ireland at the Three Candles.

Mac Póilín, Aodán (ed.). 1991. *Krino* 11. Corrandulla: Anna Livia Press.

Mahon, William J. 1981. "Images of Deformity and Blemish in the Stories of Máirtín Ó Cadhain." *Proceedings of the Harvard Celtic Colloquium* 1:159–68.

Ní Annracháin, Máire. 2003. "Literature in Irish." In *New History of Ireland*, Vol. 7: *Ireland, 1921–84*, edited by Jacqueline R. Hill, 573–86. Oxford: Oxford University Press.

———. 2007. "Athchuairt ar an Duibheagán: An Eagna i Saothar Liteartha Mháirtín Uí Chadhain." In *Léachtaí Cholm Cille* 37:208–29.

——— (ed.). 2007. *Léachtaí Cholm Cille* 37: *Saothar Mháirtín Uí Chadhain*. Maynooth: An Sagart.

———. 1980. "Ag Sméaracht i bhFásall." *Comhar* 39, no. 10 (October): 49–53.

Ní Bhroin, Verona A. 1988. "*Cré na Cille* mar Aoir." In *Léachtaí Cholm Cille* 17: *An Aoir*, 137–61.

Ní Ghairbhí, Róisín. 2008. "I dTosach do bhí an Briathar: 'Deacracht' *Cré na Cille*." *Canadian Journal of Irish Studies* 34, no. 1 (Spring): 47–52.

Nic Dhiarmada, Bríona. 2008. "Utopia, Anti-Utopia, Nostalgia and Ó Cadhain." *Canadian Journal of Irish Studies* 34, no. 1 (Spring): 53–57.

Nic Eoin, Máirín. 1981. "Éistear le mo Ghlór! Caithfear Éisteacht. . . ." In *Nua-Aois* 8:45–59.

———. 1982. *An Litríocht Réigiúnach*. Dublin: An Clóchomhar.

———. 2004. *Trén bhFearann Breac: An Díláithriú Cultúir agus Nualitríocht na Gaeilge*. Dublin: Cois Life.

———. 2009. "Seanraí Béil na Gaeilge agus Tionscnamh na Nualitríochta." In Anáil *an Bhéil Bheo: Orality and Modern Irish Culture*, edited by

Nessa Cronin, Seán Crosson, and John Eastlake, 229–40. Newcastle upon Tyne: Cambridge Scholars Press.

———. 2014. "Cultural Engagement and Twentieth-Century Irish Scholarship." In Handy and Ó Conchubhair 2014, *The Language of Gender, Power and Agency in Celtic Studies*, 181–222.

Nic Pháidín, Caoilfhionn. 1978. "*Cré na Cille* mar Úrscéal Grinn." *Comhar* 36, no. 7 (July): 21–22.

———. 1980. "*Cré na Cille*—Ealaín na Maireachtála." *Comhar* 39, no. 10 (October): 43–48.

———. 1981. "*Cré na Cille*—Scéal Chaitíona." *Lasair* 2:11–17.

Ní Mhuircheartaigh, Éadaoin. 2008. "Marbhfháisc—An Béal Marbh in *Cré na Cille*." *Bliainiris* 8:103–31.

Ó Briain, Seán. 2013. "Seachtrachas agus Inmheánachas in *Cré na Cille*." In *Saltair Saíochta, Sanasaíochta agus Seanchais: A Festschrift for Gearóid Mac Eoin*, edited by Dónall Ó Baoill, Donncha Ó hAodha, and Nollaig Ó Muraíle, 274–84. Dublin: Four Courts Press.

Ó Broin, Brian. 2006. "Máirtín Ó Cadhain's 'Cré na Cille': A Narratological Approach." *Irish University Review* 36, no. 2 (Autumn–Winter): 280–303.

———. 2008. "Racism and Xenophobia in Máirtín Ó Cadhain's *Cré na Cille*." *Studies: An Irish Quarterly Review* 97, no. 387 (Winter): 275–85.

Ó Buachalla, Breandán. 1967. "Ó Cadhain, Ó Céileachair, Ó Flaithearta." *Comhar* 26, no. 5 (May): 69–75.

Ó Cadhla, Stiofán. 2008. "The Gnarled and Stony Clods of Townland's Tip: Máirtín Ó Cadhain and the 'Gaelic' Storyteller." *Canadian Journal of Irish Studies* 34, no. 1 (Spring): 40–46.

Ó Cathasaigh, Aindrias (ed.). 1998. *Caiscín: Altanna san Irish Times*. Dublin: Coiscéim.

———. 2002. *Ag Samhlú Troda: Máirtín Ó Cadhain 1905–1970*. Dublin: Coiscéim.

———. 2005. *Daol na Réabhlóide: Poblachtachas agus Sóisialachas i Smaointeoireacht Mháirtín Uí Chadhain*. Dublin: Coiscéim.

———. 2008. "A Vision to Realise: Ó Cadhain's Politics." *Canadian Journal of Irish Studies* 34, no. 1 (Spring): 18–27.

Ó Corcora, Domhnall. 1950. "Cré na Cille." *Feasta* 3, no. 2 (May): 14–15.

Ó Corráin, Ailbhe. 1988. "Grave Comedy: A Study of *Cré na Cille* by Máirtín Ó Cadhain." In *Anglo-Irish and Irish Literature: Aspects of Language and Culture*, 2:143–48. Uppsala: Almqvist & Wiksell International.

Ó Crualaoich, Gearóid. 1981. "Domhan na Cille agus Domhan na Bréige." *Scríobh* 5:80–86.

———. 1989. "Máirtín Ó Cadhain agus Dioscúrsa na Gaeilge." In *Léachtaí Uí Chadhain*, Vol. 1: *(1980–1988)*, 168–80.

Ó Dochartaigh, Liam. 1975. "Drámaíocht na Cille: Aiste Chritice." *Feasta* 28, no. 4 (July): 13–16.

Ó Doibhlin, Breandán. 1974. "Athléamh ar *Chré na Cille*." In *Léachtaí Cholm Cille* 5: *An Fichiú hAois*, 40–53.

———. 1995. "Réamhrá." In *Athnuachan*, v–xix. Dublin: Coiscéim.

———. 1997. *Aistí Critice agus Cultúir* 2. Béal Feirste: Lagan Press.

———. 2009. *Aistí Critice agus Cultúir* 3. Dublin: Coiscéim.

Ó Drisceoil, Proinsias. 1999. "Máirtín Ó Cadhain." In *The Blackwell Companion to Modern Irish Culture*, edited by W. J. McCormack, 433–34. Oxford: Blackwell.

Ó Floinn, Tomás. 1950. "Cré na Cille." *Comhar* 9, no. 4 (April): 7–8, 30; also in Prút (ed.) 1997, *Cion Fir*.

———. 1952. "Máirtín Ó Cadhain II." *Comhar* 11, no. 6 (June): 7–8, 13–14; also in Prút (ed.), 1997, *Cion Fir*.

Ó hAnluain, Eoghan (ed.). 1989. *Léachtaí Uí Chadhain*, Vol. 1: *(1980–1988)*. Dublin: An Clóchomhar.

———. 1991. "Irish Writing: Prose Fiction and Poetry 1900–1988." In *The Field Day Anthology of Irish Writing*, Vol. 3. Derry: Field Day.

Ó hÉalaí, Pádraig. 2009. "An Leabhar Eoin: Deabhóid agus Piseogacht." In *Diasa Díograise: Aistí i gCuimhne ar Mháirtín Ó Briain*, 365–85. Conamara: Cló Iar-Chonnacht.

Ó hÉigeartaigh, Cian, and Aoileann Nic Gearailt. 2014. *Sáirséal agus Dill 1947–1981: Scéal Foilsitheora*. Indreabhán: Cló Iar-Chonnacht.

Ó hEithir, Breandán. 1973. *Thar Ghealchathair Soir: Léacht a tugadh ag Scoil Gheimhridh Merriman*. Dublin: Cumann Merriman.

———. 1977. "Cré na Cille." In *The Pleasures of Gaelic Literature*, ed. John Jordan, 72–84. Dublin: Mercier Press.

Ó Gráinne, Diarmuid. 1990. *An Dá Mháirtín*. Dublin: Comhar Teoranta.

Ó Háinle, Cathal. 1978. *Promhadh Pinn*. Maynooth: An Sagart.

———. (ed.). 1998. *Criostalú: Aistí ar Shaothar Mháirtín Uí Chadhain*. Dublin: Coiscéim.

———. 1998. "Cúig mo Láimhe Déanta." In *Criostalú: Aistí ar Shaothar Mháirtín Uí Chadhain*. Dublin: Coiscéim.

———. 2006. "Máirtín Mór Ó Cadhain: Tríonóideach." *Bliainiris* 6:9–42.

———. 2008a. *Scáthanna*. Dublin: Coiscéim.

———. 2008b. "Barbed Wire Mháirtín Uí Chadhain." In Ó Háinle 2008a, *Scáthanna*, 259–93.

———. 2009. "Máirtín Ó Cadhain." In *Dictionary of Irish Biography: From the Earliest Times to the Year 2002*, edited by James McGuire and James Quinn, Vol. 7, 136–38. Cambridge: Cambridge University Press.

Ó Laighin, Seán. 1990. *Ó Cadhain i bhFeasta*. Dublin: Clódhanna Teo.

O'Leary, Philip. 2010. *Irish Interior: Keeping Faith with the Past in Gaelic Prose 1940–1951*. Dublin: UCD Press.

Ó Murchú, Seosamh. 1982. "An Chill agus a Cré: Scrúdú ar an nGreann in *Cré na Cille*." In *Irisleabhar Mhá Nuad 1982*, 5–20.

Ó Neachtain, Joe Steve. 2013. *Ag Caint Linn Féin*. Indreabhán, Conamara: Cló Iar-Chonnacht.

Ó Tuama, Seán. 1955. "*Cré na Cille* agus *Séadna*." *Comhar* 14, no. 2 (February): 7–8, 29.

———. 1980. "Tiomna Roimh Bhás." *Comhar* 39, no. 10 (October): 55–57.

Ó hUiginn, Ruairí. 2006. "Litreacha: Máirtín Ó Cadhain chuig Seosamh Daibhéid, 19 Meán Fómhair 1951." In *Bliainiris* 6:256–70.

Prút, Liam (ed.). 1997. *Cion Fir: Aistí Thomáis Uí Fhloinn in Comhar*. Dublin: Comhar Teoranta.

Riggs, Pádraigín, and Norman Vance. 2004. "Irish Prose Fiction." In *The Cambridge Companion to Modern Irish Culture*, edited by Joe Cleary and Claire Connolly, 245–66. Cambridge: Cambridge University Press.

Titley, Alan. 1975. *Máirtín Ó Cadhain: Clár Saothair*. Dublin: An Clóchomhar.

———. 1981. "Contemporary Irish Literature." In *Crane Bag* 5, no. 2:890–96.

———. 1991. *An tÚrscéal Gaeilge*. Dublin: An Clóchomhar.

———. 1996. *Chun Doirne: Rogha Aistí*. Belfast: Lagan Press.

———. 2006. "The Novel in Irish." In *The Cambridge Companion to the Irish Novel*, edited by John Wilson Foster, 171–88. Cambridge: Cambridge University Press.

———. 2010. *Scríbhneoirí faoi Chaibidil*. Dublin: Cois Life.

Trodden Keefe, Joan. 1985. "The Graves of Connemara: Ireland's Máirtín Ó Cadhain." *World Literature Today* 59, no. 3 (Summer): 363–73.

Vance, Norman. 2002. *Irish Literature since 1800*. London: Longman.

Welch, Robert. 1993. *Changing States: Transformations in Modern Irish Writing*. London: Routledge.

Welch, Robert, and Bruce Stewart (eds.). 1996. *"Cré na Cille"* and "Máirtín Ó Cadhain." In *The Oxford Companion to Irish Literature*, edited by Robert Welch, 119, 405–6. Oxford: Oxford University Press.

Selected Audio-Visual Materials

1967. *Ó Cadhain ar an gCnocán Glas*, produced and directed by Aindreas Ó Gallchóir. Dublin: RTÉ.

1980. *There Goes Cré na Cille*, directed by Seán Ó Mórdha and scripted by Breandán Ó hEithir. Dublin: RTÉ.

2006. *Cré na Cille: Leagan Drámatúil a Réitigh Johnny Chóil Mhaidhc Ó Coisdealbha* (CDs). Dublin: RTÉ Raidió na Gaeltachta and Indreabhán: Cló Iar-Chonnacht.

2006. *Is Mise Stoc na Cille*, directed by Macdara Ó Curraidhín, produced by ROSG. Conamara: TG4.

2007. *Cré na Cille*, directed by Robert Quinn, produced by ROSG. Conamara: TG4.

2010. *Cré na Cille: 60 Bliain Os Cionn Talún*, RTÉ Raidió na Gaeltachta, produced by Dónall Ó Braonáin. Casla: RTÉ.

MÁIRTÍN Ó CADHAIN was born in 1906 and spent his formative years in An Cnocán Glas, An Spidéal (Spiddal), Conamara, County Galway. He won a scholarship to St. Patrick's College in Dublin (1924–1926), after which he returned to the Galway Gaeltacht and taught in various schools there. In 1936 his membership of the proscribed Irish Republican Army led to his dismissal from Carnmore National School in East Galway. He was interned in the Curragh camp in County Kildare during the Second World War and on his release was appointed to the Translation Staff in Dáil Éireann. He was appointed lecturer in Irish at Trinity College Dublin in 1956, becoming associate professor in 1967, professor in 1969, and fellow of Trinity College Dublin (FTCD) in 1970, the year he died. Best known for his novel *Cré na Cille* (1950), he also published several collections of short stories, including *Idir Shúgradh agus Dáiríre* (1939), *An Braon Broghach* (1948), *Cois Caoláire* (1953), *An tSraith ar Lár* (1967), *An tSraith Dhá Tógáil* (1970), and, posthumously, *An tSraith Tógtha* (1977). Two other novels, *Athnuachan* (1997) and *Barbed Wire* (2002), were published posthumously.

LIAM MAC CON IOMAIRE was born in 1937 in Casla, Conamara, County Galway. A teacher by profession, he was director of the Modern Irish Language Laboratory at University College Dublin between 1979 and 1996. He is the author of two biographies of key cultural figures, *Breandán Ó hEithir: Iomramh Aonair* (Cló Iar-Chonnacht, 2000) and *Seosamh Ó hÉanaí: Nár Fhágha mé Bás Choíche* (Cló Iar-Chonnacht, 2009). He has produced biographies of traditional singers in *A Companion to Irish Traditional Music* (Cambridge University Press, 1999 and 2011), and his *Conamara: An Tír Aineoil* (Cló Iar-Chonnacht, 1997) is a celebratory portrait series of tradition-bearers from Conamara and Árainn. He was awarded an honorary degree by National University of Ireland Galway in 2013.

TIM ROBINSON was born in 1935 and brought up in Yorkshire. He graduated in mathematics from Cambridge and worked in Vienna and London as a visual artist. In 1972 he moved to the Aran Islands, of which he produced a map and the two volumes of *Stones of Aran*. Elected to Aosdána, the affiliation of Irish artists, in 1996, he was awarded an honorary degree by National University of Ireland Galway in 1997 and made a member of the Royal Irish Academy in 2011. He was Visiting Parnell Fellow at Magdalene College, Cambridge, in 2011 and writer in residence at the Centre Culturel Irlandais, Paris, in 2012. The publication by Penguin of his Conamara trilogy (*Listening to the Wind*, 2006; *The Last Pool of Darkness*, 2008; and *A Little Gaelic Kingdom*, 2011) brought to a close a three-decade project of cartography and topographical writing.